Walter de la Mare

MEMOIRS OF A MIDGET

TELEGRAM
London San Francisco Beirut

First published by Collins Sons & Co Ltd in 1921
First paperback edition published by Oxford University Press in 1982

This edition published by Telegram in 2009

ISBN: 978-1-84659-066-5

A full CIP record for this book is available from the British Library.

Manufactured in Lebanon

TELEGRAM
26 Westbourne Grove, London W2 5RH
825 Page Street, Suite 203, Berkeley, California 94710
Tabet Building, Mneimneh Street, Hamra, Beirut
www.telegrambooks.com

MEMOIRS OF A MIDGET

To the memory of my mother

A wild beast there is in Ægypt, called orix, which the Ægyptians say, doth stand full against the dog starre when it riseth, looketh wistly upon it, and testifieth after a sort by sneesing, a kind of worship ...

Philemon Holland

Did'st thou ever see a lark in a cage? Such is the soul in the body: this world is like her little turf of grass; and the heaven o'er our heads, like her looking-glass, only gives us a miserable knowledge of the small compass of our prison ...

John Webster

Provoke them not, fair sir, with tempting words; the heavens are gracious ...

Thomas Kyd

Introduction

A few introductory and explanatory remarks are due, I think, to the reader of the following Memoirs. The Memoirs themselves will disclose how I became acquainted with Miss M. They also refer here and there to the small part I was enabled to take in straightening matters out at what was a critical juncture in her affairs, and in securing for her that independence which enabled her to live in the privacy she loved, without any anxiety as to ways and means. At the time, it is clear that she considered me a dilatory intermediary. I had not realized how extreme was her need. But she came at last to take a far too generous view of these trifling little services – services as generously rewarded, since they afforded me the opportunity of frequently seeing her, and so of becoming, as I hope, one of her most devoted friends.

One of the duties devolving on me as her sole executor – certain unusual legal proceedings having been brought to completion – was the examination of her letters and papers. Amongst these were her Memoirs – which I found sealed up with her usual scrupulous neatness in numerous small, square, brown-paper packages, and laid carefully away in a cupboard in her old nursery. They were accompanied by a covering letter addressed to myself.

Miss M.'s handwriting was even more minute than one might naturally, though not perhaps justifiably, have anticipated. Her manuscript would therefore have been difficult enough for ageing eyes to decipher, even if it had not been almost inextricably interlined, revised and corrected. Literary composition to this little woman-of-letters was certainly no 'primrose path'. The packages were therefore handed over to a trustworthy typist; and, at my direction, one complete and accurate copy was made of their contents.

After careful consideration, and after disguising the names of certain persons and places to preclude every possibility of giving offence – even Mrs. Percy Maudlen, for instance, if she ever scans these pages, may blush unrecognized! – I concluded that though I was under no absolute obligation to secure the publication of the Memoirs, this undoubtedly had been Miss M.'s intention and wish. At the same time, and for similar reasons, I decided that their publication should not take place until after my death. Instructions have therefore been left by me to this effect. Here then my editorial duties begin and end. Nothing has been altered; nothing suppressed.

Even if such a task were within my province, I should not venture to make any critical estimate of Miss M.'s work. I am not a writer; and, as a reader, have an inveterate preference to be allowed to study and enjoy my authors with as little external intervention as possible. The perusal of the Memoirs has afforded me the deepest possible pleasure. The serious-minded may none the less dismiss a midget's lucubrations as trifling; and no doubt – it could hardly be otherwise – a more practised taste than mine will discover many faults, crudities, and inconsistencies in them, though certain little prejudices on Miss M.'s side may not be so easily detectable. Whatever their merits or imperfections may be, I should be happy to think that the following pages may prove as interesting to other readers – however few – as they have been to myself.

My own prejudices, I confess, are in Miss M.'s favour. Indeed, she herself assured me in the covering letter to which reference has been made, that a chance word of mine had been her actual incentive to composition – the remark, in fact, that 'the *truth* about even the least of things – e.g. your Self, Miss M.! – may be a taper in whose beam one may peep at the truth about Everything'. I cannot recall the occasion, or this little apophthegm. Indeed only with extreme reluctance would I have helped to launch my small friend on her gigantic ordeal. As a matter of fact, she had a little way of carrying off scraps of the conversation of the 'common-sized', as a bee carries off a drop of nectar, and of transforming them into a honey all her own.

As characteristic of her is the fact that during the whole time she was engaged on her writing (and there is ample evidence in her manuscript that, whether in fatigue, disinclination, or despair, she sometimes left it untouched for weeks together) she never made the faintest allusion to it. Authors, I believe – if I may take the elder Disraeli for my authority – are seldom so secretive concerning their activities. No less characteristically, her letter to me was dated February 14th. Her Memoirs were to be my Valentine.

"'Little drops of water ...'" my dear Sir Walter,' she wrote; 'you know the rest. Nevertheless, if only I had been given but one sharp spark of genius, what "infinite pains" I should have been spared. Yet what is here concerns only my early days, and chiefly one long year of them. I might have written on – almost *ad infinitum*. But I did not, because I feared to weary us both – of myself. The years that have followed my "coming of age" have been outwardly uneventful; and other people's thoughts, I find, are not so interesting as their experiences. There's much to forgive in what I have written – the rawness, the self-consciousness, the vanity, the folly. I am older now; but am I wiser – or merely not so young?

'Just as it stands, then, I shall leave my story to, and for, you ... Again and again, as I have pored over the scenes of my memory, I have asked myself: What can life be about? What does it mean? What was my true course? Where my compass? How many times, too, have I vainly speculated what *inward* difference being a human creature of my dimensions really makes. What is – deep, deep in – at variance between Man and Midget? *You* may discover this; even if *I* never shall. For after all, life's beads are all on one string, however loosely threaded they may seem to be.

'I have tried to tell nothing but the truth about myself. But I realize that it cannot be the whole truth. For while so engaged (just as when one peers into a looking-glass in the moonlight) a something has at times looked out of some secret den or niche in me, and then has vanished. Supposing, then, my dear Sir W., my story convinces you that all these years you have unawares been harbouring in your friendship not a woman, scarcely a human being, but an ASP! Oh dear, and oh dear! Well, there are three-and-thirty ingredients (ingrediments as I used to call them, when I was a child) in that sovran antidote, Venice Treacle. Scatter a pennyweight of it upon my tombstone; and so lay my in-fi-ni-te-si-mal ap-pa-ri-ti-on!

'Maybe though, there are not so very many vital differences between "midgets" and people of the common size; no more, per-haps, than there are between them and "the Great." Even then it is possible that after reading my small, endless story you may be very thankful that you are not a Midget too.

'Whether or not, I have tried to be frank, if not a Warning. Keep or destroy what I have written as you will. But please show it to nobody until nobody would mind. And now, good-bye.'

'M.'

There was a tacit compact between Miss M. and myself that I should visit her at Lyndsey about once a month. Business, indisposition, advancing age, only too frequently made the journey impracticable. But in general, I would at such intervals find myself in her company at her old house, Stonecote; drinking tea with her, gossiping, or reading to her, while she sat in her chair beside my book, embroidering her brilliant tiny flowers and beetles and butterflies with her tiny needle, listening or day-dreaming or musing out of the high window at the prospect of Chizzel Hill.

At times she was an extremely quiet companion. At others she would rain questions on me, many of them exceedingly unconventional, on a score of subjects at once, scarcely pausing for answers which I was frequently at a loss to give. In a mixed company she was, perhaps, exaggeratedly conscious of her minute stature.

But in these quiet talks – that shrill-sweet voice, those impulsive little gestures – she forgot it altogether. Not so her visitor, who must confess to having been continually convicted in her presence of a kind of clumsiness and gaucherie – and that, I confess, not merely physical. To a stranger this experience, however wholesome, might be a little humiliating.

When interested, Miss M. would sit perfectly still, her hands tightly clasped in her lap, her eyes fixed with a piercing, yet curiously remote, scrutiny. In complete repose, her features lost this keenness, and she became an indescribably beautiful little figure, in her bright-coloured clothes, in the large quiet room. I can think of no comparison that would not seem fanciful. Herself is to some extent in her book. And yet that unique volatile presence, so frail, yet so vigorous, 'so very nearly nothing', in her own whimsical phrase, is only fitfully manifest.

Naturally enough, she loved solitude. But I am inclined to think she indulged in it to excess. It was, at any rate, in solitude that she wrote her book; and in solitude apparently that her unknown visitor found her, in the following mysterious circumstances.

The last of our reunions – and one no less happy than the rest – was towards the end of the month of March. On the morning of the following 25th of April I received a telegram summoning me to Lyndsey. I arrived there the same afternoon, and was admitted by Mrs. Bowater, Miss M.'s excellent, but somewhat Dickensian, housekeeper, then already a little deaf and elderly. I found her in extreme distress. It appeared that the evening before, about seven o'clock, Mrs. Bowater had heard voices in the house – Miss M.'s and another's. Friendly callers were infrequent; unfamiliar ones extremely rare; and Mrs. Bowater confessed that she had felt some curiosity, if not concern, as to who this stranger might be, and how he had gained admission. She blamed herself beyond measure – though I endeavoured to reassure the good woman – for not instantly setting her misgivings at rest.

Hearing nothing more, except the rain beating at the basement window, at half-past seven she went upstairs and knocked at Miss M.'s door. The large, pleasant room – her old nursery – at the top of the house, was in its usual scrupulous order, but vacant. Nothing was disarranged, nothing unusual, except only that a slip of paper had been pinned to the carpet a little beyond the threshold, with this message: 'I have been called away. – M.'

This communication, far from soothing, only increased Mrs. Bowater's anxiety. She searched the minute Sheraton wardrobe, and found that a garden hat and cape were missing. She waited awhile – unlike her usual self – at a loss what to be doing, and peering out of the window. But as darkness was coming on, and Miss M. rarely went out in windy or showery weather, or, indeed, descended the staircase without assistance, she became so much alarmed that a little before eight she set out to explore the garden with a stable lantern, and afterwards hurried off to the village for assistance.

As the reader will himself discover, this was not the first occasion on which Miss M. had given her friends anxiety. The house, the garden, the surrounding district, her old haunts at Wanderslore were repeatedly submitted at my direction to the most rigorous and protracted search. Watch was kept on the only gipsy encampment in the neighbourhood, near the Heath. Advertisements failed to bring me any but false clues. At length even hope had to be abandoned.

Miss M. had been 'called away'. By whom? I ask myself; on what errand? for what purpose? So clear and unhurried was the writing of her last message as to preclude, I think, the afflicting thought that her visitor had been the cause of any apprehension or anxiety. An even more tragic eventuality is out of the question. After the events recorded in her last chapter not only had she made me a certain promise, but her later life at Lyndsey had been, apparently, perfectly serene and happy. Only a day or two before she had laughed up at her housekeeper, 'Why, Mrs. Bowater, there's not *room* enough in me for all that's there!' Nor is it to be assumed that some 'inward' voice – her own frequent term – had summoned her away; for Mrs. Bowater immovably maintains that its tones reached her ear, though she herself was at the moment engaged in the kitchen referred to in the first chapter of the Memoirs.

Walter Dadus Pollacke,
Brunswick House, Beechwood.

Lyndsey

* * *

Chapter One

Some few years ago a brief account of me found its way into one or two country newspapers. I have been told that it reappeared, later, in better proportion, in the Metropolitan Press! Fortunately, or unfortunately, very little of this account was true. It related, among other things, that I am accustomed to wear shoes with leaden soles to them to keep me from being blown away like thistledown in the wind, that as a child I had narrowly escaped being scalded to death in a soup tureen, that one of my ancestors came from Poland, that I am an expert painter of miniatures, that I am a changeling and can speak the fairy tongue. And so on and so forth.

I think I can guess where my ingenuous biographer borrowed these fables. He meant me no harm; he was earning his living; he made judicious use of his 'no doubts' and 'it may be supposed'; and I hope he amused his readers. But by far the greater part of his account was concerned with mere *physical* particulars. He had looked at me in fancy through spectacles which may or may not have been rosy, but which certainly minified. I do not deserve his inches and ounces, however flattering his intentions may have been. It is true that my body is among the smaller works of God. But I think he paid rather too much attention to this fact. He spared any reference not only to my soul (and I am not ungrateful for that), but also to my mind and heart. There may be too much of all three for some tastes in the following pages, and especially, perhaps, of the last. That cannot be helped. Finally, my anonymous journalist stated that I was born in Rutlandshire – because, I suppose, it is the smallest county in England.

That was truly unkind of him, for, as a matter of fact, and to begin at the (apparent) beginning, I was born in the village of Lyndsey in *Kent* – the prettiest country spot, as I believe, in all that county's million acres. So it remains to this day in spite of the fact that since my childhood its little church with its decaying stones and unfading twelfth – or is it thirteenth? – century glass has been 'restored', and the lord of the manor has felled some of its finest trees, including a grove of sweet chestnuts on Bitchett Heath whose forefathers came over with the Romans. But he has not yet succeeded in levelling the barrow on Chizzel Hill. From my window I looked out (indeed, look out at this moment) to the wave-like crest of this beloved hill across a long straggling orchard, and pastures in the valley, where cattle grazed and sheep wandered, and unpolled willows stooped and silvered in the breeze. I never wearied of the hill, nor ever shall, and when, in my girlhood my grandfather, aware of this idle, gazing habit of mine, sent me from Geneva a diminutive telescope, my daydreams multiplied. His gift, as an old Kentish proverb goes, spread butter on bacon. With his spyglass to my eye I could bring a tapping green woodpecker as close as if it were actually laughing at *me,* and could all but snuff up the faint rich scent of the cowslips – paggles, as we called them, in meadows a good mile away.

My father's house, Stonecote, has a rather ungainly appearance if viewed from across the valley. But it is roomy and open and fairly challenges the winds of the equinoxes. Its main windows are of a shallow bow shape. One of them is among my first remembrances. I am seated in a bright tartan frock on a pomatum pot – a coloured picture of Mr. Shandy, as I remember, on its lid – and around me are the brushes, leather cases, knick-knacks, etc., of my father's dressing table. My father is shaving himself, his chin and cheeks puffed out with soapsuds. And now I look at him, and now at his reflection in the great looking-glass, and every time *that* happens he makes a pleasant grimace at me over his spectacles.

This particular moment of my childhood probably fixed itself on my mind because just as, with razor uplifted, he was about to attack his upper lip, a jackdaw, attracted maybe by my gay clothes, fluttered down on the sill outside, and fussing and scrabbling with wing and claw pecked hard with its beak against the glass. The sound and sight of this bird with its lively grey-blue eyes, so close and ardent, startled me. I leapt up, ran across the table, tripped over a hairbrush, and fell sprawling beside my father's watch. I hear its ticking, and also the little soothing whistle with which he was wont to comfort his daughter at any such mishap. Then perhaps I was five or six.

That is a genuine memory. But every family, I suppose, has its little pet traditions; and one of ours, relating to those early years, is connected with our kitchen cat, Miaou. She had come by a family of kittens, and I had crept, so it was said, into her shallow basket with them. Having, I suppose, been too frequently meddled with, this old mother cat lugged off her kittens one by one to a dark cupboard. The last one thus secured, she was discovered in rapt contemplation of myself, as if in debate whether or not it was her maternal duty to carry me off too. And there was I grinning up into her face. Such was our cook's – Mrs. Ballard's – story. What I actually remember is different. On the morning in question I was turning the corner of the brick-floored, dusky passage that led to the kitchen, when Miaou came trotting along out of it with her blind, blunt-headed bundle in her mouth. We were equally surprised at this encounter, and in brushing past she nearly knocked me over where I stood, casting me at the same moment the queerest animal look out of her eyes. So truth, in this case, was not so strange as Mrs. Ballard's fiction.

My father was then a rather corpulent man, with a high-coloured face, and he wore large spectacles. His time was his own, for we were comfortably off on an income derived from a half-share in the small fortune amassed by my grandfather and his partner in a paper mill. He might have been a more successful, though not perhaps a happier, man if he had done more work and planned to do less. But he only so far followed his hereditary occupations as to expend large quantities of its best 'handmade' in the composition of a monograph: *The History of Paper Making*. This entailed a vast accumulation of books and much solitude. I fancy, too, he believed in the policy of sleeping on one's first thoughts.

Since he was engaged at the same time on similar compilations with the Hop and the Cherry for theme, he made indifferent progress in all three. His papers, alas, were afterwards sold with his books, so I have no notion of what became of them or of their value. I can only hope that their purchaser has since won an easy distinction. These pursuits, if they achieved little else but the keeping of 'the man of the house' quiet and contented, proved my father, at any rate, to be a loyal and enthusiastic Man of Kent; and I have seen to it that a fine Morello cherry-tree blossoms, fruits, and flourishes over his grave.

. My father was something of a musician too, and could *pizzicato* so softly on his muted fiddle as not to jar even my too sensitive ear. He taught me to play chess on a little board with pygmy men, but he was apt to lose interest in the game when it went against him. Whereas it was then that our old friend, Dr. Grose, played his hardest. As my father's hands were rather clumsy in make, he took pains to be gentle and adroit with me. But even after shaving, his embrace was more of a discipline than a pleasure – a fact that may partly account for my own undemonstrativeness in this direction.

His voice, if anything, was small for his size, except when he discussed politics with Dr. Grose; religion or the bringing up of children with my godmother, Miss Fenne; or money matters with my mother. At such times, his noise – red face and gesticulations – affected one of his listeners, as eager as possible to pick up the crumbs, far more than ever thunder did, which is up in the clouds. My only other discomfort in his company was his habit of taking snuff. The stench of it almost suffocated me, and at tap of his finger-nail on the lid of his box, I would scamper off for shelter like a hare.

By birth he came of an old English family, though no doubt with the usual admixtures. My mother's mother was French. She was a Daundelyon. The blood of that 'sweet enemy' at times burned in her cheek like a flag; and my father needed his heaviest guns when the stormy winds did blow, and those colours were flying. At such moments I preferred to hear the engagement from a distant, not so much (again) because the mere discord grieved me, as to escape the din. But usually – and especially after such little displays – they were like two turtledoves, and I did my small best to pipe a decoy.

My father had been a man past forty when he married my mother. She about fifteen years younger – a slim, nimble, and lovely being, who could slip round and encircle him in person or mind while he was pondering whether or not to say Bo to a goose. Seven years afterwards came I. Friends, as friends will, professed to see a likeness between us. And if my mother could have been dwindled down to be of my height and figure, perhaps they would have been justified.

But in hair and complexion, possibly in ways, too, I harked back to an aunt of hers, Kitilda, who had died of consumption in her early twenties. I loved to hear stories of my great-aunt Kitilda. She sang like a bird, twice ran away from her convent school, and was so fond of water that an old gentleman (a friend of Mr. Landor's, the poet) who fell in love with her, called her 'the Naiad'.

My mother, in her youth at Tunbridge Wells, had been considered 'a beauty', and had had many admirers – at least so Mrs. Ballard, our cook, told Pollie: 'Yes, and we know who might have turned out different if things hadn't been the same,' was a cryptic remark she once made which filled two 'little pitchers' to overflowing. Among these admirers was a Mr. Wagginhorne, who now lived at Maidstone. He had pocketed his passion but not his admiration; and being an artist in the same sense that my father was an author, he had painted my mother and me and a pot of azaleas in oils. How well I remember those interminable sittings, with the old gentleman daubing along, and cracking his beloved jokes and Kentish cobbs at one and the same time. Whenever he came to see us this portrait was taken out of a cupboard and hung up in substitution for another picture in the dining-room. What became of it when Mr. Wagginhorne died I could never discover. My mother would laugh when I inquired, and archly eye my father. It was clear, at any rate, that author was not jealous of artist!

My mother was gentle with me, and had need to be; and I was happier in her company than one might think possible in a world of such fleetingness. I would sit beside her workbox and she would softly talk to me, and teach me my lessons and small rhymes to say; while my own impulse and instinct taught me to sing and dance. What gay hours we shared. Sewing was at first difficult, for at that time no proportionate needles could be procured for me, and I hated to cobble up only coarse work. But she would give me little childish jobs to do, such as arranging her silks, or sorting her beads, and would rock me to sleep with her finger to a drone so gentle that it might have been a distant bee's.

Yet shadows there were, before the darkness came. Child that I was, I would watch gather over her face at times a kind of absent-ness, as if she were dreaming of something to which she could give no name, of some hope or wish that was now never to be fulfilled. At this I would grow anxious and silent, doubting, perhaps, that I had displeased her; while, to judge from her look, I might not have been there at all.

Or again, a mischievousness and mockery would steal into her mood. Then she would treat me as a mere trivial plaything, talk-ing *small* things to me, as if our alphabet consisted of nothing but 'little o' – a letter for which I always felt a sort of pity; but small affection. This habit saddened my young days, and sometimes enraged me, more than I can say. I was *always* of a serious cast of mind – even a little priggish perhaps; and experience had already taught me that I could share my mother's thoughts and feelings more easily than she could share mine.

Chapter Two

When precisely I began to speculate *why* I was despatched into this world so minute and different I cannot say. Pretty early, I fancy, though few opportunities for comparison were afforded me, and for some time I supposed that all young children were of my stature. There was Adam Waggett, it is true, the bumpkin son of a village friend of Mrs. Ballard's. But he was some years older than I. He would be invited to tea in the kitchen, and was never at rest unless stuffing himself out with bread and dripping or dough cake – victuals naturally odious to me; or pestering me with his coarse fooling and curiosity. He was to prove useful in due season; but in those days I had a distaste for him almost as deep-rooted as that for 'Hoppy', the village idiot – though I saw poor Hoppy only once.

Whatever the reason may be, except in extremely desperate moments, I do not remember much regretting that I was not of the common size. Still, the realization was gradually borne in on me that I was a disappointment and mischance to my parents. Yet I never dared to let fall a question which was to be often in my young thoughts: 'Tell me, mamma, are you *sorry* that your little daughter is a Midget?' But then, does anyone ask questions like that until they cannot be answered?

Still, cross-examine her I did occasionally.

'Where did I come from, mamma?'

'Why, my dear, I am your mother.'

'Just', I replied, 'like Pollie's mother is *her* mother?'

She cast a glance at me from eyes that appeared to be very small, unless for that instant it was mine that I saw reflected there.

'Yes, my dear,' she replied at length. 'We come and we go.' She seemed tired with the heat of the day, so I sat quietly, holding her finger, until she was recovered.

Only, perhaps, on account of my size was there any occasion for me to be thoroughly ashamed of myself. Otherwise I was, if anything, a rather precocious child. I could walk a step or two at eleven months, and began to talk before the Christmas following the first anniversary of my birthday, August 30th. I learned my letters from the big black capitals in the Book of Genesis; and to count and cipher from a beautiful little Abacus strung with beads of silver and garnets. The usual ailments came my way, but were light come, light go. I was remarkably sinewy and muscular, strong in the chest, and never suffered from snuffling colds or from chilblains, though shoes and gloves had always been a difficulty.

I can perfectly recall my childish figure as I stood with endless satisfaction surveying my reflection in a looking-glass on the Christmas morning after my ninth birthday. My frock was of a fine puffed scarlet, my slippers loose at heel, to match. My hair, demurely parted in the middle, hung straight on my narrow shoulders (though I had already learned to plait it) and so framed my face; the eyebrows faintly arched (eyebrows darker and crookeder now); the nose in proportion; the lips rather narrow, and of a lively red.

My features wore a penetrating expression in that reflection because my keen look was searching them pretty close. But if it was a sharp look, it was not, I think, a bold or defiant; and then I smiled, as if to say, 'So this is to be my companion, then.'

It was winter, and frost was on the window that day. I enjoyed the crisp air, for I was packed warm in lamb's wool underneath. There I stood, my father's round red face beaming on one side of the table, my mother's smiling but enigmatic, scrutinizing my reflection on the other, and myself tippeting this way and that – a veritable miniature of Vanity.

Who should be ushered at this moment into the room, where we were so happy, but my godmother, Miss Fenne, come to bring my father and mother her Christmas greetings and me a little catechism sewn up in a pink silk cover. She was a bent-up old lady and a rapid talker, with a voice which, though small, jangled every nerve in my body, like a pencil on a slate. Being my godmother, she took great liberties in counselling my parents on the proper way of 'managing' me. The only time, indeed, I ever heard my father utter an oath was when Miss Fenne was just beyond hearing. She peered across at me on this Christmas morning like a bird at a scorpion: 'Caroline, Caroline,' she cried, 'for shame! The Shrimp! You will turn the child's head.'

Shrimp! I had seen the loathsome, doubled-up creatures (in their boiled state) on a kitchen plate. My blood turned to vinegar; and in rage and shame I fell all of a heap on the table, hiding from her sight my face and my hands as best I could under my clothes, and wishing that I might vanish away from the world altogether.

My father's voice boomed out in protest; my mother took me into her arms to soothe and scold me; but long after the ruffled old lady had taken her departure I brooded on this affront. 'Away, away!' a voice seemed to cry within; and I listened to it as if under a spell. All that day I nursed my wounded vanity, and the same evening, after candle light, I found myself for a moment alone in the kitchen. Pollie had gone to the wood-shed to fetch kindling, leaving the door into the garden ajar. The night air touched my cheek. Half beside myself with desire of I know not what, I sprang out from the doorstep into an inch or so of snow, and picking myself up, ran off into the darkness under the huge sky.

It was bitterly cold. Frost had crusted the virgin surface of the snow. My light footsteps can hardly have shattered its upper crystals. I ran on and on into the ghostly world, into this stiff, marvellous, gloating scene of frozen vegetation beneath that immense vacancy. A kind of stupor must have spread over my young mind. It seemed I was transported out of myself under the stars, in the mute presence of the Watchman of Heaven. I stood there lost in wonder in the grey, luminous gloom.

But my escapade was brief and humiliating. The shock of the cold, the excitement, quickly exhausted me. I threw myself down and covered my face with my hands, trying in vain to stifle my sobs. What was my longing? Where its satisfaction? Soft as wool a drowsiness stole over my sense that might swiftly have wafted me off on the last voyage of discovery. But I had been missed. A few minutes' search, and Pollie discovered me lying there by the frozen cabbage stalks. The woeful Mænad was carried back into the kitchen again – a hot bath, a hot posset, and a few anxious and thankful tears.

The wonder is that, being an only child, and a sore problem when any question of discipline or punishment arose, I was not utterly spoiled. One person at least came very near to doing so, my grandfather, Monsieur Pierre de Ronvel. To be exact, he was my step-grandfather, for my mother's charming mother, with her ringlets and crinoline, after my real grandfather's death, had married a second time. He crossed the English Channel to visit my parents when I was in my tenth year – a tall, stiff, jerky man, with a sallow face, speckled fur-like hair that stood in a little wall round his forehead, and the liveliest black eyes. His manners were a felicity to watch even at my age. You would have supposed he had come *courting* my mother; and he took a great fancy to me. He was extremely fond of salad, I remember; and I very proud of my mustard and cress – which I could gather for him myself with one of my own table-knives. So copiously he talked, with such a medley of joys and zests and surprises on his face, that I vowed soon to be mistress of my stepmother tongue. He could also conjure away reels and thimbles, even spoons and forks, with a skill that precluded my becoming a materialist for ever after. I *worshipped* my grandfather – and yet without a vestige of fear.

To him, indeed – though I think he was himself of a secular turn of mind – I owe the story of my birthday saint, St. Rosa of Lima in Peru, the only saint, I believe, of the New World. With myself pinnacled on his angular knee, and devouring like a sweetmeat every broken English word as it slipped from his tongue, he told me how pious an infant my Saint had been; how, when her mother, to beautify her, had twined flowers in her hair, she had *pinned* them to her skull; how she had rubbed quicklime on her fair cheeks to disenchant her lovers ('*ses prétendants*'), and how it was only veritable showers of roses from heaven that had at last persuaded Pope Clement to make her a saint.

'Perhaps, *bon papa*,' said I, 'I shall dig and sow too when I am grown up, like St. Rosa, to support *my* mamma and papa when *they* are very old. Do you think I shall make enough money? Papa has a very good appetite?' He stared at me, as if in consternation.

'*Dieu vous en garde, ma p'tite,*' he cried; and violently blew his nose.

So closely I took St. Rosa's story to heart that, one day, after bidding my beauty a wistful farewell in the glass, I rubbed my cheek too, but with the blue flowers of the – *brook*lime. It stained them a little, but soon washed off. In my case a needless precaution; my *prétendants* have been few.

It was a mournful day when my grandfather returned to France never to be seen by me again. Yet he was to remember me always; and at last when I myself had forgotten even my faith in his fidelity. Nearly all my personal furnishings and belongings were gifts of his from France, and many of them of his own making. There was my four-post bed, for instance; with a flowered silk canopy, a carved tester and half a dozen changes of linens and valance. There were chairs to match, a wardrobe, silk mats from Persia, a cheval glass, and clothes and finery in abundance, china and cutlery, top-boots and sabots. Even a silver-hooped bath-tub and a crystal toilet set, and scores of articles besides for use or ornament, which it would be tedious to mention. My grandfather had my measurements to a nicety, and as the years went by he sagaciously allowed for growth.

I learned to tell the time from an eight-day clock which played a sacred tune at matins and vespers; and later, he sent me a watch, the least bit too large for me to be quite comfortable, but an exquisite piece of workmanship. As my birthdays (and his) drew near, I could scarcely sleep for thinking what fresh entrancing novelty the festive morning would bring. The only one of his gifts – by no means the least ingenious – which never, after the first flush of excitement, gave me much pleasure, was a two-chambered thatched summer-house, set up on a pole, and reached by a wide, shallow ladder. The roof opened, so that on very hot days a block of ice could be laid within, the water from its slow melting running out by a gutter. But I loved sunshine. This was a plaything that ridiculously amused chance visitors; it attracted flies; I felt silly up in it: and gladly resigned it to the tits, starlings, and sparrows to quarrel over as they pleased.

My really useful furniture – of plain old Sheraton design – was set out in my bedroom. In one half of the room slept Pollie, a placid but, before her marriage, rather slow-witted creature about six years my senior. The other half was mine and had been made proportionate to my needs by a cabinet-maker from London. My father had had a low stone balcony built on beyond my window. This was fenced with fine trellis work to screen it from the colder winds. With its few extremely dwarf trees set along in green Nankin tubs, and the view it commanded, I could enjoy this eyrie for hours – never wearied of it in my youth, nor shall if I live to be a hundred.

I linger over these early recollections, simply because they are such very happy things to possess. And now for out-of-doors.

Either because my mother was shy of me, or because she thought vulgar attention would be bad for me, she seldom took me far abroad. Now and then Pollie carried me down to the village to tea with *her* mother, and once or twice I was taken to church. The last occasion, however, narrowly escaped being a catastrophe, and the experiment was not repeated. Instead, we usually held a short evening service, on Sundays, in the house, when my father read the lessons, 'like a miner prophet', as I wrote and told Miss Fenne. He certainly dug away at the texts till the words glittered for me like lumps of coal. On weekdays more people were likely to be about, and in general I was secluded. A mistake, I think. But fortunately our high, plain house stood up in a delightful garden, sloping this way and that towards orchard and wood, with a fine-turfed lawn, few 'cultivated' flowers, and ample drifts of shade. If Kent is the garden of England, then this was the garden of Kent.

I was forbidden to be alone in it. But Pollie would sometimes weary of her charge (in which I encouraged her) and when out of sight of the windows she would stray off to gossip with the gardener or with some friend from the village, leaving me to myself. To judge from the tales which I have read or have been told about children, I must have been old for my age. But perhaps the workings of the mind and heart of a girl in her teens are not of general interest. Let me be brief. A stream of water ran on the southern side all the length of the garden, under a high, rocky bank (its boundary) which was densely overhung with ash and willow, and hedges of brier and bramble looped with bindweed, goose-grass, and traveller's joy. On the nearer bank of this stream which had been left to its wild, I would sit among the mossy rocks and stones and search the green tops of my ambush as if in quest of Paradise.

When the sun's rays beat down too fiercely on my head I would make myself an umbrella of wild angelica or water parsnip.

Caring little for playthings, and having my smallest books with me chiefly for silent company, I would fall into a day-dream in a world that in my solitude became my own. In this fantastic and still world I forgot the misadventure of my birth, which had now really begun to burden me, forgot pride, vanity, and chagrin; and was at peace. There I had many proportionate friends, few enemies. An old carrion crow, that sulked out a black existence in this beauty, now and then alarmed me with his attentions; but he was easily scared off. The lesser and least of living things seemed to accept me as one of themselves. Nor (perhaps because I never killed them) had I any silly distaste for the caterpillars, centipedes, and satiny black slugs. Mistress Snail would stoop out at me like a foster-mother. Even the midges, which to his frenzy would swarm round my father's head like swifts round a steeple, left me entirely unmolested. Either I was too dry a prey, or they misliked the flavour of my blood.

My eyes dazzled in colours. The smallest of the marvels of flowers and flies and beetles and pebbles, and the radiance that washed over them, would fill me with a mute, pent-up rapture almost unendurable. Butterflies would settle quietly on the hot stones beside me as if to match their raiment against mine. If I proffered my hand, with quivering wings and horns they would uncoil their delicate tongues and quaff from it drops of dew or water. A solemn grasshopper would occasionally straddle across my palm, and with patience I made quite an old friend of a harvest mouse. They weigh only two to the halfpenny. This sharp-nosed furry morsel would creep swiftly along to share my crumbs and snuggle itself to sleep in my lap. By and by, I suppose, it took to itself a wife; I saw it no more. Bees would rest there, the panniers of their thighs laden with pollen: and now and then a wasp, his jaws full of wood or meat. When sunbeetles or ants drew near, they would seem to pause at my whisper, as if hearkening. As if in their remote silence pondering and sharing the world with me. All childish fancy, no doubt; for I proved far less successful with the humans.

But how, it may be asked, seeing that there must have been a shrill piping of birds and brawling of water among the stones, how could Mademoiselle's delicate ear endure *that* racket? Perhaps it is because the birds being loose in the hollow of space is carried away into its vacancy their cries. It is, too, the harsh, rather than the shrill, that frets me. As for the noise of the water, it was so full and limpid, yet made up of such infinitely entangled chimings and drummings, that it would lull me into a kind of trance, until to a strange eye I must have appeared like a lifeless waxen mammet on my stone.

What may wholly have been another childish fancy was that apart from the silvery darting flies and the rainbow-coloured motes in the sunbeams, fine and airy invisible shapes seemed to haunt and hover around me when all was still. Most of my fellow creatures to my young nose had an odour a good deal denser than the fainter scented flowers, and I can fancy such a fog, if intensified, would be distressing to beings so bodiless and rare. Whereas the air I disturbed and infected with my presence can have been of but shallow volume.

Fairies I never saw – I had a kind of fear and distaste for them even in books. Nor for that matter – perhaps because the stream here was too tumbling and opaque – a kingfisher. But whatever other company may have been mine, I had the clouds and the water and the insects and the stones – while pimpernel, mouse-tail, tormentil, the wild strawberry, the feathery grasses seemed to have been made expressly for my delight. Ego-centric Midget that I was!

Chapter Three

Not that in an existence so passive riddles never came my way. As one morning I brushed past a bush of lads' love (or maidens' ruin, as some call it), its fragrance sweeping me from top to toe, I stumbled on the carcass of a young mole. Curiosity vanquished the first gulp of horror. Holding my breath, with a stick I slowly edged it up in the dust and surveyed the white heaving nest of maggots in its belly with a peculiar and absorbed recognition. 'Ah ha!' a voice cried within me, 'so this is what is in wait; this is how things are'; and I stooped with lips drawn back over my teeth to examine the stinking mystery more closely. That was a lesson I have never unlearned.

One of a rather different kind had another effect. I was sitting in the garden one day watching in the distance a jay huffling and sidling and preening its feathers on a bit of decrepit fencing. Suddenly there fell a sharp crack of sound. In a flash, with a derisive chattering, the jay was flown: and then I saw Adam Waggett, half doubled up, stealing along towards the place. I lay in wait for him. With catapult dangling in one hand, the other fist tight shut, he came along like a thief. And I cried hollowly out of my concealment, 'Adam, what have you there?'

Such a picture of foolish shame I have never seen. He was

compelled none the less to exhibit his spoil, an eye-shut, twinkle-tailed, needle-billed Jenny Wren crumpled up in his great, dirty paw. Fury burnt up in me like a fire. What I said to him I cannot remember, but it was nothing sweet; and it was a cowed Adam Waggett that loafed off as truculently as he could towards the house, his catapult and victim left behind him. But that was his lesson rather than mine, and one which *he* never forgot.

When in my serener moods Pollie's voice would be heard slyly hallooing for me, I would rouse up with a shock to realize again the little cell of my body into which I had been confined. Then she and I would eat our luncheon, a few snippets of biscuit, a cherry or two, or slice of apple for me, and for her a hunch of bread and bacon about half my size in length and thickness. I would turn my back on her, for I could not endure to see her gobble her meal, having an abhorrence of cooked flesh, and a dainty stomach. Still, like most children I could be greedy, and curious of unfamiliar foods. To a few forbidden black currants which I reached up and plucked from their rank-smelling bush, and devoured, skin and all, I owe lesson Number 3. This one, however, had to be repeated.

Childhood quickly fleets away. Those happy, unhappy, faraway days seem like mere glimpses of a dragon-fly shimmering and darting over my garden stream, though at the actual time they more closely resembled, perhaps, a continuous dream broken into bits of vivid awakening.

As I grew older, my skirts grew longer, my desire for independence sharper, and my wits more inquiring. On my seventeenth birthday I put up my hair, and was confirmed by a bishop whom my godmother persuaded to officiate in the house. It was a solemn occasion; but my mother was a good deal concerned about the lunch, and with the ballooning lawn sleeves and the two square episcopal finger-tips disposed upon my head. The experience cast a peaceful light into my mind and shook my heart, but it made me for a time a little self-conscious of both my virtue and my sins. I began to brood not only on the deplorable state of my own soul, but also on Pollie's and Mrs. Ballard's, and became for a time a diminutive Miss Fenne. I suppose innocence is a precarious bliss. On the other hand, if one's mind is like a dead mole's belly, it is wise, I think, to examine it closely but not too often, and to repeat that confirmation for one's self every morning and evening.

As a young child I had been, of course, as naturally religious as a savage or an angel. But even then, I think, I never could quite believe that Paradise was a mere Fenne-land.

Once I remember in the midst of my multiplication table I had broken out unannounced with, 'Then *God* made the world, mamma?'

'Yes, my dear.'

'And all things in the forests and the birds in the sky and – and moles, and this?' I held down my limp, coral-coloured arithmetic.

'Yes,' said she.

I wondered awhile, losing myself, as if in wanderings like Ariel's, between the clouds. 'What, mamma, did He make them of?' my voice interrupted me.

'He made them', said my mother steadily, 'of His Power and Love.'

Rapidly I slid back into her company. 'And can we, can I, make things of *my* power and love?'

'I suppose, my dear,' replied my mother reflectively and perhaps thinking of my father in his study, over his Paper and Hops, 'it is only *that* in life that is really worth doing.'

'Then,' I said sagely, 'I *suspects* that's how Mullings does the garden, mamma.'

Long before Miss Fenne's and the bishop's visitation my mother had set about teaching me in earnest. A governess – a Miss Perry – was our first experiment. Alas, apart from her tendency to quinsy, it was I who was found wanting. She complained of the strain on her nerves. My mother feared that quinsy was catching; and Miss Perry had no successor. Reading was always a difficulty. My father bought me as tiny old books as could be found, including a dwarf Bible, a midget Pickering Shakespeare, and a grammar (with a menagerie for frontispiece) from which I learned that 'irony is a figure which intends the reverse of what it speaks, and under the masque of praise, conceals the most biting satyr'; and the following stanza:

> Hail Energeia! hail my native tongue
> Concisely full, and musically strong;
> Thou with the pencil hold'st a glorious strife,
> And paint'st the passions equal to the life.

My mother agreed that 'strung' would be preferable to 'strong', and explained that 'the passions' did not signify merely ill-temper; while, if I pecked over-nicely at my food, my father would cry 'Hail Energeia!', a challenge which rarely failed to persuade me to set to.

My grandfather sent me other pygmy books from Paris, including a minute masterpiece of calligraphy, *Une Anthologie de Chansons pour une Minuscule Aimante et Bien-aimée par P. de R.* These I could easily carry about with me. I soon learned to accustom my arms and shoulders to bulkier and more cumbrous volumes. My usual method with a common-sized book was to prop it up towards the middle of the table and then to seat myself at the edge. The page finished, I would walk across and turn over a fresh leaf. Thus in my solitude I studied my lessons and read again and again my nursery favourites, some of them, I gather, now undeservedly out of fashion.

Perhaps even better than fiction or folk-tales, I liked books of knowledge.

There were two of these in particular, *The Observing Eye; or Lessons to Children on the Three Lowest Divisions of Animal Life – The Radiated, Articulated, and Molluscuous*, and *The Childhood of the World*. Even at nine I remarked how nimbly the anonymous author of the former would skip from St. Paul to the lobster; and I never wearied of brooding on Mr. Clodd's frontispiece. This depicts a large-headed and seemingly one-legged little girl in a flounced frock lying asleep under a wall on which ivy is sprawling. For pillow for herself and her staring doll there lies on the ground a full-sized human skull, and in the middle distance are seen the monoliths of Stonehenge. Beyond these gigantic stones, and behind the far mountains, rises with spiky rays an enormous Sun.

I was that child; and mine her sun that burned in heaven, and he a more obedient luminary than any lamp of man's. I would wonder what she would do when she awoke from sleep. The skull, in particular, both terrified and entranced me – the secret of all history seemed to lie hidden in the shadows beneath its dome. Indeed I needed no reminder from Mr. Clodd that 'Children (and some grown-up people too) are apt to think that things are wonderful only when they are big, which is not true.'

I knew already, out of nowhere, that 'the bee's waxen cell is more curious than the chimpanzee's rough hut' (though I should have dearly liked to see the latter); and that 'an ant is more won-derful than the huge and dull rhinoceros'. Such is childishness, however: I pitied the poor rhinoceros his 'dull'. Over such small things as a nut, a shell, a drop of rainwater in a buttercup, a frond of frost (for there were cold winters at Lyndsey in those days), I would pore and pore, imbibing the lesson that the eye alone if used in patience will tell its owner far more about an object than it can merely see.

Among my few framed pictures I cannot resist mentioning one by a painter of the name of Bosch. Below the middle of it kneeled naked Adam and Eve with exquisite crimped hair on their shoulders; and between them stood God. All above and beneath them roamed the animals, birds, insects, and infinitesimals of Eden, including a long-tailed monkey on an elephant, a jerboa, a dancing crocodile, and – who but our cat Miaou, carrying off a mouse! An astonishing, inexhaustible piece of thoughtfulness. I loved Mynheer Bosch.

Shameful dunce Miss M. may remain, but she did in her childhood supremely enjoy any simple book about the things of creation great or small. But I preferred my own notions of some of them. When my father of a dark, clear night would perch me up at a window to see the stars – Charles's Wain and the Chair – and told me that they were huge boiling suns, roaring their way through the vast pits of space, I would shake my head to myself. I was grateful for the science, but preferred to keep them just 'stars'. And though I loved to lave my hands in a trickle of light that had been numberless years on its journey to this earth, that of a candle also filled me with admiration, and I was unfeignedly grieved that the bleak moon was naught but a sheer hulk, *sans* even air or ice or rain or snow.

How much pleasanter it would be to think that her shine was the reflection of our cherry orchards, and that her shadows were just Kentish hay-ricks, barns, and oast-houses. It was, too, perhaps rather tactless of my father to beguile me with full-authors' grown accounts of the Lives of the Little. Accomplished writers they may be, but – well, never mind. As for the Lives of the Great, I could easily adjust Monsieur Bon Papa's spyglass and reduce them to scale.

My father taught me also to swim in his round bath; and on a visit to Canterbury purchased for me the nimblest little dun Shetland pony, whom we called Mopsa. I learned to become a fearless rider. But hardy though her race may be, perhaps I was too light a burden to satisfy Mopsa's spirits. In a passing fit of temper she broke a leg. Though I had stopped my ears for an hour before the vet came, I heard the shot.

My mother's lessons were never very burdensome. She taught me little, but she taught it well – even a morsel of Latin. I never wearied of the sweet oboe-like nasal sound of her French poems, and she instilled in me such a delight in words that to this day I firmly believe that things are at least twice the better and richer for being called by them. Apart from a kind of passionate impatience over what was alien to me – arithmetic for instance, and 'analysis' – and occasional fits of the sulks, which she allowed to deposit their own sediment at leisure, I was a willing, and, at times, even a greedy scholar. Apparently from infancy I was of a firm resolve to match my wits with those of the common-sized and to be 'grown-up' some day.

So much for my education, a thing which it seems to me is likely to continue – and specially in respect of human nature – as long as I keep alive. With so little childish company, without rivalry, I was inclined to swell myself out with conceit and complacency. 'It's easy holding down the latchet when nobody pulls the string.' But whatever size we may be, in soul or body, I have found that the world wields a sharp pin, and is pitiless to bubbles.

Though inclined to be dreamy and idle when alone, I was, of course, my own teacher too. My senses were seven in number, however few my wits. In particular I loved to observe the clustering and gathering of plants, like families, each of a shape, size, and hue, each in their kind and season, though tall and lowly were intermingled. Now and then I would come on some small plant self-sown, shining and flourishing, free and clear, and even the lovelier for being alone in its kind amid its greater neighbours. I prized these discoveries, and if any one of them was dwarfed a little by its surroundings I would cosset it up and help it against them. How strange, thought I, if men so regarded each other's intelligence. If from pitying the dull-witted the sharp-witted slid to mere toleration, and from toleration to despising and loathing, what a contest would presently begin between the strong-bodied stupid and the feeble-bodied clever, and how soon there would be no strong-bodied stupid left in the world! They would dwindle away and disappear into Time like the mammoth and the woolly bear. And then I began to be sorry for the woolly bear and to wish I could go and have a look at him. Perhaps this is putting my old head on those young shoulders, but when I strive to re-enter the thoughts of those remote days, how like they seem to the noisy wasting stream beside which they flowed on, and of whose source and destination I was unaware.

All this egotism recalls a remark that Mrs. Ballard once made apropos of some little smart repartee from Miss M. as she sat beside her pasteboard and slapped away at a lump of dough, 'Well *I* know a young lady who's been talking to the young man that rubbed his face with a brass candlestick.'

Chapter Four

In the midst of my eighteenth year fortune began to darken. My mother had told me little of the world, its chances and changes, cares and troubles. What I had learned of these came chiefly from books and my own speculations. We had few visitors and from all but the most familiar I was quickly packed away. My mother was sensitive of me, for both our sakes. But I think in this she was mistaken, for when my time came, Life found me raw, and it rubbed in the salt rather vigorously.

My father had other views. He argued for facing the facts, though perhaps those relating to fruit and paper are not very intimidating. But he seldom made his way against my mother, except in matters that concerned his own comfort. He loved me fondly, but throughout my childhood seems to have regarded me as a kind of animated marionette. When he came out from his Mills and Pockets it amused him to find me nibbling a raspberry beside his plate. He'd rub his round stubbly head, and say, 'Well, mamma, and how's Trot done this morning?' or he would stoop and draw ever so heedfully his left little finger down my nose to its uttermost tip, and whisper, 'And so to Land's End, my love.' Now and then I would find his eyes fixed on me as if in stupefaction that I was actually his daughter.

But now that I was getting to be a young woman and had put up my hair, and the future frowned near, this domestic problem began seriously to concern him. My mother paled at the very mention of it. I remember I had climbed up on to his writing desk one morning, in search of a pair of high boots which I had taken off in his study the evening before. We had been fishing for sticklebacks. Concealed from view, while the wind whined at the window, I heard a quarrel between my father and mother about me which I will never repeat to mortal ear. It darkened my mind for days, and if ... but better not.

At this time anxiety about money matters must have begun its gnawing in my poor father's brains. And I know what *that* means. He had recommended to others and speculated himself in some experiment in the cultivation of the trees from which the Chinese first made paper, and had not only been grossly cheated, but laughed at in the press. *The Kentish Courier* – I see his ears burning now – had referred to him as 'the ingenious Mr. Tapa'; and my mother's commiseration had hardly solaced him: 'But, my dear, you couldn't have gone to Canton by yourself. We must just draw in our horns a little.' The ingenious Mr. Tapa patted the hand on his shoulder, but his ears burned on.

'Besides,' my mother added, with a long, sighing breath, as she seated herself again, 'there are the books.' He plucked his spectacles off, and gazed vaguely in her direction: 'Oh, yes, yes, there are the books.'

Nor was he long daunted by this attack. He fell in love with some notion of so pickling hop-poles that they would last for ever. But the press was no kinder to his poles than to his mulberries.

And then befell the blackest misfortune of my life. I had been ill; and for a few days had been sleeping in one of the spare bedrooms in a cot beside my mother, so that she should be near me if I needed her. This particular evening, however, I had gone back to my own room. We cannot change the past, or foresee the future. But if only Pollie had not been a heavy sleeper; if only I had escaped that trivial ailment – how tangled is life's skein! It was the May after my eighteenth birthday and full moonlight.

Troubled in mind by my illness and other worries and mortifications, my mother, not fully aroused perhaps, got up in the small hours and mounted the stone staircase in order to look in on me. I was awake, and heard the rustling of her nightdress and the faint touch of her slippered feet ascending from stone to stone. I guessed her errand, and in my folly thought I would pretend to be asleep and give her a 'surprise'. I drew my curtains and lay motionless on my back as if I were dead. With eyes closed, listening, I smilingly waited.

Then suddenly I heard a muffled, gasping cry; and all was utterly, icily still. I flung aside the silk curtains and leapt out of bed.

The moonlight was streaming in a lean ray across the floor of my room. I ran down this luminous pathway into the dusk at the open door. At the stair-head beyond, still and silent, I saw my poor dear. On through the cold dark air I ran, and stood in her loosened hair beside her head. It lay unstirring, her cheek colourless, her hand stretched out, palm upward, on the stone. I called into her ear, first gently and pleadingly, then loud and shrill. I ran and chafed her fingers, then back again, and stooped, listening with my cheeks to her lips. She exhaled a trembling sigh. I called and called; but my shrillness was utterly swallowed up in the vast night-hung house. Then softly in the silence her lids unsealed and her eyes, as if wonderful with a remote dream, looked up into my face. 'My dear,' she whispered, wakefulness gathering faintly into her gaze, 'my dear, is it you?' There was an accent in her voice that I had never heard before. Perhaps her tranceful eyes had magnified me. Then once more the lids closed down and I was alone. I fell on my knees beside her and crouched, praying into her heedless ear.

It was my first acquaintance with calamity, and physically powerless to aid her, I could think of nothing for a moment but to persuade her to speak to me again. Then my senses returned to me. To descend that flight of stairs – down which hitherto I had always been carried – would waste more precious time than I could spare. There seemed to be but one alternative – to waken Pollie. I ran back into my bedroom and tugged violently at the slack of her bedclothes. A mouse might as well have striven to ring Great Paul. She breathed on with open mouth, flat on her back, like a log. Then a thought came to me.

There was a brass-bound box under my bed, a full fifteen inches long, though shallow, in which my grandfather had lately sent me some gowns and finery from Paris. With some little difficulty I lugged and pushed this all across the room, and out on to the staircase. My strength seemed to be super-human. One moment I flew to my mother, but now she lay in a profound sleep indeed, her cheek like marble. With a last effort I edged my box on its side between the balusters, and at some risk of falling after it, shoved it over into the moon-silvered dusk below. The house echoed with its resounding brazen clatter as it pitched from stair to stair. Then quiet. Clutching with either hand the baluster I leaned over, listening. Then a voice cried sleepily: 'Hah!' then a call, 'Caroline!'

and a moment afterwards I discerned my father ascending the staircase ...

For weeks I lay desperately ill. The chill, the anguish, and horror of that night had come upon a frame already weakened. Life was nothing but an evil dream, a world of terrifying shadows and phantoms. But our old friend Dr. Grose was familiar with my constitution, and at last I began to mend. Pollie, stricken with remorse, nursed me night and day, giving my small bed every hour she could spare in a house stricken and disordered. I was never told in so many words that my mother was dead. In my extreme weakness I learned it of the air around me, of every secret sound and movement in the house.

Morning and evening appeared my father's great face in the doorway, his eyebrows lifted high above his spectacles. To see his misery I almost wished that I might die to spare him more. When Dr. Grose gave him permission, he sat down beside my bed and stooping low, told me that my mother had remembered our last speech together on the staircase, and he gave me her last message. A thousand and one remembrances of her patience and impulsiveness, of our long hours of solitude together, of her fits of new life as if she were a tree blossoming in the Spring, of her voice, her dignified silence with Miss Fenne, her sallies with my grandfather, her absent musings – these all return to me.

Alas, that it was never in my power, except perhaps at that last moment, to be to her a true comfort and companion, anything much better, in fact, than a familiar and tragic playmate. Worse beyond words; how little I had done for her that I might have done!

But regret must not lead me into extremes. That is not the whole truth. There were occasions, I think, when she almost forgot my disabilities, when we were just two quiet, equal spirits in the world and conversed together gravely and simply, not as children, but as fellow-women. It is these I treasure dearest, while thanking her for all. Why, in the whirligig of time, if my authorities are trustworthy, and my life had fallen out differently, the problem might now have been reversed! I myself might have had natural-sized children and they a pygmy mother. The strangeness of the world.

Out of the listlessness of convalescence my interests began to renew themselves. Across the gulf that separated us I could still commune with my mother's quiet spirit. Her peace and the peace of her forgiveness began to descend on me; and her grave in my imagination has now no more sorrow than the anticipation of my own. From my windowsill loggia I could command a full 'Hundred' of Kent. Up there on the barrowed hill-top it was said that on fine days a keen eye could descry the sea to north and south; though Dr. Grose dismissed it as a piece of local presumption. Now that my mother was gone the clouds were stranger, the birds sweetly melancholy, the flowers more fleeting. Something of youth had passed away to return no more.

Half my thoughts were wasted in futile resentment at my incapacities. Yet it was a helplessness that in part was forced on me from without. Still less now could my father take me seriously. We shared our silent meals together. He would sit moping, pushing his hand over his whitening hair, or staring over his spectacles out of the window to the low whistling of some endless, monotonous tune that would haunt him for days together and fret me to distraction. Now and again he would favour me with a serious speech, and then, with a glance, perhaps hurry away to his study before I could answer. To his half-completed dissertations on Hop, Cherry, and Paper, I learned he had added another, on the

Oyster. Many of his letters were now postmarked Whitstable. He even advertised in his old enemy, the *Courier*, for information: and would break out into furious abuse at the stupidity of his correspondents. Meanwhile his appetite increased; he would nod in his chair; his clothes grew shabby; his appearance neglected. Poor dear, he missed my mother.

But I made a struggle to take her place. Every morning Pollie would carry me off to the kitchen for a discussion with Mrs. Ballard over the household affairs of the day. With her fat, floury hand, she would hide her mouth and gravely nod her head at my instructions. But I knew she was concealing her amusement. 'Oh, these men!' she once exclaimed at some new caprice of 'the master's', 'they are never happy unless they can be where they baint.' With my own hand I printed out for her a list of my father's favourite dishes. I left off my black and wore bright colours again, so that he might not be constantly reminded of the past. But when after long debate I took courage one day to propose myself as his housekeeper – I shall never forget the facial expression which he quickly rubbed off with his hand.

He fetched out of his trousers pocket a great bunch of keys, and jangled them almost ferociously in the air at me for a full minute together with tears of amusement in his eyes. Then he tossed down the last gulp or two of his port and went off. A moment after he must have realized how cruel a blow he had dealt my vanity and my love. He returned, seated himself heavily in his chair, and looked at me. Then stretching out his hand he dropped his face on to his arm. A horrible quietness spread over the room. For the first time I looked with a kind of terror at the hairy fingers and whitening head, and could not stir.

How oddly chance repeats itself. The door opened and once

more, unannounced, Miss Fenne appeared in our midst. My father hastily rose to greet her, pretending that nothing was amiss. But when she held out her clawlike hand to me to be kissed, I merely stared at her. She screwed up her countenance into a smile; mumbled that I was looking pale and peaked again; and, with difficulty keeping her eyes from mine, explained that she had come for a business talk with my father.

A few days afterwards I was standing up at the window of my mother's little sewing-room – always a favourite refuge of mine, for there the afternoon sun and the colours of evening used to beat into the corner. And I saw a small-sized woman with a large black bonnet come waddling up the drive. She was followed by a boy wheeling a square box on a two-wheeled trolley. It was Mrs. Sheppey come to be housekeeper to the widower and his daughter.

Mrs. Sheppey proved to be a harassed and muddling woman, and she came to a harassed home. My father's affairs had gone from bad to worse. He was gloomy and morose. A hunted look sometimes gleamed in his eyes, and the spectacled nose seemed to grow the smaller the more solemn its surroundings were. He spent most of the day in his dressing-gown now, had quarrelled with Dr. Grose, and dismissed Mrs. Ballard. The rooms were dirty and neglected. Pollie would maunder about with a broom, or stand idly staring out of the window. She was in love. At least, so I realize now. At the time I thought she was merely lumpish and stupid.

Only once in my recollection did Mrs. Sheppey pay my own quarters a visit. I was kneeling on my balcony and out of sight, and could watch her unseen. She stood there – tub-shaped, a knob of dingy hair sticking out from her head, her skirts suspended round her boots – passively examining my bed, my wardrobe, and my other belongings. Her scrutiny over, she threw up her hands and the whites of her eyes as if in expostulation to heaven, turned about in her cloth boots, and waddled out again. Pollie told me, poor thing, that her children had been thorns in her side. I brooded over this. Had I not myself, however involuntarily, been a thorn in *my* mother's side? I despised and yet pitied Mrs. Sheppey.

She was, if anything, frightened of me, and of my tongue, and would address me as 'little lady' in a cringing, pursed-up fashion. But I am thankful to say she never attempted to touch me or to lift me from the floor. Her memory is inextricably bound up with a brown, round pudding with a slimy treacle sauce which she used to send to table every Tuesday, Thursday, and Saturday. My father would look at it with his nose rather than with his eyes; and after perhaps its fiftieth appearance, he summoned Mrs. Sheppey with a violent tug at the bell. She thrust her head in at the door. 'Take it away,' he said, 'take it away. Eat it. Devour it. Hide it from God's sight, good woman. Don't gibber. Take it away!'

His tone frightened me out of my wits and Mrs. Sheppey out of the house. Then came the end. At the beginning of August in my twentieth year, my father, who had daily become stranger in appearance and habits, though steadfastly refusing to call in his old friend, Dr. Grose, was found dead in his bed. He was like a boy who never can quite succeed in pleasing himself or his masters. He had gone to bed and shut his eyes, never in this world to open them again.

Chapter Five

Am I sorry that almost beside myself with this new affliction, and bewildered and frightened by the incessant coming and going of strangers in the house, I refused to be carried down to bid that unanswering face goodbye? No, I have no regret on that score. The older I grow the more closely I seem to understand him. If phantoms of memory have any reality – and it is wiser, I think, to remember the face of the living rather than the stony peace of the dead – he has not forgotten his only daughter.

Double-minded creature I was and ever shall be; now puffed up with arrogance at the differences between myself and gross, common-sized humanity; now stupidly sensitive to the pangs to which by reason of these differences I have to submit. At times I have been tempted to blame my parents for my short-comings. What wicked folly – they did not choose their only child. After all, too, fellow creatures of any size seem much alike. They rarely have *nothing* to blame Providence for – the length of their noses or the size of their feet, their bones or their corpulence, the imbecilities of their minds or their bodies, the 'accidents' of birth, breeding, stations, or circumstance. Yet how secure and perhaps wholesome is Man's self-satisfaction. To what ideal does he compare himself but to a self-perfected abstraction of his own image? Even his Venus and Apollo are mere flattering reflections of his own he-or she-shapes. And what of his anthropomorphic soul?

As for myself, Dame Nature may some day take a fancy to the dwarf. 'What a pretty play it would be' – I have clean forgotten where I chanced on this amusing passage – 'What a pretty play it would be if, from the next generation onwards, the only humans born into the world should be of mere pygmy stature. Fifty years hence there would remain but few of the normal-sized in the land. Imagine these aged few, miserably stalking through the dwarfed streets, picking up a scanty livelihood in city or countryside, where their very boots would be a public danger, their very tread would set the bells in the steeples ringing, and their appetites would be a national incubus. House, shop, church, high road, furniture, vehicles abandoned or sunken to the pygmy size; wars and ceremonies, ambitions and enterprises, everything but prayers, dwindled to the petty. Would great-grandfather be venerated, cherished, admired, a welcome guest, a lamented emigrant? Would there be as many mourners as sextons at his funeral, as many wreaths as congratulations at his grave?' And so on and so forth – like Jonathan Swift.

But I must beware. Partly from fatigue and partly from dislike of the version of Miss M. that stared out of his picture at me, I had begun, I remember, to be a little fretful when old Mr. Wagginhorne was painting my portrait. And I complained pertly that I thought there were far too many azaleas on the potted bush.

'Ah, little Miss Finical,' he said, 'take care, if you please. Once there was a Diogenes whom the gods shut up in a tub and fed on his own spleen. He died ... He died', he repeated, drawing his brush slowly along the canvas, 'of dyspepsia.'

He popped round, 'Think of that.'

I can think of that to better purpose now, and if there is one thing in the world whose company I shall deplore in my coffin, that thing is a Cynic. That is why I am trying as fast as I can to put down my experiences in black and white before the black predominates.

But I must get back to my story. My poor father had left his affairs in the utmost disorder. His chief mourners were his creditors. Apart from these, one or two old country friends and distant relatives, I believe, attended his funeral, but none even of them can have been profoundly interested in the Hop, the Oyster, or the Cherry, at least in the abstract. Dr. Grose, owing to ill-health, had given up his practice and was gone abroad. But though possibly inquiry was made after the small creature that had been left behind, I stubbornly shut myself away in my room under the roof, listening in a fever of apprehension to every sinister movement in the house beneath.

Yet if a friend in need is a friend indeed, then I must confess that my treatment of Miss Fenne was the height of ingratitude. In my grief and desolation, the future seemed to be only a veil beyond the immediate present, which I had neither the wish nor the power to withdraw. Miss Fenne had no such illusions. I begged Pollie to make any excuse she could think of to prevent her from seeing me. But at last she pushed her way up, and doubtless, the news and the advice she brought were the best tonic that could have been prescribed for me.

As a child I had always associated my godmother with the crocodile (though not with Mr. Bosch's charming conception of it, in his picture of the Creation). Yet there were no tears in her faded eyes when she explained that of my father's modest fortune not a pittance remained. In a few days the house, with everything in it except my own small sticks of furniture, was to be sold by auction. I must keep my door locked against intruders. All that would be left to me was a small income of about £110 per annum, derived from money bequeathed to me by a relative of my mother's whom I had never seen.

'I fancy your father knew nothing about it,' she concluded, 'at least so your dear *mother* seemed to imply. But there! it's a sad business, a sad business. And that Tapa scandal; a lamentable affair.' Having thus prepared the way, my godmother proposed that I should take up my residence in her house, and commit my future entirely to her charge.

'You cannot be an expensive guest,' she explained, 'and I am sure you will try to be a grateful one. No truly *conscientious* godparent, my dear child, *ever* relinquishes the soul committed to her care. I sometimes wonder whether your poor dear mother realized this.'

But it was my soul, if that is brother to the spirit and can be neighbour to pride, that revolted against her proposition. I had to shut my eyes at the very remembrance of Miss Fenne's prim and musty drawing-room. Every intimation, every jerk of her trembling head, every pounce of her jewelled fingers only hardened my heart. Poor Miss Fenne. Her resentment at my refusal seemed to increase her shortness of sight. Looking in on her from my balcony, I had the advantage of her, as she faced me in the full light in her chair, dressed up in her old lady's clothes like a kind of human Alp among my pygmy belongings. I tried to be polite, but this only increased her vexation. One smart tap of the ivory ball that topped her umbrella would have been my *coup de grâce*. She eyed me, but never administered it.

At last she drew in her lips and fell silent. Then, as may happen at such moments, her ill-temper and chagrin, even the sense of her own dignity drooped away, and for a while in the quietness we were simply two ill-assorted human beings, helpless in the coils of circumstance. She composed her mouth, adjusted her bonnet strings, peered a moment from dim old eyes out of the window, then once more looked at me.

'It must be, then, as God wills,' she said in a trembling voice. 'The spirit of your poor dear mother must be judge between us. She has, we may trust, gone to a better world.'

For a moment my resolution seemed to flow away like water, and I all but surrendered. But a rook cawed close overhead, and I bit my lip. Little more was said, except that she would consider it her duty to find me a comfortable and God-fearing home. But she admonished me of the future, warned me that the world was a network of temptations, and assured me of her prayers. So we parted. I bowed her out of my domain. It was the last time we met. Two days afterwards I received her promised letter:

MY DEAR GODCHILD – Mr. Ambrose Pellew, an old *clergyman* friend of mine, in whose discretion and knowledge of the world I have every confidence, has spoken for you to an old married, respectable servant of his now living a few miles from London – a Mrs. Bowater. For the charge of thirty shillings a week she has consented to give you board, lodging, and *reasonable* attendance. In all the circumstances this seems to me to be a moderate sum. Mr. Pellew assures me that Mrs. B. is clean, honest, and a *practising* Christian. When this dreadful Sale is over, I have arranged that Pollie shall conduct you safely to what will in future be your *home*. I trust that you will be as happy there as Providence permits, though I cannot doubt that your poor dear mother and your poor father, too, for that matter, would have wished otherwise – that the roof of her old friend who was present at your Baptism and *insisted* on your Confirmation, should have been your refuge and asylum now that you are absolutely alone in the world.

However, you have rejected this proposal, and have chosen your own path. I am not your legal guardian, and I am too deeply pained to refer again to your obstinacy and ingratitude. Rest assured that, in spite of all, I shall remember you in my prayers, and I trust, D.V., that you will escape the temptations of this wicked world – a world in which it has pleased God, in spite of self-sacrificing and anxious friends, to place you at so distressing a disadvantage. But in His Sight all men are equal. Let that be your continual consolation. See Amos vii. 2; Prov. xxxi. 24-28; Eccles. xii. 1.

I remain, your affectionate godmother,

Emma E. Fenne.

P.S. – I reopen this letter to explain that your financial affairs are in the hands of Messrs. Harris, Harris and Harris, respectable solicitors of Gray's Inn. They will remit you on every quarter day – Christmas, Lady Day, June 25th and September 29th – the sum of £28 10s. od. Of this you will pay £19 10s. at once to Mrs. Bowater, who, I have no doubt, will advise you on the expenditure of what remains on wearing apparel, self-improvement, missions, charity, and so on. It grieves me that from the wreckage of your father's affairs you must not anticipate a further straw of assistance. All his money and property will be swallowed up in the dreadful storm that has broken over what we can only trust is a tranquil resting place. R.I.P. – E. E. F.

So sprawling and straggling was my godmother's penmanship that I spelled her letter out at last with a minifying glass, though rather for forlorn amusement's sake than by necessity. Not that this diminishment of her handwriting in any sense lessened the effect upon me of the sentiments it conveyed. They at once daunted me and gave me courage. For a little I hesitated, then at last I thought *out* in my heart that God might be kinder to me than Miss Fenne wished. Indeed I was so invigorated by the anticipation of the 'wicked world', that I all but called her a crocodile to her phantasmal face. Couldn't I – didn't I – myself 'mean well' too? What pictures and prospects of the future, of my journey, of Mrs. Bowater and the 'network' pursued each other through my brain. And what a darkness oppressed me when a voice kept repeating over in my mind – *Harris and Harris and Harris*, as if it were a refrain to one of my grandfather's *chansons*. Messrs. *Harris and Harris and Harris* – I *saw* all three of them (dark men with whiskers), but trusted profoundly they would never come to see *me*.

Nor from that day to this, through all my giddying 'ups' and sobering 'downs' have I ever for a moment regretted my decision – though I might have conveyed it with a little better grace. My body, perhaps also my soul, would have been safer in the seclusion of my godmother's house. But my spirit? I think it would have beaten itself to death there like a wasp on a window-pane. Whereas – well, here I am.

Chapter Six

Those last few days of August dragged on – days of a burning wind-less heat. Yet, as days, I enjoyed them. On some upper branch of my family tree must have flourished the salamander. Indeed I think I should have been a denizen of Venus rather than of this colder, darker planet. I sat on my balcony, basking in the hot sunshine, my thoughts darting hither and thither like flies under a ceiling – those strange, winged creatures that ever seem to be attempting to trace out in their flittings the starry 'Square of Pegasus'. In spite of my troubles and forebodings, and fleeting panics, my inward mind was calm. I carefully packed away my few little valuables. The very notion of food gave me nausea, but that I determined to conquer, since of course to become, at either extreme, a slave to one's stom-ach, is a folly.

The noise and tramplings of the men in the rooms beneath never ceased, until Night brought quiet. The Sale lasted for two days. A stale and clouded air ascended even into my locked bed-room from the human beings (with their dust and tobacco and perfumes and natural presences) collected together in the heat of the great dining-room. A hum, a murmur, the scuffling of feet toiling downstairs with some heavy and cumbrous burden, the cries of the auctioneer, the coarse voices and laughter, the tinkle of glass – the stretching hours seemed endless; and every minute of them knelled the fate of some beloved and familiar object. I was glad my father couldn't hear the bidding, and sorry that perhaps he did not know that the most valuable of his curios – *how* valuable I was to learn later – was safely hidden away in an upper room. So passed my birthday – the twentieth – nor tapped me on the shoulder with, 'Ah, but, my dear, just you wait till I come again!'

None the less I thought a good deal about birthdays that afternoon, and wondered how it was that we human beings can bear even to go on living between two such mysteries as the beginning and the end of life. Where was my mother now? Where was I but two-and-twenty years ago? What was all this 'Past', this 'History', of which I had heard so much and knew so little? Just a story? Better brains than mine have puzzled over these questions, and perhaps if I had studied the philosophers I should know the answers. In the evenings, wrapped up in a shawl, Pollie carried me downstairs, and we took a sober whispering walk in the hush and perfumes of the deserted garden. Loud rang the tongues of the water over the stones. The moths were fluttering to their trysts, and from some dark little coign the cricket strummed me a solo. Standing up there in the starry night the great house looked down on me like an elder brother, mute but compassionate.

By the second day after the conclusion of the Sale, the removers' vans and carts should have gutted the rooms and be gone. It had, therefore, been arranged that Pollie should as usual share my bedroom the last night, and that next day we should set off on our journey. After luncheon – the flavour of its sliced nectarine (or is it of one that came later?) is on my tongue at this moment – all the rest of the house being now hollow and vacant, Pollie put on her hat, thrust the large door key into her pocket, and went off to visit her mother in the village and to fetch a clean nightdress. She promised to return before dark. Her shoes clattered down the stone stairs, the outer door boomed like a gun. I spread out my hands in the air, and as if my four-poster could bear witness, cried softly, 'I am alone.' Marvel of marvels, even as I sit here today gazing at my inkpot, there in its original corner stands that same old four-poster. Pollie is living down in the village with her husband and her two babies; and once more: I am alone. Is there anything in life so fascinating, so astonishing, as these queer, common little repetitions? Perhaps on the Last Day – but I anticipate.

I read a little; wrote on the flyleaf of my diminutive Johnson, 'September 1st, Lyndsey for the last time. – M.'; arranged my morrow's clothes on a chair, then sat down in my balcony to do nothing, to be nothing, merely to dream. But Nature decreed otherwise. Soon after six by my grandfather's clock – it struck the hour out of its case, as if out of a sepulchre – a storm, which all the afternoon had been steadily piling its leaden vapours into space, began to break. Chizzel Hill with its prehistoric barrow was sunk to a green mound beneath those lowering cloudy heights, pooling so placid and lovely a blue between them. The very air seemed to thicken, and every tree stood up as if carved out of metal. Of a sudden a great wind, with heavy plashing drops of rain, swept roaring round the house, thick with dust and green leaves torn from the dishevelled summer trees. There was a hush. The darkness intensified, and then a vast sheet of lightning seemed to picture all Kent in my eyes, and the air was full of water.

One glance into the obscure vacancy of the room behind me persuaded me to remain where I was, though the rain drove me further and further into the corner of my balcony. Cold, and a

little scared by the glare and din, yet not unhappy, I cowered close
up against the glass, and, shading my eyes as best I could from the
flames of the lightning, I watched the storm. How long I sat there
I cannot say. The clamour lulled and benumbed my brain into a
kind of trance. My only company was a blackbird which had flown
or been blown into my refuge, and with draggled feathers stared
black-eyed out of the greenery at me. It was gathering towards
dark when the rain and lightning began to abate, and the sullen
thunder drew away into the distance, echoing hollowly along the
furthest horizons. At last, with teeth chattering, and stiff to my
bones, I made my way into the room again, and the benighted
blackbird went squawking to his nest.

Slipping off my gown and shoes, and huddling myself in the
blankets and counterpane of my bed, I sat there pondering what
next was to be done. It would soon be night; and Pollie seemed
unlikely to appear until all this turmoil was over. I was not only
alone, but forsaken and infinitely solitary, a mere sentient living
speck in the quiet sea of light that washed ever and again into the
gloomiest recesses of the room. And that familiar room itself seemed
now almost as cold and inhospitable as a neglected church. I could
hear the dark, vacant house beneath echoing and murmuring at
every prolonged reverberation of thunder, and sighing through
all its crannies and keyholes. My bedhangings softly shook in the
air. Gone beyond recovery were my father and mother; and I now
realized how irrevocably. I was no longer a child; and the responsibilities of life were now wholly on my own shoulders.

Yet I was not utterly forlorn. The great scene comforted me,
and now and then I prayed, almost without thinking and without
words, just as a little tune will keep recurring in the mind. And
now, darkness being spread over the garden, in the east the moon

was rising. Moreover, a curious sight met my eyes; for as the storm settled, heavy rain in travelling showers was still occasionally skirting the house; and when, between the heaped-up masses of cloud, the distant lightning gleamed a faint vaporous lilac, I saw motionless in the air, and as if suspended in their falling between earth and sky, the multitudinous glass-clear, pear-shaped drops of water. At sight of these jewels thus crystalling the dark air I was filled with such a rapture that I actually clapped my hands. And presently the moon herself appeared, as if to be my companion. Serene, remote, she glided at last from cover of an enormous bluff of cloud into the faint-starred vault of space, seemed to pause for an instant in contemplation of the dark scene, then went musing on her way. Beneath her silver all seemed at peace, and it was then that I fell asleep.

And while I slept, I dreamed a dream. My dreams often commit me to a quiet and radiant life, as if of a reality less strange to me than that of waking. Others are a mere uneasiness and folly. In the old days I would sometimes tell my dreams to Mrs. Ballard; and she would look them up in a frowsy book she kept in the dresser drawer, a brown, grease-stained volume entitled *Napoleon's Book of Fate*. Then she would promise me a prince for a husband, or that I would be a great traveller across the sea, or that I must beware of a red-haired woman, and nonsense of that kind. But this particular dream remains more vividly in my memory than any.

Well, I dreamed that I was walking in a strange garden – an orchard. And, as it seemed, I was either of the common human size, or this was a world wherein of human beings I was myself of the usual stature. The night was still, like the darkest picture, yet there must have been light there, since I could see as I walked. The grasses were coarse and deep, but they did not encumber my feet, and presently I found myself standing beneath a tree whose branches in their towering sombre heaviness seemed to be made of iron. Dangling here and there amid the pendulous leaves hung enormous fruits – pears stagnant and heavy as shaped lumps of lead or of stone. Why the sight of these fruits in the obscure luminosity of the air around them laid such a spell upon me, I cannot say. I stood there in the dew-cold grass, gazing up and up into those monstrous branches as if enchanted, and then of a sudden the ground under my feet seemed faintly to tremble as if at a muffled blow. One of the fruits in my dream, now come to ripeness, had fallen stone-like from above. Then again – thud! Realization of the dreadful danger in which I stood swept over me. I turned to escape, and awoke, shivering and in a suffocating heat, to discover in the moonlight that now flooded my room where in actuality I was.

Yet still, as it seemed, the dying rumour of the sound persisted, and surely, I thought, it must be poor, careless Pollie, her key forgotten, come back in the darkness after the storm, and hammering with the great knocker on the door below. Hardly a minute had passed indeed before the whole house resounded again with her thumping. One seldom finds Courage keeping tryst on the outskirts of sleep, and there was a vehemence in the knocking as if Pollie was in an extremity of fear at finding herself under the vacant house alone in the night. The thought of going to her rescue set my teeth chattering. I threw back the bedclothes and gazed at the moon, and the longer I sat there the more clearly I realized that I must somehow descend the stairs, convey to her that I was safe, and, if possible, let her in.

Three steep stone flights separated us, stairs which I had very rarely ascended or descended except in her arms. I thrust my foot out; all was still; I must go at once. But what of light? The moon was on this side of the house. It might be pitch dark on the lower landings and in the hall. On the stool by her bedside stood Pollie's copper candlestick, with an inch or two of candle in it and a box of matches. It was a thick-set tallow candle and none too convenient for me to grasp. With this alight in my hand, the stick being too cumbersome, I set out on my errand. The air was cool; the moon shone lustily. Just waked from sleep my mind was curiously exalted. I sallied out into the empty corridor. A pace or two beyond the threshold my heart seemed to swell up in my body, for it seemed that at the head of the staircase lay stretched the still form of my mother as I had found her in the cold midnight hours long ago. It was but a play of light, a trick of fantasy. I recovered my breath and went on.

To leap from stair to stair was far too formidable a means of progression. I should certainly have dashed out my brains. So I must sit, and jump sitting, manipulating my candle as best I could. In this sidling, undignified fashion, my eyes fixed only on the stair beneath me, I mastered the first flight, and paused to rest. What a medley of furtive sounds ascended to my ear from the desolate rooms below: the heavy plash of raindrop from the eaves, scurry and squeak of mouse, rustle of straw, a stirring – light as the settling of dust, crack of timber, an infinitely faint whisper; and from without, the whistle of bat, the stony murmur of the garden stream, the hunting screech of some predatory night-fowl over the soaked and tranquil harvest fields. And who, Who? – that shape? ... I turned sharply, and the melted tallow of the guttering candle welled over and smartly burned the hand that held it. The pain gave me confidence. But better than that, a voice from below suddenly broke out, not Pollie's but Adam Waggett's, hollaing in the porch. Adam – the wren-slaughterer – prove me a coward?

No, indeed. All misgiving gone, I girded my dressing-gown tighter around me, and continued the descent.

It was a jolting and arduous business, and as I paused on the next landing, I now looked into the moon-bathed vacancy of my father's bedroom. Dismantled, littered with paper and the fragments of wood and glass of a picture my mother had given him, a great hole in the plaster, a broken chair straddling in the midst – a hideous spectacle it was. An immense moth with greenly glowing eyes, lured out of its roosting place, came fluttering round my candle, fanning my cheek with its plumy wings. I shaded the flame and smiled up at the creature which, not being of a kind that is bent on self-slaughter, presently wafted away. The lower I descended the filthier grew my journey. My stub of candle was fast wasting; and what use should I be to Pollie's messenger? When indeed in the muck and refuse left by the Sale, I reached the door, it was too late. He was now beating with his fists at the rear of the house; and I must needs climb down the last flight of the back wooden staircase used by the servants. When at last the great stagnant kitchen came into view, it was my whole inward self that cried out in me. Its stone flags were swarming with cockroaches.

These shelled, nocturnal, sour-smelling creatures are among the few insects that fill me with horror. By comparison the devil's coachman may be worse-tempered, but he is a gentleman. The very thought of one of them rearing itself against my slippered foot filled me with disgust; and the males were winged. They went scurrying away into hiding, infants seemingly to their mothers, whisper, whisper – I felt sick at the sight. There came a noise at the window. Peering from round my candle flame I perceived Adam's dusky face, with its long nose, staring in at me through the glass. At sight of the plight I was in, he burst into a prolonged guffaw of laughter.

This enraged me beyond measure. I stamped my foot, and at last he sobered down enough to yell through the glass that Pollie's mother had sent him to see that I was safe and had forgotten to give him the house-key. Pollie herself would be with me next morning.

I waved my candle at him in token that I understood. At this the melted grease once more trickled over and ran scalding up my arm. The candle fell to the floor, went out; the pale moonshine spread through the air. I could see Adam's conical head outlined against the soft light of the sky; though he could no longer see me. Horror of the cockroaches returned on me. Instantly I turned tail, leaving the lump of tallow for their spoil.

How, in that dark, high house, I managed to remount those stairs, I cannot conceive. Youth and persistency, I suppose. I doubt if I could do it now. Utterly exhausted and bedraggled I regained my bedroom at last without further misadventure. I sponged the smoke and grime from face and hands in my wash-bowl, hung my dressing-gown where the morning air might refresh it, and was soon in a dead sleep, from which I think even the Angel Gabriel would have failed to arouse me.

Chapter Seven

When I awoke, the morning sky was gay with sunshine, there was a lisping and gurgling of starlings on the roof, the roar of the little river in flood after the rains shook the air at my window, and there sat Pollie, in her outdoor clothes, the rest of the packing done and she awaiting breakfast. Unstirringly from my pillow I scrutinized the plump, red-cheeked face with its pale-blue prominent eyes dreaming out of the window; and sorrow welled up in me at the thought of the past and of how near drew our separation. She heard me move, and kneeling and stooping low over my bed, with her work-roughened finger she stroked the hand that lay on my coverlet. A pretty sight I must have looked – after my night's experiences. We whispered a little together. She was now a sedate, young woman, but still my Pollie of the apples and novelettes. And whether or not it is because early custom is second nature, she is still the only person whom my skin does not a little creep against when necessity calls for a beast of burden.

Her desertion of me the night before had been caused by the untimely death of one of her father's three Alderney cows – a mild, horned creature, which I had myself often seen in the meadows cropping among the buttercups, and whose rich-breathed nose I had once had the courage to ask to stroke with my hand. This ill-fated beast at first threat of the storm had taken shelter with her companions under an oak. Scarcely had the lightnings begun to play when she was struck down by a 'thunderbolt'. It was a tragedy after Pollie's heart. She had (she said) fainted dead off at news of it – and we bemoaned the event in concert. In return I told her my dream of the garden. Nothing would then content her but she must fetch from under her mattress *Napoleon's Book of Fate*, a legacy from Mrs. Ballard.

'But, Pollie,' I demured; 'a dream is only a dream.'

'Honest, miss,' she replied, thumbing over the pages, 'there's some of 'em means what happens and comes true, and they'll tell secrets too if they be searched about. More'n a month before Mrs. Ballard fell out with master she dreamed that one of the speckled hens had laid an egg in the kitchen dresser. There it was clucking among the crockery. And to dream of eggs, the book says, is to be certain sure of getting the place you are after, and which she wrote off to a friend in London and is there now!'

What more was there to say? So presently Pollie succeeded in turning to 'Pears' in the grease-grimed book, and spelled out slowly:

> PEARS. – To dream of pears is in-di-ca-tive of great wealth (which means riches, miss), and that you will rise to a much higher spear than the one you at present occupy. To a woman they denote that she will marry a person far above her in rank (lords and such-like, miss, if you please), and that she will live in great state. To persons in trade they denote success and future prosper-ity and eleviation. They also indi- indicate constancy in love and happiness in the marriage state.

Her red cheeks grew redder with this exertion of scholarship, and

I burst out laughing. 'Ah, miss,' she cried in confusion, 'laugh you may, and that's what Sarah said to the angel. But mark my words if something of it don't hap out like what the book says.'

'Then, Pollie,' said I, 'there's nothing for it but to open a butcher's shop. For live in great state I can't and won't, not if the Prince of Wales himself was to ask me in marriage.'

'Lor, miss,' retorted Pollie in shocked accents, 'and him a married man with grown-up sons and all.' But she forgave me my mockery. As for the Dream Book, doubtless young Bonaparte must often have dreamed of pears in Corsica; and no less indubitably have I lived in 'great state' – though without much alleviation.

But the day was hasting on. My toilet must be made, and the preparations for our journey completed. Now that the dawn of my new fortunes was risen, expectancy filled my mind, and the rain-freshened skies and leaves of the morning renewed my spirits. Our train – the first in my experience – was timed to leave our country railway station at 3.30 pm. By one o'clock, all the personal luggage that I was to take with me had been sewn up in a square of canvas, and corded. The rest of my belongings – my four-poster, etc. – were to be stowed in a large packing-case and sent after me. First impressions endure. No great store of sagacity was needed to tell me that. So I had chosen my clothes carefully, determined to show my landlady that I meant to have my own way and not be trifled with. My dear Mrs. Bowater! – she would be amused to hear that.

Pollie bustled downstairs. I stood in the midst of the sunlit, dismantled room, light and shadow at play upon ceiling and walls, and sun-pierced air a silvery haze of dust. A host of memories and thoughts, like a procession in a dream, traversed my mind. A strangeness, too – as if even this novel experience of farewell was a

vague recollection beyond defined recall. Pollie returned with the
new hat in the paper bag in which she had brought it from home:
and I was her looking-glass when she had put it on. Then from
top to basement she carried me through every room in the house,
and there on the kitchen floor, mute witness of the past, lay the
beetle-gnawn remnant of my candle-stub. We wandered through
the garden, glinting green in the cool flocking sunbeams after the
rain; and already vaunting its escape from Man. Pollie was returning to Lyndsey – I not! My heart was too full to let me linger by
the water. I gazed at the stones and the wild flowers in a sorrowful
hunger of farewell. Trifles, soon to be dying, how lovely they were.
The thought of it swallowed me up. What was the future but an
emptiness? Would that I might vanish away and be but a portion
of the sweetness of the morning. Even Pollie's imperturbable face
wore the appearance of make-belief; for an instant I surprised the
whole image of me reflected in her round blue eye.

The Waggett's wagonette was at the door, but not – and I was
thankful – not *my* Adam, but the old Adam, his father. My luggage
was pushed under the seat. I was set up, to be screened as far as possible from the wind, beside Pollie and behind Mr. Waggett – no
stranger to me with his neat, dark whiskers, for in the old days, at
dinner parties, he would wait at table. I see him now – as gentle-
manlike as a Devil's Coach-horse – entering the kitchen with his
little black bag. Only once I swiftly turned my head over my shoulder toward the house. Then we were outside the iron gates, and
bumping along through the puddles between the bowery hedges
towards the station.

I thought of my father and mother lying side by side, beyond
the sullen drift of nettles, under the churchyard wall. Miss Fenne
had taken me there many weeks before in her faded barouche

with the gaunt white mare. Not a word had I breathed to her of my anguish at sight of the churchyard. The whole afternoon was a nightmare. She regaled the journey with sentiments on death and the grave. Throughout it, I was in danger of slipping out of her sight; for the buttons on the sage-green leather seat were not only discomfort but had failed to aid me to sit upright; and nothing would have induced me to catch at the trimmings of her dolman to save myself from actually falling off into the pit of her carriage. There sat her ancient coachman; clutter-clutter plodded the hoofs; what a monstrous, monstrous world – and she cackling on and on – like a hen over its egg.

But now the novelty of this present experience, the flowery cottages, Mr. Waggett's square, sorrel nag, the ballooning north-westerly clouds, the aromatic rusty hedgrows, the rooks in the cornfields – all these sights and sounds called joy into my mind, and far too soon the bright-painted railway station at the hill-bottom hove into sight, and our drive was over. I was lifted down into Pollie's arms again. Then followed a foolish chaffering over the tickets, which Mr. Waggett had volunteered to purchase for us at the rounded window. The looming face beyond had caught sight of me, and the last words I heard bawled through for any to hear were: 'Lor, Mr. Waggett, I'd make it a *quarter* for 'ee if it was within regulations. But 'tain't so, the young lady's full natural size in the eye of the law, and I couldn't give in to 'ee not even if 'twas a honeymooning you was after.' No doubt it was wholesome to learn as quickly as possible how easy a butt I was to be for the jests of the good-humoured. On that occasion it was a bitter pill. I felt even Pollie choke down a laugh into her bosom. My cheek whitened, but I said nothing.

An enormous din at the moment shattered around me, ten

thousand times harsher to my nerves than any mere witticism could be. My first 'steam-monster' was entering the station. All but stunned by its clatter, I barely had the presence of mind to thank Mr. Waggett for the little straw basket of three greengages, and the nosegay of cherry-pie which he had thrust into my arms. My canvas-wrapped package was pushed in under the seat, the door was slammed to, the guard waved his green flag, Mr. Waggett touched his hat: and our journey was begun.

Fortunately Pollie and I found ourselves in an empty carriage. The scream of the whistle, the grinding jar of the wheels, the oppressive odour of Mr. Waggett's bouquet – I leaned back on her to recover my wits. But the cool air blowing in on my face and a far-away sniff from a little glass bottle with which her mother had fortified her for the journey, quickly revived me, and I was free to enjoy the novelties of steam-travel. My eyes dizzied at the wide revolving scene that was now spread out beneath the feathery vapours. How strange it was to see the green country world – meadow and stream and wooded hill – thus wheel softly by. If Pollie and I could have shared it alone, it would have been among my pleasantest memories.

But at the next stopping places other passengers climbed into the carriage; and five complete strangers soon shared the grained wood box in which we were enclosed. There was a lady in black, with her hair smoothed up under her bonnet, and a long pale nose; and up against her sat her little boy, a fine fair, staring child of about five years of age. A black-clothed, fat little man with a rusty leather bag, over the lock of which he kept clasped his finger and thumb, quietly seated himself. He cast but one dark glance about him and immediately shut his eyes. In the corner was an older man with a beard under his chin, gaiters, and a hard, wide-brimmed hat. Besides these, there was a fat country woman on the same side as Pollie and I, whom I could hear breathing and could not see, and a dried-up, bird-eyed woman opposite in a check shawl, with heavy metal ear-rings dangling at her ears. She sat staring blankly and bleakly at things close as if they were at a distance.

My spirit drank in this company. So rapt was I that I might have been a stock of wood. Gathered together in this small space they had the appearance of animals, and, if they had not been human, what very alarming ones. As long as I merely sat and watched their habits I remained unnoticed. But the afternoon sun streamed hot on roof and windows: and the confined air was soon so dense with a variety of odours, that once more my brain dizzied, and I must clutch at Pollie's arm for support. At this movement the little boy who had more than once furtively glanced at me, crouched wriggling back against his mother, and, edging his face aside, piped up into her ear, 'Mamma, is that alive?'

The train now stood motionless, a fine array of hollyhocks and sunflowers flared beyond the window, and his voice rang out shrill as a bird in the quiet of afternoon. Tiny points of heat broke out all over me, as one by one my fellow passengers turned their astonished faces in my direction. Even the man with the leather bag heard the question. The small bead-brown eyes wheeled from under their white lids and fixed me with a stare.

'Hush, my dear,' said the lady, no less intent but less open in her survey; 'hush, look at the pretty cows!'

'But she *is*, mamma. It moved. I saw that move,' he asseverated, looking along cornerwise at me out of his uptilted face.

Those blue eyes! a mingling of delight, horror, incredulity, even greed swam in their shallow deeps. I stood leaning close to Pollie's bosom, breathless and helpless, a fascinating object, no doubt. Never before had I been transfixed like this in one congregated stare. I felt myself gasp like a fish. It was the old farmer in the corner who at last came to my rescue. 'Alive! *I* warrant. Eh, ma'am?' he appealed to poor Pollie. 'And an uncommon neat-fashioned young lady, too. Off to Whipham Fair, I'll be bound.'

The bag-man turned with a creeping grin on his tallowy features and muttered some inaudible jest out of the corner of his mouth to the gipsy. She eyed him fiercely, drawing her lips from her bright teeth in a grimace more of contempt than laughter. Once more the engine hooted and we glided on our way.

'I *want* that, mamma,' whispered the child. 'I *want* that dear little lady. Give that teeny tiny lady a biscuit.'

At this new sally universal merriment filled the carriage. We were jogging along in fine style. This, then, was Miss Fenne's 'network'. A helpless misery and bitterness swept through me, the heavy air swirled; and then – whence, from whom, I know not – self-possession returned to me. Why, I had *chosen* my fate: I must hold my own.

My young admirer, much against his mother's inclination, had managed to fetch out a biscuit from her reticule – a star-shaped thing, graced with a cone of rose-tinted sugar. Still crouching back like a chick under her wing, he stretched his bribe out at arm's length towards me, in a pink, sweat-sparked hand. All this while Pollie had sat like a lump beside me, clutching her basket, a vacant, flushed smile on her round face. I drew myself up, and supporting myself by her wicker basket, advanced with all the dignity at my command to the peak of her knees, and, stretching out my hand in return, accepted the gift. I even managed to make him an indulgent little bow, feigned a nibble at the lump of food, then planted it on the dusty ledge beneath the carriage window.

A peculiar silence followed. With a long sigh the child hid his face in his mother's sleeve. She drew him closer and smiled carefully into nothingness. 'There,' she murmured, 'now mother's treasure must sit still and be a good boy. I can't think why papa didn't take – second-class tickets.'

'But nor did that kind little lady's papa,' returned the child stoutly.

The kindly old farmer continued to gloat on me, gnarled hands on knees. But I could not bear it. I quietly surveyed him until he was compelled to rub his face with his fingers, and so cover its retreat to his own window. The gipsy woman kept her ferocious, birdlike stare on me, with an occasional stealthy glance at Pollie. The bag-man's lids closed down. For the rest of the journey – though passengers came and went – I kept well back, and was left in peace. It was my first real taste of the world's curiosity, mockery, aversion, and flattery. One practical lesson it taught me. From that day forward I never set out on any such journey unless thickly veiled. For then, though the inquisitive may see me, they cannot tell whether or not I see them, or what my feelings may be. It is a real comfort; though, from what I have read, it appears to be the condition rather of a ghost than of a normal young lady.

But now the sun had begun to descend and the rays of evening to stain the fields. We loitered on from station to station. To my relief Pollie had at last munched her way through the pasties and sweetmeats stowed in her basket. My nosegay of cherry-pie was fainting for want of water. In heavy sleep the bagman and gipsy sat woodenly nodding and jerking side by side. The lady had delicately composed her face and shut her eyes. The little boy slumbered serenely with his small red mouth wide open. Languid and heavy, I dared not relax my vigilance. But in the desolation that gathered over me I almost forgot my human company, and returned to the empty house which seemingly I had left for ever – the shadows of yet another nightfall already lengthening over its flowers and sward.

Could I not hear the silken rustle of the evening primrose unfolding her petals? Soon the cool dews would be falling on the stones where I was wont to sit in reverie beside the flowing water. It seemed indeed that my self had slipped from my body, and hovered entranced amid the thousand jargonings of its tangled lullaby. Was there, in truth, a wraith in me that could so steal out; and were the invisible inhabitants in their fortresses beside my stream conscious of its presence among them, and as happy in my spectral company as I in theirs?

I floated up out of these ruminations to find that my young pasha had softly awakened and was gazing at me in utter incredulity from sleep-gilded eyes. We exchanged a still, protracted, dwelling smile, and for the only time in my life I actually *saw* a fellow creature fall in love!

'Oh, but mamma, mamma, I do *beseech* you,' he called up at her from the platform where he was taking his last look at me through the dingy oblong window, 'please, please, I want her for mine! I want her for mine!'

I held up his biscuit in my hand, laughing and nodding. The whistle knelled, out narrow box drew slowly out of the station. As if heartbroken, he took his last look at me, petulantly flinging aside his mother's hand. He had lost me for ever, and Pollie and I were alone again.

Beechwood

* * *

Chapter Eight

Still the slow train bumped on, loath to drag itself away from the happy harvest fields. Darkness was near when we ourselves alighted at our destination, mounted into a four-wheeled cab, and once more were in motion in the rain-laid dust. On and on rolled Pollie and I and our luggage together, in such ease and concealment after the hard wooden seats and garish light that our journey began to seem – as indeed I wished for the moment it might prove – interminable. One after another the high street lamps approached, flung their radiance into our musty velvet cabin, and went gliding by. Ever and again the luminous square of a window beyond the outspread branches of a tree would float on. Then suddenly our narrow solitude was invaded by the bright continuous flare flung into it from a row of shops.

Never before had I been out after nightfall. I gazed enthralled at the splendours of fruit and cakes, silks and sweet-meats packed high behind the glass fronts. Wasn't I myself the heiress of £110 a year? Indeed I was drinking in Romance, and never traveller surveyed golden Moscow or the steeps of Tibet with keener relish than I the liquid amber, ruby, and emerald that summoned its customers to a wayside chemist's shop. Twenty – what a child I was! I smile now at these recollections with an indulgence not unmixed with envy. It is Moscow survives, not the artless traveller.

After climbing a long hill – the wayside houses steadily thinning out as we ascended – the cab came to a standstill. The immense, shapeless old man who had so miraculously found our way for us, and who on this mild August evening was muffled up to his eyes in a thick ulster, climbed down backwards from his box and opened the door. At the same moment, as if by clockwork, opened another door – that of the last house on the hill. I was peering out of the cab, then, at my home; and framed in that lighted oblong stood Mrs. Bowater. All utterly different from what I had foreseen: this much smaller house, this much taller landlady, and – dear me, how fondly I had trusted that she would not for the first time set eyes on her lodger being *carried* into her house. I had in fancy pictured myself bowing a composed and impressive greeting to her from her own hearthrug. But it was not to be.

Pollie lifted me out, settled me on her arm, and my feet did not touch *terra firma* again until she had ascended the five stone steps and we were within the passage.

'Lor, miss; then here we are,' she sighed breathlessly, then returned to the cabman to pay him his fare. Even dwarfed a little perhaps by my mourning, there I stood, breathed upon by the warm air of the house, in the midst of a prickly doormat, on the edge of the shiny pattern oilcloth that glossed away into the obscurity from under the gaslight in front of me; and there stood my future landlady. For the first time, with head thrown back, I scanned a countenance that was soon to become so familiar and so endeared. Mrs. Bowater's was a stiff and angular figure. She, too, was in black, with a long, springside boot. The bony hands hung down in their peculiar fashion from her elbows. A large cameo brooch adorned the flat chest. A scanty velvet patch of cap failed to conceal the thin hair sleekly parted in the middle over the high narrow temples. The long dark face with its black, set eyes, was almost without expression, except that of a placid severity. She gazed down at me, as I up at her, steadily, silently.

'So this is the young lady,' she mused at last, as if addressing a hidden and distant listener. 'I hope you are not over-fatigued by your journey, miss. Please to step in.'

To my ear, Mrs. Bowater's was what I should describe as a low, roaring voice, like falling water out of a black cloven rock in a hillside; but what a balm was its sound in my ear, and how solacing this dignified address to jaded nerves still smarting a little after my victory on the London, Chatham, and Dover Railway. Making my way around a grandfather's clock that ticked hollowly beside the door, I followed her into a room on the left of the passage, from either wall of which a pair of enormous antlers threatened each other under the discoloured ceiling. For a moment the glare within and the vista of furniture legs confused my eyes. But Mrs. Bowater came to my rescue.

'Food was never mentioned,' she remarked reflectively, 'being as I see nothing to be considered except as food so-called. But you will find everything clean and comfortable; and I am sure, miss, what with your sad bereavements and all, as I have heard from Mr. Pellew, I hope it will be a home to you. There being nothing else as I suppose that we may expect.'

My mind ran about in a hasty attempt to explore these sentiments. They soothed away many misgivings, though it was clear that Mrs. Bowater's lodger was even less in dimensions than Mrs. Bowater had supposed. 'Clean': after so many months of Mrs. Sheppey's habits, it was this word that sang in my head. Wood, glass, metal flattered the light of gas and coal, and for the first time I heard my own voice float up into my new 'apartment': 'It looks *very* comfortable, thank you, Mrs. Bowater; and I am quite sure I shall be happy in my new abode.' There was nothing intentionally affected in this formal little speech.

'Which being so,' replied Mrs. Bowater, 'there seems to be trouble with the cabman, and the day's drawing in, perhaps you will take a seat by the fire.'

A stool nicely to my height stood by the steel fender, the flames played in the chimney; and for a moment I was left alone. 'Thank God,' said I, and took off my hat, and pushed back my hair ... Alone. Only for a moment, though. Its mistress gone, as fine a black cat as ever I have seen appeared in the doorway and stood, green-eyed, regarding me. To judge from its countenance, this must have been a remarkable experience.

I cried seductively, 'Puss.'

But with a blink of one eye and a shake of its forepaw, as if inadvertently it had trodden in water, it turned itself about again and disappeared. In spite of all my cajoleries, Henry and I never were to be friends.

Whatever Pollie's trouble with the cabman may have been, Mrs. Bowater made short work of it. Pollie was shown to the room in which she was to sleep that night. I took off my bodice and bathed face, hands, and arms to the elbow in the shallow bowl Mrs. Bowater had provided for me. And soon, wonderfully refreshed and talkative, Pollie and I were seated over the last meal we were to share together for many a long day.

There were snippets of bread and butter for me, a little omelette, two sizes too large, a sugared cherry or two sprinkled with

'hundreds and thousands', and a gay little bumper of milk gilded
with the enwreathed letters, 'A Present from Dover'. Alack-a-day for
that omelette! I must have kept a whole family of bantams steadily engaged for weeks together. But I was often at my wits' end to
dispose of their produce. Fortunately Mrs. Bowater kept merry fires
burning in the evening – 'Ladies of some sizes can't warm the air as
much as most,' as she put it. So at some little risk to myself among
the steel fire-irons, the boiled became the roast. At last I made a
clean breast of my horror of eggs, and since by that time my landlady and I were the best of friends, no harm came of it. She merely
bestowed on me a grim smile of unadulterated amusement, and the
bantams patronized some less fastidious stomach.

My landlady was a heavy thinker, and not a copious – though a
leisurely – talker. Minutes would pass, while with dish or duster in
hand she pondered a speech; then perhaps her long thin lips would
only shut a little tighter, or a slow, convulsive rub of her lean forefinger along the side of her nose would indicate the upshot. But I
soon learned to interpret these mute signs. She was a woman who
disapproved of most things, for excellent, if nebulous, reasons;
and her silences were due not to the fact that she had nothing to
say, but too much.

Pollie and I talked long and earnestly that first evening at Beechwood. She promised to write to me, to send me all the gossip of
the village, and to come and see me when she could. The next
morning, after a sorrowful breakfast, we parted. Standing on the
table in the parlour window, with eyes a little wilder than usual,
I watched her pass out of sight. A last wave of her handkerchief,
and the plump-cheeked, fair-skinned face was gone. The strangeness and solitude of my situation flooded over me.

For a few days, strive as she might, Mrs. Bowater's lodger moped.

It was not merely that she had become more helpless, but of far less importance. This may, in part, be accounted for by the fact that, having been accustomed at Lyndsey to live at the top of a high house and to look down on the world, when I found myself foot to foot with it, so to speak, on Beechwood Hill, it alarmingly intensified the *sense* of my small stature. Use and habit however. The relative merits of myself and of the passing scene gradually readjusted themselves with a proper respect for the former. Soon, too, as if from heaven, the packing-case containing my furniture arrived. Mrs. Bowater shared a whole morning over its unpacking, ever and again standing in engrossed consideration of some of my minute treasures, and, quite unaware of it, heaving a great sigh. But how to arrange them in a room already over-occupied.

Chapter Nine

A carpenter of the name of Bates was called in, so distant a relative of Mrs. Bowater's apparently that she never by nod, word, or look acknowledged the bond. Mr. Bates held my landlady in almost speechless respect. 'A woman in a thousand,' he repeatedly assured me, when we were grown a little accustomed to one another; 'a woman in *ten* thousand. And if things hadn't been what they was, you may understand, they might have turned out different. Ah, miss, there's one looking down on us could tell a tale.' I looked up past his oblong head at the ceiling, but only a few flies were angling round the chandelier.

Mrs. Bowater's compliments were less indirect. 'That *Bates*,' she would say, surveying his day's handiwork after he was gone, 'is all thumbs.'

He was certainly rather snail-like in his movements, and spent most of his time slowly rubbing his hands on the stiff apron that encased him. But I minded his thumbs far less than his gluepot.

Many years have passed, yet at the very whisper of his name, that inexpressible odour clouds up into my nose. It now occurs to me for the first time that he never sent in his bill. Either his memory failed him, or he carpentered for love. Level with the wide table in the window recess, strewn over with my small Persian mats, whereon I sat, sewed, read, and took my meals, Mr. Bates constructed a broad shelf, curtained off on three sides from the rest of the room. On this wooden stage stood my four-poster, wardrobe, and other belongings. It was my bedchamber. From table to floor he made a staircase, so that I could easily descend and roam the room at large. The latter would have been more commodious if I could have persuaded Mrs. Bowater to empty it a little. If I had *kept on* looking at the things in it I am sure I should have gone mad. Even tact was unavailing. If only there had been the merest tinge of a Cromwell in my character, the baubles that would have been removed!

There were two simpering plaster figures – a Shepherd and Shepherdess – nearly half my height on the chimney-piece, whom I particularly detested; also an enlarged photograph in a discoloured frame on the wall – that of a thick-necked, formidable man, with a bush of whisker on either cheek, and a high, quarrelsome stare. He made me feel intensely self-conscious. It was like a wolf looking all day into a sheep-fold. So when I had my meals, I invariably turned my back on his portrait.

I went early to bed. But now that the autumnal dusks were shortening, an hour or two of artificial light was necessary. The flare of the gas dazzled and stupefied me, and gave me a kind of hunted feeling; so Mrs. Bowater procured for me a couple of fine little glass candlesticks. In bed I sometimes burned a wax-light in a saucer, a companionable thing for night-thoughts in a strange place. Often enough I sat through the evening with no other illumination than that of the smouldering coals, so that I could see out of the window. It was an endless source of amusement to withdraw the muslin curtains, gaze out over the darkened fields beyond the roadway, and let my day-dreams wander at will.

At nine o'clock Mrs. Bowater would bring me my supper – some fragments of rusk, or of bread, and milk. My food was her constant anxiety. The difficulty, as she explained, was to supply me with *little* enough to eat – at least of cooked food: 'It dries up in the winking of an eye.' So her cat, Henry, fared more sumptuously than ever, though the jealous creature continued to reject all my advances, and as far as possible ignored my existence. 'Simple victuals, by all means, miss,' Mrs. Bowater would admit. 'But if it don't enjoy, the inside languishes; and you are not yet of an age that can fall back on skin and bone.'

The question of food presently introduced that of money. She insisted on reducing her charges to twenty shillings a week. 'There's the lodging, and there's the board, the last being as you might say all but unmentionable; and honesty the best policy though I have never tried the reverse.' So, in spite of all my protestations, it was agreed. And thus I found myself mistress of a round fifty-eight pounds a year over and above what I paid to Mrs. Bowater. Messrs. Harris, Harris, and Harris were punctual as quarter-day: and so was I. I '*at once*' paid over to my landlady £13 and whatever other sum was needful. The 'charity' my godmother had recommended began, and, alas, remained at home. I stowed the rest under lock and key in one of my grandfather's boxes which I kept under my bed. This was an imprudent habit, perhaps. Mrs. Bowater advocated the Penny Bank. But the thought of my money being so handy and *palpable* reassured me. I would count it over in my mind, as if it were a means to salvation; and became, in consequence, near and parsimonious.

Occasionally when she had 'business' to transact, Mrs. Bowater would be off to London. There she would purchase for me any little trifle required for the replenishment of my wardrobe. Needing so little, I could afford the finest materials; my sovereign was worth at least sixty shillings. Rather than 'fine', Mrs. Bowater preferred things 'good'; and for this 'goodness', I must confess, she sometimes made rather alarming sacrifices of appearance. Still, I was already possessed of a serviceable stock of clothes, and by aid of one of my dear mother's last presents to me, a shiny Swiss miniature workbox with an inlaid picture of the Lake of Geneva on the lid, I soon became a passable needlewoman.

I love bright, pure colours, and, my sweeping and dusting and bedmaking over, and my external mourning for my father at an end, a remarkably festive figure would confront me in my cheval glass of an afternoon. The hours I spent in dressing my hair and matching this bit of colour with that. I would talk to myself in the glass, too, for company's sake, and make believe I was a dozen different characters. I was young. I pined for life and companionship, and having only my own – for Mrs. Bowater was rather a faithful feature of the landscape than a fellow being – I made as much, and as many, of myself as possible.

Another question that deeply engaged my landlady was my health. She mistrusted open windows, but strongly recommended 'air'. What insidious maladies she spied around me! Indeed that September was unusually hot. I sat on my table in the window like a cricket in an oven, sorely missing my high open balcony, the garden, and the stream. Once and again Mrs. Bowater would take me for a little walk after sunset. Discretion to her was much the better part of valour; nor had I quite recovered from my experiences in the train. But such walks – though solitary enough at that hour of the day – were straggly and irksome. Pollie's arm had been a kind of second nature to me; but Mrs. Bowater, I think, had almost as fastidious a disinclination to carrying me as I have to being carried.

I languished for liberty. Being a light sleeper, I would often awake at daybreak and the first call of the birds. Then the hill – which led to Tyddlesdon End and Love (or Loose) Lane – was deserted. Thought of the beyond haunted me like a passion. At a convenient moment I intimated to Mrs. Bowater how secure was the street at this early hour, how fresh the meadows, and how thirsty for independent outings her lodger. 'Besides, Mrs. Bowater, I am not a child, and who could see me?'

After anxious and arduous discussion, Mr. Bates was once more consulted. He wrapped himself in a veritable blanket of reflection, and all but became unconscious before he proposed a most ingenious device. With Mrs. Bowater's consent, she being her own landlady and amused at the idea, he cut out of one of the lower panels of her parlour door a round-headed opening just of an easy size to suit me. In this aperture he hung a delicious little door that precisely fitted it. So also with the door into the street – to which he added a Bramah lock. By cementing a small square stone into the corner of each of the steps down from the porch, he eased *that* little difficulty. May Heaven bless Mr. Bates! With his key round my neck, stoop once, stoop twice, a scamper down his steps, and I was free – as completely mistress of my goings-out and of my comings-in as every self-respecting person should be.

'That's what my father would have called a good job, Mr. Bates,' said I cordially.

He looked yearningly at me, as if about to impart a profound secret; but thought better of it. 'Well, miss, what I say is, a job's a *job*; and if it *is* a job, it's a job that should be made a job *of*.'

As I dot the i's and cross the t's of this manuscript, I often think – a little ruefully – of Mr. Bates.

As soon as daybreak was piercing into my region of the sky, and before Mrs. Bowater or the rest of the world was stirring, I would rise, make my candlelit toilet, and hasten out into the forsaken sweet of the morning. If it broke wet or windy, I could turn over and go to sleep again. A few hundred yards up the hill, the road turned off, as I have said, towards Tyddlesdon End and Loose Lane – very stony and steep. On the left, and before the fork, a wicket gate led into the woods and the park of empty 'Wanderslore'. To the verge of these deserted woods made a comfortable walk for me.

If, as might happen, any other wayfarer was early abroad, I could conceal myself in the tussocks of grass and bushes that bordered the path. In my thick veil, with my stout green parasol and inconspicuous shawl, I made a queer and surprising figure no doubt. Indeed, from what I have heard, the ill fame of Wanderslore, acquired a still more piquant flavour in the town by reports that elf-folk had been descried on its outskirts. But if I sometimes skipped and capered in these early outings, it was for exercise as well as suppressed high spirits. To be prepared, too, for the want of such facilities in the future, I had the foresight to accustom myself to Mrs. Bowater's steep steps as well as to my cemented-in 'Bateses', as I called them. My only difficulty was to decide whether to practise on them when I was fresh at the outset of my walk, or fatigued at the end of it. Naturally people grow 'peculiar' when much alone: self plays with self, and the mimicry fades.

These little expeditions, of course, had their spice of danger, and it made them the more agreeable. A strange dog might give me a fright. There was an old vixen which once or twice exchanged glances with me at a distance. But with my parasol I was a match for most of the creatures which humanity has left unslaughtered. My sudden appearance might startle or perplex them. But if few were curious, fewer far were unfriendly. Boys I feared most. A hulking booby once stoned me through the grass, but fortunately he was both a coward and a poor marksman. Until winter came, I doubt if a single sunshine morning was wasted. Many a rainy one, too, found me splashing along, though then I must be a careful walker to avoid a sousing.

The birds renewed their autumn song, the last flowers were blossoming. Concealed by scattered tufts of bracken where an enormous beech forked its roots and cast a golden light from its withering leaves, I would spend many a solitary hour. Above the eastern tree-tops my Kent stretched into the distance beneath the early skies. Far to my left and a little behind me rose the chimneys of gloomy Wanderslore. Breathing in the gentle air, the dreamer within would stray at will. There I kept the anniversary of my mother's birthday; twined a wreath for her of ivy-flowers and winter green; and hid it secretly in a forsaken blackbird's nest in the woods.

Still I longed for my old home again. Mrs. Bowater's was a stuffy and meagre little house, and when meals were in preparation, none too sweet to the nose. Especially low I felt, when a scrawling letter was now and then delivered by the postman from Pollie. Her spelling and grammar intensified my homesickness. Miss Fenne, too, had not forgotten me. I pored over her spidery epistles till my head ached. Why, if I had been so rash and undutiful, was she so uneasy? Even the texts she chose had a parched look. The thought of her spectacling my minute handwriting and examining the proof that I was still a child of wrath, gave my pride a silly qualm. So Mrs. Bowater came to my rescue, and between us we concocted replies to her which, I am afraid, were not more intelligible for a tendency on my landlady's part to express my sentiments in the third person.

This little service set her thinking of Sunday and church. She was not, she told me, 'what you might call a religious woman', having been compelled 'to keep her head up in the world, and all not being gold that glitters'. She was none the less a regular attendant at St. Peter's – a church a mile or so away in the valley, whose five bells of a Sabbath evening never failed to recall my thoughts to Lyndsey and to dip me into the waters of melancholy. I loved their mellow clanging in the lap of the wind, yet it was rather doleful to be left alone with my candles, and only Henry sullenly squatting in the passage awaiting his mistress's return.

'Not that you need making any *better*, miss,' Mrs. Bowater assured me. 'Even a buttercup – or a retriever dog, for that matter – being no fuller than it can hold of what it is, in a manner of speaking. But there's the next world to be accounted for, and hopes of reunion on another shore, where, so I understand, mere size, body or station, will not be noticeable in the sight of the Lamb. *Not* that I hold with the notion that only the good so-called will be there.'

This speech, I must confess, made me exceedingly uncomfortable.

'Wherever I go, Mrs. Bowater,' I replied hastily, 'I shall not be happy unless you are there.'

'D.V.,' said Mrs. Bowater grimly, 'I will.'

Still, I remained unconverted to St. Peter's. Why, I hardly know: perhaps it was her reference to its pew rents, or her description of the vicar's daughters (who were now nursing their father at Tunbridge Wells), or maybe even it was a stare from her husband which I happened at that precise moment to intercept from the wall. Possibly if I myself had taken a 'sitting', this aura of formality would have faded away. Mrs. Bowater was a little reassured, however, to hear that my father and mother, in spite of Miss Fenne, had seldom taken me to church. They had concluded that my absence was best both for me and for the congregation. And I told her of our little evening services in the drawing-room, with Mrs. Ballard, the parlourmaid, Pollie, and the Boy on the sofa, just as it happened to be their respective 'Sundays in'.

This set her mind at rest. Turn and turn about, on one Sunday evening she went to St. Peter's and brought back with her the text and crucial fragments of Mr. Crimble's sermon, and on the next we read the lessons together and sang a hymn. Once, indeed, I embarked upon a solo, 'As pants the hart', one of my mother's favourite airs. But I got a little shaky at 'O for the wings', and there was no rambling, rumbling chorus from my father. But Sunday was not my favourite day on Beechwood Hill. Mrs. Bowater looked a little formal with stiff white 'frilling' round her neck. She reminded me of a leg of mutton. To judge from the gloom and absentmindedness into which they sometimes plunged her, quotations from Mr. Crimble could be double-edged. My real joy was to hear her views on the fashions and manners of her fellow-worshippers.

Well, so the months went by. Winter came with its mists and rains and frosts, and a fire in the polished grate was no longer an evening luxury but a daily need. As often as possible I went out walking. When the weather was too inclement, I danced for an hour or so, for joy and exercise, and went swimming on a chair. I would entertain myself also in watching through the muslin curtains the few passers-by; sorting out their gaits, and noses, and clothes, and acquaintances, and guessing their characters, occupations, and circumstances. Certain little looks and movements led me to suppose that, even though I was perfectly concealed, the more sensitive among them were vaguely uneasy under this secret scrutiny. In such cases (though very reluctantly) I always drew my eyes away: first because I did not like the thought of encroaching on their privacy, and next, because I was afraid their uneasiness might prevent them coming again. But this microscopic examination of mankind must cease with dusk, and the candle-hours passed rather heavily at times. The few books I had brought away from Lyndsey were mine now nearly by heart. So my eye would often wander up to a small bookcase that hung out of reach on the other side of the chimney-piece.

Chapter Ten

One supper-time I ventured to ask Mrs. Bowater if she would hand me down a tall, thin, dark-green volume, whose appearance had particularly taken my fancy. A simple enough request, but surprisingly received. She stiffened all over and eyed the bookcase with a singular intensity. 'The books there', she said, 'are what they call the dead past burying its dead.'

Spoon in hand, I paused, looking now at Mrs. Bowater and now at the coveted book. '*Mr.* Bowater', she added from deep down in herself, 'followed the sea.' This was, in fact, Mr. Bowater's début in our conversation, and her remark, uttered in so hollow yet poignant a tone, produced a romantic expectancy in my mind.

'Is – ' I managed to whisper at last: 'I hope Mr. Bowater isn't *dead*?'

Mrs. Bowater's eyes were like lead in her long, dark-skinned face. She opened her mouth, her gaze travelled slowly until, as I realized, it had fixed itself on the large yellowing photograph behind my back.

'Dead, no'; she echoed sepulchrally. 'Worse than.'

By which I understood that, far from being dead, Mr. Bowater was still actively alive. And yet, apparently, not much the happier for that. Instantaneously I caught sight of a rocky, storm-strewn shore, such as I had seen in my *Robinson Crusoe,* and *there* Mr. Bowater, still 'following the sea'.

'Never, never,' continued Mrs. Bowater in her Bible voice, 'never to darken these doors again!' I stole an anxious glance over my shoulder. There was such a brassy boldness in the responsive stare that I was compelled to shut my eyes.

But Mrs. Bowater had caught my expression. 'He was, as some would say,' she explained with gloomy pride, 'a handsome man. *Do* handsome he did never. But there, miss, things being as they must be, and you in the green of your youth – though hearing the worst may be a wholesome physic if taken with care, as I have told Fanny many a time ...' She paused to breathe. 'What I was saying is, there can be no harm in your looking at the book if that's all there's to it.' With that she withdrew the dry-looking volume from the shelf and laid it on the table beside my chair.

I got down, opened it in the middle (as my father had taught me, in order to spare the binding), opened it on a page inkly black as night all over, but starred with a design as familiar to me as the lines on the palm of my hand.

'But, oh! Mrs. Bowater!' I cried, all in a breath, running across, dragging back the curtain and pointing out into the night; 'look, look, it's there! It's Orion!'

There, indeed, in the heavens beyond my window, straddling the dark, star for star the same as those in the book, stood the Giant, shaking his wondrous fires upon the air. Even Mrs. Bowater was moved by my enthusiasm. She came to the table, compared at my direction chart with sky, and was compelled rather grudgingly to admit that her husband's book was at least true to the facts. Stooping low, I read out a brief passage. She listened. And it seemed a look of girlhood came into the shadowy face uplifted towards the window. So the stars came into my life, and faithful friends they have remained to this day.

Mrs. Bowater's little house being towards the crest of the hill, with sunrise a little to the left across the meadows, my window commanded about three-fifths of the southern and eastern skies. By day I would kneel down and study for hours the charts, and thus be prepared for the dark. Night after night, when the weather was fair, or the windy clouds made mock of man's celestial patternings, I would sit in the glow of the firelight and summon these magic shiners each by name – Bellatrix, huge Betelgeuse, Aldebaran, and the rest. I would look at one, and, while so doing, watch another. This not only isolated the smaller stars, but gradually I became aware that they were one and all furtively signalling to *me*! About a fortnight later my old Lyndsey friend, the Dogstar, topped the horizon fringe of woodland. I heard myself shout at him across the world. His sudden molten bursts of crimson betwixt his emeralds and sapphires filled me with an almost ridiculous delight.

By the middle of December I had mastered all the greater stars in my region, and with my spyglass a few even of the Gammas and Deltas. But much of the zenith and all the north was closed to me, and – such is human greed – I began to pine beyond measure for a sight of Deneb, Vega, and the Chair. This desire grew unendurable, and led me into a piece of genuine foolhardiness. I determined to await the first clear still night and then to sally out and make my way, by hook or crook, up to my beech-roots, from which I should be able to command a fair stretch of the northern heavens. A quiet spell favoured me.

I waited until Mrs. Bowater had gone to her bedroom, then muffled myself up in my thickest clothes and stole out into the porch.

At my first attempt, one glance into the stooping dark was enough. At the second, a furtive sighing breath of wind, as I breasted the hill, suddenly flapped my mantle and called in my ear. I turned tail and fled. But never faint heart won fair constellation. At the third I pressed on.

The road was deserted. No earthly light showed anywhere except from a lamp-post this side of the curve of the hill. I frisked along, listening and peering, and brimming over with painful delight. The dark waned; and my eyes grew accustomed to the thin starlight. I gained the woods unharmed. Rich was my reward. There and then I begged the glimmering Polestar to be true to Mr. Bowater. Fear, indeed, if in a friendly humour, is enlivening company. Instead of my parasol I had brought out a carved foreign knife (in a sheath at least five inches long) which I had discovered on my parlour what-not.

The whisperings of space, the calls of indetectable birds in the wastes of the sky, the sudden appearance of menacing or sinister shapes which vanished or melted themselves into mere stocks or stones as I drew near – my heart gave many an anguished jump. But quiet, and the magnificence of night, vanquished all folly at last. It seemed to me that a Being whom one may call Silence was brooding in solitude where living and human visitants are rare, and that in his company a harmless spirit may be at peace. Oblivious of my ungainly knife, yet keeping a firm arm on it, self seemed to be the whole scene there, and my body being so small I was perhaps less a disturber than were most intruders of that solemn repose.

Why I kept these night-walks secret, I cannot say. It was not apprehension of Mrs. Bowater. She would have questioned my discretion, but would not, I think, have attempted to dissuade me from them against my will. No. It may be that every true astronomer is a miser at heart, and keeps some Lambda or Mu or lost nebula his eternal friend, named with his name, but unrecorded on any chart. For my part I hoarded the complete north for a while.

A fright I got one night, however, kept me indoors for the better part of a week. In my going out the little house door had been carelessly left unlatched. Algol and the red planet Mars had been my quarry among the floating woolpack clouds. The wind was lightly blowing from the north-west after the calm. I drew down my veil and set off briskly and light-heartedly for home.

The sight of the dark-looking hole in the door quickly sobered me down. All was quiet, however, but on entering my room, there was a strangeness in the air, and that not due to my landlady's forlorn trumpetings from above. Through the floating vaporous light I trod across to my staircase and was soon in bed. Hardly had my eyes closed when there broke out of the gloom around me a dismal, appalling cry. I soon realized that the creeping horror this caused in me was as nothing compared with that of the poor beast, lured, no doubt, into the house by Henry, at finding itself beneath a strange roof.

'Puss, puss,' I pleaded shakenly; and again broke out that heart-sick cry.

Knife in hand, I descended my staircase and edging as far as possible from the baleful globes greenly burning beneath a mahogany chair, I threw open both doors and besought my unwelcome visitor to take his departure. The night wind came fluttering; there was the blur of a scuttering, shapeless form, and in the flash of an eye I was sprawling on the floor. A good deal shaken, with a nasty scratch on my thigh, but otherwise unharmed, I waved my hand after the fugitive and returned to bed.

The blood soon ceased to flow. Not daring to send my blood-stained nightgown to the wash, I concealed it behind my dresses in the wardrobe, and the next fine morning carried it off with me and buried it as deeply as I could in a deserted rabbit-burrow in the woods. Such is an evil conscience that, first, I had the fancy that during my digging a twig had inexplicably snapped in the undergrowth; and next, for 'burnt offering', I made Mrs. Bowater the present of an oval hand-glass set in garnets (one of my grandfather's gifts). This she took down to a local jeweller's to be mounted with a pin, and wore it on Sundays in place of her usual cameo depicting the Three Graces disporting themselves under a Palm-tree beside a Fountain.

Meanwhile I had heard a little more about the 'Fanny' whom Mrs. Bowater had mentioned. My landlady was indeed a slow confider. Fanny, I gathered, had a post as mistress at a school some forty miles away. She taught the little boys 'English'. The fleeting Miss Perry returned to mind, and with a faint dismay I heard that Fanny would soon be returning home for the Christmas holidays. Mrs. Bowater's allusions to her were the more formidable for being veiled. I dreaded the invasion. Would she not come 'between us'?

Then by chance I found hidden in my star-book the photograph of an infant in arms and of a pensive, ringleted woman, who, in spite of this morsel in her lap, seemed in her gaze out of nowhere to be vaguely afraid. On the back was scrawled in pencil: 'F.: six weeks' – and an extremely cross six weeks 'F.' looked. For some inexplicable reason I pushed back this lady's photograph into the book, and said nothing about it. The suspicion had entered my mind that Fanny was only a daughter by marriage. I sank into a kind of twilight reflection at this. It seemed, in an odd fashion, to make Mrs. Bowater more admirable, her husband more formidable, and the unknown Fanny more mysterious and enigmatical. At the first opportunity I crept my way to the subject and asked my landlady if she could show me a portrait of her daughter.

The photograph she produced from upstairs had in fading almost become a caricature. It had both blackened and greyed. It depicted herself many years younger but hardly less grim in appearance in full flounced skirts, Fanny as a child of about five or six standing at her knee, and Mr. Bowater leaning with singular amenity behind her richly-carved chair, the fingers of his left hand resting disposedly on her right shoulder. I looked anxiously at the child. It was certainly crosspatch 'F.', and a far from prepossessing little creature with that fixed, level gaze. Mr. Bowater, on the other hand, had not yet adopted the wild and rigid stare which dominated the small parlour.

Mrs. Bowater surveyed the group with a lackadaisical detachment. 'Fractious! – you can see the tears on her cheeks for all what the young man could do with his woolly lamb and grimaces. It was the heyday.'

What was the heyday, I wondered. 'Was Mr. Bowater attached to her?' seemed a less intrusive question.

'Doted,' she replied, polishing the glass with her apron. 'But not to much purpose – with an eye for every petticoat.'

This seemed a difficult conversation to maintain. 'Don't you think, Mrs. Bowater,' I returned zealously, 'there is just the faintest tinge of *Mr.* Bowater in the *chin*? I don't', I added candidly, 'see the faintest glimpse of *you.*'

Mrs. Bowater merely tightened her lips.

'And is she like that now?' I asked presently.

Mrs. Bowater re-wrapped frame and photograph in their piece of newspaper. 'It's *looks,* miss, that are my constant anxiety: and you may be thankful for being as you might say preserved from the world. What's more, the father will out, I suppose, from now till Day of Judgment.'

How strangely her sentiments at times resembled my godmother's, and yet how different they were in effect. My thoughts after this often drifted to Mrs. Bowater's early married life. And so peculiar are the workings of the mind that her husband's star-chart, his sleek appearance as a young father, the mysterious reference to the petticoats, awoke in me an almost romantic interest in him. To such a degree that it gradually became my custom to cast his portrait a satirical little bow of greeting when I emerged from my bedroom in the morning, and even to kiss my hand to his invisible stare when I retired for the night. To all of which advances he made no reply.

My next bout of star-gazing presaged disaster. I say star-gazing, for it is true that I stole out after honest folk are abed only when the heavens were swept and garnished. But, as a matter of fact, my real tryst was with another Self. Had my lot been different, I might have sought that self in Terra del Fuego or Malay, or in a fine marriage. Mine was a smaller world. Bo-peep I would play with shadow and dew-bead. And if Ulysses, as my father had read me, stopped his ears against the Sirens, I contrariwise unsealed mine to the ethereal airs of that bare wintry solitude.

The spectral rattle of the parched beechleaves on the saplings, the faintest whisper in the skeleton bracken set me peeping, peering, tippeting; and the Invisibles, if they heeded me, merely smiled on me from their grave, all-seeing eyes. As for the first crystal sparkling of frost, I remember in my folly I sat down (bunched up, fortunately, in honest lamb's-wool) and remained, minute by minute, unstirring, unwinking, watching as if in my own mind the exquisite small fires kindle and flit from point to point of lichen and bark, until – out of this engrossment – little but a burning icicle was left to trudge along home.

It was December 23rd. I remember that date, and even now hardly understand the meaning or intention of what it brought me. Love for the frosty, star-roofed woods, that was easy. And yet what if – though easy – it is not enough? I had lingered on, talking in my childish fashion – a habit never to leave me – to every sudden lovely morsel in turn, when, to my dismay, I heard St. Peter's clock toll midnight. Was it my fancy that at the stroke, and as peacefully as a mother when she is alone with her sleeping children, the giant tree sighed, and the whole night stilled as if at the opening of a door? I don't know, for I would sometimes pretend to be afraid merely to enjoy the pretending. And even my small Bowater astronomy had taught me that as the earth has her poles and equator, so these are in relation to the ecliptic and the equinoctial. So too, then, each one of us – even a mammet like myself – must live in a world of the imagination which is in everlasting relation to its heavens. But I must keep my feet.

I waved adieu to the woods and unseen Wanderslore. As if out of the duskiness a kind of reflex of me waved back; and I was soon hastening along down the hill, the only thing stirring in the cold, white, luminous dust. Instinctively, in drawing near, I raised my eyes to the upper windows of Mrs. Bowater's crouching house. To my utter confusion. For one of them was wide open, and seated there, as if in wait for me, was a muffled figure – and that not my landlady's – looking out. All my fine boldness and excitement died in me. I may have had no apprehension of telling Mrs. Bowater of my pilgrimage, but not having told her, I had a lively distaste of being 'found out'.

Stiff as a post, I gazed up through the shadowed air at the vague, motionless figure – to all appearance completely unaware of my presence. But there is a commerce between minds as well as between eyes. I was perfectly certain that I was being *thought* about, up there.

For a while my mind faltered. The old childish desire gathered in me – to fly, to be gone, to pass myself away. There was a door in the woods. Better sense, and perhaps a creeping curiosity, prevailed, however. With a bold front, and as if my stay in the street had been of my own choosing, I entered the gate, ascended my 'Bateses', and so into the house. Then I listened. Faintly at last sounded a stealthy footfall overhead; the window was furtively closed. Doubt vanished. In preparation for the night's expedition I had lain down in the early evening for a nap. Evidently while I had been asleep, Fanny had come home. The English mistress had caught her mother's lodger playing truant!

Chapter Eleven

If it was the child of wrath in me that hungered at times after the night, woods, and solitude to such a degree that my very breast seemed empty within me; it was now the child of grace that prevailed. With girlish exaggeration I began torturing myself in my bed with remorse at the deceit I had been practising. Now Conscience told me that I must make a full confession the first thing in the morning; and now that it would be more decent to let Fanny 'tell on me'. At length thought tangled with dreams, and a grisly night was mine.

What was that? It was day; Mrs. Bowater was herself softly calling me beyond my curtains, and her eye peeped in. Always before I had been up and dressed when she brought in my breakfast. Through a violent headache I surveyed the stooping face. Something in my appearance convinced her that I was ill, and she insisted on my staying in bed.

'But Mrs. Bowater ...' I expostulated.

'No, no, miss; it was in a *butt* they drowned the sexton. Here you stay; and its being Christmas Eve, you must rest and keep quiet. What with those old books and all, you have been burning the candle at both ends.'

Early in the afternoon on finding that her patient was little better, my landlady went off to the chemist's to get me some physic; I could bear inactivity no longer, and rose and dressed. The fire was low, the room sluggish, when in the dusk, as I sat dismally brooding in my chair, the door opened and a stranger came in with my tea. She was dressed in black, and was carrying a light. With that raised in one hand, and my tea-tray held between finger and thumb of the other, she looked at me with face a little sidelong. Her hair was dark above her clear pale skin, and drawn, without a fringe, smoothly over her brows. Her eyes were almost unnaturally light in colour. I looked at her in astonishment; she was new in my world. She put the tray on my table, poked the fire into a blaze, blew out her candle at a single puff from her pursed lips, and seating herself on the hearthrug, clasped her hands round her knees.

'Mother told me you were in bed, *ill,*' she said, 'I hope you are better.'

I assured her in a voice scarcely above a whisper that I was quite well again.

She nestled her chin down and broke into a little laugh: 'My! how you startled me!'

'Then it *was* you,' I managed to say.

'Oh, yes; it was me, it was me.' The words were uttered as if to herself. She stooped her cheek over her knees again, and smiled round at me. 'I'm not *telling,*' she added softly.

Her tone, her expression, filled me with confusion. 'But please do not suppose', I began angrily, 'that I am not my own mistress here. I have my own key – '

'Oh, yes, your own mistress,' she interrupted suavely, 'but you see that's just what I'm *not*. And the key! why, it's just envy that's gnawing at the roots. I've never, never in my life seen anything so queer.' She suddenly raised her strange eyes on me. 'What were you doing out there?'

A lie perched on my lip; but the wide, light eyes searched me through. 'I went', said I, 'to be in the woods – to see the stars'; then added in a rather pompous voice, 'only the southern and eastern constellations are visible from *this* poky little window.'

There was no change in the expression of the two eyes that drank me in. '*I* see; and you want them all. That's odd, now,' she went on reflectively, stabbing again at the fire; 'they have never attracted me very much – angels' tin-tacks, as they say in the Sunday Schools. Fanny Bowater was looking for the moon.'

She turned once more, opened her lips, showing the firm row of teeth beneath them, and sang in a low voice the first words, I suppose, of some old madrigal: '"*She enchants me*". And if *I* had my little key, and my little secret door ... But never mind. "*Telltale Tit, her tongue shall be slit.*" It's safe with me. I'm no sneak. But you might like to know, Miss M., that my mother thinks the very world of you. And so do I, for that matter; though perhaps for different reasons.'

The calm, insolent words infuriated me, and yet her very accents, with a curious sweet rasp in them, like that in a skylark's song when he slides his last twenty feet from the clouds, were an enchantment. Ever and always there seemed to be two Fannies; one visible, her face; the other audible, her voice. But the enchantment was merely fuel for the flames.

'Will you please remember', I broke out peremptorily, 'that neither myself nor what I choose to do is any affair of yours. Mrs. Bowater is an excellent landlady; you can tell her precisely what you please; and – and' (I seemed to be choking) 'I am accustomed to take my meals alone.'

The sidelong face grew hard and solemn in the firelight, then slowly turned, and once more the eyes surveyed me under lifted brows – like the eyes of an angel, empty of mockery or astonishment or of any meaning but that of their beauty. 'There you are,' she said. 'One talks like one human being to another, and I should have thought you'd be grateful for that; and this is the result. Facts are facts; and I'm not sorry for them, good or bad. If you wish to see the last of me, here it is. I don't thrust myself on people – there's no need. But still; I'm *not* telling.'

She rose, and with one light foot on my fender, surveyed herself for a moment with infinite composure in the large looking-glass that spanned the chimneypiece.

And I? – I was exceedingly tired. My head was burning like a coal; my thoughts in confusion. Suddenly I lost control of myself and broke into an angry, ridiculous sobbing. I simply sat there, my face hidden in my dry, hot hands, miserable and defeated. And strange Fanny Bowater, what did she do?

'Heavens!' she muttered scornfully, 'I gave up snivelling when I was a baby.' Then voice, manner, even attitude suddenly changed – 'And there's mother!'

When Mrs. Bowater knocked at my door, though still in my day-clothes, I was in bed again, and my tea lay untasted on a chair beside it.

'Dear, dear,' she said, leaning anxiously over me, 'your poor cheeks are red as a firebrand, miss. Those chemists daren't put a nose outside their soaps and tooth powders. It must be Dr. Phelps to-morrow if you are no better. And as plump a little Christmas pudding boiling for you in the pot as ever you could see! Tell me, now; there's no *pain* anywhere – throat, limbs, or elsewhere?'

I shook my head. She sprinkled a drop or two of eau de Cologne on my sheet and pillow, gently bathed my temples and hands, kindled a night-light, and left me once more to my own reflections.

They were none too comfortable. One thing only was in my mind – Fanny Bowater, her face, her voice, every glance and intonation, smile, and gesture. That few minutes' talk seemed now as remote and incredible as a nightmare. The stars, the woods, my solitary delights in learning and thinking were all suddenly become empty and meaningless. She despised me: and I hated her with a passion I cannot describe.

Yet in the midst of my hatred I longed for her company again, distracting myself with the sharp and clever speeches I might have made to her, and picturing her confounded by my contempt and indifference. But should I ever see her alone again? At every sound and movement in the house, which before had so little concerned me, I lay listening, with held breath. I might have been a mummy in a Pyramid hearkening after the fluttering pinions of its spirit come back to bring it life. But no tidings came of the stranger.

When my door opened again, it was only to admit Mrs. Bowater with my supper – a bowl of infant's gruel, not the customary old lady's rusk and milk. I laughed angrily within to think that her daughter must have witnessed its preparation. Even at twenty, then, I had not grown used to being of so little consequence in other people's eyes. Yet, after all, who ever quite succeeds in being that? My real rage was not that Fanny had taken me as a midget, but as *such* a midget. Yet can I honestly say that I have *ever* taken her as mere Fanny, and not as *such* a Fanny?

The truth is she had wounded my vanity, and vanity may be

a more fractious nursling even than a wounded heart. Tired and fretful, I had hardly realized the flattering candour of her advances. Even her promises not to 'tell' of my night-wanderings, implied that she trusted in my honour not to tell of her promise. I thought and thought of her. She remained an enigma. Cold and hard – no one had ever spoken to me like that before. Yet her voice – it was as if it had run about in my blood, and made my eyes shine. A mere human sound to set me sobbing! More dangerous yet, I began to think of what Miss Bowater must be thinking of me, until, exhausted, I fell asleep, to dream that I was a child again and shut up in one of Mrs. Ballard's glass jars, and that a hairy woman who was a kind of mixture of Mrs. Bowater and Miss Fenne, was tapping with a thimbled finger on its side to increase my terror.

Next morning, thank Heaven, admitted me to my right mind again. I got out of bed and peered through the window. It was Christmas Day. A thin scatter of snow was powdering down out of the grey sky. The fields were calm and frozen. I felt, as I might say, the hunger in my face, looking out. There was something astonishingly new in my life. Everything familiar had become a little strange.

Overnight, too, someone – and with mingled feelings I guessed who – must have stolen into my room while I lay asleep. Laid out on a bedside chair was a crimson padded dressing-jacket, threaded with gold, a delicate piece of needle-work that would have gladdened my grandfather. Rolled up on the floor beside it was a thick woollen mat, lozenged in green and scarlet, and just of a size to spread beside my bed. These gifts multiplied my self-reproaches and made me acutely homesick.

What should I do? Beneath these thoughts was a quiet fizz of expectation and delight, like water under a boat. Pride and common sense fought out their battle in my mind. It was pride that lost the day. When Mrs. Bowater brought in my breakfast, she found her invalid sitting up in Fanny's handsome jacket, and the mat laid over the bedrail for my constant contemplation. Nor had I forgotten Mrs. Bowater. By a little ruse I had found out the name and address of a chemist in the town, and on the tray beside my breakfast was the fine bottle of lavender water which I had myself ordered him to send by the Christmas Eve post.

'Well there, miss, you did take me in that time,' she assured me. 'And more like a Valentine than a Christmas present; and its being the only scent so-called that I've any nose for.'

Clearly this was no occasion for the confessional, even if I had had a mind to it. But I made at least half a vow never to go star-gazing again without her knowledge. My looks pleased her better, too, though not so much better as to persuade her to counter-mand Dr. Phelps. Her yellowish long hand with its worn wedding ring was smoothing my counterpane. I clutched at it, and, shame-stricken, smiled up into her face.

'You have made me very happy,' I said. At this small remark, the heavy eyelids trembled, but she made no reply.

'Did,' I managed to inquire at last, 'did she have any breakfast before she went for the doctor?'

'A cup of tea,' said Mrs. Bowater shortly. A curious happiness took possession of me.

'She is very young to be teaching; not much older than I am.'

'The danger was to keep her back,' was the obscure reply. 'We don't always see eye to eye.'

For an instant the dark, cavernous face above me was mated by that other of birdlike lightness and beauty. 'Isn't it funny?' I observed, 'I had made quite, quite a different picture of her.'

'Looks are looks, and brains are brains; and between them you must tread very wary.'

About eleven o'clock a solemn-looking young man of about thirty, with a large pair of reddish leather gloves in his hand, entered the room. For a moment he did not see my bedroom, then, remarking circumspectly in a cheerful, hollow voice, 'So this is our patient,' he bade me good-morning, and took a seat beside my bed. A deep blush mounted up into the fair, smooth-downed cheeks as he returned my scrutiny and asked me to exhibit my tongue. I put it out, and he blushed even deeper.

'And the pulse, please,' he murmured, rising. I drew back the crimson sleeve of Fanny's jacket, and with extreme nicety he placed the tip of a square, icy forefinger on my wrist. Once more his fair-lashed eyelids began to blink. He extracted a fine gold watch from his waistcoat pocket, compared beat with beat, frowned, and turned to Mrs. Bowater.

'You are not, I assume, aware of the – the young lady's *normal* pulse?'

'There being no cause before to consider it, I am not,' Mrs. Bowater returned.

'Any *pain*?' said Dr. Phelps.

'Headache', replied Mrs. Bowater on my behalf, 'and shoots in the limbs.'

At that Dr. Phelps took a metal case out of his waistcoat, glanced at it, glanced at me, and put it back again. He leaned over so close to catch the whisper of my breathing that there seemed a danger of my losing myself in the labyrinth of his downy ear.

'H'm, a little fever,' he said musingly. 'Have we any reason to suppose that we can have taken a chill?'

The head on the pillow stirred gently to and fro, and I think its cheek was dyed with an even sprightlier red than had coloured his. After one or two further questions, and a low colloquy with Mrs. Bowater in the passage, Dr. Phelps withdrew, and his carriage rolled away.

'A painstaking young man', Mrs. Bowater summed him up in the doorway, 'but not the kind I should choose to die under. You are to keep quiet and warm, miss; have plenty of light nourishment; and physic to follow. Which, except for the last mentioned, and that mainly water, one don't have to ride in a carriage to know for one's self.'

But 'peace and goodwill': I liked Dr. Phelps, and felt so much better for his skill that before his wheels had rolled out of hearing I had leapt out of bed, dragged out the trunk that lay beneath it, and fetched out from it a treasured ivory box. On removal of the lid, this ingenious work disclosed an Oriental Temple, with a spreading tree, a pool, a long-legged bird, and a mountain. And all these exquisitely tinted in their natural colours. It had come from China, and had belonged to my mother's brother, Andrew, who was an officer in the Navy and had died at sea. This I wrapped up in a square of silk and tied with a green thread. During the whole of his visit my head had been so hotly in chase of this one stratagem that it is a marvel Dr. Phelps had not deciphered it in my pulse.

When Mrs. Bowater brought in my Christmas dinner – little but bread sauce and a sprig of holly! – I dipped in the spoon, and, as innocently as I knew how, inquired if her daughter would like to see some really fine sewing.

The black eyes stood fast, then the ghost of a smile vanished over her features; 'I'll be bound she would, miss. I'll give her your message.' Alone again, I turned over on my pillow and laughed until tears all but came into my eyes.

All that afternoon I waited on, the coals of fire that I had prepared for my enemy's head the night before now ashes of penitence on my own. A dense smell of cooking pervaded the house; and it was not until the evening that Fanny Bowater appeared.

She was dressed in a white muslin gown with a wreath of pale green leaves in her hair. 'I am going to a party,' she said, 'so I can't waste much time.'

'Mrs. Bowater thought you would like to see some *really* beautiful needlework,' I replied suavely.

'Well,' she said, 'where is it?'

'Won't you come a little closer?'

That figure, as nearly like the silver slip of the new moon as ever I have seen, seemed to float in my direction. I held my breath and looked up into the light, dwelling eyes. 'It is this,' I whispered, drawing my two hands down the bosom of her crimson dressing-jacket. 'It is only, Thank you, I wanted to say.'

In a flash her lips broke into a low clear laughter. 'Why, *that's* nothing. Really and truly I hate that kind of work; but mother often wrote of you; there was nothing better to do; and the smallness of the thing amused me.'

I nodded humbly. 'Yes, yes,' I muttered, 'Midget is as Midget wears. I know that. And – and here, Miss Bowater, is a little Christmas present from me.'

Voraciously I watched her smooth face as she untied the thread. 'A little ivory box!' she exclaimed, pushing back the lid, 'and a Buddhist temple, how very pretty. Thank you.'

'Yes, Miss Bowater, and, do you see, in the corner there, a moon? She *enchants* you.'

'So it is,' she laughed, closing the box. 'I was supposing,' she went on solemnly, 'that I had been put in the corner in positively everlasting disgrace.'

'Please don't say that,' I entreated. 'We *may* be friends, mayn't we? I am better now.'

Her eyes wandered over my bed, my wardrobe, and all my possessions. 'But yes,' she said, 'of course'; and laughed again.

'And you believe me?'

'Believe you?'

'That it was the stars? I thought Mrs. Bowater might be anxious if she knew. It was quite, quite safe, really; and I'm *going* to tell her.'

'Oh, dear,' she replied in a cold, small voice, 'so you are still worrying about that. I – I envied you.' With a glance over her shoulder, she leaned closer. 'Next time you go,' she breathed out to me, 'we'll go together.'

My heart gave a furious leap; my lips closed tight. 'I could tell you the names of some of the stars now,' I said, in a last wrestle with conscience.

'No, no,' said Fanny Bowater, 'it isn't the stars I'm after. The first fine night we'll go to the woods. You shall wait for me till everything is quiet. It will be good practice in *practical* astronomy.' She watched my face, and began silently laughing as if she were reading my thoughts. 'That's a bargain, then. What is life, Miss M., but experience? And what is experience, but knowing thyself? And what's knowing thyself but the very apex of wisdom? Anyhow it's a good deal more interesting than the Prince of Denmark.'

'Yes,' I agreed. 'And there's still all but a full moon.'

'Aha!' said she. 'But *what* a world with only one! Jupiter has scores, hasn't he? Just think of *his* Love Lanes!' She rose to her feet with a sigh of boredom, and smoothed out her skirts with her long, narrow hands. I stared at her beauty in amazement.

'I hate these parties here,' she said. 'They are not worth while.'

'You look lov – you look all right.'

'H'm; but what's that when there's no one to see.'

'But you see yourself. You *live* in it.'

The reflected face in the glass, which, craning forward, I could just distinguish, knitted its placid brows. 'Why, if that were enough, we should all be hermits. I rather think, you know, that God made man almost solely in the hope of his two-legged appreciation. But perhaps you disapprove of incense?'

'Why should I, Miss Bowater? My Aunt Kitilda was a Catholic: and so was my mother's family right back.'

'*That's* right,' said Miss Bowater. She kissed her hand to looking-glass and four-poster, flung me a last fervid smile, and was gone. And the little box I had given her lay on the table, beside my bed.

I was aroused much later by the sound of voices drawing nearer. Instinctively I sat up, my senses fastened on the sound like a vampire. The voices seemed to be in argument, then the footsteps ceased and clear on the night air came the words:

'But you made me promise *not* to write. Oh, Fanny, and you have broken your own!'

'Then you must confess', was the cautious reply, 'that I am consistent. As for the promises, you are quite, quite welcome to the pieces.'

'You mean that?' was the muffled retort.

'That', cried the other softly, 'depends entirely on what you mean by "mean". Please look happy! You'd soon grow old and uglier if there was only that scrap of moon to light your face.'

'Oh, Fanny. Will you never be serious?' – the misery in the words seemed to creep about in my own mind for shelter. They were answered by a sparkling gush of laughter, followed by a crisp, emphatic knock at the door. Fanny had returned from her party, and the eavesdropper buried her face in her pillow. So she enjoyed hurting people. And yet ...

Chapter Twelve

The next afternoon Mrs. Bowater was out when Dr. Phelps made his call. It was Fanny who ushered him into the room. He felt my pulse again, held up the phial of medicine to the light, left unconsulted my tongue, and pronounced that 'we are doing very nicely'. As indeed I was. While this professional inquiry was in progress Fanny stood silently watching us, then exclaimed that it was half-past four, and that I must have my tea. She was standing behind Dr. Phelps, and for a few seconds I watched with extreme interest but slow understanding a series of mute little movements of brows and lips which she was directing at me while he was jotting down a note in a leather pocket-book. At length I found myself repeating – as if at her dictation – a polite little invitation to him to take tea with me. The startled blue eyes lifted themselves above the pocket-book, the square, fair head was bowing a polite refusal, when, 'But, of course, Dr. Phelps,' Fanny broke in like one inspired, 'how very thoughtless of me!'

'Thank you, thank you, Miss Bowater, but – ' cried Dr. Phelps, with a smooth uplifted hand, and almost statuesque in his pose. His refusal was too late. Miss Bowater had hastened from the room.

His panic passed. He reseated himself, and remarking that it was a very cold afternoon, predicted that if the frost continued, skating might be expected. Conversation of this kind is apt so soon to faint away like a breeze in hot weather, that I kept wondering what to say next. Besides, whenever Dr. Phelps seemed impelled to look at me, he far more quickly looked away, and the sound of his voice suggested that he was uncertain if he was not all but talking to himself. To put him more at his ease I inquired boldly if he had many other midgets among his patients.

The long lashes swept his cheek; he pondered awhile on my landlady's window curtains. 'As a matter of fact perhaps *not*,' he replied at last, as if giving the result of a mathematical calculation.

'I suppose, Dr. Phelps,' I then inquired, 'there *might* be more, at any time, might there not?' Our glances this time met. He blinked.

'My father and mother, I mean,' I explained in some confusion, 'were just of the com – of the ordinary size. And what I was wondering is, whether you yourself would be sorry – in quite a general way, of course – if you found your practice going down like that.'

'Going down?'

'I mean the *patients* coming smaller. I never had the opportunity of asking our own doctor, Dr. Grose. At Lyndsey, you know. Besides, I was a child then. Now, first of all, it *is* true, isn't it, that giants are usually rather dull-witted people? So nobody would deliberately choose *that* kind of change. If, then, quality does vary with quantity, mightn't there be an improvement in the other direction? You will think I am being extremely ego – egotistical. But one must take Jack's side, mustn't one? – even if one's Jill?'

'Jack?'

'The Giant Killer.'

He looked at me curiously, and his finger and thumb once more strayed up towards the waistcoat pocket in which he kept his thermometer. But instead of taking it out, he coughed.

'There is a norm – ' he began in a voice not quite his own.

'Ah,' I cried, interrupting him, and throwing up my hands, 'there is indeed. But why, I ask myself, so vast a number of examples of it!'

It was as if a voice within were prompting me. Perhaps the excitement of Fanny's homecoming was partly to blame. 'I sit at my window here and watch the passers-by. Norms, in mere size, Dr. Phelps, every one of them, if you allow for the few little defects in the – the moulding, you know. And just think what London must be like. Why, *nobody* can be noticeable, there.'

'But surely,' Dr. Phelps smiled indulgently, though his eyelashes seemed to be in the way, 'surely variety is possible, without – er – excess. Indeed there must be variety in order to arrive at our norm, mustn't there?'

'You'd be astonished', I assured him, 'how slight the differences really are. A few inches or ounces; red or black or fawn; and age, and sex, of course; that's all. Now, isn't it true, Dr. Phelps, that almost any twenty women – unselected, you know – would weigh about a ton?' And surely there's no particular reason why just human shells should weigh as much as that. We are not lobsters. And yet, do you know, I have watched, and they really seem to enjoy being the same as one another. One would think they tried to be – manners and habits, knowledge and victuals, hats and boots, everything. And if on the outside, I suppose on the inside, too. What a mysterious thing it seems. All of them *thinking* pretty much the same: Norm *Thoughts*, you know; just five-foot-fivers. After all, one wouldn't so much mind the monotonous packages,

MEMOIRS OF A MIDGET

if the contents were different. "Forty feeding like one" – who said that? Now, truly, Dr. Phelps, don't you feel – It would, of course, be very serious at first for their mothers and fathers if all the little human babies here came midgets, but it would be amusing, too, wouldn't it? ... And it isn't quite my own idea, either.'

Dr. Phelps cleared his throat, and looked at his watch. 'But surely,' he said, with a peculiar emphasis which I have noticed men are apt to make when my sex asks intelligent or unintelligent questions, 'surely you and I are understanding one another. *I* try to make myself clear to *you*. So extremes *can* meet; at least I hope so.' He gave me a charming little awkward bow. 'Tell me, then, what is this peculiar difference you are so anxious about? You wouldn't like a pygmy England, a pygmy Universe, now, would you, Miss M.?'

It was a great pity. A pygmy England – the thought dazzled me. In a few minutes Dr. Phelps would perhaps have set all my doubts at rest. But at that moment Miss Bowater came in with the tea, and the talk took quite another turn. She just made it Fanny's size. Even Dr. Phelps looked a great deal handsomer in her company. More sociable. Nor were we to remain 'three's none'. She had finished but one slice of toast over my fire, and inflamed but one cheek, when a more protracted but far less vigorous knock than Dr. Phelps's on the door summoned her out of the room again. And a minute or two afterwards our tea-party became one of four, and its sexes (in number, at any rate) equally matched.

By a happy coincidence, just as Good King Wenceslas had looked out on the Feast of Stephen, so Mr. Crimble, the curate-in-charge at St. Peter's, had looked in. By his 'Ah, Phelps!' it was evident that our guests were well acquainted with one another;

and Fanny and I were soon enjoying a tea enriched by the cream of local society. Mr. Crimble had mild dark eyes, gold spectacles, rather full red lips, and a voice that reminded me of raspberries. I think he had heard of me, for he was very attentive, and handled my small cup and saucer with remarkable, if rather conspicuous, ingenuity.

Candles were lit. The talk soon became animated. From the weather of this Christmas we passed to the weather of last, to Dr. Phelps's prospects of skating, and thence to the good old times, to Mr. Pickwick, to our respective childish beliefs in Santa Claus, stockings, and to credulous parents. Fanny repeated some of the naïve remarks made by her pupils, and Mr. Crimble capped them with a collection of biblical *bons mots* culled in his Sunday School. I couldn't glance fast enough from one to the other. Dr. Phelps steadily munched and watched Mr. Crimble. He in turn told us of a patient of his, a Mrs. Hall, who, poor old creature, was 101, and enjoyed nothing better than playing at 'Old Soldier' with a small grandson.

'Literally, second childhood. Senile decay,' he said, passing his cup.

From Mrs. Hall we naturally turned to parochial affairs; and then Mr. Crimble, without more ado, bolted his mouthful of toast, in order to explain the inmost purpose of his visit.

He was anxious to persuade Miss Bowater to sing at the annual Parish Concert, which was to be given on New Year's Eve. Try as he might, he had been unable to persuade his vicar of the efficacy of Watch Night Services. So a concert was to be given instead. Now, would Miss Bowater, as ever, be ever so kind, and would I add my entreaties to his? As he looked at Fanny and I did too – with one of those odd turns of the mind, I was conscious that the peculiar leaning angle of his head was exactly the same as my own. Whereupon I glanced at Dr. Phelps, but he sat fair and four-square, one feeding like forty. Fanny remaining hesitant, appeal was made to him. With almost more cordiality than Mr. Crimble appeared to relish, he agreed that the musical talent available was not so abundant as it might be, and he promised to take as many of the expensive tickets as Miss Bowater would sing songs.

'I don't pretend to be musical, not like you, Crimble. But I don't mind a pleasant voice – in moderation; and I assure you, Miss Bowater, I am an excellent listener – given a fair chance, you know.'

'But then,' said Fanny, 'so am I. I believe now really – and one can judge from one's speaking voice, can't one, Mr. Crimble? – I believe you sing yourself.'

'Sing, Miss Bowater,' interjected Mr. Crimble, tipping back his chair. "The wedding guest here beat his chest, for he heard the loud bassoon." Now, conjuring tricks, eh, Phelps? With a stetho-scope and a clinical thermometer; and I'll hold the hat and make the omelette. It would bring down the house.' – 'It was his *breast* he beat; not his *chest*,' I broke in.

The six eyes slid round, as if at a voice out of the clouds. There was a pause.

'Why, exactly,' cried Mr. Crimble, slapping his leg.

'But I wish Dr. Phelps *would* sing,' said Fanny in a small voice, passing him the sugar.

'He must, he shall,' said Mr. Crimble in extreme jubilation. 'So that's settled. *Thank* you, Miss Bowater,' his eyes seemed to melt in his head at his success, 'the programme is complete.'

He drew a slip of paper from his inside pocket and brandished a silver pencil-case. 'Mrs. Browning, *The Better Land* – better and better every year. *Caller Herrin'* to follow – though what kind of herrings caller herrings are I've never been able to discover.' He beamed on me. 'Miss Finch – she is sending me the names of her songs this evening. Miss Willett and Mr. Bangor – *O That We Two*, and a queer pair they'd look; and *My Luv is Like*. Hardy annuals. Mrs. Bullace – recitations, *Abt Vogler*, and no doubt a Lord Tennyson. Flute, Mr. Piper; 'cello, Miss Oran, a niece of Lady Pollacke's; and for comic relief, Tom Sturgess, of course; though I hope he will be a little more – er – eclectic this year. And you and I', again he turned his boyish brow on me, 'will sit with Mrs. Bowater in the front row of the gallery – a claque, Phelps, eh?'

He seemed to be in the topmost height of good spirits. Well, thought I, if social badinage and *bonhomie* were as pleasant and easy as this, why hadn't my mother – ?

'But why in the gallery?' drawled Fanny suddenly from the hearthrug, with the little steel poker ready poised; 'Miss M. *dances*.'

The clear voice rasped on the word. A peculiar silence followed the lingering accents. The two gentlemen's faces smoothed themselves out, and both, I knew, though I gave them no heed, sat gazing, *not* at their hostess. But Fanny herself was looking at me now, her light eyes quite still in the flame of the candles, which, with their reflections in Mrs. Bowater's pier glass were not two, but four. It was into those eyes I gazed, yet not into, only at.

All day my thoughts had remained on her, like bubbles in wine. All day hope of the coming night and of our expedition to the woods had been, as it were, a palace in which my girlish fancy had wandered, and now, though only a few minutes ago I had been cheeping my small extemporary philosophy into the ear of Dr. Phelps, the fires of self-contempt and hatred burned up in me hotter than ever.

I forgot even the dainty dressing-jacket on my back. 'Miss Bowater is pleased to be satirical,' I said, my hand clenched in my lap.

'Now *was* I?' cried Fanny, appealing to Dr. Phelps, 'Be just to me.' Dr. Phelps opened his mouth, swallowed, and shut it again.

'I really think not, you know,' said Mr. Crimble persuasively, coming to her rescue. 'Indeed it would be extremely kind and – er – entertaining; though dancing – er – and – unless, perhaps, so many strangers ... We can count in any case on your being *present,* can we not, Miss M.?' He leaned over seductively, finger and thumb twitching at the plain gold cross suspended from his watch-chain on his black waistcoat.

'Oh, yes,' I replied, 'you can count on me for the claque.'

The room had sunk into a stillness. Constraint was in the air. 'Then that's settled. On New Year's Eve we – we all meet again. Unless, Miss Bowater, there is any hope of seeing you meanwhile – just to arrange the *titles* and so on of your songs on the programme.'

'No,' smiled Fanny, 'I see no hope whatever. You forget, Mr. Crimble, there are dishes to wash. And hadn't you better see Miss Finch first?'

Mr. Crimble cast a strange look at her face. He was close to her, and it was almost as if he had whispered, 'Fanny.' But there was no time for further discussion. Dr. Phelps, gloved and buttoned, was already at the door.

Fanny returned into the room when our guests had taken their departure. I heard their male voices in vivacious talk as they marched off in the cold dark air beneath my window.

'I thought they were never going,' said Fanny lightly, twisting up into her hair an escaped ringlet. 'I think, do you know, we had better say nothing to mother about the tea – at least not yet awhile. They are dull creatures: it's pottering about so dull and sleepy a place, I suppose. What *could* have inspired you to invite Dr. Phelps to tea? Really, really, Miss M., you are rather astonishing. Aren't you, now?'

What right had she to speak to me like this, as if we had met again after another life? She paused in her swift collection of the remnants of our feast. 'Sulking?' she inquired sweetly.

With an effort I kept my self-possession. 'You meant what you said, then? You really think I would sink to that?'

'"Sink!" To what? Oh, the dancing, you mean. How funny you should still be fretting about that. Still, you look quite entertaining when you are cross: "Diaphenia like the daffadowndilly", you know. Good Heavens! Surely we shouldn't hide any kind of lights under bushels, should we? I'm sure the Reverend Harold would agree to that. Isn't it being the least bit pedantic?'

'I should think', I retorted, 'Mr. Crimble would say anything pleasant to *any* young woman.'

'I have no doubt he would,' she agreed. 'The other cheek also, you know. But the real question is what the young woman would say in reply. You are too sensitive, Miss M.'

'Perhaps I am.' Oh that I could escape from this horrible net between us. 'I know this, anyhow – that I lay awake till midnight because you had made a kind of promise to come in. Then I – I "counted the pieces".'

Her face whitened beneath the clear skin. 'Oh, so we list –' she began, turning on me, then checked herself. 'I tell you this,' she said, her hand trembling, 'I'm sick of it all. Those – those fools! Ph! I thought that you, being as you are – snippeting along out of the night – might understand. There's such a thing as friendship on false pretences, Miss M.'

Was she, too, addressing, as she supposed, a confidant hardly more external to herself than that inward being whom we engage in such endless talk and argument? Her violence shocked me; still more her 'fools'. For the word was still next-door neighbour in my mind to the dreadful 'Raca'.

'"Understand"', I said, 'I do, if you would only let me. You just hide in your – in your own inside. You think because I am as I am that I'm only of that much account. It's you are the – foolish. Oh, don't let us quarrel. You just came. I never knew. Every hour, every minute ...' Inarticulate my tongue might be, but my face told its tale. She must have heard many similar confessions, yet an almost childish incredulity lightened in hers.

'Keep there,' she said, 'keep there! I won't be a moment.'

She hastened out of the room with the tea things, poising an instant like a bird on a branch as she pushed open the door with her foot. The slave left behind her listened to her footsteps dying away in a mingling of shame, sorrow, and of a happiness beyond words. I know now that it is not when we are near people that we reach themselves, not, I mean, in their looks and words, but only by following their thoughts to where the spirit within plays and has its being. Perhaps if I had realized this earlier, I shouldn't have fallen so easy a prey to Fanny Bowater. I waited – but that particular exchange of confidences was never to be completed. A key sounded in the latch. Fanny had but time to show herself with stooping, almost serpent-like head, in the doorway. 'To-night!' she whispered. 'And not a word, not a word!'

Chapter Thirteen

Was there suspicion in the face of Mrs. Bowater that evening? Our usual familiar talk dwindled to a few words this supper-time. The old conflict was raging in my mind – hatred of my deceit, horror at betraying an accomplice, and longing for the solemn quiet and solitude of the dark. I crushed my doubtings down and cast a dismal, hostile look at the long face, so yellow of skin and sombre in expression. When would she be gone and leave me in peace? The packed little parlour hung stagnant in the candlelight. It seemed impossible that Mrs. Bowater could not hear the thoughts in my mind. Apparently not. She tidied up my few belongings, which, contrary to my usual neat habits. I had left scattered over the table. She bade me good-night; but paused in the doorway to look back at me. But what intimacy she had meant to share with me was put aside. 'Goodnight, miss,' she repeated; 'and I'm sure, God bless you.' It was the dark, quiet look that whelmed over me. I gazed mutely, without response, and the silence was broken by a clear voice like that of a cautious mocking-bird out of a wood.

It called softly on two honeyed notes, 'Mo – ther!'

The house draped itself in quiet. Until ten had struck, and footsteps had ascended to the rooms overhead, I kept close in my bedchamber. Then I hastily put on my outdoor clothes, shivering not with cold, but with expectation, and sat down by the fire, prepared for the least sound that would prove that Fanny had not forgotten our assignation. But I waited in vain. The cold gathered. The vaporous light of the waning moon brightened in the room. The cinders fainted to a darker glow. I heard the kitchen clock with its cracked, cantankerous stroke beat out eleven. Its solemn mate outside, who had seemingly lost his voice, ticked on.

Hope died out in me, leaving an almost physical nausea, a profound hatred of myself and even of being alive. 'Well,' a cold voice said in my ear, 'that's how we are treated; that comes of those eyes we cannot forget. Cheated, cheated again, my friend.'

In those young days disappointment set my heart aching with a bitterness less easy to bear than it is now. No doubt I was steeped in sentimentality and folly. It was the vehemence of this new feeling that almost terrified me. But my mind was my world; it is my only excuse. I could not get out of *that* by merely turning a tiny key in a Bramah lock. Nor could I betake myself to bed. How sleep in such an inward storm of reproaches, humiliation, and despised love?

I drew down my veil, wrapped my shawl closer round my shoulders, descended my staircase, and presently stood in the porch in confrontation of the night. Low on the horizon, at evens with me across space, and burning with a limpid fire, hung my chosen – Sirius. The sudden sight of him pouring his brilliance into my eyes brought a revulsion of feeling. He was 'cutting me dead'. I brazened him down. I trod with exquisite caution down the steps, daring but one fleeting glance, as I turned, at Fanny's window. It was blinded, empty. Toiling on heavily up the hill, I sourly comforted myself with the vow that she should realize how little I cared, that her room had been sweeter than her company. Never more would I put trust in 'any child of man'.

Gradually, however, the quiet night received me into its peace (just as, poor soul, did the Moor Desdemona), and its influence stole into my darkened mind. The smooth, columnar boughs of the beeches lifted themselves archingly into the sky. Soon I was climbing over the moss-bound roots of my customary observatory. But this night the stars were left for a while unsignalled and unadmired. The crisped, frost-lined leaves scattered between the snake-like roots sparkled faintly. Years seemed to have passed away, dwindled in Time's hour-glass, since my previous visit. That Miss M. had ghosted herself away for ever. In my reverie the vision of Fanny re-arose into my imagination – that secret still fountain – of herself. Asleep now ... I could no more free myself from her sorcery than I could disclaim the two hands that lay in my lap. She was indeed more closely mine than they – and nearer in actuality than I had imagined.

A faint stir in the woods suddenly caught my attention. The sound neared. I pressed my hand to my breast, torn now between two incentives, two desires – to fly, to stay. And on the path by which I had come, appeared, some yards distant, in the faint trickling light, the dark figure of my dreams.

She was dressed in a black cloak, its peaked old-fashioned hood drawn over her head. The moonbeams struck its folds as she moved. Her face was bowed down a little, her hand from within clutching her cloak together. And I realized instinctively and with joy that the silence and solitude of the woods alarmed her. It was I who was calm and self-contained. She paused and looked around her – stood listening with lips divided that yet could not persuade themselves to call me by name. For my part, I softly gathered myself closer together and continued to gloat. And suddenly out of the far-away of the woods a nightbird loosed its cry: 'A-hoo ... Ahoo-oo-oo-hooh!'

There is a hunter in us all. I laughed inwardly as I watched. A few months more and I was to watch a lion-tamer ... but let me keep to one thing at a time. I needled myself in, and, almost hooting the sound through my mouth, as if in echo of the bird, I heard myself call stealthily across the air, 'Fanny! – Fanny Bowater!'

The cloaked figure recoiled, with lifted head, like the picture of a faun I have seen, and gazed in my direction. Seeing nothing of me amidst the leaves and shadows, she was about to flee, when I called again:

'It is I, Fanny. Here: here!'

Instantly she woke to herself, came near, and looked down on me. No movement welcomed her. 'I was tired of waiting,' I yawned. 'There is nothing to be frightened about.'

Many of her fellow creatures, I fancy, have in their day wearied of waiting for Fanny Bowater, but few have had the courage or sagacity to tell her so. She had not recovered her equanimity fully enough to refrain from excuses.

'Surely you did not expect me while mother was moving? I am not accustomed, Miss M., to midnight wanderings.'

'I gave up expecting you, and was glad to be alone.'

The barb fell short. She looked stilly around her. The solemn beeches were like mute giants overarching with their starry, sky-hung boughs the dark, slim figure. What consciousness had they, I wonder, of those odd humans at their roots?

'Alone! Here!' she returned. 'But no wonder. It's what you are all about.'

A peculiar elation sprang up in me at this none too intelligible remark.

'I wonder, though,' she added, 'you are not frozen like – like a pebble, sitting there.'

'But I am,' I said, laughing softly. 'It doesn't matter in me, because I'm so easy to thaw. You ought to know that. Oh, Miss Bowater, think if this were summer time and the dew and the first burning heat! Are you wrapped up? And shall we sit here, just – just for one dance of the Sisters: thou lost dove, Merope?'

For there on high – and I had murmured the last words all but inaudibly to myself – there played the spangling Pleiads, clear above her head in the twig-swept sky.

'What sisters?' she inquired, merely humouring me, perhaps.

'The Six, Fanny, look! You cannot see their Seventh – yet she is all that *that* is about.' South to north I swept my hand across the powdery firmament. 'And I myself trudge along down Watling Street; that's the Milky Way. I don't think, Fanny, I shall ever, ever be weaned. Please, may I call you that?'

She frowned up a moment into the emptiness, hesitated, then – just like a white peacock I had once seen when a child from my godmother's ancient carriage as we rolled by an old low house with terraces smooth as velvet beneath its cedars – she disposed her black draperies upon the ground at a little distance, disclosing, in so doing, beneath their folds the moon-blanched flounces of her party gown. I gazed spellbound. I looked at the white and black, and thought of what there was within their folds, and of the heart within that, and of the spirit of man. Such was my foolish fashion, following idly like a butterfly the scents of the air, flitting on from thought to thought, and so missing the full richness of the one blossom on which I might have hovered.

'Tell me some more,' broke suddenly the curious voice into the midst of this reverie.

'Well, there', I cried, 'is fickle Algol; the Demon. And over there where the Crab crawls, is the little Beehive between the Roses.'

'Præsepe,' drawled Fanny.

'Yes,' said I, unabashed, 'the Beehive. And crane back your neck, Fanny – there's little Jack-by-the-Middle-Horse; and far down, oh, far down, Berenice's Hair, which would have been Fanny Bowater's Hair, if you had been she.'

Even as I looked, a remote film of mist blotted out the infinitesimal cluster. 'And see, beyond the Chair,' I went on, laughing, and yet exalted with my theme, 'that dim in the Girdle is the Great Nebula – s-sh! And on, on, that chirruping Invisible, *that,* Fanny, is the Midget. Perhaps you cannot even dream of her: but she watches.'

'Never even heard of her,' said Fanny good-humouredly, withdrawing the angle of her chin from the Ecliptic.

'"Say not so, Horatia,"' I mocked, '"there are more things –"'

'Oh, yes, I know all about that. And these cold, monotonous old things really please you? Personally, I'd give the whole meaningless scramble of them for another moon.'

'But your old glutton has gobbled up half of them already.'

'Then my old glutton can gobble up what's left. Who taught you about them? And why,' she scanned me closely, 'why did you pick out the faintest; do you see them the best?'

'I picked out the faintest because they were meant especially for me so that I could give them to you. My father taught me a little about them; and *your* father the rest.'

'*My* father,' echoed Fanny, her face suddenly intent.

'His book. Do you miss him? Mine is dead.'

'Oh, yes, I miss him,' was the serene retort, 'and so, I fancy, does mother.'

'Oh, Fanny, I am sorry. She told me – something like that.'

'You need not be. I suppose God chooses one's parents quite deliberately. Praise Him from Whom all blessings flow!' She smoothed out her black cloak over her ankles, raised her face again into the dwindling moonlight, and gently smiled at me. 'I am glad I came, Midgetina, though it's suicidally cold. "*Pardi! on sent Dieu bien à son aise ici*". We are going to be great friends, aren't we?' Her eyes swept over me. 'Would you like that?'

'Friends', indeed! and as if she had offered me a lump of sugar.

I gravely nodded. 'But I must come to you. You can't come to me. No one has; except, perhaps, my mother – a little.'

'Oh, yes,' she replied cautiously, piercing her eyes at me, 'that *is* a riddle. You must tell me about your childhood. Not that I love children, or my own childhood either. I had enough of that to last me a lifetime. I shan't pass it on; though I promise you, Midgetina, if ever I *do* have a baby, I will anoint its little backbone with the grease of moles, bats, and dormice, and make it like you. Was your mother – ' she began again, after a pause of reflection. 'Are *you* sorry, I mean, you aren't – you aren't – ?'

Her look supplied the missing words. 'Sorry that I am a midget, Fanny? People think I must be. But why? It is all I am, all I ever was. I am myself, inside; like everybody else; and yet, you know, not quite like everybody else. I sometimes think' – I laughed at the memory – 'I was asking Dr. Phelps about that. Besides, would *you* be – alone?'

'Not when I was alone, perhaps. Still, it must be rather odd, Miss Needle-in-a-Haystack. As for being alone' – once again our owl, if owl it was, much nearer now, screeched its screech in the wintry woods – 'I hate it!'

'But surely', expostulated the wiseacre in me, 'that's what we cannot help being. We even die alone, Fanny.'

'Oh, but I'm going to help it. I'm not dead yet. Do you ever think of the future?'

For an instant its great black hole yawned close, but I shook my head.

'Well, that', replied she, 'is what Fanny Bowater is doing all the time. There's nothing', she added satirically, 'so important, so imperative for teachers as learning. And you must learn your lesson, my dear, before you are heard if – if you want to escape a slapping. Every little donkey knows that.'

'I suppose the truth is', said I, as if seized with a bright idea, 'there are two kinds of ambitions, of wants, I mean. We are all like those Chinese boxes; and some of us want to live in the biggest, the outsidest we can possibly manage; and some in the inmost one of all. The one,' I added a little drearily, 'no one can share.'

'Quite, quite true,' said Fanny, mimicking my sententiousness, 'the teeniest, tiniest, icklest one, which no mortal ingenuity has ever been able to open – and so discover the nothing inside. *I* know your Chinese boxes!'

'Poor Fanny,' I cried, rising up and kneeling beside the ice-cold hand that lay on the frosty leaves. 'All that I have shall help you.'

Infatuated thing; I stooped low as I knelt, and stroked softly with my own the outstretched fingers on which she was leaning.

I might have been a pet animal for all the heed she paid to my caress. 'Fanny,' I whispered tragically, 'will you please sing to me – if you are not frozenly cold? You remember – the *Moon Song*: I have never forgotten it; and only three notes, yet it sometimes wakes me at night. It's queer, isn't it, being you and me?'

She laughed, tilting her chin; and her voice began at once to sing, as if at the scarcely opened door of her throat, and a tune so plain it seemed but the words speaking:

> 'Twas a Cuckoo, cried 'cuck-oo'
> In the youth of the year;
> And the timid things nesting,
> Crouched, ruffled in fear;
> And the Cuckoo cried, 'cuck-oo',
> For the honest to hear.
>
> One – two notes: a bell sound
> In the blue and the green;
> 'Cuck-oo: cuck-oo: cuck-oo!'
> And a silence between.
>
> Ay, mistress, have a care, lest
> Harsh love, he hie by,
> And for kindness a monster
> To nourish you try –
> In your bosom to lie:
> 'Cuck-oo', and a 'cuck-oo',
>   And 'cuck-oo!'

The sounds fell like beads into the quiet – as if a small child had come up out of her heart and gone down again; and she callous and unmoved. I cannot say why the clear, muted notes saddened and thrilled me so. Was *she* the monster?

I had drawn back, and stayed eyeing her pale face, the high cheek, the delicate straight nose, the darkened lips, the slim black eyebrows, the light, clear, unfathomable eyes reflecting the solitude and the thin brilliance of the wood. Yet the secret of herself remained her own. She tried in vain not to be disturbed at my scrutiny.

'Well,' she inquired at last, with motionless glance fixed on the distance. 'Do you think you could honestly give me a testimonial, Miss Midget?'

It is strange. The Sphinx had spoken, yet without much enlightenment. 'Now look at me,' I commanded. 'If I went away, you couldn't follow. When you go away, you cannot escape from me. I can go back and – and *be* where I was.' My own meaning was half-concealed from me; but a startled something that had not been there before peeped out of those eyes so close to mine.

'If', she said, 'I could care like that too, yet wanted nothing, then I should be free too.'

'What do you mean?' said I, lifting my hand from the unanswering fingers.

'I mean', she exclaimed, leaping to her feet, 'that I'm sick to death of the stars and am going home to bed. Hateful listening old woods!'

I turned sharp round, as if in apprehension that some secret hearer might have caught her remark. But Fanny stretched out her arms, and, laughing a foolish tune, in affected abandonment began softly to dance in the crisp leaves, quite lost to me again. So twirling, she set off down the path by which she had come trespassing. A physical exhaustion came over me. I watched her no more, but stumbled along, with unheeding eyes, in her wake. What had I not given, I thought bitterly, and this my reward. Thus solitary, I had gone only a little distance, and had reached the outskirts of the woods, when a far from indifferent Fanny came hastening back to intercept me.

And no wonder. She had remembered to attire herself becomingly for her moonlight tryst, but had forgotten the door key. We stood looking at one another aghast, as, from eternity, I suppose, have all fellow-conspirators in danger of discovery. It was I who first awoke to action. There was but one thing to be done, and, warning Fanny that I had never before attempted to unlatch the big front door of her mother's house, I set off resolutely down the hill.

'You walk so slowly!' she said suddenly, turning back on me. 'I will carry you.'

Again we paused. I looked up at her with an inextricable medley of emotions struggling together in my mind, and shook my head.

'But why, why?' she repeated impatiently. 'We could get there in half the time.'

'If you could *fly,* Fanny, I'd walk,' I replied stubbornly.

'You mean – ' and her cold anger distorted her face. 'Oh, pride! What childish nonsense! And you said we were to be friends. Do you suppose I care whether ...?' But the question remained unfinished.

'I *am* your friend', said I, 'and that is why I will not, I *will* not give way to you.' It was hardly friendship that gleamed out of the wide eyes then. But mine the victory – a victory in which only a tithe of the spoils, unrecognized by the vanquished, had fallen to the victor.

Without another word she turned on her heel, and for the rest of our dejected journey, she might have been mistaken for a cross nurse trailing on pace for pace beside a rebellious child. My dignity was less ruffled than hers, however, and for a brief while I had earned my freedom.

Arrived at the house, dumbly hostile in the luminous night, Fanny concealed herself as best she could behind the gatepost and kept watch on the windows. Far away in the stillness we heard a footfall echoing on the hill. 'There is someone coming,' she whispered, 'you must hurry.' She might, I think, have serpented her way in by my own little door. Where the *head* leads, the heart may follow. But she did not suggest it. Nor did I.

I tugged and pushed as best I could, but the umbrella with which from a chair I at last managed to draw the upper bolt of the door was extremely cumbersome. The latch for a while resisted my efforts. And the knowledge that Fanny was fretting and fuming behind the gate-post hardly increased my skill. The house was sunken in quiet; Mrs. Bowater apparently was sleeping without her usual accompaniment; only Henry shared my labours, and he sat moodily at the foot of the stairs, refusing to draw near until at the same moment Fanny entered, and he leapt out.

Once safely within, and the door closed and bolted again, Fanny stood for a few moments listening. Then with a sigh and a curious gesture she bent herself and kissed the black veil that concealed my fair hair.

'I am sorry, Midgetina,' she whispered into its folds, 'I was impatient. Mother wouldn't have liked the astronomy, you know. That was all. And I am truly sorry for – for – '

'My dear,' I replied in firm, elderly tones, whose echo is in my ear to this very day; 'my dear, it was my mind you hurt, not my feelings.' With that piece of sententiousness I scrambled blindly through my Bates's doorway, shut the door behind me, and more disturbed at heart than I can tell, soon sank into the thronging slumber of the guilty and the obsessed.

Chapter Fourteen

When my eyes opened next morning, a strange, still glare lay over the ceiling, and I looked out of my window on a world mantled and cold with snow. For a while I forgot the fever of the last few days in watching the birds hopping and twittering among the crumbs that Mrs. Bowater scattered out on the window-sill for my pleasure. And yet – their every virtue, every grace, Fanny Bowater, all were thine! The very snow, in my girlish fantasy, was the fairness beneath which the unknown Self in her must, as I fondly believed, lie slumbering; a beauty that hid also from me for a while the restless, self-centred mind. How believe that such beauty is any the less a gift to its possessor than its bespeckled breast and song to a thrush, its sheen to a starling? It is a riddle that still baffles me. If we are all shut up in our bodies as the poets and the Scriptures say we are, then how is it that many of the loveliest seem to be all but uninhabited, or to harbour such dingy tenants; while quite plain faces may throng with animated ghosts?

Fanny did not come to share my delight in the snow that morning. And as I looked out on it, waiting on in vain, hope flagged, and a sadness stole over its beauty. Probably she had not given the fantastic lodger a thought. She slid through life, it seemed, as easily as a seal through water. But I was not the only friend who survived her caprices. In spite of her warning about the dish-washing, Mr. Crimble came to see her that afternoon. She was out. With a little bundle of papers in his hand he paused at the gate-post to push his spectacles more firmly on to his nose and cast a kind of homeless look over the fields before turning his face towards St. Peter's. Next day, Holy Innocents', he came again; but this time with more determination, for he asked to see me.

To rid myself, as far as possible, of one piece of duplicity, I at once took the bull by the horns, and in the presence of Mrs. Bowater boldly invited him to stay to tea. With a flurried glance of the eye in her direction he accepted my invitation.

'A cold afternoon, Mrs. Bowater,' he intoned. 'The cup that cheers, the cup that cheers.'

My landlady left the conventions to take care of themselves; and presently he and I found ourselves positively *tête-à-tête* over her seed cake and thin bread and butter.

But though we both set to work to make conversation, an absent intentness in his manner, a listening turn of his head, hinted that his thoughts were not wholly with me.

'Are you long with us?' he inquired, stirring his tea.

'I am quite, quite happy here,' I replied, with a sigh.

'Ah!' he replied, a little wistfully, taking a sip, 'how few of us have the courage to confess that. Perhaps it flatters us to suppose we are miserable. It is this pessimism – of a mechanical, a scientific age – which we have chiefly to contend against. We don't often see you at St. Peter's, I think?'

'You wouldn't see *very* much of me, if I did come,' I replied a little tartly. Possibly it was his 'we' that had fretted me. It seemed needlessly egotistical. 'On the other hand,' I added, 'wouldn't there be a risk of the congregation seeing nothing else?'

Mr. Crimble opened his mouth and laughed. 'I wish', he said, with a gallant little bow, 'there were more like you.'

'More like *me*, Mr. Crimble?'

'I mean,' he explained, darting a glance at the furniture of my bedroom, whose curtains, to my annoyance, hung withdrawn, 'I mean that – that you – that so many of us refuse to see the facts of life. To look them in the face, Miss M. There is nothing to fear.'

We were getting along famously, and I begged him to take some of Mrs. Bowater's black currant jam.

'But then, I have plenty of time,' I said agreeably. 'And the real difficulty is to get the facts to face me. Dear me, if only, now, I had some of Miss Bowater's brains.'

A veil seemed suddenly to lift from his face and as suddenly to descend again. So, too, he had for a moment stopped eating, then as suddenly begun eating again.

'Ah, Miss Bowater! She is indeed clever; a – a brilliant young lady. The very life of a party, I assure you. And, yet, do you know, in parochial gatherings, try as I may, I occasionally find it very difficult to get people to mix. The little social formulas, the prejudices. Yet, surely, Miss M., religion *should* be the great solvent. At least, that is my view.'

He munched away more vigorously, and gazed through his spectacles out through my window-blinds.

'Mixing people must be very wearisome,' I suggested examining his face.

'"Wearisome",' he repeated blandly. 'I am sometimes at my wits' end. No. A curate's life is not a happy one.' Yet he confessed it almost with joy.

'And the visiting!' I said. And then, alas! my tongue began to run away with me. He was falling back again into what I may call his company voice, and I pined to talk to the real Mr. Crimble, little dreaming how soon that want was to be satiated.

'I sometimes wonder, do you know, if religion is made difficult enough.'

'But I assure you,' he replied, politely but firmly, 'a true religion is exceedingly difficult. "The eye of a needle" – we mustn't forget that.'

'Ah, yes,' said I warmly; 'that "eye" will be narrow enough even for a person with my little advantages. I remember my mother's cook telling me, when I was a child, that in the old days, really wicked people if they wanted to return to the Church had to do so in a sheet, with ashes on their heads, you know, and carrying a long lighted candle. She said that if the door was shut against them, they died in torment, and went to Hell. But she was a Roman Catholic, like my grandmother.'

Mr. Crimble peered at me as if over a wall.

'I remember, too,' I went on, 'one summer's day as a very little girl I was taken to the evening service. And the singing – bursting out like that, you know, with the panting and the yowling of the organ, made me faint and sick; and I jumped right out of the window.'

'Jumped out of the window!' cried my visitor in consternation.

'Yes, we were at the back. Pollie, my nursemaid, had put me up in the niche, you see; and I dragged her hand away. But I didn't hurt myself. The grass was thick in the churchyard: I fell light, and I had plenty of clothes on. I rather enjoyed it – the air and the tombstones. And though I had my gasps, the "eye" seemed big enough when I was a child. But afterwards – when I was confirmed – I thought of Hell a good deal. I can't *see* it so plainly now. Wide, low, and black, with a few demons. *That* can't be right.'

'My dear young lady!' cried Mr. Crimble, as if shocked, 'is it wise to attempt it? It must be admitted, of course, that if we do not take advantage of the benefits bestowed upon us by Providence in a Christian community, we cannot escape His displeasure. The absence from His Love.'

'Yes,' I said, looking at him in sudden intimacy, 'I believe that.' And I pondered awhile, following up my own thoughts. 'Have you ever read Mr. Clodd's *Childhood of the World*, Mr. Crimble?'

By the momentary confusion of his face I gathered that he had not. 'Mr. Clodd? ... Ah, yes, the writer on Primitive Man.'

'This was only a little book, for the young, you know. But in it Mr. Clodd says, I remember, that even the most shocking old forms of religion were not invented by devils. They were "Man's struggles from darkness to twilight". What he meant was that no man *loves* darkness. At least,' I added, with a sudden gush of remembrances, 'not without the stars.'

'That is exceedingly true,' replied Mr. Crimble. 'And talking of stars, what a wonderful sight it was the night before last, the whole heavens one spangle of diamonds. I was returning from visiting a sick parishioner, Mr. Hubbins.' Then it was *his* foot that Fanny and I had heard reverberating on the hill! I hastily hid my face in my cup, but he appeared not to have noticed my confusion. He took another slice of bread and butter; folded it carefully in two, then peered up out of the corner of his round eye at me, and added solemnly: 'Sick, I regret to say, no longer.'

'Dead?' I cried from the bottom of my heart, and again looked at him.

Then my eyes strayed to the silent scene beyond the window,

silent, it seemed, with the very presence of poor Mr. Hubbins. 'I should not like to go to Hell in the snow,' I said ruminatingly. Out of the past welled into memory an old ballad my mother had taught me:

> 'This ae nighte, this ae nighte
> – *Every nighte and alle,*
> Fire and sleet and candle-lighte,
> *And Christe receive thy saule!*'

'Beautiful, beautiful,' murmured Mr. Crimble, yet not without a trace of alarm in his dark eyes. 'But believe me, I am not suggesting that Mr. Hubbins – His was, I am told, a wonderfully peaceful end.'

'Peaceful! Oh, but surely not in his mind, Mr. Crimble. Surely one must be more alive in that last hour than ever – just when one's going away. At any rate,' and I couldn't refrain a sigh, almost of envy, 'I hope *I* shall be. Was Mr. Hubbins a good man?'

'He was a most regular church-goer,' replied my visitor a little unsteadily; 'a family-man, one of our Sidesmen, in fact. He will be greatly missed. You may remember what Mr. Ruskin wrote of his father: "Here lies an entirely honest merchant". Mr. Ruskin, senior, was, as a matter of fact, in the wine trade. Mr. Hubbins, I believe, was in linen, though, of course, it amounts to the same thing. But haven't we,' and he cleared his throat, 'haven't we – er – strayed into a rather lugubrious subject?'

'We have strayed into a rather lugubrious world,' said I.

'Of course, of course; but, believe me, we mustn't always *think* too closely. "Days and moments quickly flying", true enough, though hardly appropriate, as a matter of fact, at this particular season in the Christian year. But, on the other hand, "we may make our lives sublime". Does not yet another poet tell us that? Although, perhaps, Mr. Hub –'

'Yes,' I interposed eagerly, the lover of books in me at once rising to the bait, 'but what do you think Longfellow absolutely *meant* by his "sailor on the main" of life being comforted, you remember, by somebody else having been shipwrecked and just leaving *footprints* in the sand? I used to wonder and wonder. Does the poem imply, Mr. Crimble, that merely to be born is to be shipwrecked? I don't think that can be so, because Longfellow was quite a cheerful man, wasn't he? – at least for a poet. For my part', I ran on, now thoroughly at home with my visitor, and on familiar ground, 'I am sure I prefer poor Friday. Do you remember how Robinson Crusoe described him soon after the rescue from the savages as "without Passions, Sullenness, or Designs", even though he did, poor thing, "have a hankering stomach after some of the Flesh"? Not that I mean to suggest', I added hastily, 'that Mr. Hubbins was in any sense a cannibal.'

'By no means,' said Mr. Crimble helplessly. 'But there,' and he brushed his knees with his handkerchief, 'I fear you are too much of a reader for me, and – and critic. For that very reason I do hope, Miss M., you will sometimes contrive to pay a visit to St. Peter's. Mother Church has room for all, you know, in her – about her footstool.' He smiled at me very kindly. 'And our organist, Mr. Temple, has been treating us to some charmingly quaint old carols – at least the words seem a little quaint to a modern ear. But I cannot boast of being a *student* of poetry. Parochial work leaves little time even for the classics:

> *Odi profanum vulgus, et arceo.*
> *Favete linguis ...*

He almost chirped the delightful words in a high, pleasant voice, but except for the first three of them, they were too many for my small Latin, and I afterwards forgot to test the aptness of his quotation. I was just about to ask him (with some little unwillingness) to translate the whole ode for me, when I heard Fanny's step at the door. I desisted.

At her entry the whole of our conversation, as it hung about in Mrs. Bowater's firelit little parlour, seemed to have become threadbare and meaningless. My visitor and I turned away from each other almost with relief – like Longfellow's shipwrecked sailors, perhaps, at sight of a ship.

Fanny's pale cheeks beneath her round beaver hat and veil were bright with the cold – for frost had followed the snow. She eyed us slowly, with less even than a smile in her eyes, facing my candles softly, as if she had come out of a dream. Whatever class of the community Mr. Crimble may have meant to include in his *Odi,* the celerity with which he rose to greet her made it perfectly clear that it was not Miss Bowater's. She smiled at the black sleeve, cuff, and signet ring outstretched towards her, but made no further advance. She brought him, too, a sad disappointment, simply that she would be unable to sing at his concert on the last night of the year. At this blow Mr. Crimble instinctively folded his hands. He looked helpless and distressed.

'But, Miss Bowater,' he pleaded, 'the printer has been waiting nearly two days for the names of your songs. The time is very short now.'

'Yes,' said Fanny, seating herself on a stool by the fire and slowly removing her gloves, 'it is annoying. I hadn't a vestige of a cold last night.'

'But, indeed, indeed,' he began, 'is it wise in this severe weather –?'

'Oh, it isn't the weather I mind,' was the serene retort, 'it's the croaking like a frog in public.'

"'A frog!'" cried Mr. Crimble beguilingly, 'oh, no!'

But all his protestations and cajoleries were unavailing. Even to a long, silent glance so private in appearance that it seemed more courteous to turn away from it, Fanny made no discernible response. His shoulders humped. He caught up his soft hat, made his adieu – a little formal, and hasty – and hurried off through the door to the printer.

When his muffled footsteps had passed away, I looked at Fanny.

'Oh, yes,' she agreed, shrugging her shoulders, 'it was a lie. I said it like a lie, so that it shouldn't deceive him. I detest all that wheedling. To come here two days running, after – And why, may I ask, if it is beneath your dignity to dance to the parish, is it not beneath mine to sing? Let the silly sheep amuse *themselves* with their bleating. I have done with it all.'

She rose, folded her gloves into a ball and her veil over her hat, and once more faced her reflection in her mother's looking-glass. I had not the courage to tell her that the expression she wore on other occasions suited her best.

'But surely,' I argued uneasily, 'things are different. If I were to dance, stuck up there on a platform, you know very well it would not be the dancing that would amuse them, but – just me. Would you care for that if you were – well, what I am?'

'Ah, but you don't know,' a low voice replied bitterly, 'you don't know. The snobs they are! I have soaked in it for years, like a pig in brine. Boxed up here in your pretty little doll's house, you suppose that all that matters is what you think of other people. But to be perfectly frank, you are out of the running, my dear. *I* have to get my own living, and all that matters is not what I think of other people but what other people think of me. Do you suppose I don't know what *he*, in his heart, thinks of me – and all the rest of them? Well, I say, wait!'

And she left me to my doll's house – a more helpless slave than ever.

Not only one 'star' the fewer, then, dazzled St. Peter's parish that New Year's Eve, but Fanny and I never again shared an hour's practical astronomy. Still, she would often sit and talk to me, and the chain of my devotion grew heavy. Perhaps she, on her side, merely basked in the flattery of my imagination. It was for her a new variety of a familiar experience. Perhaps a curious and condescending fondness for me for a while sprang up in her – as far as that was possible, for, apart from her instinctive heartlessness, she never really accustomed herself to my physical shortcomings. I believe they attracted yet repelled her. To my lonely spirit she was a dream that remained a dream in spite of its intensifying resemblance to a nightmare.

I realize now that she was desperately capricious, of a catlike cruelty by nature, and so evasive and elusive that frequently I could not distinguish her soft, furry pads from her claws. But whatever her mood, or her treatment of me, or her lapses into a kind of commonness to which I deliberately shut my eyes, her beauty remained. Whomsoever we love becomes unique in that love, and I suppose we are responsible for what we give as well as for what we accept. The very memory of her beauty, when I was alone, haunted me as intensely as if she were present. Yet in her actual company, it made her in a sense unreal. So, often, it was only the ghost of her with whom I sat and talked. How sharply it would have incensed her to know it. When she came to me in my sleep, she was both paradise and seraph, and never fiddle entranced a Paganini as did her liquid lapsing voice my small fastidious ear. Yet, however much she loved to watch herself in looking-glass or in her mind, and to observe her effects on others, she was not vain.

But the constant, unbanishable thought of anything wearies the mind and weakens the body. In my infatuation, I, too, was scarcely more than a ghost – a very childish ghost perhaps. I think if I could call him for witness, my small pasha in the train from Lyndsey would bear me out in this. As for what is called passion, the only burning of it I ever felt was for an outcast with whom I never shared so much as glance or word. Alas, Fanny, I suppose, was merely a brazen image.

Long before the dark day of her departure – a day which stood in my thoughts like a barrier at the world's end – I had very foolishly poured out most of my memories for her profit and amusement, though so immobile was she when seated in a chair beside my table, or standing foot on fender at the chimney-piece, that it was difficult at times to decide whether she was listening to me or not. What is more important, she told me in return, in her curious tortuous and contradictory fashion, a good deal about herself, and of her childhood, which – because of the endless violent roarings of her nautical father, and the taciturn discipline of poor Mrs. Bowater – filled me with compassion and heaped fuel on my love. And not least of these bonds was the secret which, in spite of endless temptation, I managed to withhold from her in a last instinctive loyalty to Mrs. Bowater – the discovery that her own mother was long since dead and gone.

She possessed more brains than she cared to exhibit to visitors like Dr. Phelps and Mr. Crimble. Even to this day I cannot believe that Mr. Crimble even so much as guessed how clever she was. It was just part of herself, like the bloom on a plum. Hers was not one of those gesticulating minds. Her efforts only intensified her Fannyishness. Oh dear, how simple things are if only you leave them unexplained. Her very knowledge, too (which for the most part she kept to herself) was to me like finding chain armour when one is in search of a beating heart. She could shed it all, and her cleverness too, as easily as a swan water-drops. What could she not shed, and yet remain Fanny? And with all her confidences, she was extremely reticent. A lift of the light shoulders, or of the clear arched eyebrows, a sarcasm, a far-away smile, at the same time illuminated and obscured her talk. These are feminine gifts, and yet past my mastery. Perhaps for this reason I admired them the more in Fanny – just as, in reading my childhood's beloved volume, *The Observing Eye*, I had admired the crab's cuirass and the scorpion's horny rings – because, being, after all, myself a woman, I faintly understood their purpose.

Thus, when Fanny told me of the school she taught in; and of the smooth-haired drawing-master who attended it with his skill, on Mondays, Wednesdays, and Fridays; and of the vivacious and saturnine 'Monsieur Crapaud', who, poked up in a room under the gables, lived in the house; or of that other parish curate who was a nephew of the headmistress's, the implacable Miss Stebbings, and who, apparently, preached Sunday after Sunday, with peculiar pertinacity on such texts as 'God is love' – when Fanny recounted to me these afflictions, graces, and mockeries of her daily routine as 'literature' mistress, I could as easily bestow on her the vivifying particulars she left out, as a painter can send his portraits to be framed.

Once and again – just as I have seen a blackbird drop plumb

from the upper boughs of a tree on a worm disporting itself in the dewy mould – once I did ask a question which produced in her one of those curious reactions which made her, rather than immaterial, an exceedingly vigilant image of her very self. 'What will you do, Fanny, when you *can't* mock at him?'

'Him?' she inquired in a breath.

'*The* him,' I said.

'What him?' she replied.

'Well,' I said, stumbling along down what was a rather black and unfamiliar alley to me, 'my father was not, I suppose, particularly wise in anything, but my mother loved him very much.'

'And *my* father,' she retorted, in words so carefully pronounced that I knew they must be dangerous, 'my father was a first mate in the mercantile marine when he married your landlady.'

'Well,' I repeated, 'what would you do, if – if *you* fell in love?'

Fanny sat quite still, all the light at the window gently beating on her face, with its half-closed eyes. Her foot stirred, and with an almost imperceptible movement of her shoulder, she replied, 'I shall go blind.'

I looked at her, dumbfounded. All the days of her company were shrivelled up in that small sentence. 'Oh, Fanny,' I whispered hopelessly, 'then you know?'

'"Know?"' echoed the smooth lips.

'Why, I mean,' I expostulated, rushing for shelter fully as rapidly as my old friend the lobster must have done when it was time to change his shell, 'I mean that's what that absurd little Frenchman is – "Monsieur Crapaud."'

'Oh, no,' said Fanny calmly, '*he* is not blind, he only has his eyes shut. Mine,' she added, as if the whole light of the wintry sky she faced were the mirror of her prediction, 'mine will be wide open.'

How did I know that for once the serene, theatrical creature was being mortally serious?

Chapter Fifteen

I grew a little weary of the beautiful snow in the days that followed my first talk with Mr. Crimble, and fretted at the close air of the house. The last day of the year the wind was still in the north. It perplexed me that the pride which from my seed had sprung up in Fanny, and had prevented her from taking part in the parish concert, yet allowed her to attend it. She set off thickly veiled. Not even Mr. Crimble's spectacles were likly to pierce her disguise. I had written a little letter the afternoon before and had myself handed it to Mrs. Bowater with a large fork of mistletoe from my Christmas bunch. It was an invitation to herself and Fanny to sit with me and 'see in' the New Year. She smiled at me over it – still her tranquil, though neglected self – and I was half-satisfied.

Her best black dress was donned for the occasion. She had purchased a bottle of ginger wine, which she brought in with some glasses and placed in the middle of the red and black tablecloth. Its white-lettered, dark-green label 'haunts me still'. The hours drew on. Fanny returned from the concert – entering the room like a cloud of beauty. She beguiled the dwindling minutes of the year with mocking echoes of it.

In a rich falsetto she repeated Mr. Crimble's 'few words' of sympathetic apology for her absence. 'I must ask your indulgence, ladies and gentlemen, for a lamentable hiatus in our programme'. She gave us Miss Willett's and Mr. Bangor's spirited rendering of *Oh, that we two*; and of the recitation which rather easily, it appeared, Mrs. Bullace had been prevailed upon to give as an encore after her *Abt Vogler: The Lady's Yes*, by Elizabeth Barrett Browning. And what a glance of light and fire she cast me when she came to stanza six of the poem:

> Lead her from the festive boards,
> Point her to the starry skies! ...

And she imitated Lady Pollacke's niece's – Miss Oran's – cello obbligato to *The Lost Chord*, with a plangency that stirred even the soul of Henry as he lay curled up in my landlady's lap. The black head split like a pomegranate as he yawned his disgust.

At this Mrs. Bowater turned her bony face on me, her hands on her knees, and with a lift of her eyes disclosed the fact that she was amused, and that she hoped her amusement would remain a confidence between us. She got up and put the cat out: and on her return had regained her solemnity.

'I suppose,' she said stiffly, staring into the sparkling fire that was our only illumination. 'I suppose, poor creatures, they did their best: and it isn't so many years ago, Fanny, since you were as put-about to be allowed to sing at one of the church concerts as a bird is to hop out of its cage.'

'Yes,' said Fanny, 'but in this world birds merely hop out of one cage into another; though I suppose the larger are the more comfortable.' This retort set Mrs. Bowater's countenance in an impassive mask – so impassive that every fitfully-lit photograph in the room seemed to have imitated her stare. 'And, mother,' added Fanny seductively, 'who *taught* me to sing?'

'The Lord knows,' cried Mrs. Bowater, with conviction, '*I* never did.'

'Yes,' muttered Fanny in a low voice, for my information, 'but does He care?' I hastily asked Mrs. Bowater if she was glad of to-morrow's New Year. As if in reply the kitchen clock, always ten minutes fast, began to chime twelve, half-choking at every stroke. And once more the soul of poor Mr. Hubbins sorrowfully took shape in a gaze at me out of vacancy.

'To them going downhill, miss,' my landlady was replying to my question, 'it is not the milestones are the pleasantest company – nor that the journey's then of much account until it is over. By which I don't mean to suggest there need be *gloom*. But to you and Fanny here – well, I expect the little that's the present for you is mostly wasted on the future.' With that, she rose, and poured out the syrupy brown wine from the green bottle, reserving a remarkably little glass which she had rummaged out of her years' hoardings for me.

Fanny herself, with musing head – her mockings over – was sitting drawn-up on a stool by the fire. I doubt if she was thinking. Whether or not, to my enchanted eyes some phantom within her seemed content merely to be her beauty. And in rest, there was a grace in her body – the smooth shoulder, the poised head that, because, perhaps, it was so transitory, seemed to resemble the never-changing – that mimicry of the unknown which may be seen in a flower, in a green hill, even in an animal. It is as though, I do think, what we love most in this life must of necessity share two worlds.

Faintly out of the frosty air was wafted the knelling of midnight.

I rose, stepped back from the firelight, drew the curtain, and stole a look into space. Away on the right flashed Sirius, and to east of him came gliding flat-headed Hydra with Alphard, the Red Bird, in his coil. So, for a moment in our history, I and the terrestrial globe were alone together. It seemed indeed that an intenser silence drew over reality as the earth faced yet one more fleeting revolution round her invisible lord and master. But no moon was risen yet.

I turned towards the shape by the fire, and without her perceiving it, wafted kiss and prayer in her direction. Cold, careless Fanny – further than Uranus. We were alone, for at first stroke of St. Peter's Mrs. Bowater had left the room and had opened the front door. She was smiling; but *was* she smiling, or was that vague bewitchingness in her face merely an unmeaning guile of which she was unaware? It might have been a mermaid sitting there in the firelight.

The bells broke in on our stillness; and fortunately, since there was no dark man in the house to bring us luck, Henry, already disgusted with the snow and blacker in hue than any whiskered human I have ever seen, seized his opportunity, and was the first living creature to cross our threshold from one year into another.

This auspicious event renewed our spirits which, in waiting, had begun to flag. From far away came a jangling murmur of shouting and instruments and bells, which showed that the rest of the parish was sharing our solemn vigil; and then, with me on my table between them, a hand of each clasping mine, Mrs. Bowater, Fanny, and I, after sipping each other's health, raised the strains of *Auld Lang Syne*. There must have been Scottish blood in Mrs. Bowater; she certainly made up for some little variation from the tune by a heartfelt pronunciation of the words. Hardly had we completed this rite than the grandfather's clock in the narrow passage staidly protested its own rendering of eternity; and we all – even Mrs. Bowater – burst out laughing.

'Good-night, Midgetina; an immense happy New Year to you,' whispered a voice to me about half an hour afterwards. I jumped out of bed and peeped through my curtains. On some little errand Fanny had come down from her bedroom, and with a Paisley shawl over her shoulders stood with head and candle thrust in at the door. I gazed at her fairness. 'Oh Fanny!' I cried. 'Oh, Fanny!'

New Year's Day brought a change of weather. A slight mist rose over the fields, it began to thaw. A kind of listlessness now came over Fanny, which I tried in vain to dispel. Yet she seemed to seek my company; often to remain silent, and occasionally to ask me curious questions as if testing one answer against another. And one discovery I made in my efforts to keep her near me: that she liked being read to. Most of the volumes in Mrs. Bowater's small library were of a nautical character, and though one of them, on the winds and tides and seas and coasts of the world, was to console me later in Fanny's absence, the majority defied even my obstinacy. Fanny hated stories of the sea, seemed to detest Crusoe; and smiled her slow, mysterious smile while she examined my own small literary treasures. By a flighty stroke of fortune, tacked up by an unskilled hand in the stained brown binding of a volume on Disorders of the Nerves, we discovered among her father's books a copy of *Wuthering Heights*, by Emily Brontë.

The very first sentence of this strange, dwelling book was a spell: '1801. – I have just returned from a visit to my landlord – the solitary neighbour that I shall be troubled with.' ... And when, a few lines farther on, I read: 'He little imagined how my heart warmed towards him when I beheld his black eyes withdraw so suspiciously under their brows' – the apparition of who but Mr. Crimble blinked at me out of the print, and the enchantment was complete. It was not only gaunt enormous Yorkshire with its fells and wastes of snow that seized on my imagination, not only that vast kitchen with its flagstones, green chairs, and firearms, but the mere music and aroma of the words, 'I beheld his black eyes'; 'a range of gaunt thorns'; 'a wilderness of crumbling griffins'; 'a huge, liver-coloured bitch pointer' – they rang in my mind, echoed on in my dreams.

And though in the wet and windy afternoons and evenings which Fanny and I thus shared, she, much more than poor Mr. Crimble, resembled Heathcliff in being 'rather morose', and in frequently expressing 'an aversion to showing displays of feeling', she was more attracted by my discovery than she condescended to confess. *Jane Eyre*, she said, was a better story, 'though Jane herself was a fool'. What cared I? To me this book was like the kindling of a light in a strange house; and that house my mind. I gazed, watched, marvelled, and recognized, as I kneeled before its pages. But though my heart was torn, and my feelings were a little deranged by the scenes of violence, and my fancy was haunted by that stalking wolfish spectre, I took no part. I surveyed all with just that sense of aloofness and absorption with which as children Cathy and Heathcliff, barefoot in the darkness of the garden, had looked in that Sunday evening on the Lintons' crimson taper-lit drawing-room.

If, in February, you put a newly gathered sprig of budding thorn into the fire; instantaneously, in the influence of the heat, it will break into bright-green tiny leaf. That is what Emily Brontë did for me. Not so for Fanny. In her 'vapid listlessness' she often pretended to yawn over *Wuthering Heights*, and would shock me with mocking criticism, or cry 'Ah!' at the poignant passages. But I believe it was pure concealment. She was really playing a part in the story. I have, at any rate, never seen her face so transfigured as when once she suddenly looked up in the firelight and caught my eye fixed on her over the book.

It was at the passage where Cathy – in her grand plaid silk frock, white trousers, and burnished shoes – returns to the dreadful Grange; and, 'dismally beclouded', Heathcliff stares out at her from his hiding-place. 'He might', I read on, 'well skulk behind the settle, at beholding such a bright, graceful damsel enter the house. "Is Heathcliff not here?" she demanded, pulling off her gloves, and displaying fingers wonderfully whitened with doing nothing and staying indoors.'

It was at this point that our eyes, as I say, Fanny's and mine, met. But she, bright, graceful damsel, was not thinking of me.

'Do you like that kind of character, Fanny?' I inquired.

My candle's flames gleamed lean and tiny in her eyes. 'Whose?' she asked.

'Why, Heathcliff's.'

She turned slowly away. 'You take things so seriously, Midgetina. It's merely a story. He only wanted taming. You'll see by-and-by.' But at that moment my ear caught the sound of footsteps, and when Mrs. Bowater opened the door to contemplate idle Fanny, the book was under my bed.

As the day drew near for Fanny's return to her 'duties', her mood brightened. She displayed before me in all their stages the new clothes which Mrs. Bowater lavished on her – to a degree that, amateur though I was in domestic economy, filled me with astonishment. I had to feign delight in these fineries – 'Ah!' whispered I to each, 'when she wears *you* she will be far, far away.' I envied the very buttons, and indeed pestered her with entreaties. I implored her to think of me at certain hours; to say good-night to herself for me; to write day by day in the first of the evening; to share the moon: 'If we both look at her at the same moment,' I argued, 'it will be next to looking at one another. You *cannot* be utterly gone: and if you see even a flower, or hear the wind ... Oh, I hope and hope you will be happy.'

She promised everything with smiling ease, and would have sealed the compact in blood if I had thought to cut my thumb for it. Thursday in Holy Week – *then* she would be home again. I stared at the blessed day across the centuries as a condemned man stares in fancy at the scaffold awaiting him; but on mine hung all my hopes. Long evenings I never saw her at all; and voices in the kitchen, when she came in late, suggested that my landlady had also missed her. But Fanny never lost her self-control even when she lost her temper; and I dared not tax her with neglecting me. Her cold looks almost suffocated me. I besought her to spend one last hour of the eve of her departure alone with me and with the stars in the woods. She promised. At eleven she came home, and went straight up into her bedroom. I heard her footsteps. She was packing. Then silence.

I waited on until sick at heart I flung myself on my knees beside my bed and prayed that God would comfort her. Heathcliff had acquired a feeble pupil. The next afternoon she was gone.

Chapter Sixteen

For many days my mind was an empty husk, yet in a constant torment of longing, day-dream, despair, and self-reproaches. Everything I looked at had but one meaning – that she was not there. I did not dare to admit into my heart a hope of the future, since it would be treason to the absent. There was an ecstatic mournfulness even in the sight of the January sun, the greening fields, the first scarcely perceptible signals of a new year. And when one morning I awoke early and heard, still half in dream, a thrush in all but darkness singing of spring, it seemed it was a voice pealing in the empty courts of paradise. What ridiculous care I took to conceal my misery from Mrs. Bowater. Hardly a morning passed but that I carried out in a bag the food I couldn't eat the day before, to hide it away or bury it. But such journeys were brief.

I have read somewhere that love is a disease. Or is it that Life piles up the fuel, a chance stranger darts a spark, and the whole world goes up in smoke? Was I happier in that fever than I am in this literary calm? Why did love for things without jealousy or envy fill me with delight, pour happiness into me, and love for Fanny parch me up, suck every other interest from my mind, and all but blind my eyes? Is that true? I cannot be sure: for to remember her ravages is as difficult as to reassemble the dismal phantoms that flock into a delirious brain. And still to be honest – there's another chance: Was she to blame? Would my mind have been at peace even in its solitary woe if she had dealt truly with me? Would anyone believe it? – it never occurred to me to remind myself that it might be a question merely of size. Simply because I loved, I deemed myself lovable. Yet in my heart of hearts that afternoon I had been twitting Mr. Crimble for saying his prayers!

But even the heart is Phœnix-like. The outer world began to break into my desolation, not least successfully when after a week or two of absence there came a postcard from Fanny to her mother with a mere 'love to M.' scrawled in its top right-hand corner. It was as if a wine-glass of cold water had been poured down my back. It was followed by yet another little 'shock'. One evening, when she had carefully set down my bowl of rusk and milk, Mrs. Bowater took up her stand opposite to me, black as an image in wood. 'You haven't been after your stars, miss, of late. It's moping you are. I suffered myself from the same greensick fantasticalities, when *I* was a girl. Not that a good result's any the better for a poor cause; but it was courting danger with your frail frame; it was indeed.'

I smile in remembrance of the picture presented by that conscience-stricken face of mine upturned to that stark monitor – a monitor no less stark at this very moment though we are both many years older.

'Yes, yes,' she continued, and even the dun, fading photograph over her head might have paled at her accents. 'I'm soliciting no divulgements; she wouldn't have gone alone, and if she did, would have heard of it from me. But you must please remember, miss, I am her mother. And you will remember, miss, also,' she added, with upper lip drawn even tighter, 'that your care is my care, and always will be while you are under my roof – and after, please God.'

She soundlessly closed the door behind her, as if in so doing she were shutting up the whole matter in her mind for ever, as indeed she was, for she never referred to it again. Thunderbolts fall quietly at times. I sat stupefied. But as I examine that distant conscience, I am aware, first, of a faint flitting of the problem through my mind as to why a freedom which Mrs. Bowater would have denied to Fanny should have held no dangers for me, and next, I realize that of all the emotions in conflict within me, humiliation stood head and shoulders above the rest. Indeed I flushed all over, at the thought that never for one moment – then or since – had I paused to consider how, on that fateful midnight, Fanny could have left the house-door *bolted* behind her. My utter stupidity: and Fanny's! All these weeks my landlady had known, and said nothing. The green gooseberries of my childhood were a far less effective tonic. But I lost no love for Mrs. Bowater in this prodigious increase of respect.

A far pleasanter interruption of my sick longings for the absent one occurred the next morning. At a loss what to be reading (for Fanny had abstracted my *Wuthering Heights* and taken it away with her), once more shudderingly pushing aside my breakfast, I turned over the dusty, faded pile of Bowater books. And in one of them I discovered a chapter on knots. Our minds are cleverer than we think them, and not only cats have an instinct for physicking themselves. I took out a piece of silk twine from my drawer and – with Fanny's phantom sulking awhile in neglect – set myself to the mastery of 'the ship boy's' science. I had learned for ever to distinguish between the granny and the reef (such is fate, this knot was also called the true lover's!), and was setting about the fisherman's bend, when there came a knock on the door – and then a head.

It was Pollie. Until I saw her round, red, country cheek, and stiff Sunday hat, thus unexpectedly appear, I had almost forgotten how much I loved and had missed her. No doubt my landlady had been the *dea ex machinâ* that had produced her on this fine sunshine morning. Anyhow she was from heaven. Besides butter, a posy of winter jasmine, a crochet bedspread, and a varnished arbour chair made especially for me during the winter evenings by her father, Mr. Muggeridge, she brought startling news. There suddenly fell a pause in our excited talk. She drew out her handkerchief and a slow crimson mounted up over neck, cheek, ears, and brow. I couldn't look quite away from this delicious sight, so my eyes wandered up in admiration of the artificial cornflowers and daisies in her hat.

Whereupon she softly blew her nose and, with a gliding glance at the shut door, she breathed out her secret. She was engaged to be married. A trying, romantic vapour seemed instantly to gather about us, in whose hush I was curiously aware not only of Pollie thus suffused, sitting with her hands loosely folded in her lap, but of myself also, perched opposite to her with eyes in which curiosity, incredulity, and even a remote consternation played upon her homely features. Time melted away, and there once more sat the old Pollie – a gawk of a girl in a pinafore, munching up green apples and replaiting her dull brown hair.

Then, of course, I was bashfully challenged to name the happy man. I guessed and guessed to Pollie's ever-increasing gusto, and at last I dared my first unuttered choice: 'Well, then, it *must* be Adam Waggett!'

'Adam Waggett! Oh, miss, him! a nose like a wine-bottle.'

It was undeniable. I apologized, and Pollie surrendered her future into my hands. 'It's Bob Halibut, miss,' she whispered hoarsely.

And instantaneously Bob Halibut's red head loomed louringly out at me. But I know little about husbands; and premonitions only impress us when they come true. Time was to prove that Pollie and her mother had made a prudent choice. Am I not now Mr. Halibut's god-sister, so to speak?

The wedding, said Pollie, was to be in the summer. 'And oh, miss' – would I come?

The scheming that followed! The sensitive draping of difficulties on either side, the old homesick longing on mine – to flee away now, at once, from this scene of my afflicted adoration. I almost hated Fanny for giving me so much pain. Mrs. Bowater was summoned to our council; my promise was given; and it was she who suggested that its being 'a nice bright afternoon', Pollie should take me for a walk.

But whither? It seemed a sheer waste of Pollie to take her to the woods. Thoughts of St. Peter's, the nocturnal splendour in the cab, a hunger for novelty, the itch to spend money, and maybe a tinge of dare-devilry – without a moment's hesitation I chose the shops and the 'town'. Once more in my black, with two thicknesses of veil canopying my head, as if I were a joint of meat in the Dog Days, I settled myself on Pollie's arm, and – in the full publicity of three o'clock in the afternoon – off we went.

We chattered; we laughed; we sniggled together like school-girls in amusement at the passers-by, in the strange, busy High Street. I devoured the entrancing wares in the shop windows – milliner, hairdresser and perfumer, confectioner; even the pyramids of jam jars and sugar cones in the grocer's, and the soaps, syrups, and sponges of Mr. Simpkins – Beechwood's pharmaceutical chemist. Out of the sovereign which I had brought with me from my treasure-chest Pollie made purchases on my behalf. For Mrs. Bowater, a muslin tie for the neck; for herself – after heated controversy – a pair of kid gloves and a bottle of frangipani; and for me a novel.

This last necessitated a visit to Mrs. Stocks's Circulating Library. My hopes had been set on *Jane Eyre*. Mrs. Stocks regretted that the demand for this novel had always exceeded her supply: 'What may be called the sensational style of fiction' (or was it friction?) 'never lays much on our hands.' She produced, instead, and very tactfully, a comparatively diminutive copy of Miss Austen's *Sense and Sensibility*. It was a little shop-soiled; 'But books keep, miss'; and she let me have it at a reduced price. Her great shears severed the string. Pollie and I once more set clanging the sonorous bell at the door, and emerged into the sunlight. 'Oh, Pollie,' I whispered, 'if only you could stay with me for ever!'

This taste of 'life' had so elated me that after fevered and silent debate I at last laughed out, and explained to Pollie that I wished to be 'put down'. Her breathless arguments against this foolhardy experiment only increased my obstinacy. She was compelled to obey. Bidding her keep some little distance behind me, I settled my veil, clasped tight my Miss Austen in my arms and set my face in the direction from which we had come. One after another the wide paving-stones stretched out in front of me. It was an extraordinary experience. I was openly alone now, not with the skulking, deceitful shades and appearances of night, or the quiet flowers and trees in the enormous vacancy of nature; but in the midst of a town of men in their height – and walking along there: by myself. It was as if I had suddenly realized what astonishingly active and domineering and multitudinous creatures we humans are. I can't explain. The High Street, to use a good old phrase, 'got up into my head'. My mind was in such a whirl of excitement that full consciousness of what followed eludes me.

The sun poured wintry bright into the house-walled gulf of a street that in my isolation seemed immeasurably vast and empty. I think my senses distorted the scene. There was the terrific glitter of glass, the clatter of traffic. A puff of wind whirled dust and grit and particles of straw into the air. The shapes of advancing pedestrians towered close above me, then, stiff with sudden attention, passed me by. My legs grew a little numb and my brain confused. The strident whistling of a butcher's boy, with an empty, blood-stained tray over his shoulder, suddenly ceased. Saucer-eyed, he stood stock still, gulped and gaped. I kept on my course. A yelp of astonishment rent the air. Whereupon, as it seemed, from divers angles, similar boys seemed to leap out of the ground and came whooping and revolving across the street in my direction. And now the blood so hummed in my head that it was rather my nerves than my ears which informed me of a steadily increasing murmur and trampling behind me.

With extraordinary vividness I recall the vision of a gigantic barouche gliding along towards me in the shine and the dust; and seated up in it a high, pompous lady who at one moment with rigid urbanity inclined her head apparently in my direction, and at the next, her face displeased as if at an offensive odour, had sunk back into her cushions, oblivious not only of Beechwood but of the whole habitable globe. Simultaneously, I was aware, even as I hastened on, first that the acquaintance whose salute she had acknowledged was Mr. Crimble, and next, that with incredible rapidity he had wheeled himself about and had instantaneously transfixed his entire attention on some object in the window of a hatter's.

Until this moment, as I say, a confused but blackening elation had filled my mind. But at sight of Mr. Crimble's rook-like stooping shoulders I began to be afraid. My shoe stumbled against a jutting paving-stone. I almost fell. Whereupon the mute concourse at my heels – spreading tail, of me, the Comet – burst into a prolonged squealing roar of delight. The next moment Pollie was at my side, stooping to my rescue. It was too late. One glance over my shoulder – and terror and hatred of the whole human race engulfed me like a sea. I struck savagely at Pollie's cotton-gloved hand. Shivering, with clenched, sticky teeth, I began to run.

Why this panic? Who could have harmed me? And yet on the thronging faces which I had flyingly caught sight of through my veil there lay an expression that was not solely curiosity – a kind of hunger, a dog-like gleam. I remember one thin-legged, ferrety, red-haired lad in particular. Well, no matter. The comedy was brief, and it was Mrs. Stocks who lowered the curtain. Attracted by all this racket and hubbub in the street, she was protruding her round head out of her precincts. Like fox to its hole, I scrambled over her wooden doorstep, whisked round her person, and fled for sanctuary into her shop. She hustled poor Pollie in after me, wheeled round on my pursuers, slammed the door in their faces, slipped its bolt, and drew down its dark blue blind.

In the sudden quiet and torpor of this musty gloom I turned my hunted eyes and stared at the dark strip of holland that hid me from my pursuers. So too did Mrs. Stocks. The round creature stood like a stone out of reach of the surf. Then she snorted.

'Them!' said she, with a flick of her duster. 'A parcel of idle herrand-boys. *I* know them: and no more decency than if you was Royalty, my dear, or a pickpocket, or a corpse run over in the street. You rest a bit, poor young thing, and compose yourself. They'll soon grow tired of themselves.'

She retired into the back part of her shop beyond the muslined door and returned with a tumbler of water. I shook my head. My sight pulsed with my heartbeats. As if congealed into a drop of poison, I stared and stared at the blind.

'Open the door,' I said. 'I'd like to go out again.'

'Oh, miss! oh, miss!' cried Pollie.

But Mrs. Stocks was of a more practical turn. After surveying my enemies from an upper window she had sent a neighbour's little girl for a cab. By the time this vehicle arrived, with a half-hearted 'Boo!' of disappointment, the concourse in the street had all but melted away, and Mrs. Stocks's check duster scattered the rest. The cab-door slammed, the wheels ground on the kerbstone, my début was over. I had been but a nine minutes' wonder.

Chapter Seventeen

We jogged on sluggishly up the hill, and at last, in our velvety quiet, as if at a preconcerted signal, Pollie and I turned and looked at one another, and broke into a long, mirthless peal of laughter – a laughter that on her side presently threatened to end in tears. I left her to recover herself, fixing my festering attention on her engagement ring – two hearts in silver encircled by six sky-blue turquoises. And in the silly, helpless fashion of one against the world, I plotted revenge.

The cab stopped. There stood the little brick house, wholly unaffected by the tragic hours which had passed since we had so gaily set out from it. I eyed it with malice and disgust as I reascended by Bateses and preceded Pollie into the passage. Once safely within, I shrugged my shoulders and explained to Mrs. Bowater the phenomenon of the cab with such success that I verily believe she was for the moment convinced that her lodger was one of those persons who prosper in the attentions of the mob – Royalty, that is, rather than pickpockets or corpses run over in the street.

With my new muslin tie adorning her neck, Mrs. Bowater took tea with us that afternoon, but even Pollie's imaginative version of our adventures made no reference to the lady in the carriage, nor did she share my intense conjecture on what Mr. Crimble can have found of such engrossing interest in the hatter's. *Was* it that the lady had feigned not to have seen me entirely for my sake; and that Mr. Crimble had feigned not to have seen me entirely for *his*? I was still poring over this problem in bed that night when there came a tap at my door. It was Pollie. She had made her way downstairs to assure herself that I was safe and comfortable. 'And oh, miss,' she whispered, as she bade me a final good-night, 'you never see such a lovely little bedroom as Mrs. Bowater have put me into – fit for a princess, and yet just quite plain! Bob's been thinking about furniture too.'

So I was left alone again with forgotten Fanny, and that night I dreamed of her. Nothing to be seen but black boiling waves flinging their yeasty, curdling crests into the clouds, and every crest the face of my ferrety 'herrand-boy'. And afloat in the midst of the welter beneath, a beloved shape whiter than the foam, with shut eyes, under the gigantic stoop of the water. Who hangs these tragic veils in the sleeping mind? Who was this I that looked out on them? I awoke, shuddering, breathed a blessing – disjointed, nameless; turned over, and soon was once more asleep.

My day's experiences in the High Street had added at least twenty-four hours to my life. So much a woman of the world was I becoming that when, after Pollie's departure, a knock announced Mr. Crimble, I greeted him with a countenance guileless and self-possessed. With spectacles fixed on me, he stood nervously twitching a small bunch of snowdrops which he assured me were the first of the New Year. I thanked him, remarked that our Lyndsey snowdrops were shorter in the stalk than these, and had he noticed the pale green hieroglyphs on the petals?

'In the white, dead nettle you have to look underneath for them: tiny black oblongs; you can't think how secret it looks!'

But Mr. Crimble had not come to botanize. After answering my inquiry after the health of Mrs. Hubbins, he suddenly sat down and announced that the object of his visit was to cast himself on my generosity. The proposal made me uncomfortable, but my timid attempt to return to Mrs. Hubbins was unavailing.

'I speak', he said, 'of yesterday's atrocity. There is no other word for it, and inasmuch as it occurred within two hundred yards of my own church, indeed of my mother's house, I cannot disclaim all responsibility for it.'

Nor could I. But I wished very heartily that he had not come to talk about *his* share. 'Oh,' said I, as airily as I could, 'you mean, Mr. Crimble, my little experience in the High Street. That was nothing. My attention was so much taken up with other things that I did not get even so much as a glimpse of St. Peter's. So you see –'

'You are kindness itself,' he interrupted, with a rapid insertion of his forefinger between his neck and his clerical collar, 'but the fact is,' and he cast a glance at me as if with the whites of his eyes, 'the fact is, I was myself a scandalized witness of the occurrence. Believe me, it cannot have hurt your sensitive feelings more than – than it hurt mine.'

'But honestly, Mr. Crimble,' I replied, glancing rather helplessly round the room, 'it didn't hurt my feelings at all. You don't feel much, you know, when you are angry. It was just as I should have foreseen. It is important to know where we are, isn't it; and where other people are? And boys will be boys, as Mrs. Bowater says, and particularly, I suppose, errand-boys. What else could I expect? It has just taught me a very useful lesson – even though I didn't much enjoy learning it. If I am ever to get used to the world (and that *is* a kind of duty, Mr. Crimble, isn't it?), the world must get used to me. Perhaps if we all knew each other's insides – our thoughts and feelings, I mean – everybody would be as peculiar there – inside, you know – as I am, outside. I'm afraid this is not making myself very clear.'

And only a few weeks ago I had been bombarding Dr. Phelps with precisely the opposite argument. That, I suppose, is what is meant by being 'deceitful on the weights'.

Mr. Crimble opened his mouth, but I continued rapidly, 'You see, I must be candid about such things to myself and try not to – to be silly. And you were merely going to be very kind, weren't you? I am a midget, and it's no good denying it. The people that hooted me were not. That's all; and if there hadn't been so many of them perhaps, I might have been just as much amused, if not even shocked at them, as they at me. We *think* our own size that's all, and I'm perfectly certain,' I nodded at him emphatically, 'I'm perfectly certain if poor Mr. Hubbins were here now, he'd – he'd bear me out.'

Bear me out – the words lingered on in my mind so distinctly, and conveyed so peculiar a picture of Mr. Hubbins's spirit and myself, that I missed the beginning of my visitor's reply.

'But I assure you,' he was saying, 'it is not merely that.' The glint of perspiration was on his forehead. 'In the Almighty's sight all men are equal. Appearances are nothing. And some of us perhaps are far more precious by very reason of – of passing afflictions, and –'

'My godmother', I interposed, 'said exactly that in a letter to me a few months ago. Not that I accept the *word,* Mr. Crimble, the 'afflictions', I mean. And as for appearances, why they are *everything,* aren't they?' I gave him as cordial an imitation of a smile as I could.

'No, no, no; yes, yes, yes,' said Mr. Crimble rapidly. 'But it was not of that, not of that in a sense that I was speaking. What I came to say this afternoon is this. I grant it; I freely confess it; I played the coward; morally rather than physically, perhaps, but still the coward. The – the hideous barbarity of the proceeding.' He had forgotten me. His eyes were fixed on the scene in his memory. He was once more at the hatter's window. There fell a painful pause.

I rose and sat down again. 'But quite, quite honestly,' I interposed faintly, 'they did me no harm. They were only inquisitive. What could you have done? Why, really and truly,' I laughed feebly, 'they might have had to *pay*, you know. It was getting – getting me cheap!'

His head was thrown back, so that he looked *under* his spectacles at me, as he cried hollowly: 'They might have stoned you.'

'Not with those pavements.'

'But I was there. I turned aside. You *saw* me?'

What persuaded me to be guilty of such a ridiculous quibble, I cannot think. Anything, perhaps, to ease his agitation: 'But honestly, honestly, Mr. Crimble,' I murmured out at him, 'I didn't *see* you see me.'

'Oh, ah! a woman's way!' he adjured me desperately, turning his head from one side to the other. 'But you must have known that I knew you knew I had seen you, you *must* confess *that*. And, well … as I say, I can only appeal to your generosity.'

'But what can I *do*? I'm not hurt. If it had been the other way round – *you* scuttling along, I mean; I really do believe *I* might have looked into the hatter's. Besides, when we were safe in the cab … I mean, I'm glad. It was experience: oh, and past. I loved it and the streets, and the shops, and all those grinning, gnashing faces, and even you … It was wildly *exciting*, Mr. Crimble, can't you *see*? And now' – I ended triumphantly – 'and now I have another novel!'

At this, suddenly overcome, I jumped up from my chair and ran off into my bedroom as if in search of the book. The curtains composed themselves behind me. In this inner quietness, this momentary release, I stood there, erect beside the bed – without a thought in my head. And I began slowly, silently – to laugh. Handkerchief to my lips, I laughed and laughed – not exactly like Pollie in the cab, but because apparently some infinitely minute being within me had risen up at remembrance of the strange human creature beyond the curtains who had suddenly before my very eyes seemed to have expanded and swollen out to double his size. Oh, what extraordinary things life was doing to me. How can I express myself? For that pip of a moment I was just an exquisite icicle of solitude – as if I had never been born. Yet there, under my very nose, was my bed, my glass, my hair-brushes and bottles – 'Here we all are, Miss M.' – and on the other side of the curtains ... And how contemptuous I had been of Pollie's little lapse into the hysterical! I brushed my hand-kerchief over my eyes, tranquillized my features, and sallied out once more into the world.

'Ah, here it is,' I exclaimed ingenuously, and lifting my *Sense and Sensibility* from where it lay on the floor beside my table, I placed it almost ceremoniously in Mr. Crimble's hands. A visible mist of disconcertion gathered over his face. He looked at the book, he opened it, his eye strayed down the title-page.

'Yes, yes,' he murmured, '*Jane Austen* – a pocket edition. Macaulay, I remember ...' He closed-to the covers again, drew finger and thumb slowly down the margin, and then leaned forward. 'But you were asking me a question. What could I have *done*? Frankly, I don't quite know. But I might have protected you, driven the rabble off, taken you – The Good Shepherd. But there, in short', and the sun of relief peered through the glooms of conscience, 'I did nothing. That was my failure. And absurd though it may seem, I could not rest until, as a matter of fact, I had unbosomed myself, confessed, knowing you would understand.' His tongue came to a standstill. 'And when,' he continued in a small, constrained voice, and with a searching, almost appealing glance, 'when Miss *Bowater* returns, you will, I hope, allow me to make amends, to prove – She would never – for – for-give ...'

The fog that had been his became mine. In an extravagance of attention to every syllable of his speech as it died away uncompleted in the little listening room I mutely surveyed him. Then I began to understand, to realize where my poor little 'generosity' was to come in.

'Ah,' I replied at last, forlornly, our eyes in close communion, 'she won't be back for months and months. And anyhow, she wouldn't, I am sure, much *mind*, Mr. Crimble.'

'Easter,' he whispered. 'Well, you will write, I suppose,' and his eye wandered off as if in search of the inkpot, 'and no doubt you will share our – your secret.' There was no vestige of interrogation in his voice, and yet it was clear that what he was suggesting I should do was only and exactly what he had come that afternoon to ask me not to do. Why, surely, I thought, examining him none too complimentarily, I am afraid, he was merely playing for a kind of stalemate. What funny, blind alleys love leads us into.

'No,' I said solemnly. 'I shall say nothing. But that, I suppose, is because I am not so brave as you are. Really and truly, I think she would only be amused. Everything amuses her.'

It seemed that we had suddenly reassumed our natural dimensions, for at that he looked at me *tinily* again, and with the suggestion, to which I was long accustomed, that he would rather not be observed while so looking.

On the whole, ours had been a gloomy talk. Nevertheless, *there,* not on my generosity, but I hope on my understanding, he reposed himself, and so reposes to this day. When the door had closed behind him, I felt far more friendly towards Mr. Crimble than I had felt before. Even apart from the Almighty, he had made us as nearly as he could – equals. I tossed a pleasant little bow to his snowdrops, and, catching sight of Mr. Bowater's fixed stare on me, hastily included *him* within its range.

Mr. Crimble, Mrs. Bowater informed me the following Sunday evening, lived with an aged mother, and in spite of his sociability and his 'fun', was a lonely young man. He hadn't, my landlady thought, yet seen enough of the world to be of much service to those who had. 'They', and I think she meant clergymen in general, as well as Mr. Crimble in particular, 'live a shut-in, complimentary life, and people treat them according. Though, of course, there's those who have seen a bit of trouble and cheese-paring themselves, and the Church is the Church when all's said and done.'

And all in a moment I caught my first real glimpse of the Church – no more just a number of St. Peterses than I was so many 'organs', or Beechwood was so many errand-boys, or, for that matter, England so many counties. It was an idea; my attention wandered.

'But he was very anxious about the concert,' I ventured to protest.

'I've no doubt,' said Mrs. Bowater shortly.

'But then,' I remarked with a sigh, 'Fanny seems to make friends wherever she goes.'

'It isn't the making,' replied her mother, 'but the keeping.'

The heavy weeks dragged slowly by, and a one-sided correspondence is like posting letters into a dream. My progress with Miss Austen was slow, because she made me think and argue with her. Apart from her, I devoured every fragment of print I could lay hands on. For when fiction palled I turned to facts, mastered the sheepshank, the running bowline, and the figure-of-eight; and wrestled on with my sea-craft. It was a hard task, and I thought it fair progress if in *that* I covered half a knot a day.

Besides which, Mrs. Bowater sometimes played with me at solitaire, draughts, or cards. In these she was a martinet, and would appropriate a fat pack at Beggar-my-neighbour with infinite gusto. How silent stood the little room, with just the click of the cards, the simmering of the kettle on the hob, and Mrs. Bowater's occasional gruff 'Four to pay'. We might have been on a desert island. I must confess this particular game soon grew a little wearisome; but I played on, thinking to please my partner, and that she had chosen it for her own sake. Until one evening, with a stifled sigh, she murmured the word, Cribbage. I was shuffling my own small pack at the moment, and paused, my eyes on their backs, in a rather wry amusement. But Fate has pretty frequently so turned the tables on me; and after that, 'One for his nob' sepulchrally broke the night silence of Beechwood far more often than 'Four to pay'.

Not all my letters to Fanny went into the post. My landlady looked a little askance at them, and many of the unposted ones were scrawled, if possible in moonlight, after she had gone to bed. To judge from my recollection of other letters written in my young days, I may be thankful that Fanny was one of those practical people who do not hoard the valueless. I can still recall the poignancy of my postscripts. On the one hand: 'I beseech you to write to me, Fanny, I live to hear. Last night was full moon again. I saw you – you only in her glass.' On the other: 'Henry has been fighting. There is a chip out of his ear. Nine centuries nearer now! And how is 'Monsieur Crapaud'?'

Wanderslore

* * *

Chapter Eighteen

At last there came a post which brought me, not a sermon from Miss Fenne, nor gossip from Pollie, but a message from the Islands of the Blest. All that evening and night it lay unopened under my pillow. I was saving it up. And never have I passed hours so studious yet so barren of result. It was the end of February. A sudden burst of light and sunshine had fallen on the world. There were green shining grass and new-fallen lambs in the meadows, and the almond tree beyond my window was in full, leafless bloom. As for the larks, they were singing of Fanny. The next morning early, about seven o'clock, her letter folded up in its small envelope in the bosom of my cloak. I was out of the house and making my way to the woods. It was the clear air of day-break and only the large stars shook faint and silvery in the brightening sky.

Frost powdered the ground and edged the grasses. But now tufts of primroses were in blow among the withered mist of leaves. I came to my 'observatory' just as the first beams of sunrise smote on its upper boughs. Yet even now I deferred the longed-for moment and hastened on between the trees, beech and brooding yew, by what seemed a faint foot-track, and at last came out on a kind of rising on the edge of the woods. From this green eminence for the first time I looked straight across its desolate garden to Wanderslore.

It was a long, dark, many-windowed house. It gloomed sullenly back at me beneath the last of night. From the alarm calls of the blackbirds it seemed that even so harmless a trespasser as I was a rare spectacle. A tangle of brier and bramble bushed frostily over its grey stone terraces. Nearer at hand in the hollow stood an angled house, also of stone – and as small compared with Wanderslore as a little child compared with its mother. It had been shattered at one corner by a falling tree, whose bole still lay among the undergrowth. The faint track I was following led on, and apparently past it. Breathless and triumphant, I presently found myself seated on a low mossy stone beside it, monarch of all I surveyed. With a profound sigh I opened my letter:

BURN THIS LETTER, AND SHOW THE OTHER TO M.

DEAR MIDGETINA. – Don't suppose, because I have not written, that Fanny is a monster, though, in fact, she is. I have often thought of you – with your stars and knick-knacks. And of course your letters have come. My thanks. I can't really answer them now because I am trying at the same time to scribble this note and to correct 'composition' papers under the very eyes of Miss Stebbings – the abhorred daughter of Argus and the eldest Gorgon. Dear me, I almost envy you, Midgetina. It *must* be fun to be like a tiny, round-headed pin in a pin-cushion and just mock at the Workbox. But all things in moderation.

When the full moon came last I remembered our *vow*. She was so dazzling, poor old wreck. And I wondered, as I blinked up at her, if you would not some day vanish away altogether – unless you make a fortune by being looked at.

I wish I could. Only would they pay enough? That is the question.

What I am writing about now is not the Moon, but – don't be amused! – a Man. Not Monsieur Crapaud, who is more absurd than ever; but someone you know, Mr. Crimble. He has sent me the most alarming letter and wants me to marry him. It is not for the first time of asking, but still a solemn occasion. Mother once said that he was like a coquette – all *at*tention and no *in*tention. Sad to say, it is the other way round. M., you see, always judges by what she fears. *I* by what his Heart tells me.

Now I daren't write back to him direct (*a*) because I wish just now to say neither Yes nor No; (*b*) because a little delay will benefit his family pride; (*c*) because it is safer not to – he's very careless and I might soon want to change my mind; (*d*) because that's how my fancy takes me; and (*e*) because I love you exceedingly and know you will help me.

When no answer comes to his letter, he will probably dare another pilgrimage to Beechwood Hill, if only to make sure that I am not in my grave. So I want you to tell him *secretly* that *I have received his letter and that I am giving it my earnest attention* – let alone my prayers. Tell me exactly how he takes this answer; then I will write to you again. I am sure, Midgetina, in some previous life you must have lived in the tiny rooms in the Palace at Mantua – you are a born *intrigante*.

In my bedroom, 11 pm. – A scheme is in my mind, but it is not yet in bloom, and you may infer from all this that I don't *care*. Often I wish this were so. I sat in front of my eight inches of grained looking-glass last night till it seemed some god(dess) *must* intervene. But no. My head was dark and empty. I could hear Mr. Oliphant cajoling with his violin in the distance – as if music had charms. Oh, dear, they give you life, and leave you to ask, Why. *You* seem to be perfectly contented in your queer little prim way with merely asking. But Fanny Bowater wants an answer, or she will make one up. Meanwhile, search for a scrap of magic mushroom, little sister, and come nearer! Some day I will tell you even more about myself. Meanwhile, believe me, petitissimost M., your affec. – F.

P.S. – *Burn this*.

P.P.S – What I mean is, that he must be *made* to realize that I will not and cannot give him an answer before I come home – unless he hears meanwhile.

Burn this: the *other* letter is for show purposes.

Fanny's 'other' was more brief:

DEAR MIDGETINA. – It is delightful to have your letters, and I am ashamed of myself for not answering them before. But I will do so the very moment there is a free hour. Would you please ask mother with my love to send me some hand-kerchiefs, some stockings, and some soap? My first are worn with weeping, my second with sitting still, and my third is mottled – and similarly affects the complexion. But Easter draws near, and I am sure I must long to be home. Did you tell mother by any chance of your midnight astronomy lesson? It has been most useful when all other baits and threats have failed to teach the young idea how to shoot. Truly a poet's way of putting it. Is Mr. Crimble still visiting his charming parishioner?

I remain,
Yours affec'ly,

FANNY BOWATER

Slowly, self-conscious word by word, lingering here and there, I read these letters through – then through again. Then I lifted my eyes and stared for a while over my left shoulder at empty Wanderslore. A medley of emotions strove for mastery, and as if to reassure herself the 'tiny, round-headed pin' kissed the signature, whispering languishingly to herself in the great garden: 'I love you exceedingly. Oh, Fanny, I love you exceedingly,' and hid her eyes in her hands. The note-paper was very faintly scented. My imagination wandered off I know not where; and returned, elated and dejected. Which the more I know not. Then I folded up the secret letter into as small a compass as I could, dragged back a loose, flat stone, hid it away in the dry crevice beneath, and replaced the stone. The other I put into my silk bag.

I emerged from these labours to see in my mind Mrs. Bowater steadfastly regarding me, and behind her the shadowy shape of Mr. Crimble, with I know not what of entreaty in his magnified dark eyes. I smiled a little ruefully to myself to think that my life was become like a pool of deep water in which I was slowly sinking down and down. As if, in sober fact, there were stones in my pocket, or leaden soles to my shoes. It was more like reading a story about myself, than *being* myself, and what was to be the end of it all? I thought of Fanny married to Mr. Crimble, as my mother was married to my father. How dark and uncomfortable a creature he looked beside Fanny's grace and fairness. And would Mrs. Crimble sit in an arm-chair and watch Fanny as Fanny had watched me? And should I be asked to tea? I was surprised into a shudder. Yet I don't think there would have been any *wild* jealousy in my heart – even if Fanny should say, Yes. I could love her better, perhaps, if she would give me a little time. And what was really keeping her back? Why did every word she said or wrote only hide what she truly meant?

So, far from mocking at the Workbox, I was only helplessly examining its tangled skeins. Nor was I criticising Fanny. To help her – that was my one burning desire, to give all I had, take nothing. In a vague, and possibly priggish, fashion, I knew, too, that I wanted to help her against herself. Her letter (and perhaps the long waiting for it) had smoothed out my old excitements. In the midst of these musings memory suddenly alighted on the question in the letter which was to be shown to Mrs. Bowater about the star-gazing. There was no need for that now. But the point was, had not Fanny extorted a promise from me *not* to tell her mother of our midnight adventure? It seemed as though without a shred of warning the fair face had drawn close in my consciousness and was looking at me low and fixedly, like a snake in a picture. Why, it was like cheating at cards! Fascinated and repelled, I sank again into reverie.

'No, no, it's cowardly, Fanny,' cried aloud a voice in the midst of this inward argument, as startling as if a stranger had addressed me. The morning was intensely still. Sunbeams out of the sky now silvered the clustered chimney shafts of Wanderslore. Where shadow lay, the frost gloomed wondrously blue on the dishevelled terraces; where sun, a thin smoke of vapour was ascending into the air. The plants and bushes around me were knobbed all over with wax-green buds. The enormous trees were faintly coloured in their twigs. A sunbeetle staggered out among the pebbles at my feet. I glanced at my hands; they were coral pink with the cold. 'I love you exceedingly – exceedingly,' I repeated, though this time I knew not to whom.

So saying, and, even as I said it, realizing that the *exceedingly* was not my own, and that I must be intelligent even if I was senti- mental, I rose from my stone, and turned to go back. I thus faced the worn, small, stone house again. Instantly I was all attention. A curious feeling came over me, familiar, yet eluding remembrance. It meant that I must be vigilant. Cautiously I edged round to the other side of the angled wall, where lay the fallen tree. Hard, dark buds showed on its yet living fringes. Rather than clamber over its sodden bole, I skirted it until I could walk beneath a lank, upthrust bough. At every few steps I shrank in and glanced around me, then fixed my eyes – as I had learned to do by my stream-side or when star-gazing – on a single object, in order to mark what was passing on the outskirts of my field of vision. Nothing, I was alone in the garden. A robin, with a light flutter of wing, perched to eye me. A string of rooks cawed across the sky. Wanderslore emptily stared. If, indeed, I was being watched, then my watcher was no less circumspect than I. Soon I was skirting the woods again, and had climbed the green knoll by which I had descended into the garden. I wheeled sharply searching the whole course of my retreat. Nothing.

When I opened my door, Mrs. Bowater and Henry seemed to be awaiting me. Was it my fancy that both of them looked censorious? Absently she stood aside to let me pass to my room, then followed me in.

'Such a lovely morning, Mrs. Bowater,' I called pleasantly down from my bedroom, as I stood taking off my cloak in front of the glass, 'and not a soul to be seen – though' (and my voice was better under command with a hairpin between my teeth) 'I wouldn't have minded if there had been. Not now.'

'Ah,' came the reply, 'but you must be cautious, miss. Boys will be boys; and', the sound tailed away, 'men, men.' I heard the door open and close, and paused, with hands still lifted to my hair, prickling cold all over at this strange behaviour. What could I have been found out in now?

Then a voice sounded seemingly out of nowhere. 'What I was going to say, miss, is – A letter's come.'

With that I drew aside the curtain. The explanation was simple.

Having let Henry out of my room, in which he was never at ease, Mrs. Bowater was still standing, like a figure in waxwork, in front of her chiffonier, her eyes fixed on the window. They then wheeled on me. '*Mr.* Bowater,' she said.

I was conscious of an inexpressible relief and of the profoundest interest. I glanced at the great portrait. 'Mr. Bowater?' I repeated.

'Yes,' she replied. 'Buenos Ayres. He's broken a leg; and so's fixed there for the time being.'

'Oh, Mrs. Bowater,' I said, 'I *am* sorry. And how terribly sudden.'

'Believe me, my young friend,' she replied musingly, 'it's never in my experience what's unprepared for that finds us least expecting it. Not that it was actually his *leg* was in my mind.'

What was chiefly in *my* selfish mind was the happy conviction that I had better not give her Fanny's letter just then.

'I do hope he's not in great pain,' was all I found to say.

She continued to muse at me in her queer, sightless fashion, almost as if she were looking for help.

'Oh, dear me, miss,' the poor thing cried brokenly, 'how should your young mind feel what an old woman feels: just grovelling in the past?'

She was gone; and, feeling very uncomfortable in my humiliation, I sat down and stared – at 'the workbox'. Why, why indeed, I thought angrily, why should I be responsible? Well, I suppose it's only when the poor fish – sturgeon or stickleback – struggles, that he really knows he's in the net.

Chapter Nineteen

One of the many perplexing problems that now hemmed me in was brushed away by Fortune that afternoon. Between gloomy bursts of reflection on Fanny's, Mr. Crimble's, Mrs. Bowater's, and my own account, I had been reading Miss Austen; and at about four o'clock was sharing Chapter XXIII with poor Elinor:

> The youthful infatuation of nineteen would naturally blind her to everything but her beauty and good nature, but the four succeeding years – years which, if rationally spent, give such improvements to the understanding – must have opened her eyes to her defects of Education, which the same period of time, spent on her side in inferior society and more frivolous pursuits.

I say I was reading this passage, and had come to the words 'and more frivolous pursuits', when an unusually imperative *rat-tat-tat* fell upon the outer door, and I emerged from my book to discover that an impressive white-horsed barouche was drawn up in the street beyond my window. The horse tossed its head and chawed its frothy bit; and the coachman sat up beside his whip in the sparkling frosty afternoon air. My heart gave a thump, and I was still seeking vaguely to connect this event with myself or with Mr. Bowater in

Buenos Ayres, when the door opened and a lady entered whose plumed and purple bonnet was as much too small for her head as she herself was too large for the room. Yet in sheer dimensions this was not a very large lady. It was her 'presence' that augmented her.

She seemed, too, to be perfectly accustomed to these special proportions, and with a rather haughty, 'Thank you', to Mrs. Bowater, winningly announced that she was Lady Pollacke, 'a friend, a mutual friend, as I understand, of dear Mr. Crimble's.'

Though a mauvish-pink in complexion, Lady Pollacke was so like her own white horse that *whinnyingly* rather than *winningly* would perhaps have been the apter word. I have read somewhere that this human resemblance to horses sometimes accompanies unusual intelligence. The poet, William Wordsworth, was like a horse; I have seen his portrait. And I should like to see Dean Swift's. Whether or not, the unexpected arrival of this visitor betrayed me into some little gaucherie, and for a moment I still sat on, as she had discovered me, literally 'floored' by my novel. Then I scrambled with what dignity I could to my feet, and chased after my manners.

'And not merely that,' continued my visitor, seating herself on a horsehair easy-chair, 'but among my still older friends is Mr. Pellew. So you see – you see,' she repeated, apparently a little dazzled by the light of my window, 'that we need no introduction, and that I know all – all the circumstances.' She lowered a plump, white-kidded hand to her lap, as if, providentially, *there* all the circumstances lay.

Unlike Mr. Crimble, Lady Pollacke had not come to make excuses, but to bring me an invitation – nothing less than to take tea with her on the following Thursday afternoon. But first she hoped – she was sure, in fact, and she satisfied herself with a candid gaze round my apartment – that I was comfortable with Mrs. Bowater; 'a thoroughly trustworthy and sagacious woman, though, perhaps, a little eccentric in address.'

I assured her that I was so comfortable that some of my happiest hours were spent gossiping with my landlady over my supper.

'Ah, yes,' she said, 'that class of person tells us such very interesting things occasionally, do they not? Yet I am convinced that the crying need in these days is for discrimination. Uplift, by all means, but we mustn't confuse. What does the old proverb say: *Festina lente*: there's still truth in that. Now, had I known your father – but there; we must not rake in old ashes. We are clean, I see; and quiet and secluded.'

Her equine glance made a rapid circuit of the photographs and ornaments that diversified the walls, and I simply couldn't help thinking what a queer little cage they adorned, for so large and handsome a bird, the kind of bird, as one might say, that is less weight than magnitude.

I was still casting my eye up and down her silk and laces when she abruptly turned upon me with a direct question: 'You seldom, I suppose, go *out*?'

Possibly if Lady Pollacke had not at this so composedly turned her full face on me – with its exceedingly handsome nose – her bonnet might have remained only vaguely familiar. Now as I looked at her, it was as if the full moon had risen. She was, without the least doubt in the world, the lady who had bowed to Mr. Crimble from her carriage that fateful afternoon. A little countenance is not, perhaps, so tell-tale as a large one. (I remember, at any rate, the horrid shock I once experienced when my father set me up on his hand one day to show me my own face, many times magnified, in his dressing-room shaving-glass.) But my eyes must have narrowed a little, for Lady Pollacke's at once seemed to set a little harder. And she was still awaiting an answer to her question.

"'Go out!'" I repeated meditatively, 'not very much, Lady Pollacke; at least not in crowded places. The boys, you know.'

'Ah, yes, the boys.' It was Mr. Crimble's little dilemma all over again: Lady Pollacke was evidently wondering whether I knew she knew I knew.

'But still', I continued cheerfully, 'it *is* the looker-on that sees most of the game, isn't it?'

Her eyelids descended, though her face was still lifted up. 'Well, so the proverb says,' she agreed, with the utmost cordiality. It was at this moment – as I have said – that she invited me to tea.

She would come for me herself, she promised. 'Now wouldn't that be very nice for us both – quite a little adventure?'

I was not perfectly certain of the niceness, but might not Mr. Crimble be a fellow-guest; and hadn't I an urgent and anxious mission with him? I smiled and murmured; and, as if her life had been a series of such little social triumphs, my visitor immediately rose; and, I must confess, in so doing seemed rather a waste of space.

'Then *that's* settled: Thursday afternoon. We must wrap up,' she called gaily through her descending veil. 'This treacherous month! It has come in like a lamb, but' – and she tugged at her gloves, still scrutinizing me fixedly beneath her eyelids, 'but it will probably go out like a lion.' As if to illustrate this prediction, she swept away to the door, leaving Mrs. Bowater's little parlour and myself to gather our scattered wits together as best we could, while her carriage rolled away.

Alas, though I love talking and watching and exploring, how could I be, even at that age a really social creature? Though Lady

Pollacke had been politeness itself, the remembrance of her bonnet in less favourable surroundings was still in my mind's eye. If anything, then, her invitation slightly depressed me. Besides, Thursday never was a favourite day of mine. It is said to have only one lucky hour – the last before dawn. But this is not tea-time. Worse still, the coming Thursday seemed to have sucked all the virtue out of the Wednesday in between. I prefer to see the future stretching out boundless and empty in front of me – like the savannas of Robinson Crusoe's island. Visitors, and I am quite sure he would have agreed with me, are hardly at times to be distinguished from visitations.

All this merely means that I was a rather green and backward young woman, and, far worse, unashamed of being so. Here was one of the greatest ladies of Beechwood lavishing attentions upon me, and all I was thinking was how splendid an appearance she would have made a few days before if she had borrowed his whip from her coachman and dispersed my little mob with it, as had Mrs. Stocks with her duster. But *noblesse oblige*; Mr. Crimble had been compelled to consider my feelings, and no doubt Lady Pollacke had been compelled to consider his.

The next day was fine, but I overslept myself and was robbed of my morning walk. For many hours I was alone.

Mrs. Bowater had departed on one of her shopping bouts. So, whoever knocked, knocked in vain; and I listened to such efforts in secret and unmannerly amusement. I wonder if ever ghosts come knocking like that on the doors of the mind; and it isn't that one won't hear, but can't. My afternoon was spent in an anxious examination of my wardrobe. Four o'clock punctually arrived, and, almost as punctually, Lady Pollacke. Soon, under Mrs. Bowater's contemplative gaze, I was mounted up on a pile of cushions, and we were bowling along in most inspiriting fashion through the fresh March air. Strangely enough, when during our progress, eyes were now bent in my direction, Lady Pollacke seemed copiously to enjoy their interest. This was especially the case when she was acquainted with their owners; and bowed her bow in return.

'Quite a little reception for you,' she beamed at me, after a particularly respectable carriage had cast its occupants' scarcely modulated glances in my direction. How strange is human character! To an intelligent onlooker, my other little reception must have been infinitely more inspiring; and yet she had almost wantonly refused to take any part in it. Now, supposing I *had* been Royalty or a corpse run over in the street ... But we were come to our journey's end.

Brunswick House was a fine, square, stone-edged edifice, dominating its own 'grounds'. Regiments of crocuses stood with mouths wide open in its rich loam. Its gate-posts were surmounted by white balls of stone; and the gravel was of so lively a colour that it must have been new laid. Wherever I looked, my eyes were impressed by the best things in the best order. This was as true of Lady Pollacke's clothes, as of her features, of her gate-posts, and her drawing-room. And the next most important thing in the last was its light.

Light simply *poured* in upon its gilt and brass and pale maroon from two high wide windows staring each other down from between their rich silk damask curtains. It was like entering an enormous bath, and it made me timid. In the midst of a large animal's skin, beneath a fine white marble chimney-piece, and under an ormolu clock, the parlour-maid was directed to place a cherry-coloured stool for me. Here I seated myself. With a fine, encouraging smile my hostess left me for a few minutes to myself. Maybe because an embroidered fire-screen that stood near reminded me of Miss Fenne, I pulled myself together. 'Don't be a ninny,' I heard myself murmur. My one hope and desire in this luxurious solitude was for the opportunity to deliver my message to Mr. Crimble. This was not only a visit, it was an adventure. I looked about the flashing room; and it rather stared back at me.

The first visitor to appear was none but Miss Bullace, whose recitation of *The Lady's 'Yes'* had so peculiarly inspirited Fanny. She sat square and dark with her broad lap in front of her, and scrutinized me as if *no* emergency ever daunted her. And Lady Pollacke recounted the complexity of ties that had brought us together. Miss Bullace, alas, knew neither Mr. Ambrose Pellew, nor my godmother, nor even my godmother's sister, Augusta Fenne. Indeed I seemed to have no claim at all on her recognition until she inquired whether it was not Augusta Fenne's cousin, Dr. Julius Fenne, who had died suddenly while on a visit to the Bermudas. Apparently it was. We all at once fell into better spirits, which were still more refreshed when Lady Pollacke remarked that Augusta had also 'gone off like that', and that the Fennes were a doomed family.

But merely to smile and smile is not to partake; so I ventured to suggest that to judge from my last letter from my godmother she, at any rate, was in her usual health; and I added, rather more cheerfully perhaps than the fact warranted, that my family seemed to be doomed too, since, so far as I was aware, I myself was the last of it left alive.

At this a sudden gush of shame welled up in me at the thought that through all my troubles I had never once remembered the kindnesses of my step-grandfather; that he too, might be dead. I was so rapt away by the thought that I caught only the last three words of Miss Bullace's murmured aside to Lady Pollacke, viz., 'not blush unseen'.

Lady Pollacke raised her eyebrows and nodded vigorously; and then to my joy Mr. Crimble and a venerable old lady with silver curls clustering out of her bonnet were shown into the room. He looked pale and absent as he bent himself down to take my hand. It was almost as if in secret collusion we had breathed the word Fanny together. Mrs. Crimble was supplied with a teacup, and her front teeth were soon unusually busy with a slice of thin bread and butter. Eating or drinking, her intense old eyes dwelt distantly but assiduously on my small shape; and she at last entered into a long story of how, as a girl, she had been taken to a circus – a circus: and there had seen ... But *what* she had seen Mr. Crimble refused to let her divulge. He jerked forward so hastily that his fragment of toasted scone rolled off his plate into the wild beast's skin, and while, with some little difficulty, he was retrieving it, he assured us that his mother's memory was little short of miraculous, and particularly in relation to the past.

'I have noticed,' he remarked, in what I thought a rather hollow voice, 'that the more advanced in years we – er – happily become, the more closely we return to childhood.'

'Senile ...' I began timidly, remembering Dr. Phelps's phrase.

But Mr. Crimble hastened on. 'Why, mother,' he appealed to her, with an indulgent laugh, 'I suppose to you I am still nothing but a small boy about that height?' He stretched out a ringless left hand about twenty-four inches above the rose-patterned carpet.

The old lady was not to be so easily smoothed over. 'You interrupted me, Harold,' she retorted, with some little show of indignation, 'in what I was telling Lady Pollacke. Even a child of that size would have been a perfect monstrosity.'

A lightning grimace swept over Miss Bullace's square features.

'Ah, ah, ah!' laughed Mr. Crimble, 'I am rebuked, I am in the corner! Another scone, Lady Pollacke?' Mrs. Crimble was a beautiful old lady; but it was with a rather unfriendly and feline eye that she continued to regard me; and I wondered earnestly if Fanny had ever noticed this characteristic.

'The fact of the matter is,' said Lady Pollacke, with conviction, 'our memories *rust* for want of exercise. Where, physically speaking, would you be, Mr. Crimble, if you hadn't the parish to tramp over? Precisely the same with the mind. Every day I make a personal effort to commit some salient fact to memory – such a fact, for a *trivial* example, as the date of the Norman Conquest. The consequence is, my husband tells me, I am a veritable encyclopædia. My father took after me. Alexander the Great, I have read somewhere, could address by name – though one may assume *not* Christian name – every soldier in his army. Thomas Babington Macaulay, a great genius, poor man, knew by heart every book he had ever read. A veritable *mine* of memory. On the other hand, I once had a parlour-maid, Sarah Jakes, who couldn't remember even the simplest of her duties, and if it hadn't been for my constant supervision would have given us port with the soup.'

'Perfectly, perfectly true,' assented Miss Bullace. 'Now mine is a verbal memory. My mind is a positive magnet for *words*. Method, of course, is everything. I weld. Let us say that a line of a poem terminates with the word *bower*, and the next line commences with *she*, I commit these to memory as one word – *Bowershee* – and so master the sequence. My old friend, Lady Bovill Porter – we were schoolfellows – recommended this method. It was Edmund Kean's, I fancy, or some other well-known actor's. How else indeed, could a great actor *realize* what he was doing? Word-perfect, you see, he is free.'

'Exactly, exactly,' sagely nodded Mr. Crimble, but with a

countenance so colourless and sad that it called back to my remembrance the picture of a martyr – of St. Sebastian, I think – that used to hang up in my mother's room.

'And you?' – I discovered Lady Pollacke was rather shrilly inquiring of me. 'Is yours a verbal memory like Miss Bullace's; or are you in my camp?'

'Ah, there,' cried Mr. Crimble, tilting back his chair in sudden enthusiasm. 'Miss M. positively puts me to shame. And poetry, Miss Bullace; even your wonderful repertory!'

'You mean Miss M. *recites*?' inquired Miss Bullace, leaning forward over her lap. 'But how entrancing! It is we, then, who are birds of a feather. And how I should adore to hear a fellow-enthusiast. Now, won't you, Lady Pollacke, join your entreaties to mine? Just a *stanza* or two!'

A chill crept through my bones. I had accepted Lady Pollacke's invitation, thinking my mere presence would be entertainment enough, and because I knew it was important to see life, and immensely important to see Mr. Crimble. In actual fact it seemed I had hopped for a moment not *out* of my cage, but merely, as Fanny had said, into another compartment of it.

'But Mr. Crimble and I were only talking,' I managed to utter.

'Oh, now, but do! Delicious!' pleaded a trio of voices.

Their faces had suddenly become a little strained and unnatural. The threat of further persuasion lifted me almost automatically to my feet. With hunted eyes fixed at last on a small marble bust with stooping head and winged brow that stood on a narrow table under the window, I recited the first thing that sprang to remembrance – an old poem my mother had taught me, *Tom o' Bedlam*:

The moon's my constant mistress,
　　And the lovely owl my marrow;
　　　　The flaming drake,
　　　　And the night-crow, make
　　Me music to my sorrow.

I know more than Apollo;
　　For oft when he lies sleeping,
　　　　I behold the stars
　　　　At mortal wars,
　　And the rounded welkin weeping.

The moon embraces her shepherd,
　　And the Queen of Love her warrior;
　　　　While the first does horn
　　　　The stars of the morn,
　　And the next the heavenly farrier ...

Throughout these first three stanzas all went well. So rapt was my audience that I seemed to be breaking the silence of the seas beyond their furthest Hebrides. But at the first line of the fourth – at 'With a heart' – my glance unfortunately wandered off from the unheeding face of the image and swam through the air, to be caught, as it were like fly by spider, by Miss Bullace's dark, fixed gaze, that lay on me from under her flat hat.

"'With a heart'", I began; and failed. Some ghost within had risen in rebellion, sealed my tongue. It seemed to my irrational heart that I had – how shall I say it? – betrayed my 'stars', betrayed Fanny, that she and they and I could never be of the same far, quiet company again. So the 'furious fancies' were never shared. The blood ran out of my cheek; I stuck fast; and shook my head.

At which quite a little tempest of applause spent itself against the walls of Lady Pollacke's drawing-room, an applause reinforced by that of a little round old gentleman, who, unnoticed, had entered the room by a farther door, and was now advancing to greet his guest. He was promptly presented to me on the beast-skin, and with the gentlest courtesy begged me to continue.

'"With a heart", now; "with a heart …"' he prompted me, 'a most important organ, though less in use nowadays than when *I* was a boy.'

But it was in vain. Even if he had asked me only to whisper the rest of the poem into his long, pink ear, for his sake alone, I could not have done so. Moreover, Mr. Crimble was still nodding his head at his mother in confirmation of his applause; and Miss Bullace was assuring me that mine was a poem entirely unknown to her, that, 'with a few little *excisions*', it should be instantly enshrined in her repertory – 'though perhaps a little bizarre!' and that if I made trial of Lady Bovill Porter's *Bowershee* method, my memory would never again play me false.

'The enunciation – am I not right, Sir Walter? – as distinct from the elocution – was flawless. And really, quite remarkable vocal power!'

Amidst these smiles and delights, and what with the brassy heat of the fire and the scent of the skin, I thought I should presently faint, and caught, as if at a straw, at the bust in the window.

'How lovely!' I cried, with pointing finger …

At that, silence fell, but only for a moment. Lady Pollacke managed to follow the unexpected allusion, and led me off for a closer inspection. In the hushed course of our progress thither I caught out of the distance two quavering words uttered as if in expostulation, 'apparent intelligence'. It was Mrs. Crimble addressing Sir Walter Pollacke.

'Classical, you know,' Lady Pollacke was sonorously informing me, as we stood together before the marble head. 'Charming pose, don't you think? Though, as we see, only a fragment – one of Sir Walter's little hobbies.'

I looked up at the serene, winged, sightless face, and a whisper sounded on and on in my mind in its mute presence, 'I know more than Apollo; I know more than Apollo.' How strange that this mere deaf-and-dumbness should seem more real, more human even, than anything or anyone else in Lady Pollacke's elegant drawing-room. But self-possession was creeping back. 'Who', I asked, '*is* he? And who sculped him?'

'Scalped him?' cried Lady Pollacke, poring down on me in dismay.

'Cut him out?'

'Ah, my dear young lady,' said a quiet voice, 'that I cannot tell you. It is the head of Hypnos, Sleep, you know, the son of Night and brother of Death. One wing, as you see, has been broken away in preparation for this more active age, and yet ... only a replica, of course'; the voice trembled into richness, 'but an exceedingly pleasant example. It gives me rare pleasure, rare pleasure,' he stood softly rocking, hands under coat-tails, eyes drinking me in, 'to – to have your companionship.'

What pleasure his words gave *me,* I could not – can never – express. Then and there I was his slave for ever.

'Walter,' murmured Lady Pollacke, as if fondly, smiling down on the rotund old gentleman, 'you are a positive peacock over your little toys; is he not, Mr. Crimble? Did you ever hear of a *woman* wasting her affections on the inanimate. Even a doll, I am told, is an infant in disguise.'

But Mr. Crimble had approached us not to discuss infants or woman, but to tell Lady Pollacke that her carriage was awaiting me.

'Then pity 'tis, 'tis true,' cried she, as if in Miss Bullace's words. 'But *please,* Miss M., it must be the briefest of adieus. There are so many of my friends who would enjoy your company – and those delightful recitations. Walter, will you see that everything's quite – er – convenient?'

I am sure Lady Pollacke's was a flawless *savoir faire*, yet, when I held out my hand in farewell, her cheek crimsoned, it seemed, from some other cause than stooping. The crucial moment had arrived. If one private word was to be mine with Mr. Crimble, it must be now or never. To my relief both gentlemen accompanied me out of the room, addressing their steps to mine. Urgency gave me initiative. I came to a standstill in the tessellated marble of the hall, and this time proffered my hand to Sir Walter. He stooped himself double over it; and I tried in vain to dismiss from remembrance a favourite reference of Pollie's to the guinea-pig held up by its tail.

I wonder now what Sir W. would have said of *me* in *his* auto-biography! 'And *there* stood a flaxen spelican in the midst of the hearthrug; blushing, poor tiny thing, over her little piece like some little bread-and-butter miss fresh from school.' Something to that effect? I wonder still more who taught him so lovable a skill in handling that spelican?

'There; good-bye,' said he, 'and the blessing, my dear young lady, of a fellow fanatic.'

He turned about and ascended the staircase. Except for the parlour-maid who was awaiting me in the porch, Mr. Crimble and I were alone.

Chapter Twenty

'Mr. Crimble,' I whispered, 'I have a message.'

A tense excitement seized him. His face turned a dusky yellow. How curious it is to see others as they must sometimes see ourselves. Should *I* have gasped like that, if Mr. Crimble had been Fanny's Mercury?

'A letter from Miss Bowater,' I whispered, 'and I am to say,' the cadaverous face was close above me, its sombre melting eyes almost bulging behind their glasses, 'I am to say that she is giving yours "*her earnest attention, let alone her prayers*".'

I remember once, when Adam Waggett as a noisy little boy was playing in the garden at home, the string of his toy bow suddenly snapped! Mr. Crimble drew back as straight and as swiftly as that. His eyes rained unanswerable questions. But the parlourmaid had turned to meet me, and the next moment she and I were side by side in Lady Pollacke's springy carriage *en route* for my lodgings. I had given my message, but never for an instant had I anticipated it would have so overwhelming an effect.

There must have been something inebriating in Lady Pollacke's tea. My mind was still simmering with excitement. And yet, during the whole of that journey, I spent not a moment on Mr. Crimble's or Fanny's affairs, or even on Brunswick House, but on the dreadful problem whether or not I ought to 'tip' the parlour-maid, and if so, with how much. Where had I picked this enigma up? Possibly from some chance reference of my father's. It made me absent and harassed. I saw not a face or a flower; and even when the parlourmaid was actually waiting at my request in Mrs. Bowater's passage, I stood over my money-chest, still incapable of coming to a decision.

Instinct prevailed. Just as I could not bring myself to complete *Tom o' Bedlam* with Miss Bullace looking out of her eyes at me, so I could not bring myself to offer money to Lady Pollacke's nice prim parlour-maid. Instead I hastily scrabbled up in tissue paper a large flat brooch – a bloodstone set in pinchbeck – a thing of no intrinsic value, alas, but precious to me because it had been the gift of an old servant of my mother's. I hastened out and lifting it over my head, pushed it into her hand.

Dear me, how ashamed of this impulsive action I felt when I had regained my solitude. Should I not now be the jest of the Pollacke kitchen and drawing-room alike? – for even in my anxiety to attain Mr. Crimble's private ear, I had half-consciously noticed what a cascade of talk had gushed forth when Mr. Crimble had closed the door of the latter behind him.

That evening I shared with Mrs. Bowater my experiences at Brunswick House. So absorbed was I in my own affairs that I deliberately evaded any reference to hers. Yet her pallid face, seemingly an inch longer and many shades more austere these last two days, touched my heart.

'You won't think', I pleaded at last, 'that I don't infinitely prefer being here, with you? Isn't it, Mrs. Bowater, that you and I haven't quite so many things to *pretend* about? It is easy thinking of others when there are only one or two of them. But whole drawing-roomsful! While here; well, there is only just you and me.'

'Why, miss,' she replied, 'as for pretending, the world's full of shadows, though substantial enough when it comes to close quarters. If we were all to look at things just bare in a manner of speaking, it would have to be the Garden of Eden over again. It can't be done. And it's just that that what's called the gentry know so well. We must make the best use of the mess we can.'

I was tired. The thin, sweet air of spring, wafted in at my window after the precocious heat of the day, breathed a faint, reviving fragrance. A curious excitement was in me. Yet her words, or perhaps the tone of her voice, coloured my fancy with vague forebodings. I pushed aside my supper, slipped off my fine visiting clothes, and put on my dressing-gown. With lights extinguished, I drew the blind, and strove for a while to puzzle out life's riddle for myself. Not for the first or the last time did wandering wits cheat me of the goal, for presently in the quiet out of my thoughts, stole into my imagination the vision of that dreaming head my eyes had sheltered on.

'Hypnos,' I sighed the word; and – another face, Fanny's, seemed to melt into and mingle with the visionary features. Why, why, was my desperate thought, why needed *she* allow the world to come to such close quarters? Why, with so many plausible reasons given in her letter for keeping poor Mr. Crimble waiting, had she withheld the one that counted for most? And what was it? I knew in my heart that *that* could not be 'making the best use of the mess'. Surely, if one just told only the truth, there wasn't anything else to tell. It had taken me some time to learn this lesson.

A low, rumbling voice shook up from the kitchen. Mrs. Bowater was talking to herself. Dejection drew over me again at the thought of the deceit I was in, and I looked at my love for Fanny as I suppose Abraham at the altar of stones looked at his son Isaac. Then suddenly a thought far more matter of fact chilled through my mind. I saw again Mr. Crimble huddling down towards me in that echoing hall, heard my voice delivering Fanny's message, and realized that half of what I had said had been written in mockery. It had been intended for my eye only – '*Let alone my prayers.*' In the solitude of the darkness the words had a sound far more sinister than even Fanny can have intended.

Mr. Crimble, however, had accepted them apparently in good faith – to judge at least from the letter which reached me the following morning:

> DEAR MISS M. – Thank you. I write with a mind so overburdened that words fail me. But I realize that Miss Bowater has no truer friend than yourself, and shall be frank. After that *terrible* morning you might well have refused to help me. I cannot believe that you will – for her sake. This long concealment, believe me, is not of my own seeking. It cannot, it must not, continue, a moment beyond the necessity. For weeks, nay, months, I have been tortured with doubts and misgivings. Her pride, her impenetrable heedlessness; oh, indeed, I realize the difficulties of her situation. I dare not speak till she gives consent. Yet silence puts me in a false position, and tongues, as perhaps even you may be aware, begin to wag. Nor is this my first attempt, and – to be more frank than I feel is discreet – there is my mother (quite apart from *hers*) now, alas, aged and more dependent on my affection and care than ever. To make a change now – the talk, the absence of Christian *charity*, my own temperament and calling! I pray for counsel to guide my stumbling bark on this sea of *darkest* tempest.
>
> Can F. decide that her affections are such as could justify her in committing her future to me? Am I justified

in asking her? You, too, must have many anxieties – anxieties perhaps unguessed at by those of coarser fibre. And though I cannot venture to ask your confidences, I do ask for your feminine intuition – even though this may seem an *intrusion* after my sad discomfiture the other day. And yet, I assure you, it was not corporeal fear – are not we priests the police of the City Beautiful? Might I not have succeeded merely in making us *both* ridiculous? But that is past, and the dead past must bury its dead: there is no gentler sexton.

Need I say that this letter is not the fruit of any mere *impulse*. The thought, the very image of her never leaves my consciousness night or day; and I get no rest. I am almost afraid at the power she has of imprinting herself on the mind. I implore you to be discreet, without needless deception. I will wait patiently. My last desire is to *hasten* an answer – unless, dear Miss M., one in the affirmative. And would it be possible – indeed the chief purpose of this letter was to make this small request – would it be possible to give me one hour – no tea – this afternoon? There was a phrase in your whispered message – probably because of the peculiar acoustic properties of Brunswick House – that was but half-caught. We must not risk the faintest shadow of misunderstanding.

Believe me, yours most gratefully, though 'perplexed in the extreme',

HAROLD CRIMBLE

P.S. – I feel at times that it is incumbent on one to burn one's boats; even though out of sight the further shore.

And the letter! would it be even possible to share a glance at *that*?

My old habit of hunting in the crannies of what I read had ample opportunity here. Two things stood out in my mind! a kind of astonishment at Mr. Crimble's 'stumbling bark' which he was

WALTER DE LA MARE

asking *me* to help steer, and inexpressible relief that Fanny's letter was buried beyond hope of recovery before he could call that afternoon. The more I pitied and understood his state of mind, the more helpless and anxious I felt. Then, in my foolish fashion, I began again picturing in fancy the ceremony that would bring Mr. Crimble and my landlady into so close a relationship. Why did he fear the wagging of tongues so much? I didn't. Would Miss Bullace be a bridesmaid? Would I? I searched in my drawer and read over the 'Form of Solemnization of Matrimony'. I came to 'the dreadful day of judgment', and to 'serve' and 'obey', and shivered. I was not sure that I cared for the way human beings had managed these things. But at least, bridesmaids *said* nothing, and if I –

While I was thus engaged Mrs. Bowater entered the room. I smuggled my prayer-book aside and gave her Fanny's letter. She was always a woman of few words. She folded it reflectively; took off her spectacles, replaced them in their leather case, and that in her pocket.

'Soap, handkerchiefs, stockings' she mused, 'though why in the world she didn't *say* "silk" is merely Fanny's way. And I am sure, miss,' she added, 'she must have had one peculiar moment when the thought occurred to her of the bolt.'

'But, Mrs. Bowater,' I cried in snake-like accents, 'you *said* you were "soliciting no divulgements".'

Mrs. Bowater's mouth opened in silent laughter. 'Between you' – she began, and broke off. 'Gracious goodness, but here's that young man, Mr. Crimble, calling again.'

Mr. Crimble drank tea with me, though he ate nothing. And now, his darkest tempest being long since stilled, I completely absolve myself for amending the message which Lady Pollacke's tessellated hall had mercifully left obscure. He sat there, almost like a goldfish – though black in effect beyond description – gaping for the crumb that never comes. 'She bade me,' I muttered my false-hood, 'she bade me say secretly that she has had your letter, that she is giving it her earnest attention, her earnest attention, *alone, and in her prayers.*'

The dark liquid pupils appeared for one sheer instant to rotate, then he turned away, and, as if quite helplessly, stifled an unsheltered yawn.

'Alone', he cried desperately. 'I see myself, I see myself in her young imagination!'

I think he guessed that my words were false, that his ear had not been as treacherous as all that. Whether or not, no human utterance have I ever heard so humble, tragic, final. It knelled in my ear like the surrender of all hope. And yet it brought me, personally, some enlightenment. It was with Mr. Crimble's eyes that I now scanned not only his phantom presence in Fanny's imagination, but my own, standing beside him – a 'knick-knack' figure of fun, pygmied beneath the flappets of his clerical coat, like a sunbeetle by a rook. The spectacle strengthened me without much affecting Fanny. She was no longer the absolute sultana of my being. I could *think* now, as well as adore.

How strange it is that when our minds are needled to a sharp focus mere 'things' swarm so close. There was not a single ornament or book or fading photograph in Mrs. Bowater's parlour that in this queer privacy did not mutely seem to cry, 'Yes, here am I. This is how things go.'

I leant forward and looked at him. 'We mustn't care what she sees, what she thinks, if only we can go on loving her.'

'Can, can!' echoed Mr. Crimble, 'I have prayed on my knees *not* to.'

This was a sharp ray on my thoughts of love. 'But, why?' I said. 'Even when I was a child, I knew by my mother's face that I must go on, and should go on, loving her, Mr. Crimble, whether she loved me or not. One can't make a bad mistake in giving, can one? And yet – well, you must remember that I cannot but have been a – a disappointment; that as long as I live I can't expect any great affection, any disproportionate one, I mean.'

'But, but,' he stumbled on, 'a daughter's affection – it's different. I mustn't brood on my trouble. It unhinges me. Why, the clock stops. But nevertheless may God bless you for that.'

'But surely,' I persisted, smiling as cheerfully as I could, '*Nil desperandum*, Mr. Crimble. And you know what they say about fish in the sea.'

His eye rolled round on me as if a serpent had spoken. 'I am sorry, I am sorry,' he repeated rapidly, in the same low, unemphatic undertone as if to himself. 'I must just wait. You have never seen a sheep – a bullock, shall we call him? – being driven to the slaughter-house. On, on – from despair to despair. That's my position.' His face was emptied of expression, his eye fixed.

These words, his air, his look, this awful private thing – I can't say – it shocked and frightened me beyond words. But I answered him steadily none the less. 'Listen, Mr. Crimble,' I said, 'look at *me*, here, what I am. I have had my desperate moments too – more alone in the world than you can ever be! And I swear before God that I will never, never be *not* myself.' I wonder what the listener thought of this little challenge, not perhaps what Mr. Crimble did.

• 'Well,' he replied, with sudden calm, 'that's the courage of the martyrs, and not all of them perhaps have been Christians, if history is to be credited. Yes, and in sober truth, I assure you, *you*, that I would go to the stake for – for Miss Bowater.'

He rose, and in that instant of dignity I foresaw what was never to be – lawn sleeves encasing those loose, black arms. He had somehow wafted me back to my Confirmation.

'And the letter? I have no wish to intrude. But her actual words. I mayn't see *that*?'

'You will please forgive me,' I entreated helplessly, 'it is buried; because, you see, Fanny – you see, Mrs. Bowater –'

'Ah,' he said. 'It is this deception which dismays, scandalizes me most. But you will keep me informed?'

He seized his soft round hat, and it was on this cold word we parted. I stood by the window, with hand stretched out to summon him back. But no word of comfort or hope came to my aid, and I watched him out of sight.

Chapter Twenty-One

That night I wrote to Fanny, copying out my letter from the scrawling draft from which I am copying it now:

DEAR FANNY. – I have given Mr. Crimble your message; first, exactly in your own words, though he did not quite hear them and then, leaving out a little. You may be angry at what I am going to say – but I am quite sure you ought to answer him *at once*. Fanny, he's *dreadfully* fond of you. I never even dreamed people were like that – in such torture for what can't be, unless you mean you *do* care, but are too proud to tell him so. If he knows you have no heart for him, he may soon be better. This sounds hateful. But I am not such a pin in a pincushion as not to know that even the greatest sorrows and disappointments wear out. Why, isn't that beech-tree we sat under a kind of cannibal of its own dead leaves?

Your private letter is quite safe; though I prefer not to burn it – indeed, *cannot* burn it. You know how I have longed for it. But please, if possible, don't send me two in future. It doesn't seem fair; and your mother knew already about our star-gazing. You see, how else could the door have been bolted!! But it's best to have been found out – next, I mean, to telling oneself.

What day are you coming home? I look at it, as if it were a lighthouse – even though it is out of sight. Shall we go on with *Wuthering Heights* when you do come? I saw the 'dazzling' moon – but there, Fanny, what I want most to beg of you is to write to Mr. Crimble – all that you feel, even if not all that you think. No, perhaps I mean the reverse. He must have been wondering about you long before I began to. And there it was, all sunken in; no one could have guessed his longing by looking at him. I am afraid it must affect his health.

And now good-bye. I have made a vow to myself not to think into things too much. Your affectionate friend (as much of her as there is) –

MIDGETINA.

P.S. – Please tell me the *day* you are coming; and that shall be my birthday.

Fanny was prompt in reply:

DEAR MIDGETINA. – It's a strange fact, but while, to judge from your letter, *you* seem to be growing smaller, I (in spite of Miss Stebbings's water porridge) am growing fatter. Now, which is the tragedy? I *may* come home on the 30th. If so, kill the fatted calf; I will supply the birthday-cake. How foolish of you to keep letters. I never do, lest I should remember the answers. Anyhow, I shall not write again. But if, by any chance, Mr. Crimble should make another call, will you explain that my chief motive in not singing at the concert was because I should have been a second mezzo-soprano. One of two in one concert *must* be superfluous. Perhaps I did not explain this clearly; nor did I say how charming I thought my double was.

I am tired – of overwork. I have finished *Wuthering Heights*. It is a mad, untrue book. The world is not like Emily Brontë's conception of it. It is neither dream nor nightmare, Midgetina, but wide, wide awake. And I am convinced that the poets are only cherubs with sugar-sticks to their little rosebud mouths. I abominate whitewash. As for 'putting people out of their misery' and cannibal beech-trees! no, fretful midge! If you could see me sitting here looking down on rows and rows of vacant and hostile faces – though one or two are infatuated enough – you would realize that such a practice would lead me into miscellane-ous infanticide.

Personally, I never did think into things too painfully; though as regards 'telling', the reverse is *certainly* the wiser course. So you will forgive so short, and perhaps none too sweet, a letter from your affecte. – F.

Enclosed with this was a narrow slip of paper!

I shall *not* write to you know who. Think, if you like, but don't *feel* like a microscope. He is only in love. And how-ever punctilious your own practice may be, pray, Miss M., do not preach – at any rate to your affecte. but unregener-ate friend. – F.

I believe I drafted and destroyed three answers to this letter. It broke down my defences far more easily than had the errand-boys. It shamed me for a prig, a false friend, a sentimentalist. And the 'fretful midge' rankled like salt in a wounded heart. Yet Fanny was faithless even to her postscript. A sheaf of narcissuses hooded in blue tissue paper was left at the house a day or two afterwards. It was accompanied by Mr. Crimble's card in a little envelope tied in with the stalks!

I am given a ray of hope.

Mrs. Bowater had laid this offering on my table with a peculiar grimace, whether scornful or humorous, it was impossible to detect. 'From Mr. Crimble, miss. Why, one might think he had two irons in the fire!'

I sat gazing at this thank-offering long after she had gone – the waxy wings, the crimson-rimmed corona, the pale-green cluster of pistil and stamen. The heavy perfume stole over my senses, bringing only weariness and self-distaste to my mind. Fly that I was, caught in a web – once more I began a letter to Fanny, imploring her to write to her mother, to tell her everything. But that letter, too, was torn up into tiny pieces and burnt in the fire.

Next morning, heavily laden with my parasol, a biscuit or two in my bag, my *Sense and Sensibility* and a rug in my arms, I set off very early for Wanderslore, having arranged with Mrs. Bowater over night that she should meet me under my beech at a quarter to one.

Under the flat, bud-pointed branches, I pressed on between clusters of primrose, celandine, and wild wood-anemone, breathing in the earthy freshness of grass and moss. And presently I came out between the stones and jutting roots in sight of the vacant windows. I stood for a moment confronting their black regard, then descended the knoll and was soon making myself comfortable beside the garden house. But first I managed to clamber up on a fragment of the fallen masonry and peep in at its low windows. A few dead, last year's flies laid dry on their backs; dusty, derelict spider-webs; a litter of straw, and a few potsherds – the place was empty. But it was mine, and the very remembrance of which it whispered to me – the picture of my poor father's bedroom that night of the storm – only increased my sense of possession.

What was wrong with me just then, what I had sallied out in hope to be delivered from, was the unhappy conviction that my life was worthless, and I of no use in the world. I had taught myself to make knots in string, but actual experience seemed to have proved that most human fumblings resulted only in 'grannies' and not in the true lover's variety. They secured nothing, only tangled and jammed. I was young then, and yet as heavily burdened with other people's responsibilities as was poor Christian with the bundle of his sins. But my bundle, too, in that lovely, desolate loneliness at last fell off my shoulders.

Could I not still be loyal in heart and mind to Fanny, even though now I knew how little she cared whether I was loyal or not? I even climbed up behind Mr. Crimble's thick spectacles and looked down again at myself from that point of vantage. Whether or not I was his affair, I could try to make him mine – perhaps even persuade Fanny to love him.

Oh, dear; was not every singing bird in that wilderness, every unfolding flower and sunlit March leaf welcoming the spirit within me to their quiet habitation? As if in response to this naïve thought, welled up in my memory the two last stanzas of my *Tom o' Bedlam*, which, either for pride or shame, had stuck in my throat on the skin mat in Lady Pollacke's sky-lit drawing-room!

> With a heart of furious fancies,
> Whereof I am commander!
> With a burning spear,
> And a horse of air,
> To the wilderness I wander.

> With a knight of ghosts and shadows,
> I summoned am to tourney:
> Ten leagues beyond
> The wide world's end;
> Methinks it is no journey.

Parasol for spear, the youngest Miss Shanks's pony for horse of air, there was I (even though common-sized boots might reckon it a mere mile or so), ten leagues at least beyond – Mrs. Bowater's. Nor, like her husband, had I broken my leg; nor had Fanny broken my heart. All would come right again. Why, what a waste of Fanny it would be to make her Mrs. Crimble. My bishop, according to Miss Fenne, had had quite a homely helpmeet, 'little short of a frump, Caroline, as I remember her thirty years ago'. Perhaps if I left off my fine colours and bought a nice brown stuff dress and a bonnet, might not Mr. Crimble change his mind ...? I have noticed that as soon as I begin to laugh at myself, the whole world seems to smile in return.

Absurd, contrary, volatile creature that I was – a kind of thankfulness spread over my mind. I turned on to my knees where I sat and repeated the prayers which in my haste to be off I had neglected before coming out. And thus kneeling, I opened my eyes on the garden again, bathed delicately in the eastern sunshine. There was my old friend, Mr. Clodd's *Nature*, pranking herself under the nimble fingers of spring; and in her sight as well as in the sight of my godmother's God and Mr. Crimble's Almighty, and, possibly, of Dr. Phelps's Norm, were not, in deed and in truth, all men equal? How mysterious and how entrancing. If 'sight', then *eyes*: but whose? where? I gazed round me dazzledly, and if wings had been mine, would have darted through the thin, blue-green veil and been out into the morning.

Poor she-knight! romantical Miss Midge! she had no desire to hunt Big Game, or turn steeplejack; her fancies were not dangerously 'furious'; but, as she knelt there, environed about by that untended garden, and not so ridiculously pygmy either, even in the ladder of the world's proportion – saw-edged blade of grass, gold-cupped moss, starry stonecrop, green musky moschatel, close-packed pebble, wax-winged fly – well, I know not how to complete the sentence except by remarking that I am exceedingly glad I began to write my Life.

I realized too that it is less flattering to compare oneself with the very little things of the world than with the great. Given time, I might scale an Alp; I could only *kill* an ant. Besides, I am beginning to think that one of the pleasantest ways of living is in one's memory. How much less afflicting at times would my present have been if I had had the foresight to remind myself how beguiling it would appear as the past. Even my old sharpest sorrows have now hushed themselves to sleep, and those for whom I have sorrowed are as quiet.

Having come to a pause in my reflections, I opened my *Sense and Sensibility* at Chapter XXXV. Yet attend to Miss Austen I could not. She is one of those compact and cautious writers that will not feed a wandering mind; and at last, after three times re-reading the same paragraph, an uneasy conviction began to steal over me. There was no doubt now in my mind. I was being watched. Softly, stealthily, I raised my eyes from my book and with not the least motion of head or body, glanced around me. Whereupon, as if it had been playing sentinel out of the thicket near at hand, a blackbird suddenly jangled its challenge, and with warning cries fled away on its wings towards the house.

Chapter Twenty-Two

The instantly I discovered the cause of the bird's alarm. At first I fancied that this strange figure was at some little distance. Then I realized that his stature had misled me, and that he could not be more than twenty or thirty yards away. Standing there, with fixed, white face and black hair, under a flowering blackthorn, he remained as motionless and as intent as I. He was not more than a few inches, apparently, superior in height to myself.

'So,' I seemed to whisper, as gaze met gaze, 'there!' hardly certain the while if he was real or an illusion. Indeed, if, even then before my eyes, he had faded out into the tangle of thorn, twig, and thin-spun blossom above and around him, it would not have greatly astonished, though it would have deeply disappointed me. With a peculiar, trembling curiosity, I held him with my gaze. If he would not disclose himself, then must I.

Slowly and deliberately my cold hand crept out and grasped my parasol. Without for a moment removing my eyes from this interloper's face, I pushed its ribbed silk tent taut into the air. Click! went the tiny spring; and at that he stirred.

'Who are you: watching me?' I cried in a low, steady voice across the space that divided us. His head had stooped a little.

I fancied – and feared – that he was about to withdraw. But after a pause he drew himself up and came nearer, casting, as he approached, his crooked shadow away from the sun on the close-cropped turf beside him.

To this day I sometimes strive in vain to see, quite clearly in my mind, that face, as it appeared, at that first meeting. A different memory of it obtrudes itself; yet how many, many times have I searched his features for news of himself, and looked passingly – and once with final intensity – into those living eyes. But I recollect that his clothes looked slightly out of keeping and grotesque amid the green things of early spring. It seemed he had wasted in them. So, too, the cheek had wasted over its bone, and seemed parched; the thin lips, the ears slightly pointed. And then broke out his low, hollow voice. Scarcely rising or falling, the mere sound of it seemed to be as full of meaning as the words.

He looked at me, and at all I possessed, as if piece by piece – as if he had been a long time searching for them all. Yet he now seemed to avoid my eyes, though they were serenely awaiting his. Indeed from this moment almost to the last, I was never at a loss or distressed in his company. He never called me out of myself beyond an easy and happy return, though he was to creep into my imagination as easily as a single bee creeps into the thousand-celled darkness of its hive.

Whenever I parted from him, his remembrance was like that of one of those strange figures which thrust themselves as if out of the sleep-world into the mind's wakefulness; vividly, darkly, impress themselves upon consciousness, and then are gone. So I sometimes wonder if I ever really knew him, if he was ever perfectly real to me; like Fanny, for instance. Yet he made no pretence to be mysterious, and we were soon talking together almost as naturally as if we were playmates of childhood who had met again after a long separation.

He confessed that, quite unknown to me, he had watched me come and go in the cold mornings of winter, when frost had soon driven me home again out of the bare, frozen woods. He had even been present, I think, when Fanny and I had shared – or divided – the stars between us. A faint distaste at any rate showed itself on his face when he admitted that he had seen me not alone. I was unaccustomed to that kind of interest, and hardly knew whether to be pleased or angry.

'But you know I come here to be alone,' I said as courteously as possible.

'Yes,' he answered, with face turned away. 'That's how I saw you.'

Without my being aware of it, too, he played a kind of chess with me, seizing each answer in turn for hook on which to hang another question. What had I to conceal? Of my short history, though not of myself, I told him freely; yet asked him few questions in return. Nor at that time did I even consider how strange a chance had brought two such human beings as he and I to this place of meeting. Yet, after all, whales are but little creatures by comparison with the ocean in which they roam, and glow-worm will keep tryst with glow-worm in forests black as night.

Through all he said was woven a thread of secrecy. So low and monotonous was his voice (not lifting itself much, but only increasing in resonance when any thought angered or darkened his mind); so few were his gestures that he might have been talking in his sleep. Not once that long morning did he laugh, not even when I mischievously proffered him my parasol (as he sat a few paces away) to screen him from the March sun! Solemnly he shared Mrs. Bowater's biscuits with me, scattering the crumbs to a robin that hopped up between us, as if he had been invited to our breakfast.

His head hung so low between his heavy shoulders that it reminded me of a flower stooping for want of water. Not that there was anything limp or fragile or gentle in his looks. He was, far rather, clumsy and ugly in appearance, yet with a grace in his look like that of an old, haggled thorn-tree when the wind moves its branches. And anyhow, he was come to be my friend – out of the unknown. And when I looked around at the serene wild loveliness of the garden, it seemed to be no less happy a place because it was no longer quite a solitude.

'You read,' he said, glancing reflectively, but none too complimentarily, at my book.

'It isn't wise to think too much,' I replied solemnly, shutting Miss Austen up. 'Besides, as I haven't the opportunity of seeing many people in the flesh, you know, the next best thing is to meet them in books – specially in this kind of book. If only I were Jane Austen; my gracious, I would enjoy myself! Her people are just the same as people are now – inside. I doubt if leopards really want to change their spots. But of course' – I added, since he did not seem inclined to express any opinion – 'I read other kinds of books as well. That's the best of being a dunce – there's so much to learn! Just lately I have been learning to tie knots.'

I laughed and discovered that I was blushing.

He raised his eyes slowly to my face, then looked so long and earnestly at my hands, that I was forced to hide them away under my bag. Long before I had noticed that his own hands were rather large and powerful for his size. Fanny's face I had loved to watch for its fairness and beauty – it would have been as lovely if she had not been within. To watch Mrs. Bowater's was like spelling out bits of a peculiar language. I often found out what she was feeling or thinking by imitating her expression, and then translating it, after she was gone. This young man's kept me engrossed because of the self that brooded in it – its dark melancholy, too; and because even then, perhaps, I may have remotely and vaguely realized that flesh and spirit could not be long of one company. He himself was, as it were, a foreigner to me, and I felt I must make the best and most of him before he went off again.

Perhaps memory reads into this experience more than in those green salad days I actually found there. But of this at least I am certain – that the morning sped on unheeded in his company, and I was even unconscious of how cold I was until he suddenly glanced anxiously into my face and told me so. So now we wandered off together towards the great house – which hitherto I had left unapproached. We climbed the green-stained scaling steps from terrace to terrace, tufted with wallflower and snapdragon amongst the weeds, cushioned with bright moss, fretted with lichen. Standing there, side by side with him, looking up – our two figures alone, on the wide flowerless weed-grown terrace – hale, sour weeds some of them, shoulder-high – I scrutinized the dark, shut windows.

What was the secret that had kept it so long vacant, I inquired. Mrs. Bowater had never given me any coherent answer to this question. My words dropped into the silence, like a pebble into a vast, black pool of water.

'There was a tale about,' he replied indifferently, and yet, as I fancied, not so indifferently as he intended, 'that many years ago a woman' – he pronounced the word almost as if it had reference to a different species from ourselves – 'that a woman had hanged herself in one of its upper rooms.'

'Hanged herself!' It was the kind of fable Mrs. Ballard used to share with Adam Waggett's mother over their tea and shrimps. Frowning in horror and curiosity, I scanned his face. Was this the water I could dip for in his well? Alas, how familiar I was to become with the bucket.

He made a movement with his hands; at which I saw the poor creature up there in the darkness, suspended lifeless, poor, poor human, with head awry.

'Why?' I asked him, pondering childishly over this picture.

'It was mere gossip,' he replied, 'and true or not, such as "they" make up to explain their own silly superstitions. Just thinking long enough and hard enough would soon invite an evil spirit into any old empty house. Human beings are no better than sheep, though they don't always see the dogs and shepherds that drive them.'

'And does it,' I faltered, glancing covertly up the walls, and conscious of a novel vein of interest in this strangely inexhaustible world, 'does the evil spirit ever look out of the windows?'

He turned his face to me, smiling; and inquired if I had ever heard the phrase, 'the eyelids of the dawn'. 'There's Night, too,' he said.

'But whose spirit? Whose?' I persisted. 'When I am here alone in the garden, why, it is just peace. How could that be, if an evil spirit haunted here?'

'Yes,' he said, 'but a selfish, solitary peace. Dead birds don't sing. Don't come when you can't get back; or the clouds are down.'

'You are trying to frighten me,' I said, in a louder voice. 'And I have been too much alone for that. Of course things must look after themselves. Don't *we*? And you said an *evil* spirit. What is the good of dreaming when you are wide awake?'

'Then', said he, almost coldly, 'do you deny that Man is an evil spirit? He distorts and destroys.'

But with that the words of my mother came back to me out of a far-away morning: 'He made us of His Power and Love.' Yet I could not answer him, could only wait, as if expectant that by mere silence I should be able to share the thoughts he was thinking. And, all the while, my eyes were brooding in some dark chamber of my mind on Fanny, and not, as they well might have, on the dark bark of Mr. Crimble tossing in jeopardy beneath its fleeting ray of hope.

Truly this stranger was making life very interesting, even if he was only prodding over its dead moles. And truly I was an incorrigibly romantic young lady; for when, with a glance at my grandfather's watch, I discovered that it was long past noon, and told him I must be gone; without a single moment's hesitation, I promised to come again to meet him on the very first fine morning that showed. So strong within me was the desire to do so, that a profound dismay chilled my mind when, on turning about at the end of the terrace – for he had shown no inclination to accompany me – I found that he was already out of sight. I formally waved my hand towards where he had vanished in case he should be watching; sighed, and went on.

It was colder under the high, sunless trees. I gathered my cloak closer around me, and at that discovered not only that Miss Austen had been left behind, but that Fanny's letter still lay in undisturbed concealment beneath its stone. It was too late to return for them now, and a vague misgiving that had sprung up in me amid the tree-trunks was quieted by the assurance that for these – rather than for any other reason – I must return to Wanderslore as soon as I could. So, in remarkably gay spirits, I hastened light-heeled on my way in the direction of civilized society, of nefarious Man, and of my never-to-be-blessed-too-much Mrs. Bowater.

Chapter Twenty-Three

My landlady was already awaiting me at the place appointed, and we walked off together towards the house. It had been a prudent arrangement, for we met and passed at least half a dozen strangers before we arrived there, and one and all by the unfeigned astonishment with which they turned to watch our two figures out of sight (for I stooped once or twice, as if to tie my shoelace, in order to see), clearly proved themselves to belong to that type of humanity to which my new acquaintance had referred frigidly as THEY. Vanity of vanities, when one old loitering gentleman did not so much as lift an eyelid at me – he was so absorbed in his own thoughts – I felt a pang of annoyance.

As soon as I was safely installed in my own room again, I confided in Mrs. Bowater a full account of my morning's adventure. Not so much because I wished to keep free of any further deceit, as because I simply couldn't contain myself, and *must* talk of my Stranger. She heard me to the end without question, but with an unusual rigidity of features. She compressed her lips even tighter before beginning her catechism.

'What was the young man's name,' she inquired, 'and where did he live?'

My hope had been that she herself would be able to supply these little particulars. With a blank face, I shook my head: 'We just talked of things in general.'

'I see,' she said, and glanced at me, as if over her spectacles. Her next question was even less manageable. 'Was the young fellow a gentleman?'

Alas! she had fastened on a flaw in my education. This was a problem absolutely new to me. I thought of my father, of Mr. Waggett, Dr. Grose, Dr. Phelps, the old farmer in the railway train, of Sir Walter Pollacke, my bishop, Heathcliff Mr. Bowater, Mr. Clodd, even Henry – or rather all these male phantoms went whisking across the back of my mind, calling up every other two-legged creature of the same gender within sight or hearing. Meanwhile, Mrs. Bowater stood like Patience on her Brussels carpet, or rather like Thomas de Torquemada, watching these intellectual contortions.

'Well, really, do you know, Mrs. Bowater,' I was forced to acknowledge at last, with a sigh and a smile, 'I simply can't say. I didn't think of it. That seems rather on *his* side, doesn't it? But to be quite, quite candid, perhaps *not* a gentleman; not *exactly*, I mean.'

'Which is no more than I supposed,' was her comment, 'and if *not* – and any kind of not, miss – what was he, then? And *if* not, why, you can never go there again!'

'Indeed, but I must,' I said, as if to myself.

'With your small knowledge of the world,' she retorted unmovedly, 'you must, if you please, be guided by those with more. Who isn't a gentleman couldn't be desirable company if chanced on like a stranger in a young lady's lonely rambles. And *how* tall did you say? And what's more,' she continued, not pausing for an answer, and gathering momentum on her way, 'if he *is* a gentleman, I'd better come along with you, miss, and see for myself.'

A rebellious and horrified glance followed her retreating figure out of the room. So this was the reward for being open and above-board. What a ridiculous figure I should cut, tippeting along behind my landlady. What would my stranger think of me? What would she think of him? *Was* he a 'gentleman'? To decide whether or not the Spirit of Man is an evil spirit had been an easy problem by comparison. *Gentle man* – why, of course, self muttered in shame to self convicted of yet another mean little snobbery. He had been almost absurdly gentle – had treated me as if I were an angel rather than a young woman.

But the nettlerash produced by Mrs. Bowater's bigotry was not to be so easily allayed as all that. It had invited yet another kind of THEM in. An old, green, rotting board hung over the wicket gate that led up the stony path into Wanderslore – 'Trespassers will be prosecuted'. Why couldn't one put boards up in the Wanderslore of one's mind? My landlady had never inquired if Lady Pollacke was a gentlewoman. How mechanical things were in their unex-pectedness. That morning I had gone out to free myself from the Crimble tangle, merely to return with a few more knots in the skein.

A dead calm descended on me. I was adrift in the Sargasso Sea – in the Doldrums, and had dropped my sextant overboard. Even a long stare at the master-mariner on the wall gave me no help. Yet I must confess that these foolish reflections made me happy. I would share them with Fanny – perhaps with the 'gentleman' himself, some day. I leaned over the side of my small vessel, more deeply interested in the voyage than I had been since Pollie had carried me out of my girlhood into the Waggett's wagonette. And as I sat there, simmering over these novelties, a voice, clear as a cockcrow, exclaimed in my mind, 'If father hadn't died, I'd have had nothing of all this.' My hands clenched damp in my lap at this monstrosity. But I kept my wits and managed to face it. 'If father hadn't died', I answered myself, 'you don't know *what* would have happened. And if you think that, because I am happy now, anything could make me *not* wish him back, it's a lie.' But I remained a little less comfortable in mind.

The evening post brought me a letter and a registered parcel. I turned them over and over, examining the unfamiliar handwriting, the bright red seals; but all in vain. In spite of my hard-won knotlore, I was still kneeling over the package and wrestling with string and wax, when Mrs. Bowater, folding *her* letter away in its envelope, announced baldly: 'She's not coming home, it seems, at all these holidays, having been invited by some school friend into the country – Merriden, or some such place. Not that you might expect Fanny to write plain, when she doesn't *mean* plain.'

'Oh, Mrs. Bowater! Not at all?'

Cold fogs of disappointment swept in, blotting out my fool's paradise. That inward light without which life is dark indeed died in eclipse. The one thought and desire which I now realized I had been feeding on from hour to hour, had been snatched away. To think that they had been nothing but waste. 'Oh, Fanny,' I whispered bitterly to myself, 'oh, Fanny!' But the face I lifted to her mother showed only defiance.

'Well,' I muttered, 'who cares? Let's hope she will enjoy herself better than mooning about in this dingy old place.'

Mrs. Bowater merely continued to look quietly over the envelope at me.

'Oh, but you know, Mrs. Bowater,' I quaked miserably, 'it's not dingy to *me*. Surely a promise is a promise, whoever you make it to!'

With that I stooped my face over the stuffy-smelling brown paper, and attacked the last knot with my teeth. With eyes still a little asquint with resentment I smoothed away the wrappings from the shape within. Then every thought evaporated in a sigh. For there, of a delicate veined fairness against the white paper, lay a minute copy in ivory of none but lovely Hypnos. Half-blindly I stared at it – lost in a serenity beyond all hope of my poor, foolish life – then lifted it with both hands away from my face: 'A present – to me! Look!' I cried, 'look!'

Mrs. Bowater settled her face over the image as if it had been some tropical and noxious insect I was offering for her inspection. But I thrust it into her hand and opened my letter:

> My Dear Young Lady. – I am no poet, and therefore cannot hope to share with you the music of 'the flaming drake', but we did share my Hypnos. Only a replica, as I told you, but none the less one of the most beautiful things I possess. Will you, then, give me the pleasure of accepting the contents of the little package I am having posted with this – as a small token of the delight your enthusiasm gave.
>
> Yours most sincerely,
>
> WALTER POLLACKE
>
> P.S. – Lady Pollacke tells me that we may perhaps again look forward to your company to tea in a few days; please do not think, then, of acknowledging this little message by post.

But I did acknowledge it, not with that guardedness of the feelings which Miss Austen seemed to recommend, but from the very depths of my heart. Next morning came Lady Pollacke's invitation:

> DEAR MISS M. – I hasten to renew my invitation of last Thursday. Will you give us the pleasure of your company at tea on Friday afternoon? Mrs. Monnerie – the younger daughter, as you will remember, of Lord B. – has expressed an exceedingly warm wish to make your acquaintance, and Mr. Pellew, who is giving us a course of sermons at St. Peter's, during Holy Week, will also be with us. May we, perhaps, share yet another of those delightful recitations?
>
> > Believe me,
> > > Yours sincerely,
> > > > LYDIA PRESTON POLLACKE

I searched my memory for memorial of Lord B.; alas, in vain. This lapse made the thought of meeting his younger daughter a little alarming. Yet I must confess to having been pleasantly flattered by these attentions. Even the black draught administered by Fanny, who had not even thought it worth her while to send me a word of excuse or explanation, lost much of its bitterness. I asked Mrs. Bowater if she supposed I might make Sir Walter a little present in return for his. Would it be a proper thing to do, would it be *lady*like?

'What's meant kindly,' she assured me, after a moment's reflection, 'even if taken amiss, which, to judge from his letter, it won't be, is nothing to be thought of but only *felt*.'

This advice decided me, and early on my Friday morning I trimmed and freshened up as well as I could one of my grandfather's dwarf cedar-trees which, in the old days, had stood on my window balcony. Its branches were now a little dishevelled, but it was still a fresh and pretty thing in its grey-green pot.

Chapter Twenty-Four

With this dwarf tree in my arms, when came the auspicious afternoon, I followed Lady Pollacke's parlour-maid – her neat little bonnet tied with a bow under her ear – down my Bateses, and was lifted by Mrs. Bowater into the carriage. How demure a greeting we exchanged when, the maid and I having seated ourselves together under its hood, my glance fell upon the bloodstone brooch pinned conspicuously for the occasion near the topmost button of her trim, outdoor jacket. It gave me so much confidence that even the sudden clatter of conversation that gushed over me in the doorway of Lady Pollacke's drawing-room failed to be disconcerting. The long, flowery room was thronged with company, and everybody was talking to everybody else. On my entry, as if a seraph had spoken, the busy tongues sank instantly to a hush. I stood stilettoed by a score of eyes. But Sir Walter had been keeping good watch for me, and I at once delivered my great pot into his pink, outstretched hands.

'My dear, dear young lady,' he cried, stooping plumply over me, 'the pleasure you give me! A little masterpiece! and real old Nankin. Alas, my poor Hypnos!'

'But it is me, *me*,' I cried. 'If I could only tell you!'

A murmur of admiration rippled across the room, in which I distinctly heard a quavering, nasal voice exclaim, 'Touching, touching!'

The words – as if a pleasant sheep had bleated – came, I fancied, from a rather less fashionable lady with a lorgnette, who was sitting almost alone on the outskirts of the room, and who I afterwards discovered was only a widowed sister of Lady Pollacke's. But I could spare her but one startled glance, for, at the same moment, I was being presented to the younger daughter of Lord B. Mrs. Monnerie sat amply reclining in an immense gilded chair – a lady with a large and surprising countenance. Lady Pollacke's '*younger*' had misled my fancy. Far from being the slim, fair, sylphlike thing of my expectations, Mrs. Monnerie cannot have been many years the junior of my godmother, Miss Fenne.

Her skin had fallen into the queerest folds and puckers. Her black swimming eye under a thick eyebrow gazed down her fine, drooping nose at me with a dwelling expression at once indulgent, engrossed, and amused. With a gracious sweep of her hand she drew aside her voluminous silk skirts so that I could at once instal myself by her side in a small, cane-seated chair that had once, I should fancy, accommodated a baby Pollacke, and had been brought down from the nursery for this occasion.

Thus, then, I found myself – the exquisitely self-conscious centre of attention – striving to nibble a biscuit, nurse my child-size handleless teacup, and respond to her advances at one and the same time.

Lady Pollacke hung like a cloud at sunset over us both, her cheek flushed with the effort to be amused at every sentence which Mrs. Monnerie uttered and to share it as far as possible with the rest of her guests.

'A little pale, eh?' mused Mrs. Monnerie, brooding at me with her great eye. 'She wants sea-air; sea-air – just to *tinge* that roseleaf porcelain. I must arrange it.'

I assured her that I was in the best of health.

'Not at all,' she replied. 'All young people boast of their health. When I was your age every thought of illness was as black as a visitation of the devil. *That's* the door where we must lay all such evils, isn't it, Mr. Pellew?'

A lean, tall, birdlike figure, the hair on his head still showing traces of auburn, disengaged itself from a knot of charmed spectators.

'Ah,' he said. 'But I doubt, now,' he continued, with a little deprecating wave of his teacup at me, 'if Miss M. can remember me. When we first met we were precisely one week old, precisely one week old.'

Why, like Dr. Phelps, Mr. Pellew referred to me as *we* I had not time to consider, for he was already confiding to Mrs. Monnerie that he had never baptized an infant who more strenuously objected to Holy Water than had I. I looked at his long, fair eyelashes and the smile-line on his cheek as he bent with a sort of jocular urbanity over her chair, but could not recall his younger face, though during my christening I must, of course, have gazed at him even more absorbedly.

'"Remember" you – I'll be bound she did,' cried Mrs. Monnerie with enthusiasm, 'or was it the bachelor thumb? The mercy is you didn't drop her into the font. Can you swim, my dear?'

'I couldn't at a week,' I replied as archly as possible. 'But I *can* swim; my father taught me.'

'But how wonderful!' broke our listeners into chorus.

'There we are, then,' asserted Mrs. Monnerie; 'sea-bathing! And are *we* a swimmer, Mr. Pellew?'

Mr. Pellew seemed not to have caught her question. He was

assuring me that Miss Fenne had kept him well informed – well informed of all my doings. He trusted I was comfortable with the excellent Mrs. Bowater, and hoped that some day I should be able to pay a visit to his rectory in Devonshire. 'Mrs. Pellew, he knew ...' What he knew about Mrs. Pellew, however, was never divulged, for Mrs. Monnerie swallowed him up!

'Devonshire, my dear Mr. Pellew! no, indeed. Penthouse lanes, red-hot fields, staring cows. Imagine it! She would be dried up like a leaf. What she wants is a mild but bracing sea-air. It shall be arranged. And who is this Mrs. Bowater?'

At this precise moment, among the strange faces far above me, I descried that of Mr. Crimble, modestly peering out of the background. He coughed, and in a voice I should scarcely have recognized as his, informed Mrs. Monnerie that my landlady was 'a most res – an admirable woman.' He paused, coughed again, swept my soul with his glance – 'I assure you, Mrs. Monnerie, in view of – of all the circumstances, one couldn't be in better hands. Indeed the house is on the crest of the hill, well out of the town, yet not a quarter of an hour's walk from my mother's.'

'Hah!' remarked Mrs. Monnerie, with an inflection that I am sure need not have brought a warmth to my cheek, or a duskier pallor to Mr. Crimble's.

'You have perhaps heard the tragic story of Wanderslore,' persisted Mr. Crimble; 'Miss M.'s – er – lodgings are immediately adjacent to the park.'

'Hah!' repeated Mrs. Monnerie, even more emphatically. 'Mrs. Bowater, eh? Well, I must see for myself. And I'm told, Miss M.,' she swept down at me, 'that you have a beautiful gift for recitation.' She looked round, patted her lap imperiously, and cried, 'Come, now, who's to break the ice?'

In *fact,* no doubt, Mrs. Monnerie was not so arbitrary a mistress of Lady Pollacke's little ceremony as this account of it may suggest. But that is how she impressed me at the time. She the sun, and I the least – but I hope not the least grateful – of her obsequious planets. Lady Pollacke at any rate set immediately to breaking the ice. She prevailed upon a Miss Templemaine to sing. And we all sat mute.

I liked Miss Templemaine's appearance – brown hair, straight nose, dark eyelashes, pretty fringe beneath her peak-brimmed hat. But I was a little distressed by her song, which, so far as I could gather, was about two persons with more or less broken hearts who were compelled to part and said, 'Ah' for a long time. Only physically distressed, however, for though I seemed to be shaken in its strains like a linnet in the wind, its adieux were protracted enough to enable me to examine the rest of the company at my leisure. Their eyes, I found, were far more politely engaged the while in gazing composedly down at the carpet or up at the ceiling. And when I did happen to intercept a gliding glance in my direction, it was almost as if with a tiny explosion that it collided with mine and broke away.

Mrs. Monnerie's eyelids, on the other hand, with a faintly fluttering motion, remained closed from the first bar to the last – a method of appreciation I experimented with for a moment but quickly abandoned; while at the first clash of the keys, Sir Walter had dexterously contrived to slide himself out of the room by the door at which he had unexpectedly entered it on my first visit. Such was the social situation when, after murmurs of gratitude and applause, Miss Templemaine took up her gloves and rose from the piano, and Mrs. Monnerie reopened herself to the outer world with the ejaculation, 'That's right. *Now*, my dear!'

The summons was to me. My moment had come, but I was prepared for it. In my last ordeal I had broken down because I had chosen a poem that was a kind of secret thing in my mind. So, after receiving Lady Pollacke's letter, I had hunted about for a recitation as short, but less personal: one, I mean, whose sentiments I didn't mind. And since Mrs. Bullace had chosen two of Mrs. Browning's pieces for her triumph on New Year's Eve, I argued that she knew the parish taste, and that I could do no better. Of course, too, composure over what I was going to do was more important than the composition.

'Prepared for it,' I said just now, but I meant it only in the sense that one prepares for a cold bath. There was still the plunge. I clasped my hands, stood up. Ceiling and floor gently rocked a little. There seemed to be faces – faces everywhere, and every eye in them was fixed on me. Thus completely encompassed, I could find no refuge from them, for unfortunately my Hypnos was completely obliterated from view by the lady with the lorgnette. So I fixed my attention, instead, on the window, where showed a blank break of clear, fair, blue sky between the rain-clouds of afternoon. A nervous cough from Lady Pollacke plunged me over, and I announced my title: *The Weakest Thing*, by Elizabeth Barrett Browning:

> Which is the weakest thing of all
>   Mine heart can ponder?
> The sun, a little cloud can pall
>   With darkness yonder!
> The cloud, a little wind can move
>   Where'er it listeth;
> The wind, a little leaf above,
>   Though sere, resisteth!

What time that yellow leaf was green,
 My days were gladder:
Now on its branch each summer-sheen
 May find me sadder!
Ah, me! a *leaf* with sighs can wring
 My lips asunder –
Then is my heart the weakest thing
 Itself can ponder.

Yet, Heart, when sun and cloud are pined
 And drop together;
And at a blast which is not wind,
 The forests wither,
Thou, from the darkening, deathly curse
 To glory breakest –
The Strongest of the Universe
 Guarding the weakest.

The applause, in which Miss Templemaine generously joined, was this time quite unconcealed, and Lady Pollacke's sister's last 'Touching' had hardly died away when Mrs. Monnerie added *her* approbation.

'Charming, perfectly charming,' she murmured, eyeing me like a turtle-dove. 'But tell me, my dear, why that particular poem? It seemed to have even less sense than usual.'

'No-o; ye-es,' breathed Lady Pollacke, and many heads nodded in discreet accord.

'Doesn't – er – perhaps, Mrs. Browning dwell rather assiduously on the tragic side of life?' Mr. Crimble ventured to inquire.

Lady Pollacke jerked her head, either in the affirmative or in the negative, and looked inquiringly at Mrs. Monnerie, who merely drooped her eyes a little closer towards me and smiled, almost as if she and I were in a little plot together.

'What do *you* say, Miss M.?'

'Well, Mrs. Monnerie,' I replied a little nervously, for all eyes were turned on me, 'I don't think I know myself what *exactly* the poem means – the who's and what's – and what the blast was which was not wind. But I thought it was a poem which every one would understand as much as *possible* of.'

To judge from the way she quivered in her chair, though quite inaudibly, Mrs. Monnerie was extremely amused at this criticism.

'And that is why you chose it?'

'Well, yes,' said I; 'you see, when one is listening to poetry, not reading it to oneself, I mean, one hasn't time to pry about for all its bits of meaning, but only just to get the general – general –'

'Aroma?' suggested Mrs. Monnerie.

'Yes – aroma.'

'And the moral?'

The silence that hung over this little exchange was growing more and more dense. Luckless Miss M.! She only plunged herself deeper into it by her reply that, 'Oh, there's nothing very much in the moral, Mrs. Monnerie. That's quite ordinary. At least I read about that in *prose*, why, before I was seven!'

'Touch – ' began that further voice, but was silenced by a testy lift of Mrs. Monnerie's eyelid. 'Indeed!' she said, 'and couldn't you, wouldn't you, now, give me the prose version? That's more my mark.'

'It was in a little nursery lesson-book of mine, called *The Observing Eye*; letters about snails and coral insects and spiders and things – ' I paused. 'A book, rather, you know, for Sundays. But my – my family and I – '

'Oh, but do,' cried Lady Pollacke in a voice I should hardly have recognized, 'I *adore* snails.'

Once more I was cornered. So I steeled myself anew, and stumbled through the brief passage in the squat, blue book. It tells how:

> The history of each one of the animals we have now considered, teaches us that our kind God watches over the wants and the pleasures of the meanest of His creatures. We see that He gives to them, not only the sagacity and the instruments which they need for catching their food, but that He also provides them with some means of defending themselves. We learn by their history that the gracious Eye watches under the mighty waters, as well as over the earth, and that no creature can stop doing His will without His eye seeing it.

Chapter Twenty-Five

Once more I sat down, but this time in the midst of what seemed to me a rather unpleasant silence, as if the room had grown colder! a silence which was broken only by the distant whistlings of a thrush. At one and the same moment both Mr. Pellew and Mr. Crimble returned to teacups which I should have supposed must have, by this time, been empty, and Lady Pollacke's widowed sister folded up her lorgnette.

'My dear Miss M.,' said Mrs. Monnerie dryly, with an almost wicked ray of amusement in her deep-set eyes, 'wherever the top of Beechwood Hill may be, and whatever supplies of food may be caught on its crest, there is no doubt that *you* have been provided with the means of defending yourself. But tell me now, what do you think, perhaps, Mr. *Pellew's* little "instruments" are? Or, better still – mine? Am I a mollusc with a hard shell, or a scorpion with a sting?'

Lady Pollacke rose to her feet and stood looking down on me like a hen, though not exactly a motherly one. But this was a serious question over which I must not be flustered, so I took my time. I folded my hands, and fixed a long, long look on Mrs. Monnerie. Even after all these years, I confess it moves me to recall it.

'Of course, really and truly,' I said at last, as deferentially as I could, 'I haven't known you long enough to say. But I should think, Mrs. Monnerie, you always knew the truth.'

I was glad I had not been too impetuous. My reply evidently pleased her. She chuckled all over.

'Ah,' she said reposefully, 'the truth. And that is why, I suppose, like Sleeping Beauty, I am so thickly hedged in with the thorns and briers of affection. Well, well, there's one little truth we'll share alone, you and I.' She raised herself in her chair and stooped her great face close to my ear: 'We must know more of one another, my dear,' she whispered. 'I have taken a great fancy to you. We must meet again.'

She hoisted herself up. Sir Walter Pollacke had hastened in and stood smiling, with arm hooked, and genial, beaming countenance in front of her. Mr. Crimble had already vanished. Mr. Pellew was talking earnestly with Lady Pollacke. Conversation broke out like a storm-shower, on every side. For a while I was extraordinarily alone.

Into this derelict moment a fair-cheeked, breathless lady descended, and surreptitiously thrusting a crimson padded birthday book and a miniature pencil into my lap, entreated my autograph – 'Just your signature, you know – for my small daughter. How she would have *loved* to be here!'

This lady cannot have been many years older than I, and one of those instantaneous, fleeting affections sprang up in me as I looked up at her for the first and only time, and seemed to see that small daughter smiling at me out of her face.

Alas, such is vanity. I turned over the leaves to August 30th and found printed there, for motto, a passage from Shakespeare:

> He that has had a little tiny wit –
> With hey, ho, the wind and the rain –
> Must make content with his fortunes fit,
> For the rain it raineth every day.

The 29th was little less depressing, from Samuel Taylor Coleridge:

> He prayeth best who loveth best
> All creatures great and small.

This would never do. I bent double over the volume, turned back hastily three or four leaves, and scrawled in my name under August 25th on a leaf that bore the quotation:

> Fie on't! ah, fie! 'tis an unweeded garden,
> That grows to seed; things rank and gross in nature
> Possess it merely. That it should come to this!

and beneath the quotation, the signature of Josephine Mildred Spratte.

'Thank you, *thank* you, she will be overjoyed,' blushed the fair-haired lady. A sudden hunger for solitude seized upon me. I rose hastily, conscious for the first time of a headache, caused, no doubt, by the expensive and fumey perfumes in the air. Threading my way between the trains and flounces and trouser-legs around me, at last my adieux were over. I was in the porch – in the carriage. The breezes of heaven were on my cheek. My blessed parlour-maid was once more installed beside me. Yet even now the Pollacke faces were still flocking in my mind. The outside world was very sluggishly welling in. Looking up so long had stiffened my neck. I fixed my eyes on the crested back buttons of Lady Pollacke's stiff-looking coachman, and committed myself to my thoughts.

It was to a Miss M., with one of her own handkerchiefs laid over her brows, and sprinkled with vinegar and lavender water, that Mrs. Bowater brought in supper that evening. We had one of our broken talks together, none the less. But she persisted in desultory accounts of Fanny's ailments in her infancy; and I had to drag in Brunswick House by myself. At which she poked the fire and was mum. It was unamiable of her. I longed to share my little difficulties and triumphs. Surely she was showing rather too much of that discrimination which Lady Pollacke had recommended.

She snorted at Mr. Pellew, she snorted at my friendly parlourmaid and even at Mrs. Monnerie. Even when I repeated for her ear alone my nursery passage from *The Observing Eye,* her only comment was that to judge from *some* fine folk she knew of, there was no doubt at all that God watched closely over the pleasures of the meanest of His creatures, but as for their doing His will, she hadn't much noticed it.

To my sigh of regret that Fanny had not been at home to accompany me, she retorted with yet another onslaught on the fire, and the apophthegm, that the world would be a far better place if people kept themselves *to* themselves.

'But, Mrs. Bowater,' I argued fretfully, 'if I did that, I should just – distil, as you might say, quite away. Besides, Fanny would have been far, far the – the gracefullest person there. Mrs. Monnerie would have taken a fancy to *her*, now, if you like.'

Mrs. Bowater drew in her lips and rubbed her nose. 'God forbid,' she said.

But it was her indifference to the impression that I myself had made on Mrs. Monnerie that nettled me the most. 'Why, then, who *is* Lord B.?' I inquired impatiently at last, pushing back the bandage that had fallen over my eyes.

'From what I've heard of Lord B.,' said Mrs. Bowater shortly, 'he was a gentleman of whom the less heard of's the better.'

'But surely,' I protested, 'that isn't Mrs. Monnerie's fault any more than Fanny's being so lovely – I mean, than I being a midget was my father's fault? Anyhow,' I hurried on, 'Mrs. Monnerie says I look pale, and must go to the sea.'

Mrs. Bowater was still kneeling by the fire, just as Fanny used to kneel. And, like Fanny, when one most expected an answer, she remained silent; though, unlike Fanny, it seemed to be not because she was dreaming of something else. How shall I express it? – there fell a kind of loneliness between us. The severe face made no sign.

'Would you – would you miss me?' some silly self within piped out pathetically.

'Why, for the matter of that,' was her sardonic reply, 'there's not very much of you to miss.'

I rose from my bed, flung down the bandage, and ran down my little staircase. 'Oh, Mrs. Bowater,' I said, burying my face in her camphory skirts, 'be kind to me; be kind to me! I've nobody but you.'

The magnanimous creature stroked my vinegar-sodden hair with the tips of her horny fingers. 'Why there, miss. I meant no harm. Isn't all the gentry and nobility just gaping to snatch you up? You won't want your old Mrs. Bowater very long. What's more, you mustn't get carried away by yourself. You never know where that journey ends. If sea it is, sea it must be. Though, Lord preserve us, the word's no favourite of mine.'

'But suppose, suppose, Mrs. Bowater,' I cried, starting up and smiling enrapturedly into her face, 'suppose we could go together!'

'That', she said, with a look of astonishing benignity, 'would be just what I was being led to suppose was the height of the impossible.'

At which, of course, we at once began discussing ways and means. But, delicious though this prospect seemed, I determined that nothing should persuade me to go unless all hope of Fanny's coming home proved vain. Naturally, from Fanny memory darted to Wanderslore. I laughed up at my landlady, holding her finger, and suggested demurely that we should go off together on the morrow to see if my stranger were true to his word.

'We have kept him a very long time, and if, as you seem to think, Mrs. Monnerie isn't such a wonderful lady, you may decide that after all *he* is a gentleman.'

She enjoyed my little joke, was pleased that I had been won over, but refused to accept my reasoning, though the topic itself was after her heart.

'The point is, miss, not whether your last conquest is a wonderful lady, or a grand lady, or even a perfect lady for the matter of that, but, well, a *lady*. It's that's the kind in my experience that comes nearest to being as uncommon a sort as any sort of a good woman.'

This was a wholly unexpected vista for me, and I peered down its smooth, green, aristocratic sward with some little awe.

'As for the young fellow who made himself so free in his manners,' she went on placidly, so that I had to scamper back to pick her up again, 'I have no doubt seeing will be believing.'

'But what *is* the story of Wanderslore?' I pressed her none too honestly.

The story – and this time Mrs. Bowater poured it out quite freely – was precisely what I had been told already, but with the addition that the young woman who had hanged herself in one of its attics had done so for jealousy.

'Jealousy! But of whom?' I inquired.

'Her husband's, not her own: driven wild by his.'

'You really mean', I persisted, 'that she couldn't endure to live any longer because her husband loved her so much that he couldn't bear anybody else to love her too?'

'In some such measure,' replied Mrs. Bowater, 'though I don't say he didn't help the other way round. But she was a wild, scattering creature. It was just her way. The less she cared, the more they flocked. She couldn't *collect* herself, and say, "Here I am; who are you?" so to speak. Ah, miss, it's a sickly and dangerous thing to be too much admired.'

'But you said "scattering": was she mad a little?'

'No. Peculiar, perhaps, with her sidelong, startled look. A lovelier I've never seen.'

'You've seen her!'

'Thirty years ago, perhaps. Alive *and* dead.'

'Oh, Mrs. Bowater, poor thing, poor thing.'

'That you may well say, for lovely in the latter finding she was not.'

My eyes were fixed on the fire, but the picture conjured up was dark even amidst the red-hot coals. 'And he? did he die too? At least his jealousy was broken away.'

'And I'm not so sure of that,' said Mrs. Bowater. 'It's like the men to go on wanting, even when it comes to scrabbing at a grave. And there's a trashy sort of creature, though well-set-up enough from the outside, that a spark will put in a blaze. I've no doubt he was that kind.'

I thought of my own sparks, but questioned on: 'Then there's nothing else but – but her ghost there now?'

'Lor, *ghosts,* miss, it's an hour, I see, when bed's the proper place for you and me. I look to be scared by that kind of gentry when they come true.'

'You don't believe, then, in *Destroyers*, Mrs. Bowater?'

'Miss, it's those queer books you are reading,' was the evasive reply. '"Destroyers!" Why, wasn't it cruel enough to drive that poor feather-brained creature into a noose!'

Candle and I and drowsing cinders kept company until St. Peter's bell had told only the sleepless that midnight was over the world. It seemed to my young mind that there was not a day, scarcely an hour, I lived, but that Life was unfolding itself in ever new and ravishing disguises. I had not begun to be in the least tired or afraid of it. Smallest of bubbles I might be, tossing on the great waters, but I reflected the universe. What need of courage when no danger was apparent? Surely one need not mind being different if that difference added to one's share in the wonderful banquet. Even Wanderslore's story was only of what happened when the tangle was so harshly knotted that no mortal fingers could unravel it. And though my own private existence now had Mrs. Monnerie – and all that *she* might do and mean and be – to cope with, as well as my stranger who was yet another queer story and as yet mine alone, these complications were enticing. One must just keep control of them; that was all. At which I thought a little unsteadily of Fanny's 'pin', and remembered that that pin was helping to keep her and Mr. Crimble from being torn apart.

He had seemed so peering a guest at Brunswick House. Mrs. Monnerie hadn't so much as glanced at him when he had commented on Mrs. Browning's poems. There seemed to be a shadow over whatever he did. It was as though there could be a sadness in the very coursing of one's blood. How thankful I felt that mine hadn't been a really flattering reply to Mrs. Monnerie's question. She was extremely arrogant, even for a younger daughter of a lord. On the other hand, though, of course, the sheer novelty of me had had something to do with it, she had certainly singled me out afterwards to know what I *thought*, and in thoughts there is no particular size, only effusiveness – no, *piercingness*. I smiled to myself at the word, pitied my godmother for living so sequestered a life, and wondered how and why it was that my father and mother had so obstinately shut me away from the world. If only Fanny was coming home – what a difference she would find in her fretful Midge! And with that, I discovered that my feet were cold and that my headache had ached itself away.

Chapter Twenty-Six

There had been no need to reserve the small hours for these rumi-nations. The next few days were wet and windy; every glance at the streaming panes cast my mind into a sort of vacancy. The wind trumpeted smoke into the room; I could fix my mind on nothing. Then the weather faired. There came 'a red sky at night', and Spica flashing secrets to me across the darkness; and that supper-time I referred as casually as possible to Mr. Anon.

'I suppose one *must* keep one's promises, Mrs. Bowater, even to a stranger. Would half-past six be too early to keep mine, do you think? Would it look too – forward? Of course he may have forgotten all about me by this time.'

Mrs. Bowater eyed me like an owl as I bent my cheeks over my bowl of bread and milk, and proceeded to preach me yet another little sermon on the ways of the world. Nevertheless, the next morning saw us setting out together in the crisp, sparkling air to my tryst, with the tacit understanding that she accompanied me rather in the cause of propriety than romance.

Owing, I fancy, to a bunion, she was so leisurely a walker that it was I who must set my pace to hers. But the day promised to be warm, and we could take our ease. As we wandered on among the early flowers and bright, green grass and under the beeches, a mildness lightened into her face. Over her long features lay a vacant yet happy smile, of which she seemed to be unaware. This set me off thinking in the old, old fashion; comparing my lot with that of ordinary human beings. How fortunate I was. If only she could have seen the lowlier plants as I could – scarcely looking down on any, and of the same stature as some among the taller of them so that the air around me was dyed and illumined with their clear colours, and burthened with their breath.

The least and humblest of them – not merely crisp-edged lichen, speckle-seed whitlow-grass and hyssop in the wall – are so close to earth, the wonder, indeed, is that common-sized people ever see them at all. They must, at any rate, I thought, commit themselves to their stomachs, or go down on their knees to see them *properly*. So, on we went, Mrs. Bowater and I, she pursuing her private musings, and I mine.

I smiled to myself at remembrance of Dr. Phelps and his blushes. After all, if humanity should 'dwindle into a delicate littleness', it would make a good deal more difference than he had supposed. What a destruction would ensue, among all the lesser creatures of the earth, the squirrels, moles, voles, hedgehogs, and the birds, not to mention the bees and hornets. *They* would be the enemies then – the traps and poisons and the nets! No more billowy cornfields a good yard high, no more fine nine-foot hedges flinging their blossoms into the air. And all the long-legged, 'doubled', bloated garden flowers, gone clean out of favour. It would be a little world, would it be a happier? The dwarfed Mrs. Bowaters, Dr. Phelpses, Miss Bullaces, Lady Pollackes.

But there was little chance of such an eventuality – at least in my lifetime. It was far likelier that the Miss M.'s of the world would continue to be a by-play. Yet, as I glanced up at my companion, and called to mind other such 'Lapland Giants' of mine, I can truthfully avouch that I did not much envy their extra inches. So much more thin-skinned surface to be kept warm and unscratched. The cumbersome bones, the curious distance from foot and finger-tip to brain, too; and those quarts and quarts of blood. I shuddered. It was little short of a miracle that they escaped continual injury; and what an extended body in which to die.

On the other hand, what real loss was mine – with so much to my advantage? These great spreading beech-trees were no less shady and companionable to me than to them. Nor, thought I, could moon or sun or star or ocean or mountain be any the less silvery, hot, lustrous, and remote, forlorn in beauty, or vast in strangeness, one way or the other, than they are to ordinary people. Could there be any doubt at all, too, that men had always coveted to make much finer and more delicate things than their clumsiness allowed?

What fantastic creatures they were – with their vast mansions, pyramids, palaces, scores of sizes too large for either carcass or mind. Their Satan a monster on whose wrist the vulture of the Andes could perch like an aphis on my thumb; yet their Death but skeleton-high, and their Saviour of such a stature that wellnigh without stooping He could have laid His fingers on my head.

Time's sands had been trickling fast while I thought these small thoughts that bright spring daybreak. So, though we had loitered on our way, it seemed we had reached our destination on the wings of the morning. Alas, Mrs. Bowater's smile can have been only skin-deep; for, when, lifting my eyes from the ground

I stopped all of a sudden, spread out my hands, and cried in triumph, 'There! Mrs. Bowater'; she hardly shared my rapture.

She disapproved of the vast, blank 'barn of a place', with its blackshot windows and cold chimneys. The waste and ruination of the garden displeased her so much that I grew a little ashamed of my barbarism.

'It's all going to wrack and ruin,' she exclaimed, snorting at my stone summer-house no less emphatically than she had snorted at Mrs. Monnerie. 'Not a walkable walk, nor the trace of a border; and was there ever such a miggle-maggle of weeds! A fine house in its prime, miss, but now, money melting away like butter in the sun.'

'But,' said I, standing before her in the lovely light amid the dwelling dewdrops, 'really and truly, Mrs. Bowater, it is only going back to its own again. What you call a miggle-maggle is what these things were made to be. They are growing up now by themselves; and if you could look as close as I can, you'd see they breathe only what each can spare. They are just racing along to live as wildly as they possibly can. It's the tameness,' I expostulated, flinging back my hood, 'that would be shocking to *me*.'

Mrs. Bowater looked down at me, listening to this high-piped recitative with an unusual inquisitiveness.

'Well, that's as it may be,' she retorted, 'but what *I'm* asking is, Where's the young fellow? He don't seem to be as punctual as they were when I was a girl.'

My own eyes had long been busy, but as yet in vain.

'I did not come particularly to see him,' was my airy reply. 'Besides, we said no time – *any* fine day. Shall we sit down?'

With a secretive smile Mrs. Bowater spread a square of waterproof sheeting over a flat stone that had fallen out of the coping of the house, unfolded a newspaper over the grass, and we began our breakfast. Neither of us betrayed much appetite for it; she, I fancy, having already fortified herself out of her brown teapot before leaving the house, and I because of the odour of india-rubber and newspaper – an odour presently intensified by the moisture and the sun. Paying no heed to my fastidious nibblings, she munched on reflectively, while I grew more and more ill at ease, first because the 'young fellow' was almost visibly sinking in my old friend's esteem, and next because her cloth-booted foot lay within a few inches of the stone beneath which was hidden Fanny's letter.

'It'll do you good, the sea,' she remarked presently, after sweeping yet one more comprehensive glance around her, 'and we can only hope Mrs. Monnerie will be as good as her word. A spot like this – trespassing or not – is good for neither man nor beast. And when you are young the more human company you get, with proper supervising, the better.'

'Were *you* happy as a girl, Mrs. Bowater?' I inquired after a pause.

Our voices went up and up into the still, mild air. 'Happy enough – for my own good,' she said, neatly screwing up her remaining biscuits in their paper bag. 'In my days children were brought up. Taught to make themselves useful. I would as soon have lifted a hand against my mother as answer her back.'

'You mean, she – she whipped you?'

'If need be,' my landlady replied complacently, folding her thread-gloved hands on her lap and contemplating the shiny toe-caps of her boots. 'She had large hands, my mother; and plenty of temper kept well under control. What's more, if life isn't a continual punishment for the stupidities and wickedness of others, not to mention ourselves, then it must be even a darker story than was ever told me.'

'And was, Mrs. Bowater, Mr. Bowater your – your first –' I looked steadily at a flower at my foot in case she might be affected at so intimate a question, and not wish me to see her face.

'If Mr. Bowater was not the first,' was her easy response, 'he may well live to boast of being the last. Which is neither here nor there, for we may be sure he's enjoying attentive nursing. Broken bones are soon mended. It's when things are disjointed from the root that the wrench comes.'

The storm-felled bole lay there beside us, as if for picture to her parable. I began to think rather more earnestly than I had intended to that morning. In my present state of conscience, it was never an easy matter to decide whether Mrs. Bowater's comments on life referred openly to things in general or covertly to me in particular. How fortunate that the scent of Fanny's notepaper was not potent enough to escape from its tomb. And whether or not, speech seemed less dangerous than silence.

'It seems to me, Mrs. Bowater,' I began rather hastily, 'at least to judge from my own father and mother, that a man *depends* very much on a woman. Men don't seem to grow up in the same way, though I suppose they are practical enough as men.'

'If it were one female,' was the reply, 'there'd be less to be found fault with. That poor young creature over there took her life for no better reason, even though the reason was turned inside out as you may say.'

I met the frightful, louring stare of the house. 'What was her name?' I whispered – but into nothing, for, bolt upright as she was, Mrs. Bowater had shut her eyes, as if in preparation for a nap.

A thread-like tangle of song netted the air. We were, indeed, trespassers. I darted my glance this way and that, in and out of the pale green whispering shadows in this wild haunt. Then, realizing by some faint stir in my mind that the stiff, still, shut-away figure beside me was only feigning to be asleep, I opened the rain-warped covers of my *Sense and Sensibility*, and began plotting how to be rid of her for a while, so that my solitude might summon my stranger, and I might recover Fanny's letter.

Then once more I knew. Raising my eyes, I looked straight across at him, scowling there beneath his stunted thorn in a drift of flowers like fool's parsley. He was making signs, too, with his hands. I watched him pensively, in secret amusement. Then swifter than Daphne into her laurel, instantaneously *he* vanished, and *I* became aware that its black eyes were staring out from the long face of the motionless figure beside me, as might an owl's into an aviary.

'Did you hear a bird, Mrs. Bowater?' I required innocently.

'When I was a girl,' said the mouth, 'sparrowhawks were a common sight, but I never heard one sing.'

'But isn't a sparrowhawk quite a large bird?'

'We must judge,' said Mrs. Bowater, 'not by the size, but the kind. Elseways, miss, your old friend might have been found sleeping, as they say, at her box.' She pretended to yawn, gathered her legs under her, and rose up and up. 'I'll be taking a little walk round. And you shall tell your young acquaintance that I mean him no harm, but that I mean you the reverse; and if show himself he won't, well, here I sit till the Day of Judgment.'

An angry speech curled the tip of my tongue. But the simple-faced flowers were slowly making obeisance to Mrs. Bowater's black, dragging skirts, and when she was nearly out of sight I sallied out to confront my stranger.

His face was black with rage and contempt. '*That* contaminating scarecrow; who's she?' was his greeting. 'The days I have waited!'

The resentment that had simmered up in me on his behalf now boiled over against him. I looked at him in silence.

'That contaminating scarecrow, as you are pleased to call her, is the best friend I have in the world. I need no other.'

'And I', he said harshly, 'have no friend in *this* world, and need you.'

'Then,' said I, 'you have lost your opportunity. Do you suppose I am a child – to be insulted and domineered over only because I am alone? Possibly,' and my lips so trembled that I could hardly frame the words, 'it is *your* face I shall see when I think of those windows.'

I was speaking wiselier than I knew. He turned sharply, and by a play of light it seemed that at one of them there stood looking down on us out of the distance a shape that so had watched for ever, leering darkly out of the void. And there awoke in me the sense of this stranger's extremity of solitude, of his unhappy disguise, of his animal-like patience.

'Why,' I said, 'Mrs. Bowater! You might far rather be *thanking* her for – for –'

'Curses on her,' he choked, turning away. 'There was everything to tell you.'

'What everything?'

'Call her back now,' he muttered furiously.

'That,' I said smoothly, 'is easily done. But, forgive me, I don't know your name.'

His eyes wandered over the turf beneath me, mounted slowly up, my foot to my head, and looked into mine. In their intense regard I seemed to be but a bubble floating away into the air. I shivered, and turned my back on him, without waiting for an answer. He followed me as quietly as a sheep.

Mrs. Bowater had already come sauntering back to our breakfast table, and with gaze impassively fixed on the horizon, pretended not to be aware of our approach.

I smiled back at my companion as we drew near. 'This, Mrs. Bowater,' said I, 'is Mr. Anon. Would you please present him to Miss Thomasina of Bedlam?'

For a moment or two they stood facing one another, just as I have seen two insects stand – motionless, regardful, exchanging each other's presences. Then, after one lightning snap at him from her eye, she rose to my bait like a fish. 'A pleasant morning, sir,' she remarked affably, though in her Bible voice. 'My young lady and I were enjoying the spring air.'

Back to memory comes the darkness of a theatre, and Mrs. Monnerie breathing and sighing beside me, and there on the limelit green of the stage lolls ass-headed Bottom the Weaver cracking jokes with the Fairies.

My Oberon addressed Mrs. Bowater as urbanely as St. George must have addressed the Dragon – or any other customary monster.

He seemed to pass muster, none the less, for she rose, patted her sheet, pushed forward her bonnet on to her rounded temples, and bade him a composed good-morning. She would be awaiting me, she announced, in an hour's time under my beech-tree.

'I think, perhaps, *two*, Mrs. Bowater,' I said firmly.

She gave me a look – all our long slow evening firelit talks together seemed to be swimming in its smile; and withdrew.

The air eddied into quiet again. The stretched-out blue of the sky was as bland and solitary as if a seraph sat dreaming on its eastern outskirts. Mr. Anon and I seated ourselves three or four feet apart, and I watched the sidelong face, so delicately carved against the green; yet sunken in so sullen a stare.

Standing up on his feet against the background of Mrs.

Bowater's ink-black flounces, with his rather humped shoulders and straight hair, he had looked an eccentric, and, even to my view, a stunted figure. Now the whole scene around us seemed to be sorting itself into a different proportion before my eyes. He it was who was become the unit of space, the yard-stick of the universe. The flowers, their roots glintily netted with spider-webs, nodded serenely over his long hands. A peacock butterfly with folded colours sipped of the sunshine on a tuft nearly at evens with his cheek. The very birds sang to his size, and every rift between the woodlands awaited the cuckoo. Only his clothes were grotesque, but less so than in my parlour Mr. Crimble's skirts, or even Lady Pollacke's treacherous bonnet.

I folded my white silk gloves into a ball. A wren began tweeting in a bush near by. 'I am going away soon,' I said, 'to the sea.'

The wren glided away out of sight amongst its thorns. I knew by his sudden stillness that this had been unwelcome news. 'That will be very pleasant for me, won't it?' I said.

'The sea?' he returned coldly, with averted head. 'Well, *I* am bound still further.'

The reply fretted me. I wanted bare facts just then. 'Why are you so angry? What is your name? And where do you live?' It was my turn to ask questions, and I popped them out as if from a *Little by Little*.

And then, with his queer, croaking, yet captivating voice, he broke into a long, low monologue. He gave me his name – and 'Mr. Anon' describes him no worse. He waved his hand vaguely in the direction of the house he lived in. But instead of apologizing for his ill-temper, he accused me of deceiving and humiliating him; of being, so I gathered, a toy of my landlady's, of betraying and soiling myself.

Why all this wild stuff only seemed to flatter me, I cannot say. I listened and laughed, pressing flat with both hands the sorry covers of my book, and laughed also low in my heart.

'Oh, contempt!' he cried. 'I am used to that.'

The words curdled on his tongue as he expressed his loathing of poor Mrs. Bowater and her kind – mere Humanity – that ate and drank in musty houses stuck up out of the happy earth like warts on the skin, that battened on meat, stalked its puddled streets and vile, stifling towns, spread its rank odours on the air, increased and multiplied. Monstrous in shape, automatic, blinded by habit, abandoned by instinct, monkey-like, degraded!

What an unjust tirade! He barked it all out at me as if the blame were mine; as if *I* had nibbled the Apple. I turned my face away, smiling, but listening. Did I realize, he asked me, what a divine fortune it was to be so little, and in this to be All. On and on he raved: I breathed air 'a dewdrop could chill'; I was as near lovely naught made visible as the passing of a flower; the mere mattering of a dream. And when I died my body would be but a perishing flake of manna, and my bones ...

'Yes, a wren's picking,' I rudely interrupted. 'And what of my soul, please? Why, you talk like – like a poet. Besides, you tell me nothing new. I was thinking all that and more on my way here with my landlady. What has *size* to do with it? Why, when I thought of my mother after she was dead, and peered down in the place of my imagination into her grave, I saw her spirit – young, younger than I, and bodiless, and infinitely more beautiful even than she had been in my dreams, floating up out of it, free, sweet, and happy, like a flame – though shadowy. Besides, I don't see how you can help *pitying* men and women. They seem to fly to one another for company; and half their comfort is in their numbers.'

Never in all my life had I put my thoughts into words like this; and he – a stranger.

There fell a silence between us. The natural quietude of the garden was softly settling down and down like infinitesimal grains of sand in a pool of water. It had forgotten that humans were harbouring in its solitude. And still he maintained that his words were not untrue, that he knew mankind better than I, that to fall into their ways and follow their opinions and strivings was to deafen my ears, and seal up my eyes, and lose my very self. 'The Self everywhere,' he said.

And he told me, whether in time or space I know not, of a country whose people were of my stature and slenderness. This was a land, he said, walled in by enormous, ice-capped mountains couching the furnace of the rising sun, and yet set at the ocean's edge. Its sand-dunes ring like dulcimers in the heat. Its valleys of swift rivers were of a green so pale and vivid and so flower-encrusted that an English – even a Kentish – spring is but a coarse and rustic prettiness by comparison. Vine and orange and trees of outlandish names gave their fruits there; yet there also willows swept the winds, and palms spiked the blue with their fans, and the cactus flourished with the tamarisk. Geese, of dark green and snow, were on its inland waters, and a bird clocked the hours of the night, and the conformation of its stars would be strange to my eyes. And such were the lowliness and simplicity of this people's habitations that the most powerful sea-glass, turned upon and searching their secret haunts from a ship becalmed on the ocean, would spy out nothing – nothing there, only world wilderness of snow-dazzling mountain top and green valley, ravine, and condor, and what might just be Nature's small ingenuities – mounds and traceries. Yet within all was quiet loveliness, feet light as goldfinch's, silks fine as gossamer, voices as of a watery beading of silence. And their life being all happiness they have no name for their God. And it seems – according to Mr. Anon's account of it – that such was the ancient history of the world, that Man was so once, but had swollen to his present shape, of which he had lost the true spring and mastery, and had sunk deeper and deeper into a kind of oblivion of the mind, suffocating his past, and now all but insane with pride in his own monstrosities.

All this my new friend (and yet not so *very* new, it seemed) – all this he poured out to me in the garden, though I can only faintly recall his actual words, as if, like Moses, I had smitten the rock. And I listened weariedly, with little hope of understanding him, and with the suspicion that it was nothing but a Tom o' Bedlam's dream he was recounting. Yet, as if in disproof of my own incredulity, there sat I; and over the trees yonder stood Mrs. Bowater's ugly little brick house; and beyond that, the stony, tapering spire of St. Peter's, the High Street. And I looked at him without any affection in my thoughts, and wished fretfully to be gone. What use to be lulled with fantastic pictures of Paradise when I might have died of fear and hatred on Mrs. Stocks's doorstep; when everything I said was 'touching, touching'?

'Well,' I mockingly interposed at last, 'the farthing dip's guttering. And what if it's all true, and there *is* such a place, what then? How am I going to get there, pray? Would you like to mummy me and shut me up in a box and *carry* me there, as they used to in Basman? Years and years ago my father told me of the pygmy men and horses – the same size as yours, I suppose – who lived in caves on the banks of the Nile. But I doubt if I believed in them much, even then. I am not so ignorant as all that.'

The life died out of his face, just as, because of a cloud carried up into the sky, the sunlight at that moment fled from Wanderslore. He coughed, leaning on his hands, and looked in a scared, empty, hunted fashion to right and left. 'Only that you might stay,' he scarcely whispered. '... I love you.'

Instinctively I drew away, lips dry, and heart numbly, heavily beating. An influence more secret than the shadow of a cloud had suddenly chilled and darkened the garden and robbed it of its beauty. I shrank into myself, cold and awkward, and did not dare even to glance at my companion.

'A fine thing', was all I found to reply, 'for a toy, as you call me. I don't know what you mean.'

Miserable enough that memory is when I think of what came after, for now my only dread was that he might really be out of his wits, and might make my beloved, solitary garden for ever hateful to me. I drew close my cape, and lifted my book.

'There is a private letter of mine hidden under that stone,' I said coldly. 'Will you please be so good as to fetch it out for me? And you are never, never to say that again.'

The poor thing looked so desperately ill and forsaken with his humped shoulders – and that fine, fantastic story still ringing in my ears! – that a kind of sadness came over me, and I hid my face in my hands.

'The letter is not there,' said his voice.

I drew my fingers from my face, and glared at him from between them; then scrambled to my feet. Out swam the sun again, drenching all around us with its light and heat.

'Next time I come', I shrilled at him, 'the letter *will* be there. The thief will have put it back again! Oh, how unhappy you have made me!'

Chapter Twenty-Seven

I stumbled off, feeling smaller and smaller as I went, more and more ridiculous and insignificant, as indeed I must have appeared; for distance can hardly lend enchantment to any view of *me*. Not one single look did I cast behind; but now that my feelings began to quiet down, I began also to think. And a pretty muddle of mind it was. What had enraged and embittered me so? If only I had remained calm. Was it that my pride, my vanity, had in some vague fashion been a punishment of him for Fanny's unkindness to me?

'But he stole, he *stole* my letter,' I said aloud, stamping my foot on a budding violet; and – there was Mrs. Bowater. Evidently she had been watching my approach, and now smiled benignly.

'Why, you are quite out of breath, miss; and your cheeks! ... I hope you haven't been having words. A better spoken young fellow than I had fancied; and I'm sure I ask his pardon for the "gentleman".'

'Ach,' I swept up at my beech tree, now cautiously unsheathing its first green buds in the lower branches, 'I think he must be light in his head.'

'And that often comes', replied Mrs. Bowater, with undisguised *bonhomie*, 'from being heavy at the heart. Why, miss, he may be a young nobleman in disguise. There's unlikelier things even than that, to judge from that trash of Fanny's. While, as for fish in the sea – it's sometimes wise to be contented with what we can catch.'

Who had been talking to me about fish in the sea – quite lately? I thought contemptuously of Pollie and the Dream Book. 'I am sorry,' I replied, nose in air, 'but I cannot follow the allusion.'

The charge of vulgarity was the very last, I think, which Mrs. Bowater would have lifted a finger to refute. My cheeks flamed hotter to know that she was quietly smiling up there. We walked on in silence.

That night I could not sleep. I was afraid. Life was blackening my mind like the mould of a graveyard. I could think of nothing but one face, one voice – that scorn and longing, thought and fantasy. What if he did love me a little? I might at least have been kind to him. Had I so many friends that I could afford to be harsh and ungrateful? How dreadfully ill he had looked when I scoffed at him. And now what might *not* have happened to him? I seemed lost to myself. No wonder Fanny ... My body grew cold at a thought; the palms of my hands began to ache.

Half-stifled, I leapt out of bed, and without the least notion of what I was doing, hastily dressed myself, and fled out into the night. I must find him, talk to him, plead with him, before it was too late. And in the trickling starlight, pressed against my own gatepost – there he was.

'Oh,' I whispered at him in a fever of relief and shame and apprehensiveness, 'what are you doing here? You must go away at once, at once. I forgive you. Yes, yes; I forgive you. But – at once. Keep the letter for me till I come again.' His hand was wet with the dew. 'Oh, and never say it again. Please, please, if you care for

me the least bit in the world, never, never say what you did again.'
I poured out the heedless words in the sweet-scented quiet of
midnight. 'Now – now go,' I entreated. 'And indeed, indeed I am
your friend.'

The dark eyes shone quietly close to mine. He sighed. He lifted
my fingers, and put them to my breast again. He whispered unintelligible words between us, and was gone. No more stars for me
that night. I slept sound until long after dawn ...

Softly as thistledown the days floated into eternity; yet they were
days of expectation and action. April was her fickle self; not so
Mrs. Monnerie. Her letter to Mrs. Bowater must have been a
marvel of tact. Apartments had been engaged for us at a little
watering-place in Dorsetshire, called Lyme Regis. Mrs. Bowater
and I were to spend at least a fortnight there alone together, and
after our return Mrs. Monnerie herself was to pay me a visit, and
see with her own eyes if her prescription had been successful. After
that, perhaps, if I were so inclined, and my landlady agreed with
Mr. Pellew that it would be good for me, I might spend a week or
two with her in London. What a twist of the kaleidoscope. I had
sown never a pinch of seed, yet here was everything laughing and
blossoming around me, like the wilderness in Isaiah.

Indeed my own looking-glass told me how wan and languishing a Miss M. was pining for change of scene and air. She rejoiced
that Fanny was enjoying herself, rejoiced that she was going to enjoy
herself too. I searched Mrs. Bowater's library for views of the sea, but
without much reward. So I read over Mr. Bowater's Captain Maury
– on the winds and monsoons and tide-rips and hurricanes, freshened up my *Robinson Crusoe*, and dreamed of the Angels with the
Vials. In the midst of my packing (and I spread it out for sheer

amusement's sake) Mr. Crimble called again. He looked nervous, gloomy, and hollow-eyed.

I was fast becoming a mistress in affairs of the sensibilities. Yet, when, kneeling over my open trunk, I heard him in the porch, I mimicked Fanny's 'Dash!' and wished to goodness he had postponed his visit until only echo could have answered his knock. It fretted me to be bothered with him. And now? What would I not give to be able to say I had done my best and utmost to help him when he wanted it? Here is a riddle I can find no answer to, however long I live: How is it that our eyes cannot foresee, our very hearts cannot forefeel, the future? And how should we act if that future were plain before us? Yet, even then, what could I have said to him to comfort him? Really and truly I had no candle with which to see into that dark mind.

In actual fact my task was difficult and delicate enough. In spite of her vow not to write again, yet another letter had meanwhile come from Fanny. If Mr. Crimble's had afforded 'a ray of hope', this had shut it clean away. It was full of temporizings, wheedlings, evasions – and brimming over with Fanny.

It suggested, too, that Mrs. Bowater must have misread the name of her holiday place. The half-legible printing of the postmark on the envelope – fortunately I had intercepted the postman – did not even begin with an M. And no address was given within. I was to tell Mr. Crimble that Fanny was overtired and depressed by the term's work, that she simply couldn't set her 'weary mind' to anything, and as for decisions:

> He seems to think only of himself. You couldn't believe, Midgetina, what nonsense the man talks. He can't *see* that all poor Fanny's future is at stake, body and soul. Tell him if he *wants* her to smile, he must sit in patience on a pedestal,

and smile too. One simply can't trust the poor creature with cold, sober facts. His mother, now – why, I could read it in your own polite little description of her at your Grand Reception – she smiles and smiles. So did the Cheshire Cat.

'But oh, dear Fanny, time and your own true self, God helping, would win her over.' So writes H. C. That's candid enough, if you look into it; but it isn't sense. Once hostile, old ladies are *not* won over. They don't care much for mind in the young. Anyhow, one look at me was enough for her – and it was followed by a sharp little peer at poor Harold! She guessed. So you see, my dear, even for youthful things, like you and me, time gathers roses a jolly sight faster than we can, and it would have to be the *fait accompli*, before a word is breathed to her. That is, if I could take a deep breath and say yes.

But I can't. I ask you: can you *see* Fanny Bowater a Right Reverendissima? No, nor can I. And not even gaiters or an apron here and now would settle the question offhand. Why I confide all this in you (why, for that matter, it has all been confided in *me*), I know not. You want nothing, and if you did, you wouldn't want it long. Now, would you? Perhaps that is the secret. But Fanny wants a good deal. She cannot even guess how much. So, while Miss Stebbings and Beechwood Hill for ever and ever would be hell before purgatory, H. C. and St. Peter's would be merely the same thing, with the fires *out*. And I am quite sure that, given a chance, heaven is our home.

Oh, Midgetina, I listen to all this; mumbling my heart like a dog a bone. What the devil has it got to do with *me*, I ask myself? Who set the infernal trap? If only I could stop thinking and mocking and find someone – not 'to love me' (between ourselves, there are far too many of *them* already), but capable of making me love him. They say a woman can't be driven. I disagree. She *can* be driven – mad. And apart from that, though twenty men only succeed in giving me hydrophobia, one could persuade me to drink, if only his name was Mr. Right, as Mother succinctly puts it.

But first and last, I am having a real, if not a particularly sagacious, holiday, and can take care of myself. And next and last, play, I *beseech* you, the tiny good Samaritan between me and poor, plodding blinded H. C. – even if he does eventually have to go on to Jericho.

And I shall ever remain, your most affec. – F.

How all this baffled me. I tried, but dismally failed, to pour a trickle of wine and oil into Mr. Crimble's wounded heart, for his sake and for mine, not for Fanny's, for I knew in myself that his 'Jericho' was already within view.

'I don't understand her; I don't understand her,' he kept repeating, crushing his soft hat in his small, square hands. 'I cannot reach her; I am not in touch with her.'

Out of the fount of my womanly wisdom I reminded him how young she was, how clever, and how much flattered.

'You know, then, there are – others?' he gulped, darkly meeting me.

'That, surely, is what makes her so precious,' I falsely insinuated.

He gazed at me, his eyes like an immense, empty shop window. 'That thought puts ... I can't'; and he twisted his head on his shoulders as if shadows were around him; 'I can't bear to think of her and – with – *others*. It unbalances me. But how can you underrstand? ... A sealed book. Last night I sat at my window. It was raining. I know not the hour! and Spring!' He clutched at his knees, stooping forward. 'I repudiated myself, thrust myself out. Oh, believe me, we are not alone. And there and then I resolved to lay the whole matter before' – his glance groped towards the door – 'before, in fact, her *mother*. She is a woman of sagacity, of proper feeling in her station, though how she came to be the mother of ... but that's neither here nor there. We mustn't probe. Probably she thinks ... but what use to consider it? One word to her – and Fanny would be lost to me for ever.' For a moment it seemed his eyes closed on me. 'How can I bring myself to speak of it?' a remote voice murmured from beneath them.

I looked at the figure seated there in its long black coat; and far away in my mind whistled an ecstatic bird – 'The sea! the sea! You are going away – out, out of all this.'

So, too was Mr. Crimble, if only I had known it. It was my weak and cowardly acquiescence in Fanny's deceits that was speeding him on his dreadful journey. None the less, a wretched heartless impatience fretted me at being thus helplessly hemmed in by my fellow creatures. How clumsily they groped on. Why couldn't they be happy in just living free from the clouds and trammels of each other and of themselves? The selfish helplessness of it all. It was, indeed, as though the strange fires which Fanny had burnt me in – which any sudden thought of her could still fan into a flickering blaze – had utterly died down. Whether or not, I was hardened; a poor little earthenware pot fresh from the furnace. And with what elixir was it brimmed.

I rose from my chair, walked away from my visitor, and peered through my muslin curtains at the green and shine and blue. A nursemaid was lagging along with a sleeping infant – its mild face to the sky – in a perambulator. A faint drift of dandelions showed in the stretching meadow. Kent's blue hems lay calm; my thoughts drew far away.

'Mr. Crimble,' I cried in a low voice, 'is she *worth* all our care for her?'

'"Our" – "our"?' he expostulated.

'Mine, then. When I gave her, just to be friends, because – because I loved her, a little ivory box, nothing of any value, of course, but which I have loved and treasured since childhood, she left it without a thought. It's in my wardrobe drawer – shall I show it to you? I *say* it was nothing in itself; but what I mean is that she just makes use of me, and with far less generosity than – than other people do. Her eyes, her voice, when she moves her hand, turns her head, looks back – oh, I know! But', and I turned on him in the light, 'does it mean anything? Let us just help her all we can, and – keep away.'

It was a treachery past all forgiveness: I see that now. If only I had said: 'Love on, love on! ask nothing.' But I did not say it. A contempt of all this slow folly was in my brain that afternoon. Why couldn't the black cowering creature take himself off? What concern of mine was his sick, sheepish look? What particle of a fig did he care for Me? Had he lifted a little finger when I myself bitterly needed it? I seemed to be struggling in a net of hatred.

He raised himself in his chair, his spectacles still fixed on me; as if some foul insect had erected its blunt head at him.

'Then *you* are against her too,' he uttered, under his breath. 'I might have known it, I might have known it. I am a lost man.'

It was pitiful. 'Lost fiddlesticks!' I snapped back at him, with bared teeth. 'I wouldn't – I've never harmed a fly. Who, I should like to know, came to *my* help when ...?' But I choked down the words. Silence fell between us. The idiot clock chimed five. He turned his face away to conceal the aversion that had suddenly overwhelmed him at sight of me.

'I see,' he said, in a hollow, low voice, with his old wooden, artificial dignity. 'There's nothing more to say. I can only thank you,

and be gone. I had not realized. You misjudge her. You haven't the
– How could it be expected? But there! thinking's impossible.'

How often had I seen my poor father in his last heavy days
draw his hand across his eyes like that? Already my fickle mind
was struggling to find words with which to retract, to explain
away that venomous outbreak. But I let him go. The stooping,
hatted figure hastened past my window; and I was never to see
him again.

Chapter Twenty-Eight

Yet, in spite of misgivings, no very dark foreboding companioned me that evening. With infinite labour I concocted two letters:

> DEAR MR. CRIMBLE – I regret my words this afternoon. Bitterly. Indeed I do. But still truth is important, isn't it? *One we know* hasn't been too kind to either of us. I still say that. And if it seems inconsiderate, please remember Shakespeare's lines about the beetle (which I came across in a Birthday Book the other day) – a creature I detest. Besides, we can return good for evil – I can't help this sounding like hypocrisy – even though it *is* an extremely tiring exchange. I *feel* small enough just now, but would do anything in the world that would help in the way we both want. I hope that you will believe this and that you will forgive my miserable tongue. Believe me, ever yours sincerely – M.M.

My second letter was addressed to Fanny's school, 'c/o Miss Stebbings':

> DEAR FANNY – He came again today and looks like a corpse. I can do no more. You must know how utterly miserable you are making him; that I can't, and won't, go on being so doublefaced. I don't call *that* being the good Samaritan. Throw the stone one way or the other, however many birds it may

kill. That's the bravest thing to do. A horrid boy I knew as a child once aimed at a jay and killed – a wren. Well, there's only one wren that I know of – your M.

P.S. – I hope this doesn't sound an angry letter. I thought only the other day how difficult it must be being as fascinating as you are. And, of course, we are *what* we are, aren't we, and cannot, I suppose, help acting like that? You can't think how he looked, and talked. Besides, I am sure you will enjoy your holiday much more when you have made up your mind. Oh, Fanny, I can't say what's in mine. Every day there's something else to dread. And all that I do seems only to make things worse. *Do* write! and, though, of course, it isn't my affair, do have a '*sagacious*' holiday, too.

Mrs. Bowater almost squinted at my two small envelopes when she licked the stamps for me. 'We can only hope', was her one remark, 'that when the secrets of all hearts are opened, they'll excuse some of the letters we reach ourselves to write.' But I did not ask her to explain.

Lyme Regis was but a few days distant when, not for the first time since our meeting at Mrs. Bowater's gatepost, I set off to meet Mr. Anon – this time to share with him my wonderful news. When showers drifted across the sun-shafted sky we took refuge under the shelter of the garden-house. As soon as the hot beams set the raindrops smouldering, so that every bush was hung with coloured lights, we returned to my smoking stone. And we watched a rainbow arch and fade in the windy blue.

He was gloomy at first; grudged me, I think, every moment that was to be mine at Lyme Regis. So I tempted him into talking about the books he had read; and about his childhood – far from as happy as mine. It hurt me to hear him speak of his mother. Then I asked him small questions about that wonderful country he had told me of, which, whether it had any real existence or not, filled me with delight as he painted it in his imagination. He was doing his best to keep his word to me, and I to keep our talk from becoming personal.

If I would trust myself to him, friend to friend – he suddenly broke out in a thick, low voice, when I least expected it – the whole world was open to us; and he knew the way.

'What way?' said I. 'And how about poor Mrs. Bowater? How strange you are. Where do you live? May I know?'

There was an old farmhouse, he told me, on the other side of the park, and near it a few cottages – at the far end of Loose Lane. He lodged in one of these. Against my wiser inclinations he persuaded me to set off thither at once and see the farm for myself.

On the further side of Wanderslore, sprouting their pallid green frondlets like beads at the very tips of their black, were more yews than beeches. We loitered on, along the neglected bridle-path. Cuckoos were now in the woods, and we talked and talked, as if their voices alone were not seductive enough to enchant us onwards. Sometimes I spelled out incantations in the water; and sometimes I looked out happily across the wet, wayside flowers; and sometimes a robin flittered out to observe the intruders. How was it that human company so often made me uneasy and self-conscious, and nature's always brought peace?

'Now, you said', I began again, 'that they have a God, and that they are so simple He hasn't a name. What did you mean by that? There can't be one God for the common-sized, and one for – for me; now, can there? My mother never taught me that; and I have thought for myself.' Indeed I had.

'"God!"' he cried; 'why, what is all this?'

All this at that moment was a clearing in the woods, softly

shimmering with a misty, transparent green, in whose sunbeams a thousand flies darted and zigzagged like motes of light, and the year's first butterflies fluttered and languished.

'But if I speak,' I said, 'listen, now, my voice is just swallowed up. Out of just a something it faints into a nothing – dies. No, no' (I suppose I was arguing only to draw him out), 'all this cares no more for me than – than a looking-glass. Yet it is mine. Can you see Jesus Christ in these woods? Do you believe we are sinners and that He came to save us? I do. But I can see Him only as a little boy, you know, smiling, crystal, intangible; and yet I do not *like* children much.'

He paused and stared at me fixedly. '*My* size?' he coughed.

'Oh, size,' I exclaimed, 'how you harp on that!' – as if *I* never had. 'Did you not say yourself that the smaller the body is, the happier the ghost in it? Bodies, indeed!'

He plunged on, hands in pockets, frowning, clumsy. And up there in the north-west a huge cloud poured its reflected lights on his strange face. Inwardly – with all my wits in a pleasant scatter – I laughed; and outwardly (all but) danced. Solemnly taking me at my word, and as if he were reading out of one of his dry old books, he began to tell me his views about religion, and about what we are, qualities, consciousness, ideas, and that kind of thing. As if you could be anything at any moment but just that moment's whole self. At least, so it seemed then: I was happy. But since in his earnestness his voice became almost as false to itself as was Mr. Crimble's when he had conversed with me about Hell, my eyes stole my ears from him, and only a few scattered sentences reached my mind.

Nevertheless I enjoyed hearing him talk, and encouraged him with bits of questions and exclamations. Did he believe, perhaps, in the pagan gods? – Mars and all that? Was there, even at this very moment, cramped up among the moss and the roots, a crazy, brutal Pan in the woods? And those delicious Nymphs and Naiads! What would he do if one beckoned to him? – or Pan's pipes began wheedling?

'Nymphs!' he grunted, 'aren't you –'

'Oh,' I cried, coming to a pause beside a holly tree so marvellously sparkling with waterdrops on every curved spine of it that it took my breath away: 'let's talk no more thoughts. They are only mice gnawing. I can hear *them* at night.'

'You cannot sleep?' he inquired, with so grave a concern that I laughed outright.

'Sleep! with that Mr. Crimble on my nerves?' I gave a little nod in my mind to my holly, and we went on.

'Crimble?' he repeated. His eyes, greenish at that moment, shot an angry glance at me from under their lids. 'Who is he?'

'A friend, a friend,' I replied, 'and, poor man, as they say, in love. Calm yourself, Mr. Jealousy; not with me. I am three sizes too small. With Miss Bowater. But there,' I went on, in dismay that mere vanity should have let this cat out of its bag, 'that's not my secret. We mustn't talk of that either. What I really want to tell you is that we haven't much time. I am going away. Let's talk of Me. Oh, Mr. Anon, shall I ever be born again, and belong to my own world?'

It seemed a kind of mournful serenity came over his face. 'You say you are going away,' he whispered, pointing with his finger, 'and yet you expect me to talk about *that*.'

We were come to the brink of a clear rain-puddle, perhaps three or four feet wide, in the moss-greened, stony path, and '*that*' was the image of myself which lay on its surface against the far blue of the sky – the under-scarlet of my cape, my face, fair hair, eyes. I trembled a little. His own reflection troubled me more than he did himself.

'Come,' I said, laying a hand on his sleeve, 'the time's so short, and indeed I *must* see your house, you know: you have seen mine. Ah, but you should see Lyndsey and Chizzel Hill, and the stream in my father's garden. I often hear *that* at night, Mr. Anon. I would like to have died a child, however long I must live.'

But now the cloud had completely swallowed up the sun; a cold gust of wind swept hooting down on us, and I clung to his arm. We pushed on, emerged at last from the rusty gates, its eagles green and scaling, and came to the farm. But not in time. A cloud of hail had swirled down, beating on our heads and shoulders. It all but swept me up into the air. Catching hands, we breasted and edged on up the rough, miry lane towards a thatched barn, open on one side and roofing a red and blue wagon. Under this we scrambled, and tingling all over with the buffetings of the wind and the pelting of hailstones, I sat laughing and secure, watching, over my sodden skirts and shoes, the sweeping, pattering drifts paling the green.

Around us in the short straw and dust stalked the farmer's fowls, cackling, with red-eyed glances askew at our intrusion. Ducks were quacking. Doves flew in with whir of wing. I thought I should boil over with delight. And presently a sheep-dog, ears down and tail between its legs, slid round the beam of the barn door. Half in, half out, it stood bristling, eyes fixed, head thrust out. My companion drew himself up and with a large stone in his hand, edged, stooping and stealthily – and very much, I must confess, like the picture of a Fuegian I have seen in a book – between the gaudy wheels of the wagon, and faced the low-growling beast.

I watched him, enthralled. For a moment or two he and the sheep-dog confronted each other without stirring. Then with one sharp bark, the animal flung back its head, and with whitened eye, turned and disappeared.

'Oh, *bravissimo*!' said I, mocking up at Mr. Anon from under my hood. 'He was cowed, poor thing. *I* would have made friends with him.'

We sat on in the sweet, dusty scent of the stormy air. The hail turned to rain. The wind rose higher. I began to be uneasy. So heavily streamed the water out of the clouds that walking back by the way we had come would be utterly impossible for me. What's to be done now? I thought to myself. Yet the liquid song of the rain, the gurgling sighs and trumpetings of the wind entranced me; and I turned softly to glance at my stranger. He sat, chin on large-boned hands, his lank hair plastered on his hollow temples by the rain, his eyes glassy in profile.

'I am glad of this,' he muttered dreamily, as if in response to my scrutiny. 'We are here.'

A scatter of green leaf-sheaths from a hawthorn over against the barn was borne in by the wind.

'I am glad too,' I answered, 'because when you are at peace, so I can be; for that marvellous land you tell me of is very far away. Why, who – ?' But he broke in so earnestly that I was compelled to listen, confiding in me some queer wisdom he had dug up out of his books – of how I might approach nearer and nearer to the brink between life and reality, and see all things as they are, in truth, in their very selves. All things visible are only a veil, he said. A veil that withdraws itself when the mind is empty of all thoughts and desires, and the heart at one with itself. That is divine happiness, he said. And he told me, too, out of his far-fetched learning, a secret about myself.

It was cold in the barn now. The fowls huddled close. Rain and wind ever and again drowned the low, alluring, far-away voice wandering on as if out of a trance. Dreams, maybe; yet I have learned since that one half of his tale is true; that at need even an afflicted spirit, winged for an instant with serenity, may leave the body and, perhaps, if lost in the enchantments beyond, never turn back. But I swore to keep his words secret between us. I had no will to say otherwise, and assured him of my trust in him.

'My very dear,' he said, softly touching my hand, but I could make no answer.

He scrambled to his feet and peered down on me. 'It is not my peace. All the days you are away ...' He gulped forlornly and turned away his head. 'But that is what I mean. Just nothing, all this' – he made a gesture with his hands as if giving himself up a captive to authority – 'nothing but a sop to a dog.'

Then stooping, he drew my cape around me, banked the loose hay at my feet and shoulders, smiled into my face, and bidding me wait in patience a while, but not sleep, was gone.

The warmth and odour stole over my senses. I was neither hungry nor thirsty, but drugged with fatigue. With a fixed smile on my face (a smile betokening, as I believe now, little but feminine vanity and satisfaction after feeding on that strange heart), my thoughts went wandering. The sounds of skies and earth drowsed my senses, and I nodded off into a nap. The grinding of wheels awoke me. From a welter of dreams I gazed out through the opening of the barn at a little battered cart and a shaggy pony. And behold, on the chopped straw and hay beside me, lay stretched out, nose on paw, our enemy, the sheep-dog. He thumped a friendly tail at me, while he growled at my deliverer.

Thoughtful Mr. Anon. He had not only fetched the pony-cart, but had brought me a bottle of hot milk and a few raisins. They warmed and revived me. A little light-witted after my sleep in the hay, I clambered up with his help into the cart and tucked myself in as snugly as I could with my draggled petticoats and muddy shoes. So with myself screened well out of sight of prying eyes, we drove off.

All this long while I had not given a thought to Mrs. Bowater. We stood before her at last in her oil-cloth passage, like Adam and Eve in the Garden. Her oldest bonnet on her head, she was just about to set off to the police station. And instead of showing her gratitude that her anxieties on my account were over, Mrs. Bowater cast us the blackest of looks. Leaving Mr. Anon to make our peace with her, I ran off to change my clothes. As I emerged from my bedroom, he entered at the door, in an old trailing pilot coat many sizes too large for him, and I found to my astonishment that he and my landlady had become the best of friends. I marvelled. This little achievement of Mr. Anon's made me *like* him – all of a burst – ten times as much, I believe, as he would have been contented that I should *love* him.

Indeed the 'high tea' Mrs. Bowater presided over that afternoon, sitting above her cups and saucers just like a clergyman, is one of the gayest memories of my life. And yet – she had left the room for a moment to fetch something from the kitchen, and as, in a self-conscious hush, Mr. Anon and I sat alone together, I caught a glimpse of her on her return pausing in the doorway, her capped head almost touching the lintel – and looking in on us with a quizzical, benign, foolish expression on her face, like that of a grown-up peeping into a child's dolls' house. So swirling a gust of hatred and disillusionment swept over me at sight of her, that for some little while I dared not raise my eyes and look at Mr. Anon. All affection and gratitude fled away. Miss M. was once more an Ishmael!

Lyme Regis

* * *

Chapter Twenty-Eight

Out of a cab from a livery stable Mrs. Bowater and I alighted at
our London terminus next morning, to find positively awaiting us
beside the wooden platform a first-class railway carriage – a pala-
tial apartment. Swept and garnished, padded and varnished – a
miracle of wealth! At this very moment I seem to be looking up
in awe at the orange-rimmed (I think it was orange) label stuck
on the glass whose inscription I afterwards spelled out backwards
from within! 'Mrs. Bywater and Party'. As soon as we and our luggage were safely settled, an extremely polite and fatherly guard
locked the door on us. At this Mrs. Bowater was a little troubled
by the thought of how we should fare in the event of an accident.
But he reassured her.

'Never fear, ma'am; accidents are strictly forbidden on this
line. Besides *which*,' he added, with a solemn, turtle-like stare, 'if I
turn the key on the young lady, none of them young a-ogling Don
Jooans can force their way in. Strict orders, ma'am.'

To make assurance doubly sure, Mrs. Bowater pulled down
the blinds at every stopping-place. We admired the scenery. We
read the warning against pickpockets, and I translated it out of
the French. After examining the enormous hotels depicted in the

advertisement, we agreed there was nothing like home comforts. Mrs. Bowater continued to lose and find in turn our tickets, her purse, her spectacle-case, her cambric pocket-handkerchief, not to mention a mysterious little screw of paper, containing lozenges I think. She scrutinized our luxury with grim determination. And we giggled like two schoolgirls as we peeped together through the crevices of the blinded windows at the rich, furry passengers who ever and again hurried along, casting angry glances at our shrouded windows.

It being so early in the year – but how mild and sweet a day – there were few occupants of the coach at Axminster. As I had once made a (frequently broken) vow to do at once what scared me, I asked to be perched up on the box beside the lean, brick-faced driver. Thus giddily exalted above his three cantering roan horses, we bowled merrily along. With his whip he pointed out to me every 'object of interest' as it went floating by – church and inn, farm and mansion.

'Them's peewits,' he would bawl. 'And that's the self-same cottage where lived the little old 'ooman what lived in a shoe.' He stooped over me, reins in fist, with his seamed red face and fiery little eye, as if I were a small child home for the holidays. Evening sunlight on the hilltops and shadowy in the valleys. And presently the three stepping horses – vapour jetting from their nostrils, their sides panting like bellows – dragged the coach up a hill steeper than ever. 'And that there,' said the driver, as we surmounted the crest – and as if for emphasis he gave a prodigious tug at an iron bar beside him, 'that there's the Sea.'

The Sea. Flat, bow-shaped, hazed, remote, and of a blue stilling my eyes as with a dream – I verily believe the saltest tears I ever shed in my life smarted on my lids as the spirit in me fled away, to

be alone with that far loveliness. A desire almost beyond endur-
ance devoured me. 'Yes,' cried hidden self to self, 'I can never,
never love him; but he shall take me away – away – away. Oh, how
I have wasted my days, sick for home.'

But small opportunity was given me for these sentimental
reflections. Nearly at the foot of even another hill, and one so pre-
cipitous that during its rattling descent I had to cling like a spider
to the driver's strap, we came to a standstill; and in face of a gaping
knot of strangers I was lifted down – with a 'There! Miss Nan-
tuckety', from the driver – from my perch to the pavement.

The lodgings Mrs. Monnerie had taken for us proved to be the
sea rooms in a small, white, bow-windowed house on the front,
commanding the fishing-boats, the harbour, and the stone Cobb.
I tasted my lips, snuffed softly with my nose, stole a look over the
Bay, and glanced at Mrs. Bowater. Was she, too, half-demented
with this peculiar and ravishing experience? I began to shiver; but
not with cold, with delight.

Face creased up in a smile (the wind had stiffened the skin),
cheeks tingling, and ravenously hungry, I watched the ceremoni-
ous civilities that were passing between landlady and landlady;
Mrs. Bowater angular and spare; Mrs. Petrie round, dumpy,
smooth, and a little bald. My friend Mrs. Monnerie was evidently
a lady whose lightest word was Sesame. Every delicacy and luxury
that Lyme out of its natural resources can have squandered on
King George III was ours without the asking.

Mrs. Bowater, it is true, at our sea-fish breakfast next morning,
referred in the first place to the smell of drains; next to fleas; and
last to greasy cooking. But who should have the privilege of calling the Kettle black unless the Pot? Moreover, we were 'first-class'
visitors, and *had* to complain of something. I say 'we', but since, in

the first place, all the human houses that I have ever entered have been less sweet to the nose than mere country out-of-doors; since next (as I discovered when I was a child) there must be some ichor or acid in my body unpleasing to Man's parasites; and since, last, I cannot bear cooked animals; these little inconveniences, even if they had not existed solely in Mrs. Bowater's fancy, would not have troubled me.

The days melted away. We would sally out early, while yet many of Lyme's kitchen chimneys were smokeless, and would return with the shadows of evening. How Mrs. Bowater managed to sustain so large a frame for so many hours together on a few hard biscuits and a bottle of cold tea, I cannot discover. Her mood, like our weather that April, was almost always 'set fair', and her temper never above a comfortable sixty degrees. We hired a goat-chaise, and with my flaxen hair down my back under a sun-bonnet, I drove Reuben up and down the Esplanade – both of us passable ten-year-olds to a careless observer. My cheeks and hands were scorched by the sun; Mrs. Bowater added more and more lilac and white to her outdoor attire; and Mrs. Petrie lent her a striped, and once handsome parasol with a stork's head for handle, which had been left behind by a visitor – otherwise unendeared.

On warm mornings we would choose some secluded spot on the beach, or on the fragrant, green-turfed cliffs, or in the Uplyme meadows. Though I could never persuade Mrs. Bowater to join me, I sometimes dabbled in the sun in some ice-cold, shallow, seaweedy pool between the rocks. Then, while she read the newspaper, or crocheted, I also, over book or needle, indulged in endless reverie. For hours together, with eyes fixed on the glass-green, tumbling water, I would listen to its enormous, far, phantom bells and voices, happier than words can tell. And I would lie at full length, basking in the heat, for it was a hot May, almost wishing that the huge furnace of the sun would melt me away into a little bit of glass! and what colour would that have been, I wonder? If a small heart can fall in love with the whole world, that heart was mine. But the very intensity of this greed and delight – and the tiniest shell or pebble on the beach seemed to be all but exploding with it – was a severe test of my strength.

One late twilight, I remember, as we idled homeward, the planet Venus floating like a luminous water-drop in the primrose of the western sky, we passed by a low white-walled house beneath trees. And from an open window came into the quiet the music of a fiddle. What secret decoy was in that air I cannot say. I stopped dead, looking about me as if for refuge, and drinking in the while the gliding, lamenting sounds.

Curiously perturbed, I caught at Mrs. Bowater's skirt. Sky and darkening headland seemed to be spinning around me – melting out into a dream. 'Oh, Mrs. Bowater,' I whispered, as if I were drowning, 'it is strange for us to be here.'

She dropped herself on the grass beside me, brushing with her dress the scent of wild thyme into the dewy air, and caught my hands in hers. Her long face close to mine, she gently shook me: 'Now, now; now, now!' she called. 'Come back, my pretty one. See! It's me, me, Mrs. Bowater ... The love she's been to me!'

I smiled, groped with my hand, opened my eyes in the dimness to answer her. But a black cloud came over them; and the next thing I recall is waking to find myself being carried along in her arms, cold and half lifeless; and she actually breaking ever and again into a shambling run, as she searched my face in what seemed, even to my scarcely conscious brain, an extravagant anxiety.

WALTER DE LA MARE

Four days afterwards – and I completely restored – we found on the breakfast table of our quiet sea-room an unusually bountiful post: a broad, impressive-looking letter and a newspaper for Mrs. Bowater, and a parcel, from Fanny, for me. Time and distance had divided me from the past more than I had supposed. The very sight of her handwriting gave me a qualm. 'Fanny! Oh, my heavens,' cried a voice in me, 'what's wrong now?'

But removing the brown paper I found only a book, and it being near to my size as books go, I opened it with profound relief. My joy was premature. The book Fanny had sent me was by Bishop Jeremy Taylor, *Holy Living and Dying: with Prayers containing the Whole Duty of a Christian*. I read over and over this title with a creeping misgiving and dismay, and almost in the same instant, detected, lightly fastened between its fly-leaves, and above its inscription – 'To Midgetina: In Memoriam' – an inch or two of paper, pencilled over in Fanny's minutest characters.

A slow, furtive glance discovered Mrs. Bowater far too deeply absorbed to have noticed my small movements. She was sitting bolt upright, her forehead drawn crooked in an unusual frown. An open letter lay beside her plate. She was staring into, rather than at, her newspaper. With infinite stealth I slipped Fanny's scrap of paper under the tablecloth, folded it small, and pushed it into my skirt pocket. 'A present from Fanny,' I cried in a clear voice at last.

But Mrs. Bowater, with drooping, pallid face, and gaze now fixed deep on a glass case containing three stuffed, aquatic birds, had not heard me. I waited, watching her. She folded the newspaper and removed her spectacles. 'On our return', she began inconsequently, 'the honourable Mrs. Monnerie has invited you to stay in her London house – not for a week or two; for good. That's all as it should be, I suppose, seeing that pay's pay and mine is no other call on you.'

The automatic voice ceased with a gasp. Her thoughts appeared to be astray. She pushed her knotted fingers up her cheeks almost to her eyes.

'It's said', she added, with long straight mouth, 'that that unfortunate young man, Mr. Crimble – is ill.' She gave a glance at me without appearing to see me, and left the room.

What was amiss? Oh, this world! I sat trembling in empty dread, listening to her heavy, muffled footfall in the room above. The newspaper, with a scrawling cross on its margin, lay beside Mrs. Monnerie's large, rough-edged envelope. I could bear the suspense no longer. On hands and knees I craned soundlessly forward over the white tablecloth, across the rank dish of coagulating bacon fat, and stole one or two of the last few lines of grey-black print at the foot of the column: 'The reverend gentleman leaves a widowed mother. He was an only son, and was in his twenty-ninth year.'

'Leaves' – 'was' – the dingy letters blurred my sight. Footsteps were approaching. I huddled back to my carpet stool on the chair. Mrs. Petrie had come to clear away the breakfast things. Stonily I listened while she cheerfully informed me that the glass was still rising, that she didn't recollect such weather not for the month for ten years or more. 'You must be what I've heard called an 'alcyon, miss.' She nodded her congratulations at me, and squinnied at the untasted bacon.

'I am going for a breath of air, Mrs. Petrie,' came Mrs. Bowater's voice through the crack of the door. 'Will you kindly be ready for your walk, miss, in half an hour?'

Left once more to myself, I heard the alarm clock on the mantelpiece ticking as if every beat were being forced out of its works, and might be its last. An early fly or two – my strange, familiar friends – darted soundlessly beneath the ceiling. The sea was shimmering like an immense looking-glass. More pungent than I had ever remembered it, the refreshing smell of seaweed eddied in at the open window.

With dry mouth and a heart that jerked my body with its beatings, I unfolded Fanny's scrap of paper!

> WISE M. – I have thrown the stone. And now I am fey for my own poor head. Could you – and – will you absolutely secretly send me any money you can spare? £15 if possible. I'm in a hole – full fathom five – but mean to get out of it. I ask you, rather than mother, because I remember you said once you were putting money by out of that young lady's independence of yours. Notes would be best! if not, a Post Office Order to this address, somehow. I must trust to luck, and to your wonderful enterprise, if you would be truly a dear. It's only until my next salary. If you can't – or won't – help me, damnation is over my head; but I bequeathe you a kiss all honey and roses none the less, and am, pro tem., your desperate F.
>
> P.S. – Be sure not to give M. this address; and in a week or two we shall all be laughing and weeping together over the Prodigal Daughter.

Fanny, then, had not heard our morning news. I read her scribble again and again for the least inkling of it, my thoughts in disorder. That sprawling cross on the newspaper; this gibbering and dancing as of a skeleton before my eyes; and 'the stone', 'the stone'. What did it mean? The word echoed on in my head as if it had been shouted in a vault. I was deadly frightened and sick, stood

up as if to escape, and found only my own distorted face in Mrs.
Petrie's flower-and-butterfly-painted chimney glass.

'You, you!' my eyes cried out on me. And a furious storm –
remorse, grief, horror – broke within. I knew the whole awful
truth. Like a Shade in the bright light, Mr. Crimble stood there
beyond the table, not looking at me, its face turned away. Unspeakable misery bowed my shoulders, chilled my skin.

'But you said "ill",' I whispered angrily up at last at Mrs. Bowater's bonneted figure in the doorway. 'I have looked where the
cross is. He is dead!'

She closed the door with both hands and seated herself on a
chair beside it.

'I've traipsed that Front, miss – striving to pick up the ends. It
doesn't bear thinking of: that poor, misguided young man. It's hid
away ...'

'What did he die of, Mrs. Bowater?' I demanded.

She caught at the newspaper, folded it close, nodded, shook
her head. 'Four nights ago,' she said. And still, some one last shred
of devotion – not of fidelity, not of fear, for I longed to pour out
my heart to her – sealed my lips. *Holy Living and Dying. Holy
Living and Dying.* I read over and over the faded gilt letters on
the cover of Fanny's gift, and she in her mockery, desperate, too.
'Damnation' – the word echoed on in my brain.

But poor Mrs. Bowater was awaiting no confession from me.
She had out-trapsed her strength. When next I looked round at
her, the bonneted head lay back against the rose-garlanded wall-
paper, the mouth ajar, the eyelids fluttering. It was my turn now
– to implore her to 'come back'; and failing to do so, I managed at
last to clamber up and tug at the bell-pull.

Chapter Thirty

I surveyed with horror the recumbent, angular figure stretched out on the long, narrow, horsehair sofa. The shut eyes – it was selfish to leave me like this.

'There, miss, don't take on,' Mrs. Petrie was saying. 'The poor thing's coming round now. Slipping dead off out of things – many's the time I've wished I could – even though you *have* come down for a bit of pleasuring.'

But it was Lyme Regis's solemn, round-shouldered doctor who reassured me. At first sight of him I knew Mrs. Bowater was not going to die. He looked down on her, politely protesting that she must not attempt to get up. 'This unseasonable heat, perhaps. The heart, of course, not so strong as it might be.' He ordered her complete rest in bed for a few days – light nourishment, no worry, and he would look in again. Me, he had not detected under the serge window-curtain, though he cast an uneasy glance around him, I fancied, on leaving the room.

After remaining alone under the still, sunshiny window until I could endure it no longer, I climbed up the steep, narrow stairs to Mrs. Bowater's bedroom, and sat awhile clasping the hand that hung down from the bed. The blind gently ballooned in the breeze. Raying lights circled across the ceiling, as carriage and cart glided by on the esplanade. Fearful lest even my finger-tips should betray me to the flat shape beneath the counterpane, I tried hard to think. My mind was in a whirl of fears and forebodings; but there was but one thing, supremely urgent, facing me now. I must forget my own miseries, and somehow contrive to send Fanny the money she needed.

Somehow; but how? The poor little hoard which I had saved from my quarterly allowances lay locked up on Beechwood Hill in my box beneath my bed. By what conceivable means could I regain possession of it, unknown to Mrs. Bowater?

Conscience muttered harsh words in my ear as I sat there holding that cold, limp hand with mine, while these inward schemings shuttled softly to and fro.

When my patient had fallen asleep, I got downstairs again – a more resolute if not a better woman. Removing latch and box keys from their ribbon round my neck, I enclosed them in an envelope with a letter:

> DEAR MR. ANON – I want you, please, to help me. The large one of these two keys unlocks my little house door; the smaller one a box under my bed. Would you please let yourself in at Mrs. Bowater's to-morrow evening when it's dark – there will be nobody there – take out Twenty Pounds which you will find in the box, and send them to *Miss Fanny Bowater, the Crown and Anchor Hotel, B –*. I will thank you when I come.
>
> Believe me, yours very sincerely,
>
> M.M.

It is curious. Many a false, pandering word had sprung to my tongue when I was concocting this letter in my mind beside Mrs.

Bowater's bed, and even with Mrs. Petrie's stubby, ink-corroded pen in my hand. Yet some last shred of honesty compelled me to be brief and frigid. I was simply determined to be utterly open with *him,* even though I seemed to myself like the dark picture of a man in a bog struggling to grope his way out. I dipped my fingers into a vase of wall-flowers, wetted the gum, sealed down the envelope, and wrote on it this address: 'Mr. –, Lodging at a cottage near the Farm, North-west of Wanderslore, Beechwood, Kent.' And I prayed heaven for its safe delivery.

For Fanny no words would come – nothing but a mere bare promise that I would help her as soon as I could – an idiot's message. The next three days were an almost insupportable solitude. From Mr. Anon no answer could be expected, since in my haste I had forgotten to give him Mrs. Petrie's address. I brooded in horror of what the failure of my letter to reach him might entail. I shared Fanny's damnation. Wherever I went, a silent Mr. Crimble dogged my footsteps. Meanwhile, Mrs. Bowater's newspaper, I discovered, lay concealed beneath her pillow.

At length I could bear myself no longer, and standing beside her bed, asked if I might read it. Until that moment we had neither of us even referred to the subject. Propped up on her pillows, her long face looking a strange colour against their whiteness, she considered my request.

'Well, miss,' she said at last, 'you know too much to know no more.'

I spread out the creased sheets on the worn carpet, and read slowly the smudged, matter-of-fact account from beginning to end. There were passages in it that imprinted themselves on my memory like a photograph. Mr. Crimble had taken the evening service that last day looking 'ill and worn, though never in what may be described as robust health, owing to his indefatigable devotion to his ecclesiastical and parochial duties'. The service over, and the scanty congregation dispersed, he had sat alone in the vestry for so unusual a time that the verger of St. Peter's, a Mr. Soames, anxious to get home to his supper, had at length looked in on him at the door, to ask if his services were required any further. Mr. Crimble had 'raised his head as if startled', and 'had smiled in the negative', and then, 'closing the eastern door behind him', had 'hastened' out of the church. No other human eye had encountered him until he was found at 11.27 pm. in an outhouse at the foot of his mother's garden. 'The head of the unfortunate gentleman was wellnigh severed from the body.' 'He was an only son, and was in his twenty-ninth year. Universal sympathy will be extended by all to the aged lady who is prostrated by this tragic occurrence.'

Propped on my hands and knees, fearful that Mrs. Bowater might interrupt me before I was prepared, I stared fixedly at the newspaper. I understood all that it said, yet it was as strange to me as if it had been written in Hebrew. I had seen, I had known, Mr. Crimble. Who, then, was this? My throat drew together as I turned my head a little and managed to inquire: 'What is an inquest, Mrs. Bowater?'

'Fretting out the why's and wherefores,' came the response, muffled by a handkerchief pressed close to her mouth.

'And – *this* "why"?' I whispered, stooping low.

'That's between him and his Maker,' said the voice. 'The poor young man had set his heart on we know where. As we make our bed so we must lie on it, miss. It's for nobody to judge; though it may be a lesson.'

'Oh, Mrs. Bowater, then you knew I knew.'

'No, no. Not *your* lesson, miss. I didn't mean that. It's not for you to fret yourself, though I must say – I have always made it a habit, though without prying, please God, to be aware of more than interference could set right. Fanny and I have talked the affair over till we couldn't look in each other's faces for fear of what we might say. But she's *Mr.* Bowater's child, through and through, and my firm hand was not firm enough, maybe. You did what you could. It's not in human conscience to ask more than the natural frame can bear.'

Did what I could ... I cowered, staring at my knuckles, and it seemed that a little concourse of strangers, heads close together, were talking in my mind. My eyes were dry; I think the spectre of a smile had dragged up my lips. Mrs. Bowater raised herself in her bed, and peered over at me.

'It's the letters,' she whispered at me. 'If he hasn't destroyed them, they'll be read to the whole parish.'

I crouched lower. 'You'll be thankful to be rid of me. I shall be thankful to be rid of myself, Mrs. Bowater.'

She thrust a long, skinny arm clean out of the bed. 'Come away, there; come away,' she cried.

'Oh,' I said, 'take me away, take me away. I can't bear it, Mrs. Bowater. I don't *want* to be alive.'

'There, miss, rest now, and think no more.' She smoothed my hair, clucked a little low, whistling tune, as if for lullaby. 'Why, there now,' she muttered sardonically, 'you might almost suppose I had been a mother myself!'

There was silence between us for a while, then, quietly raising herself, she looked down at me on the pillow, and, finding me to be still awake, a long smile spread over her face! 'Why, we don't seem neither of us to be much good at day-time sleeping.'

Chapter Thirty-One

A morning or two afterwards we set out on our homeward journey – the sea curdling softly into foam on its stones, a solitary ship in the distance on its dim, blue horizon. We were a dejected pair of travellers, keeping each a solemn face turned aside at the window, thinking our thoughts and avoiding, as far as we could, any interchange of looks that might betray them one to the other. For the first time in our friendship Mrs. Bowater was a little short and impatient with me over difficulties and inconveniences which I could not avoid, owing to my size.

Her key in the lock of the door, she looked down on me in the porch, a thin smile between nose and cheek. 'No place like home there mayn't be, miss,' she began, 'but –' The dark passage was certainly uninviting; the clock had stopped. 'I think I'll be calling round for Henry,' she added abruptly.

I entered the stagnant room, ran up my stairs, my heart with me – and paused. Not merely my own ghost was there to meet me; but a past that seemed to mutter 'Never again, never again', from every object on shelf and wall. Yet a faint, sweet, unfamiliar odour lay on the chilly air. I drew aside the curtain and looked in. Fading on the coverlet of my bed lay a few limp violets, ivory white and faintly rosy.

I was alone in the house, concealed now even from Mr. Bowater's frigid stare. Yet at sight of these flowers a slight vertigo came over me, and I had to sit on my bed for a moment to recover myself.

Then I knelt down, my heart knocking against my side, and dragged from out its hiding-place the box in which I kept my money. Gritty with the undisturbed dust of our absence, it was locked. I drew back, my hand on my mouth. What could be the meaning of this? My stranger had come and gone. Had he been so stupidly punctilious that, having taken out the twenty pounds, he had relocked an almost empty box?

Or had he, at the last moment? ... This riddle distressed me so much that instantly I was seized with a violent headache. But nothing could be done for the present. I laid by the violets in a drawer, pushed back the box, and, making as good a pretence at eating my supper as I could, prepared for the night.

One by one the clocks in hall and kitchen struck out the hours, and, the wind being in the east, borne on it came the chimes of St. Peter's. Automatically I counted the strokes, turning this way and that, as if my life depended on this foolish arithmetic, yet ready, like Job, to curse the day I was born. What had my existence been but a blind futility, my thought for others but a mask of egotism and selfishness? Yet, in all this turmoil of mind, I must have slept, for suddenly I found myself stiff, drawn-up, and wide awake – listening to a cautious, reiterated tapping against my window-pane. A tallow night-light burned beside me in a saucer of water. For the first time in my life – at least since childhood – I had been afraid to face the dark. Why, I know not; but I at once leapt out of bed and blew out that light. The night was moonless, but high and starry. I peered through the curtains, and a shrouded figure became visible in the garden – Fanny's.

Curtain withdrawn, we looked each at each through the cold, dividing glass in the gloom – her eyes, in the night-spread pallor of her skin, as if congealed. The dark lips, with an exaggerated attempt at articulation, murmured words, but I could catch no meaning. The face looked almost idiotic in these contortions. I shuddered, shook my head violently. She drew back.

Terrified that she would be gone – in my dressing-gown and slippers I groped my way across the room and was soon, with my door open, in the night air. She had heard me, and with a beckon of her finger, turned as if to lead me on.

'No, no,' I signalled, 'I have no key.' With a gesture she drew close, stooped, and we talked there together, muttering in the porch.

'Midgetina,' she whispered, smiling bleakly, 'it's this wretched money. I must explain. I'm at my wits' end – in awful trouble – without it.'

Huddled close, I wasted no time in asking questions. She must come in. But this she flatly refused to do. Yet money, money was her one cry: and that she must have before she saw her mother again. Not daring to tell her that I was in doubt whether or not my savings were still in my possession, I pushed her hand away as she knelt before me on the upper-most step. 'I must fetch it,' I said.

By good fortune my money-box was not the weightiest of my grandfather's French trunks – not the brass-bound friend-in-need of my younger days, and it contained little but paper. I hoisted it on to my bed, and, as I had lately seen the porters do at the railway station, contrived to push under it and raise it on to my shoulder. Its edge drove in on my collar-bone till I thought it must snap.

Thus laden, I staggered cautiously down the staircase, pushed slowly across the room, and, so, out into the passage and towards the rounded and dusky oblong of the open door.

On the threshold Fanny met me, gasping under this burden, and at sight of me some blessed spirit within her seemed to give her pause. 'No, no,' she muttered, and drew back as if suddenly ashamed of her errand. On I came, however, and prudence prevailed. With a sound that might have been sigh or sob she snatched the load from me and gathered it in, as best she could, under her cloak.

'Oh, Midgetina!' she whispered meaninglessly. 'Now we must talk.' And having wedged back the catch of my door, we moved quickly and cautiously in the direction of Wanderslore.

We climbed on up the quiet hill. The cool, fragrant night seemed to be luring us on and on, to swallow us up. Yet, *there* shone the customary stars; there, indeed, to my amazement, as if the heavenly clock of the universe had set back its hands on my behalf, straddled the constellation of Orion.

Come to our beech tree, now a vast indistinguishable tent of whispering, silky leaves, Fanny seated herself upon a jutting root, and I stood panting before her.

'Well?' she said, with a light, desolate laugh.

'Oh, Fanny, "well"!' I cried.

'Can't you trust me?'

'Trust you?'

'Oh, oh, mocking-bird! – with all these riches?'

I cast a glance up into the leafy branches, and seated myself opposite to her.

'Fanny, Fanny. Have you heard?'

'"Heard,"' she says! It was her turn to play the parrot. 'What am I here for, but to hear more? But never mind; that's all over. Has mother –'

'"All over," Fanny!' I interrupted her. 'All over? But, the letters?'

'What letters?' She stared at me, and added, looking away. 'Oh, mine?' She gave out the word with a long, inexhaustible sigh. 'That was all right. He did not hide, he burned. Neither to nor from; not even to his mother. Every paper destroyed. I envy *her* feelings! He just gave up, went out, *Exit*. I envy that, too.'

'Not even to you, Fanny? Not a word even to you?'

The figure before me crouched a little closer together. 'They said', was her evasive reply, 'that there is melancholia in the family.'

I think the word frightened me even more than its meaning. 'Melancholia,' I repeated the melodious syllables. 'Oh, Fanny!'

'Listen, Midgetina,' her voice broke out coldly. 'I can guess easily enough what's saving up for me when I come home – which won't be yet awhile, I can assure you. I can guess, too, what your friends, Lady Pollacke and Co., are saying about me. *Let* them rave. That can't be helped. I shall bear it, and try to grin. Maybe there would be worse still, if worse were known. But your worse I won't have, not even from you. I was not his keeper. I did *not* play him false. I deny it. Could I prevent him – caring for me? Was he man enough to come openly? Did he say to his mother "Take her or leave her, I mean to have her" – as *I* would have done? No, he blew hot and cold. He temporized; he – he was a coward. Oh, this everlasting dog-fight between body and mind! Ages before you ever crept upon the scene he pestered and pestered me – until I have almost retched at the sound of church bells. What was it, I ask you, but sheer dread of what the man might go and *do* that kept me shilly-shallying? And what's more, Miss Wren, who told me to throw the stone? Pff, it sickens me, this paltering world. I can't and won't see things but with my reason. My reason, I tell you. What else is a schoolma'am for? Did he want me for *my* sake? Who begged and begged that his beautiful love should be kept secret? There was once a philosopher called Plato, my dear. He poisoned Man's soul.'

Flesh and spirit, Fanny must have been very tired. Her voice fluttered on like a ragged flag.

'But listen, listen!' I entreated her. 'I haven't blamed you for that, Fanny. I swear it. I mean, you can't help *not* loving. I know that. But perhaps if only we had – It's a dreadful thing to think of him sitting there alone – the vestry – and then looking up "with a smile". Oh, Fanny, with a smile! I dare hardly go into his mind – and the verger looking in. I think of him all day.'

'And I all night,' came the reply, barked out in the gloom. 'Wasn't the man a Christian, then?'

'Fanny,' I covered my eyes. 'Don't say that. We shall both of us just suffocate in the bog if you won't even let yourself listen to what you are saying.'

'Well,' she said doggedly, 'be sure you shall suffocate last, Miss Midge. There's ample perch-room for you on Fanny's shoulder.' I felt, rather than saw, the glance almost of hatred that she cast at me from under her brows.

'Mock as you like at me,' was my miserable answer, 'I have kept my word to you – all but; and it was I who helped – oh, yes, I know that.'

'Ah, "all but"!' her agile tongue caught up the words. 'And what else, may I ask?'

I took a deep breath, with almost sightless eyes fixed on the beautiful, mysterious glades stretching beneath us. 'He came again. Why, it was not very many days ago. And we talked and talked, and I grew tired, yes, and angry at last. I told him you were only making use of me. You were. I said that all we could do was just to go on loving you – and keep away. I know, Fanny, I cannot be of any account; I don't understand very much. But that is true.'

She leaned nearer, as if incredulous, her face as tranquil in its absorption as the planet that hung in the russet-black sky in a rift of the leaves.

'Candid, and candid,' she scoffed brokenly, and all in a gasp.

The voice trailed off. Her mouth relaxed. And suddenly my old love for her seemed to gush back into my heart. A burning, inarticulate pity rose up in me.

'Listen, Midgetina,' she went on. 'That was honest. And I can be honest, too. I don't care *what* you said. If you had called me the vilest word they can set their tongue to, I'd still have forgiven you. But would you have me give in? Go under? Have you ever *seen* Mother Grundy? I tell you, he haunts me – the blackness, the deadness. That outhouse! Do you suppose I can't see inside that? He sits by my bed. I eat his shadow with my food. At every corner in the street his black felt hat bobs and disappears. If even he hadn't been so solemn, so insignificant! ...' Her low, torturing laugh shook under the beechen hollow.

'And I say this' – she went on slowly, as if I sat at a distance, 'if he's not very careful I shall go the same way. I can't bear that – *that* kind of spying on me. Don't you suppose you can sin *after* death? If only he had given me away – betrayed me! We should at least have been square. But that,' she jerked back her head. 'That's only one thing. I had not meant to humble myself like this. You seem not to care what humiliations I have to endure. You sit there, oh, how absurd for me, watching and watching me, null and void and meaningless. Yet you are human: you feel. You said you loved me – oh, yes. But touch me, come here' – she laid her hand almost fondly on her breast – 'and be humanly generous, no. That's no more your nature than – than a changeling's. Contamination, perhaps!'

Her eyes fretted round her, as if she had lost her sense of direction.

'And now there's this tongueless, staring ghost.' She shuddered, hiding her face in her hands. 'The misery of it all.'

'Fanny, Fanny,' I besought her. 'You know I love you.' But the words sounded cold and distant, and some deadly disinclination held me where I was, though I longed to comfort her. 'And at times, I confess it, I have hated you too. You haven't always been very kind to me. I was trying to cure myself. You were curing me. But still I go on – a little.'

'It's useless, useless,' she replied, dropping her hands into her lap and gazing vacantly on the ground. 'I can't care; I can't even cry. And all you say is only pity. I don't want that. Would you still pity me, I wonder, if you knew that even though I had come to take this wretched money from you, I meant to taunt you, to accuse you of lying to me?'

'Taunt,' 'lying.' My cheek grew hot. I drew back my head with a jerk and stared at her. 'I don't understand you.'

'There. What did I say! She doesn't understand me,' she cried with a sob, as if calling on the angels to bear witness to her amazement. 'Well, then, let Fanny tell you, Miss M., whoever and whatever you may be, that she, yes, even she, can understand that unearthliness, too. Oh, these last days! I have had my fill of them.

Take all: give nothing. There's no other means of grace in a world like this.'

'But you said "taunt" me,' I insisted, with eyes fixed on the box that lay between the blunt-headed fronds of the springing bracken. 'What did you mean by that? I did my best. Your mother was ill. She fainted, Fanny, when the newspaper came. I couldn't come back a single hour earlier. So I wrote to – to a friend, sending him my keys, and asking him to find the money for you. I know my letter reached him. Perhaps' – I hesitated, in dread of what might be hanging over our heads, 'perhaps the box is empty.'

But I need not have wasted myself. The puzzle was not quite inexplicable. For the moment Fanny's miseries seemed to have vanished. Animation came into her face and voice and movements as she told me how, the night before, thinking that her mother and I might have returned from Lyme Regis, she had come tapping. And suddenly as she stood in the garden, her face close to the glass, an utterly strange one had thrust itself into view, and the figure of 'a ghastly gloating little dwarfish creature' had appeared in the porch.

At first she had supposed – but only for an instant – that it was myself. 'Of course, Mother had mentioned him in her letters, but' – and Fanny opened her eyes at me – 'I never guessed he was, well, like *that*.'

Then in her folly, and without giving him the least opportunity to explain his presence there, she had begun railing at him, and had accused him of forcing his way in to rob the house! 'And he stood there, hunched up, looking at me – out of my own house.' The very picture of Fanny helplessly standing there at her own door, and of these two facing each other like that in the porch – this ridiculous end to my fine stratagem, filled me with a miserable amusement. I leaned back my head where I sat, shrilly and dismally laughing and laughing, until tears sprang pricklingly into my eyes. If any listener had been abroad in the woods that night, he would, I think, have hastened his departure.

But Fanny seemed to be shocked at my levity. She peered anxiously into the clear night-glooms around us.

'And what!' I said, still striving to regain command over myself. 'What happened then? Oh, Fanny, not a policeman?'

But her memory of what had followed was confused, or perhaps she had no wish to be too exact. All that I could win from her for certain was that after an angry and bitter talk between herself and Mr. Anon, he had simply slammed my door behind him and dared her to do her worst.

'That was pretty brave of him,' I remarked.

'Oh,' said Fanny amiably, 'I am not blaming your friend, Midgetina. He seemed to be perfectly *competent*.'

Yet even now I remained unsatisfied. If Fanny had come secretly to Beechwood, as she had suggested, and had spent the night with a friend, solely to hear the last tidings of Mr. Crimble, what was this other trouble, so desperate that she had lost both her wits and her temper at finding Mr. Anon there? Supposing the house had been empty? My curiosity overcame me, and the none too ingenuous question slipped from my tongue! 'Did you want some of the money for mourning, then, Fanny?'

Her dark, pale face, above the black, enveloping cloak, met my look with astonishment.

'Mourning!' she cried, 'why, that would be the very – No, not mourning, Midgetina. I owe a little to a friend – and not money only,' she added with peculiar intensity. 'Of course, if you have any doubts about lending it –'

'Give, not lend,' said I.

'Yes, but how are we to get at it? I can't lug *that* thing about, and you say *he* has the key. Shall we *smash* it open?'

The question came so hurriedly that I had no time to consider what, besides money – and of course friendship – could be owed to a friend, and especially to a friend that made her clench her teeth on the word.

'Yes, smash it open,' I nodded. 'It's only a box.'

'But such a pretty little box!'

With knees drawn up, and shivering now after my outburst of merriment, I watched her labours. My beloved chest might keep out moth and rust, it was no match for Fanny. She wound up a large stone in her silk scarf. A few heavy and muffled blows, the lock surrendered, and the starlight dripped in like milk from heaven upon my hoard.

'Why, Midgetina,' whispered Fanny, delicately counting the notes over between her long, white fingers, 'you are richer than I supposed – a female Crœsus. Wasn't it a great risk? I mean', she continued, receiving no answer, 'no wonder he was so cautious. And how much may I take?'

It seemed as if an empty space, not of yards but of miles, had suddenly separated us. 'All you want,' said I.

'But I didn't – I *didn't* taunt you, now, did I?' she smiled at me, with head inclined to her slim shoulder, as if in mimicry of my ivory Hypnos.

'There was nothing to taunt me about. Mayn't *I* have a friend?'

'Why,' she retorted lightly, mechanically recounting the bits of paper, 'friend indeed! What about all those Pollackes and Monneries mother's so full of? You will soon be flitting to quite another sphere. It's the *old* friends that then will be left mourning. You won't sit moon-gazing then, my dear.'

'No, Fanny,' I said stubbornly, 'I've had enough of that, just for the present.'

'Sst!' she whispered swiftly, raising her head and clasping the notes to her breast beneath her cloak, 'what was that?'

We listened. I heard nothing – nothing but sigh of newborn leaf, or falling of dead twig cast off from the parent tree. It was early yet for the nightingale.

'Only the wind,' said she.

'Only the wind,' I echoed scornfully, 'or perhaps a weasel.'

She hurriedly divided my savings and thrust my share into my lap. I pushed it in under my arm.

'Good heavens, Midgetina!' she cried, aghast. 'You are almost naked. How on earth was I to know?'

I clutched close my dressing-gown and stumbled to my feet, trying in vain to restrain my silly teeth from chattering. 'Never mind about me, Fanny,' I muttered. 'They don't waste inquests on changelings.'

'My God!' was her vindictive comment, 'how she harps on the word. As if I had nothing else to worry about.' With a contemptuous foot she pushed my empty box under cover of a low-growing yew. Seemingly Wanderslore was fated to entomb one by one all my discarded possessions.

Turning, she stifled a yawn with a sound very like a groan. 'Then it's *au revoir,* Midgetina. Give me five minutes' start ... You know I am grateful?'

'Yes, Fanny,' I said obediently, smiling up into her face.

'Won't you kiss me?' she said. '*Tout comprendre*, you know, *c'est tout pardonner.*'

'Why, Fanny,' I replied; 'no, thank you. I prefer plain English.'

But scarcely a minute had separated us when I sprang up and pursued her a few paces into the shadows, into which she had disappeared. To forgive all – how piteously easy now that she was gone. She had tried to conceal it, brazen it out, but unutterable wretchedness had lurked in every fold of her cloak, in the accents of her voice, in every fatigued gesture. Her very eyes had shone the more lustrously in the starlight for the dark shadows around them. But understand her – I could not even guess what horrible secret trouble she had been concealing from me. And beyond that, too – a hideous, selfish dread – my guilty mind was haunted by the fear of what she might do in her extremity.

'Fanny, Fanny,' I called falsely into the silence. 'Oh, come back! I love you; indeed I love you.'

How little blessed it is at times even to give. No answer came. I threw myself on the ground. And I strove with myself in the darkness, crushing out every thought as it floated into my mind, and sinking on and on into the depths of unconsciousness.

'Oh, my dear, my dear,' came the whisper of a tender, guttural voice in my ear. 'You are deathly cold. Why do you grieve so? She is gone. Listen, listen. They have neither love nor pity. And I – I cannot live without you.'

I sat up, black with rage. My stranger's face glimmered obscurely in the gloom.

'Oh, if you spy on me again!' I rasped at him. 'Live without me, what do I care? – you can go and –'

But, thank God, the *die without me* was never uttered. I haven't *that* to haunt me. Some hidden strength that had been mine these few days melted away like water. 'Not now, not now!' I entreated him. I hastened away.

London

* * *

London

Chapter Thirty-Two

And then – well, life plays strange tricks. In a week or two London had swallowed me up. How many times, I wonder, had I tried in fancy to picture Mrs. Monnerie's town house. How romantic an edifice fancy had made of it. Impressive in its own fashion, it fell far short of these ignorant dreams. It was No. 2 of about forty, set side by side, their pillared porticoes fronting a prodigious square. Its only 'garden', chiefly the resort of cats, children, nursemaids, an old whiskered gentleman in a bath chair, and sparrows, was visible to every passer-by through a spear-headed palisade of railings. Broad paving-stones skirted its areas, and over each descent of steps hung a bell-pull.

On cloudless days the sun filled this square like a tank with a dry glare and heat in which even my salamanderish body sometimes gasped like a fish out of water. When rain fell out of the low, grey skies, and the scaling plane-trees hissed and the sparrows chirped, my spirits seemed to sink into my shoes. And fair or foul, London soot and dust were enemies alike to my eyes, my fingers, and my nose.

Even my beloved cloud-burdened north-west wind was never quite free of smuts and grit; and when blew the east! But it must be remembered how ignorant and local I was. In my long carriage journey to Mrs. Monnerie's through those miles and miles of grimed, huddling houses, those shops and hoardings and steeples, I had realized for the first time that its capital is not a part of *England*, only a sprawling human growth in it; and though I soon learned to respect it as *that*, I could never see without a sigh some skimpy weed struggling for life in its bricked-up crevices. It was nearly all dead, except for human beings, and that could not be said of Lyndsey, or even of Beechwood Hill.

Maybe my imagination had already been prejudiced by a coloured drawing which Mr. Wagginhorne had sent me once for a Valentine when I was a child. It hangs up now in that child's nursery for a memento that I have been nearly dead. In the midst of it on a hill, in gold and faded carmine, encircled with great five-pointed blue stars, and with green, grooved valleys radiating from its castellated towers, is a city – *Hierusalem*. A city surmounted by a narrow wreathing pennon on which inscribed in silver are the words: 'Who heareth the Voice of My Spirit? And how shall they who deceive themselves resort unto Me?'

Scattered far and near about this central piece, and connected with it by thin lines like wandering paths radiating from its gates across mountain, valley, and forest, lie, like round web-like smudges, if seen at a distance, the other chief cities of the world: Rome, Venice, Constantinople, Paris, and the rest. London sprawls low in the left-hand corner. The strongest glass cannot exhaust the skill and ingenuity of the maker of this drawing (an artist who, Mr. Wagginborne told me, was mad, poor thing – a man in a frenzy distemper – his very words). For when you peer close into this London, it takes the shape of a tusked, black, hairy boar, sprawling with hoofs outspread, fast asleep. And between them, and even actually diapering the carcass of the creature, is a perfect labyrinth of life – a high crowned king and queen, honey-hiving bees, an old man with a beard as if in a swoon, robbers with swords, travellers with beasts and torches, inns, a cluster of sharp-coloured butterflies (of the same proportion) fluttering over what looks like a clot of dung, a winding river, ships, trees, tombs, wasted unburied bodies, a child issuing from an egg, a phœnix taking flight; and so on. There is no end to this poor man's devices. The longer you look, the more strange things you discover. Yet at distance of a pace or two, his pig appears to fade into nothing but a cloudy-coloured cobweb – one of the many around his bright-dyed *Hierusalem*.

Now I cannot help wondering if this peculiar picture may not already have tinged a young mind with a curious horror of London; even though my aversion may have needed no artificial aid.

Still I must not be ungrateful. These were vague impressions; and as an actual fact, Mrs. Monnerie had transported me into the very midst of the world of rank and fashion. Her No. 2 was now my home. The spaciousness, the unnatural solitude, the servants who never so much as glanced at me until after my back was turned, the hushed *opulency*, the formality! It was impossible to be just my everyday Miss M. My feet never found themselves twirling me round before their mistress was aware of it. I all but gave up gossiping with myself as I went about my little self-services.

Parochial creature that I was – I missed Mrs. Bowater's 'home-liness'. To have things out of proportion to my body was an old story. To that, needless to say, I was perfectly accustomed. But here things were at first out of all proportion to my taste and habits, a very different thing. It is, in fact, extremely difficult in retrospect to get side by side again with those new experiences – with a self that

was at one moment intoxicated and engrossed, and the next humili-
ated and desperately ill at ease, at the novelty of her surroundings.

I had a maid, too, Fleming, with a pointed face and greenish eyes, who, unlike Mrs. Bowater, did not snort, but sniffed at
things. Whether I retired for the night or rose in the morning, it
was always to the accompaniment of a half-audible sniff. And I was
never perfectly certain whether that sniff was one of the mind, or of
the body, or of both. I found it hard to learn to do *little* enough for
myself. Fleming despised me – at least so I felt – even for emptying
my wash-basin, or folding my nightgown. Worse, I was never sure
of being alone: she stole about so softly on her duties. And then
the 'company'.

Not that the last black days at Beechwood were not even
blacker for the change. At first I tried to think them quietly over,
to ravel out my mistakes, and to get straight with my past. But
I couldn't in all that splendour. I had to spend much more time
in bewaring of *faux pas*, and in growing accustomed to being a
kind of tame, petted animal – tame even to itself, I mean. So Mrs.
Bowater's went floating off into the past like a dingy little house
on the edge of a muddy river. Amid that old horror and anxiety,
even my dear Pollie's wedding day had slipped by unheeded. How
often my thoughts went back to her now. If only *she* could have
been my Fleming.

I tried to make amends for my forgetfulness – even to the
extent of pocketing my pride, and commissioning Fleming to purchase for me (out of the little stock of money left me by Fanny) a
cradle, as a wedding present for Pollie, and a chest of tools for her
husband. Oddly enough, she did not sniff at this request. Her green
eyes almost sparkled. At the very word, wedding, she seemed to
revive into a new woman. And Pollie completely forgave me:

DEAR MISS M. – We was mother and all very sorry and grieved you couldn't come though it passed off very satisfactory. As for forgetting please don't mention the word, Lyndsey have never been the same since the old house was empty. It all passed off very satisfactory though with such torrents of rain there was a great pool in the churchyard which made everybody in high spirits. And William and I can't thank you enough for those beautiful gifts you have sent us. Will have been a carpenter since he was a boy but there's things there miss he says he never heard on in his born days but will be extreamly useful when he comes to know what for. And Mother says it was just like your good kind heart to think of what you sent me. You can't think how handsome it looks in the new-papered room and I'm sure I hope if I may say so it may be quite as useful as Will's tools, and its being pretty late to marry it isn't as if I was a slip of a girl. And of course I have mother. Though if any does come you may be sure it will be a Sunday treat being too fine for ordinary.

Please God miss I hope you are keeping well and happy in your new surroundings and that dream will come true. It was a dreadful moment that day by the shops but I'm thankful all came well. If you ever writes to Mrs. B. I trust you will mention me to her kindly not being much of a letter writer. If you could have heard the things she said of you your ears would burn miss you were such a treasure and to judge from her appearance she must have seen her troubles. And being a married woman helps to see into things though thank God I'm well and happy and William hopes to keep me so.

Well, I must now close trusting that you are in the best of health. Your old Pollie.

Miss Fenne have been very poorly of late so I've heard though not yet took to her bed – more peculiar than ever about Church and such like. Adam Waggett being W.'s

oldest friend though not my choice was to have been Best
Man but he's in service in London and couldn't come.

But if I pined for Pollie's company, how can I express what the
absence of Mrs. Bowater meant to me? Even when I had grown
used to my new quarters, I would sometimes wake myself calling
her name in a dream. She had been almost unendurably kind to
me that last May morning in Wanderslore, when she had come
to fetch me from yet another long adieu – to Mr. Anon. After
he had gone, she and I had sat on for a while in that fresh spring
beauty, a sober and miserable pair. Miserable on my side for miserable reasons. Then, if ever, had been the moment wherein to
clear my breast and be in spirit as well as heart at one with her. Yet
part for honesty and part for shame, I had remained silent. I could
only comfort myself with remembering that we should soon meet
again, and that the future might be kinder. Well, sometimes the
future is kinder, but it is never the same thing as the past.

'They may perhaps talk about that unfortunate – about that
poor young Mr. Crimble, miss,' was one of my landlady's last remarks,
as she sat staring rigidly at the great, empty house. 'We all take good
care to spread about each other's horrors; and what else is a newspaper for? If so; well, I shouldn't ask it, I suppose. But I've been
thinking maybe my Fanny wasn't *everything* to blame. We've had it
out together, she and I, though only by letter. She was frightened
of me as much as anything, though goodness knows I tried to
bring her up a God-fearing child. She had no one, as she thought,
to go to – and him a weak creature for all his obstinacy and, as
you might say, penned in by his mother and his cloth. They say
the Catholics don't marry, and there's nothing much to be wondered at in that. Poor young fellow, he won't bear much thinking

on, even when he's gone out of mind. I'm fearing now that what's come about may make her wilder and harder. Help her all you can, if only in your thoughts, miss; she sets more store by you than you might guess.'

'Indeed, indeed, I will,' I said.

'You see, miss,' Mrs. Bowater monotoned on, 'I'm nothing much better than an aunt for Fanny, with no children of my own for guidance; and him there helpless with his broken leg in Buenos Ayres.' The long, bonneted face moved round towards me. 'Do you feel *any* smouldering affections for the young gentleman that's just gone?'

This was an unexpected twist to our talk, but in some little confusion, I met it as candidly as I could.

'I am fonder of Fanny – and, of course, of you, Mrs. Bowater; oh, far, far. But – I don't quite know how to express it – I am, as you might say, in my own *mind* with him. I think he knows a little what I am, in myself I mean. And besides, oh, well, it isn't a miserable thing to feel that just one's company makes *anybody* happy.'

Mrs. Bowater considered this reply for some little time.

'He didn't *look* any too happy just now, to judge from his back view,' she remarked oracularly. 'And when I was – But there, miss, I'm thinking only of your comfort, and I'm not quite as comfortable as might be over that there Mrs. Monnerie. Generous she may be, though not noticing it much perhaps from a purse with no bottom to it, judging from what I've seen. God bless you, one way or the other. And perhaps you'll sometimes remember the bits of Sundays we've shared up there – you and the old Dragon.'

A smile and a tear battled for the dark eye that looked down on me. Indeed, seldom after came a Sunday evening with its clanking bells and empty, London hush, but it brought back to me with a pang my hymns and talks with 'the old Dragon'. Not that anyone I ever saw at Mrs. Monnerie's appeared to work so hard as to *need* a day of rest. There was merely a peculiar empty sensation on Sundays of there being nothing 'to do'.

A flight of stone steps and a pillared porch led up to her great ornamental door. Beyond was a hall compared with which the marbles of Brunswick House were mere mosaic. An alabaster fountain, its jet springing lightly from a gilded torch held by a crouching faun, cooled, and discreetly, murmured a ceaseless 'Hush!' in the air. On either hand, a wide, shallow staircase ascended to an enormous gilded drawing-room, with its chairs and pictures; and to the library. The dining-room stood opposite the portico. When Mrs. Monnerie and I were alone, we usually shared a smaller room with her parrot, Chakka; her little Chinese dog, Cherry – whose whimper had a most uncomfortable resemblance to the wild and homesick cry of my seagulls at Lyme Regis – and her collections of the world's smaller rarities. It is only, I suppose, one more proof of how volatile a creature I used to be that I took an intense interest in the contents of these cabinets for a few days, and then found them nothing but a vexation. No doubt this was because of an uneasy suspicion that Mrs. Monnerie had also collected *me*.

She could be extremely tactful in her private designs, yet she 'showed me off' in a fashion that might have turned a far less giddy head than her *protégée's*, and perhaps cannot have been in the best of taste.

So sure had she been of me, that, when I arrived, a room on the first floor of No. 2 had already been prepared for my reception. A wonderful piece of fantasticalness – like a miniature fairy palace, but without a vestige of any *real* make-believe in it. It was panelled and screened with carvings in wood, inlaid with silver and mother-of-pearl – dwarfs and apes and misshapen gods and goddesses leering and gaping out at one from amidst leafy branches, flowers, and fruits, and birds, and butterflies. The faintest sniff of that Indian wood – whatever it was – recalls to this day that nightmare scenery. Its hangings were of a silk so rich that they might have stood on edge on the floor. These screens and tapestries guarded a privacy that rarely, alas, contained a Miss M. worth being in private *with*.

The one piece of chagrin exhibited by Mrs. Monnerie in those early days of our acquaintance was at my insistence on bringing at least a few of my familiar sticks of furniture and chattels with me from Mrs. Bowater's. Their plain Sheraton design, she thought, was barbarously out of keeping with the rest. It was; but I had my way.

Not the least precious of these old possessions, though dismal for its memories, was the broken money chest which Fanny had pushed in under the yew in the garden at Wanderslore. Tacked up in canvas, its hinges and lock repaired, it had been sent on to me a week or two after my farewells to Beechwood, by Mr. Anon. Inside it I found the nightgown I had buried in the rabbit's hole, Fanny's letter from under its stone, my *Sense and Sensibility*, and last, pinned on to a scrap of kingfisher coloured silk, a pair of earrings made out of two old gold coins. Apart from a few withered flowers, they are the only thing I possess that came from Wanderslore. Long afterwards, I showed these earrings to Sir W. P. He told me they were quarter Rose Nobles of Edward III's reign, and only a quarter of a quarter of an ounce in weight. They weigh pretty heavy for me now, however.

My arrangement with Mrs. Monnerie had been that, however

long I might stay with her, I should still be in the nature of a visitor; that No. 2, in fact, should be my town house, and Mrs. Bowater's my country. But I was soon to realize that she intended Mrs. Bowater to have a very small share in me. She pretended to be jealous of me, to love me for my own sweet sake; and even while I knew it was mere pretence, it left its flattery on my mind; and for the first time in my life I feigned to be even smaller than I was; would mince my speeches, affect to be clever, even ogle the old lady, until it might be supposed we were a pair of queerly-assorted characters in a charade.

Nevertheless, I had had the obstinacy to insist that I should be at liberty to stay with Mrs. Bowater whenever I wished to do so; and I was free to invite any friend to visit me I chose. 'And especially, my dear, any one an eighth as exquisite,' Mrs. Monnerie had kindly put it. It may seem a little strange that all these obligations should have been on her side. But Mrs. Monnerie's whims were far more vigorous than most people's principles. The dews of her loving kindness descended on me in a shower, and it was some little time before I began to feel a chill.

Not the least remarkable feature of No. 2 was its back view. The window of my room came down almost to the floor. It 'commanded' an immense zinc cistern – George, by name – a Virginia creeper, groping along a brick wall, similar cisterns smalling into the distance, other brick walls and scores of back windows. Once, after contemplating this odd landscape for some little time, it occurred to me to speculate what the back view from the House of Life was like; but I failed to conceive the smallest notion of it. I rarely drew my curtains, and, oddly enough, when I did so, was usually in a vacant or dismal mood. My lights were electric. One simply twisted a tiny ivory button. At first their clear and coloured globes, set like tiny tulips in a candelabra, charmed my fancy. But, such is custom, I soon wearied of them, and pined for the slim, *living* flame of candles – even for my coarse old night-light swimming in its grease in a chipped blue and white saucer.

Chapter Thirty-Three

Mrs. Monnerie had rifled her collections for my use – pygmy Venetian glass, a silver-gilt breakfast and tea service, pygmy porcelain. There were absurd little *mechanical* knick-knacks – piping birds, a maddening little operatic clock of which I at last managed to break the mainspring, a musical chair, and so on. My bath was of jade; my table a long one of ebony inlaid with ivory, with puffing cherub faces at each corner representing the four winds. My own few possessions, I must confess, looked not only worn but provincial by comparison. But I never surprised myself actually talking to any of Mrs. Monnerie's exquisite novelties as to my other dumb, old, wooden friends. She delighted in them far more than I.

I suppose, really to enjoy such pomp and luxury, one should be positively born in the purple; and then, I suppose, one must be careful that the dye does not go to the bone. Whether or not, I have long since come to the conclusion that I am vulgar by nature – like my mother tongue. And at times in spite of my relief at being free of the blackness that had craped in my last days at Beechwood, I often found myself hungering for my Bowater parlour – even for its smell. Another thing I learned gradually at No. 2 was that I had been desperately old-fashioned; and that is, to some extent, to belong to the dead.

Mrs. Monnerie's chief desire, no doubt, was to give her new knick-knack a suitable setting. But it may also have reminded her childlessness – for she, too, like Mrs. Bowater, was 'nothing much better than an aunt' – of her childhood. Of course I affected as much pleasure in it as I could, and was really grateful. But she greatly disliked being thanked for anything, and would blandly shut her eyes at the least manifestation of gratitude. 'Humour me, humour me, humour me,' she once petulantly nodded at me; 'there are at least a hundred prayers in the Prayer Book, my pet, to one thanksgiving, and that's human nature all over.' It was what my frame must have *cost* that scandalized me. When, one day, after rhapsodizing (not without a shudder) over a cape and hat, which she had given me, composed solely of the shimmering emerald feathers of the humming-bird, I rather tactlessly reminded her of my £110 a year, and of my determination to live within it, her eyelids pinched me a glance as if I had explained in public that I had been bitten by a flea.

Yet as time went on, a peculiar affection sprang up in me for this crowded and lonely old woman. It has survived sore trials. She was by turns generous and mean, honeyed and cantankerous, impulsive and scheming. Like Mrs. Bowater, she disapproved of the world in general, and yet with how different a result. A restless, darting mind lay hidden behind the great mask of her countenance, with its heavy-lidded eyes and tower of hair. She loved to sit indolently peering, musing, and gossiping, twiddling the while perhaps some little antique toy in her capacious lap. I can boast, at any rate, that I was a spellbound listener, and devoured her peculiar wandering, satirical talk as if it had been manna from heaven.

It was the old, old story. Talking to me was the next most private thing to talking to herself; and I think she enjoyed for a while the company of so queer a confessor. Once, I remember, she confided to me the whole story of a girlish love affair, at least forty years old. I could hardly believe my eyes as I watched her; she looked so freshened and demure and spirited. It was as if she were her own twenties just dressed up. But she had a dry and acrid tongue, and spared nothing and nobody. To her and to Mrs. Bowater I owe nearly all my stock of worldly wisdom. And now I shall never have time, I suppose, to sort it out.

Mr. Monnerie, as Fleming confided in me one day – and the aristocracy was this extremely reticent and contemptuous creature's favourite topic of conversation – Mr. Monnerie had been a banker, and had made a late and dazzling marriage; for Mrs. Monnerie's blood was as blue as Caddis Bay on a cloudless morning. I asked Fleming if she had ever seen 'Lord B.' and what kind of man he was. She never had; but remarked obscurely that he must have lived mainly on porridge, he had sown so many wild oats.

This information reminded me of an old rhyme I had once learned as a child, and used to shout about the house:

> Come all you young men, with your wicked ways;
> Sow your wild, wild oats in your youthful days;
> That we may live happy when we grow old –
> Happy, and happy, when we grow old:
> The day is far spent, the night's coming on;
> So give us your arm, and we'll joggle along – joggle and
>   joggle and joggle along.

Fleming herself, I learned, had come from Ash, and was therefore, I suppose, of an Anglo-Saxon family, though she was far from stupid and rather elegant in shape. Because, I suppose, I did not like her, I was rather aggrieved she had been born in Kent. Mr. and Mrs. Monnerie, she told me, had had no children. The fair young man, Percy Maudlen, with the tired smile and beautiful shoes, who came to tea or luncheon at No. 2 at least once a week, was Mrs. Monnerie's only nephew by blood; and the still fairer Susan Monnerie, who used to float into my room ever and anon like a Zephyr, was the only one Mrs. Monnerie cared to see of her three nieces by marriage. And yet the other two, when they were invited to luncheon, were far more docile and considerate in the opinions and sentiments they expressed. *That* seemed so curious to me: there was no doubt that Mrs. Monnerie belonged to the aristocracy, and yet there always appeared to be quarrels going on in the family – apart, of course, from births, deaths, and marriages, which seemed of little consequence. She enjoyed relatives in every county in England and Scotland; while I had not one, now, so far as I knew, not even in Kent.

Marvell, the butler – he had formerly been Mr. Monnerie's valet – was another familiar object of my speculations. His rather solemn, clean-shaven countenance and steady grey eyes suggested a severe critic of mankind. Yet he seemed bent only on giving pleasure and smoothing things over, and stooped my dish of sliced cherries or apricots over my shoulder with a gesture that was in itself the cream of flattery. It astonished me to hear that he had a grown-up son in India; and though I never met Mrs. Marvell, I felt a prodigious respect for her.

I would look up and see him standing so smooth and benevolent behind Mrs. Monnerie's chair that he reminded me of my bishop, and I doubt if ever she crisply uttered his delightful name but it recalled the pleasant chime of a poem which my mother had taught me: *The Nymph Complaining of the Death of her Faun.*

I should have liked to have a long talk with Mr. Marvell – any time of the day when he wasn't a butler, I mean – but the opportunity never came.

One day, when he had left us to ourselves, I ventured to quote a stanza of this poem to Mrs. Monnerie:

> With sweetest milk and sugar first
> I it at my own fingers nursed;
> And as it grew, so every day
> It waxed more white and sweet than they –
> It had so sweet a breath! and oft
> I blushed to see its foot more soft
> And white – shall I say? – than my hand,
> Nay, any lady's in the land ...

'Charming, charming, Poppet,' she cooed, much amused, pushing in a nut for Chakka. 'Many shades whiter than *your* wrinkled old claw, you old wretch. *Another* sagacious old bird, my dear, though past blushing, I fear, at any lady's hand.'

Nothing would content her but that I must recite my *bon mot* again when her nephew Percy dandled in to tea that afternoon. He sneered down on me with his pale eyes, and with finger and thumb exposed yet another inch of silk sock, but made no comment.

'Manners, my dear Percy, maketh man,' said his aunt. 'Congratulate Miss M.'

If Percy Maudlen had had no manners at all, I think I should at that moment have seen the pink tip of his tongue; for if ever any human being detested my small person it was he. For very good reasons, probably, though I never troubled to inquire into them, I disliked him, too, beyond expression. He was, of course, a superior young man with a great many similar ancestors looking out of his face, yet he resembled a weasel. But Susan Monnerie – the very moment I saw her I loved her; just as one loves a field of butter-cups or a bush of may. For some little time she seemed to regard me as I suppose a linnet regards a young cuckoo that has been hatched out in her nest (though, of course, a squab cuckoo is of much the same size as its foster-mother). But she gradually grew accustomed to me, and even realized at last that I was something a little more – and also perhaps less – human than either Chakka or Cherry or a Dresden china shepherdess.

I would look at her just for pleasure's sake. Her hair was of the colour of undyed silk, with darker strands in it; her skin pale; and she had an odd little stutter in her light young voice when she was excited. I would often compare her with Fanny. What curious dif-ferences there were between them. She was graceful, but as if she had been taught to be. Unlike Fanny, she was not so fascinatingly just a beautiful body – with that sometimes awful Someone look-ing out of its windows. There was a lovely delicacy in her, as if, absurd though it may sound, every bit of her had been selected, actually picked out, from the finest materials. Perhaps it was her food and drink that had helped to make her so; for I don't think Miss Stebbings's diet was more than wholesome, or that follow-ing the sea in early life makes a man rich enough to afford many dainties for his children. Anyhow, there was nothing man-made in Fanny; and if there are women-shaped mermaids I know what looks will be seen in their faces.

However that may be, a keen, roving spirit dwelt in Susan's clear, blue eyes. I never discovered in her any malice or vanity, and this, I think, frequently irritated Mrs. Monnerie. Susan, too, used to ask me perfectly sane and ordinary questions; and I cannot describe what a flattery it was. I had always supposed that men and women were *intended* to talk openly to one another in this world; but it was an uncommonly rare luxury for me at Mrs. Monnerie's. I could talk freely enough to Susan, and told her a good deal about my early days, though I kept my life at Beechwood Hill more or less to myself.

And that reminds me that Mrs. Bowater proved to have been a good prophet. It was one day at luncheon. Mrs. Monnerie happened to cast a glance at the *Morning Post* newspaper which lay open on a chair near by, showing in tall type at the top of the column: 'Sudden Death of Sir Jasper Goodge.' Sir Jasper Goodge, whose family history, it seemed, was an open book to her, reminded her whimsically of another tragedy. She put back her head and, surveying me blandly as I sat up beside her, inquired if I had known at all intimately that unfortunate young man, Mr. Crimble.

'I remember him bobbing and sidling at me that delightful afternoon when – what do you think of it, Susan? – Poppet and I discovered in each other an unfashionable taste for the truth! A bazaar in aid of the Pollacke Blanket Fund, or something of the kind.'

The recollection seemed to have amused her so much that for the moment I held my breath and ignored her question.

'But why was Mr. Crimble unfortunate?' inquired Susan, attempting to make Cherry beg for a breadcrumb. I glanced in consternation at Marvell, who at the moment was bringing the coffee things into the room. But he appeared to be uninterested in Mr. Crimble.

'Mr. Crimble was unfortunate, my dear,' said Mrs. Monnerie complacently, 'because he cut his throat.'

'Ach! how horrible. How can you say such things. Get down, you little silly! Please, Aunt Alice, there must be something pleasanter to talk about than that? Everybody knows about the hideous old Sir Jasper Goodge; so it doesn't much matter what one says of him. But ... ' In spite of her command the little dog still gloated on her fingers.

'There may be things pleasanter, my dear Susan,' returned Mrs. Monnerie complacently, 'but there are few so illuminating. In Greek tragedy, I used to be told, all such horrors have the effect of what is called a purgation. Did Mr. Crimble *seem* that kind of young man, my dear? And why was he so impetuous?'

'I think, Mrs. Monnerie,' said I, 'he was in trouble.'

'H'm,' said she. 'He had a very sallow look, I remember. So he discussed his troubles? But not with *you*, my fairy?'

'Surely, Aunt Alice,' exclaimed Susan hotly, 'it isn't quite fair or nice to bring back such ghastly memories. Why,' she touched my hand with the tips of her light fingers, 'she is quite cold already.'

'Poppet's hands are always cold,' replied her aunt imperturbably. 'And I suspect that she and I know more about this wicked world than has brought shadows to your young brow. We'll return to Mr. Crimble, my dear, when Susan is butterflying elsewhere. She is so shockingly easily shocked.'

But it was Susan herself who returned to the subject. She came into my room where I sat reading – a collection of the tiniest little books in the most sumptuous gilt morocco had been yet another of Mrs. Monnerie's kindnesses – and she stood for a moment musing out through my silk window blinds at the vast zinc tank on the roof.

'Was that true?' she said at last. 'Did you really know someone who killed himself? Who was he? What was he like?'

'He was a young man – in his twenty-ninth year,' I replied automatically, 'dark, short, with gold spectacles, a clergyman. He was the curate at St. Peter's – Beechwood, you know.' I was speaking in a low voice, as if I might be overheard.

It was extraordinary how swiftly Mr. Crimble had faded into a vanishing shadow. From the very instant of his death the world had begun to adjust itself to his absence. And now nothing but a memory – a black, sad memory.

But Susan's voice interrupted these faint musings. 'A clergyman!' she was repeating. 'But why – why did he – do that?'

'They said melancholia. I suppose it was just impossible – or *seemed* impossible – for him to go on living.'

'But what made him melancholy? How awful. And how can Aunt Alice have said it like that?'

'But surely,' I argued, in my old contradictory fashion, and spying about for a path of evasion, 'it's better to call things by their proper names. What is the body, after all? Not that I mean one has any right to – to *not* die in one's own bed.'

'And do you really think like that? – the body of no im-portance? You? Why, Miss M., Aunt Alice calls you her "pocket Venus", and she means it, too, in her own sly way.'

'It's very kind of her,' said I, breathing more freely. 'Someone I know always calls me Midgetina, or Miss Midge, anything of that sort. I don't mean, Miss Monnerie, that it doesn't *matter* what we are called. Why, if that were so, there wouldn't be any Society at all, would there? We should all be – well – anonymous.' Deep inside I felt myself smile. 'Not that that makes much difference to good poetry.'

Susan sighed. 'How zigzaggedly you talk. What has poetry to do with Mr. Crimble? – that was his name, wasn't it?'

'Well, it hasn't very much,' I confessed. 'He hadn't the time for it.'

Susan seated herself on a cushion on the floor – and with how sharp a stab reminded me of Fanny and the old, carefree days of *Wuthering Heights*.

Surely – in spite of Fanny – life had definitely taken a tinge of Miss Brontë's imagination since then. But it was only the languor of Susan's movements, and that because she seemed a little tired, rather than merely indolent. And if from Fanny's eyes had now stooped a serpent and now a blinded angel; from these clear blue ones looked only a human being like myself. Even as I write that 'like myself', I ponder. But let it stay.

'So you really did know him?' Susan persisted. 'And it doesn't seem a nightmare even to think of him? And who, I say, made it impossible for him to go on living?' So intense was her absorption in these questions that when they ceased her hands tightened round her knees, and her small mouth remained ajar.

'You said *what* just now,' I prevaricated, looking up at her.

At this her blue eyes opened so wide I broke into a little laugh.

'No, no, no, Miss Monnerie,' I hastened to explain, 'not *me*. It isn't my story, though I was in it – and to blame. But please, if you would be so kind, don't mention it again to Mrs. Monnerie, and don't think about it any more.'

'Not think about it! *You* must. Besides, thoughts sometimes think themselves. I always supposed that things like that only happened to quite – to different people, you know. Was *he*?'

'*Different*?' I couldn't follow her. 'He was the curate of St. Peter's – a friend of the Pollackes.'

'Oh, yes, the Pollackes,' said she; and having glanced at me again, said no more.

The smallest confidence, I find, is a short cut to friendship. And after this little conversation there was no ice to break between Susan Monnerie and myself, and she often championed me in my little difficulties – even if only by her silence.

Chapter Thirty-Four

Miss Monnerie's visits were less punctual though more frequent than Percy Maudlen's. 'And where is the toadlet?' I heard him drawl one afternoon as I was being carried downstairs by the light-footed Fleming, on the padded tray which Mrs. Monnerie had had made for the purpose.

'The toadlet, my dear Percy, is about to take a little gentle exercise with me in the garden, and you shall accompany us. If you were the kind of fairy-tale hero I used to read of in my nursery, you would discover the charm, and live happy ever after. But I see nothing of the heroic in you, and little of the hereafter. Miss M. is a feast of mercies.'

'H'm. Providence packs his mercies into precious small quarters at times,' he yawned.

'Which suggests an uncivil speculation,' replied his aunt, 'on the size of your hat.'

'But candidly, Aunt Alice,' he retorted, 'is your little *attachée* quite all there – I mean, all of her that there is? Personally I wouldn't touch her, if I could help it, with a pair of tongs ... A nasty trick!'

Then, 'Hah!' cried Mrs. Monnerie in a large, pleasant voice, 'here *is* Miss M. Percy has been exposing a wounded heart, precious one. He is hurt because you look at him as if there were positively nothing more of him than what is there to see.'

'Not at all, Aunt Alice,' Percy drawled, with a jerk of his cane. 'It was for precisely the opposite reason. Who knows you ain't a witch, Miss M.? Distilled? Heavens, Aunt Alice! you are not bringing Cherry *too*?'

Yes, Cherry was coming too, with his globular eye and sneering nose. And so poor Percy, with a cold little smile on his fine pale features, had to accommodate himself to Mrs. Monnerie's leisurely pace, and she to mine, while Cherry disdainfully shuffled in our rear. We were a singular quartette, though there were only two or three small children in the palisaded garden to enjoy the spectacle; and they, after a few polite and muffled giggles, returned to their dolls.

It was a stifling afternoon. As I trod the yellow gravel the quivering atmosphere all but blinded me with its reflected glare. The only sounds to be heard were the clang of a milkman's handcart, and the pirouettes of a distant piano.

'And what,' Mrs. Monnerie suddenly inquired, looking down on me, with mauve-tinted cheek, from under her beribanded, long-handled parasol, 'what is Miss M. thinking about?'

As a matter of fact I was walking at that moment in imagination with Mrs. Bowater at Lyme Regis, but I seized the opportunity of hastening round from between aunt and nephew so that I could screen myself from the sun in Mrs. Monnerie's ample shadow, and inquired why London gardeners were so much attached to geraniums, lobelias, calceolarias, and ice-plants? Mightn't one just as well *paint* the border, Mrs. Monnerie, red, yellow, and blue? Then it would last – rain, snow, anything.

'Now I'll wager, Percy, you hadn't noticed *that*,' said Mrs. Monnerie in triumph.

'I make it a practice', he replied, 'never to notice the obvious. It is merely a kind of least common denominator, as I believe you call 'em, and', he wafted away a yawn with his glove, 'I take no interest in vulgar fractions.'

I took a little look at him out of the corner of my eye, and wished that as a child I had paid more heed to my arithmetic lessons. 'Look, Mrs. Monnerie,' I cried piteously, 'poor Cherry's tongue is dangling right out of his head. He looks *so* hot and tired.'

She swept me a radiant, if contorted, gleam. 'Percy, would you take pity on poor dear Cherry? Twice round, I think, will be as much as I can comfortably manage.'

So Percy had to take poor dear Cherry into his arms, just like a baby; and the quartette to all appearance became a trio.

But my existence at No. 2 was not always so monotonous as that. Mrs. Monnerie, in spite of her age, her ebony cane, and a tendency to breathlessness, was extremely active and alert. If life is a fountain, she preferred to be one of the larger bubbles as near as possible to its summit. She almost succeeded in making me a minute replica of herself. We shared the same manicurist, milliner, modiste, and coiffeur. And since it was not always practicable for Mahometta to be carried off to these delectable mountains, they were persuaded to attend upon her, and that as punctually as the fawn-faced man, Mr. Godde, who came to wind the clocks.

Whole mornings were spent in conclave in Mrs. Monnerie's boudoir – Susan sometimes of our company. Julius Cæsar, so my little Roman history told me, had hesitated over the crossing of one Rubicon. Mrs. Monnerie and I confabulated over the fording of a dozen of its tributaries a day. A specialist – a singularly bald man in a long black coat – was called in. He eyed me this way, he eyed me that – with far more deference than I imagine Mr. Pellew can have paid me at my christening. He assured Mrs. Monnerie of his confirmed belief that the mode of the moment was not of the smallest consequence so far as I was concerned. 'The hard, small hat,' he smiled; 'the tight-fitting sleeve!' And yet, to judge by the clothes he did recommend, I must have been beginning to look a pretty dowd at Mrs. Bowater's.

'But even if Madam prefers to dress in a style of her own choice,' he explained, 'the difference, if she will understand, must still be *in* the fashion.'

But he himself – though Mrs. Monnerie, I discovered after he was gone, had not even noticed that he was bald – he himself interested me far more than his excellent advice; and not least when he drew some papers out of a pocket-book, and happened to let fall on the carpet the photograph of a fat little boy with an immense mop of curls. So men – quite elderly, practical men, can blush, I thought to myself; for Dr. Phelps had rather flushed than blushed; and my father used only to get red.

Since nothing, perhaps, could make me more exceptional in appearance than I had been made by Providence, I fell in with all Mrs. Monnerie's fancies, and wore what she pleased – pushing out of mind as well as I could all thought of bills. I did more than that. I really began to enjoy dressing myself up as if I were my own doll, and when alone I would sit sometimes in a luxurious trance, like a lily in a pot. Yet I did not entirely abandon my old little Bowater habit of indoor exercise. When I was secure in my room I would sometimes skip. And on one of Fleming's afternoons 'out' I even furbished up what I could remember of my four kinds of Kentish hop-scotch, with a slab of jade for dump. But in the very midst of such recreations I would surprise myself lost in a kind of vacancy. Apart from its humans and its furniture, No. 2 was an empty house.

I do not mean that Mrs. Monnerie was concerned only with externals. Sir William Forbes-Smith advised that a little white meat should enrich my usual diet of milk and fruit, and that I should have sea-salt baths. The latter were more enjoyable than the former, though both, no doubt, helped to bring back the strength sapped out of me by the West End.

My cheekbones gradually rounded their angles; a livelier colour came to lip and skin, and I began to be as self-conscious as a genuine beauty. One twilight, I remember, I had slipped across from out of my bath for a pinch of the 'crystals' which Mrs. Monnerie had presented me with that afternoon; for my nose, also, was accustoming itself to an artificial life. An immense cheval looking-glass stood there, and at one and the same instant I saw not only my own slim, naked, hastening figure reflected in its placid deeps, but, behind me, that of Fleming, shadowily engrossed. With a shock I came to a standstill, helplessly meeting her peculiar stare. Only seven yards or so of dusky air divided us. Caught back by this unexpected encounter, for one immeasurable moment I stood thus, as if she and I were mere shapes in a picture, and reality but a thought.

Then suddenly she recovered herself, and with a murmur of apology was gone. Huddled up in my towel, I sat motionless, shrunken for a while almost to nothing in the dense sense of shame that had swept over me. Then suddenly I flung myself on my knees, and prayed – though what about and to whom I cannot say. After which I went back and bathed myself again.

The extravagances of Youth! No doubt, the worst pang was

that though vaguely I knew that my most secret solitude had been for a while destroyed, that long intercepted glance of half-derisive admiration had filled me with something sweeter than distress. If only I knew what common-sized people really feel like in similar circumstances. Biographies tell me little; and can one trust what is said in novels? The only *practical* result of this encounter was that I emptied all Mrs. Monnerie's priceless crystals forthwith into my bath, and vowed never, never again to desert plain water. So, for one evening, my room smelt like a garden in Damascus.

As for Fleming, she never, of course, referred to this incident, but our small talk was even smaller than before. If, indeed, to Percy, 'toadlet' was the aptest tag for me; for Fleming, I fancy 'stuck-up' sufficed. Instinct told her that she was only by courtesy a *lady's*-maid.

Less for her own sake than for mine, Mrs. Monnerie and I scoured London for amusement, even though she was irritated a little by my preference for the kind which may be called instructive. The truth is, that in all this smooth idleness and luxury a hunger for knowledge had seized on me; as if (cat to grass) my mind were in search of an antidote.

Mrs. Monnerie had little difficulty in securing 'private views'. She must have known everybody that is anybody – as I once read of a Countess in a book. And I suppose there is not a very large number of this kind of person. Whenever our social engagements permitted, we visited the show places, galleries, and museums. Unlike the rest of London, I gazed at Amenhotep's Mummy in the late dusk of a summer evening; and we had much to say to one another; though but one whiff of the huge round library gave me a violent headache. When the streets had to be faced, Fleming came with us in the carriage, and I was disguised to look as much like a child as possible – a process that made me feel at least twenty years older. The Tower of London, the Zoo, Westminster Abbey, St. Paul's – each in turn fell an early prey to my hunger for learning and experience. As for the Thames, the very sight of it seemed to wash my small knowledge of English history clear as crystal.

Mrs. Monnerie yawned her way on – though my comments on these marvels of human enterprise occasionally amused her. I made amends, too, by accompanying her to less well-advertised show-places, and patiently sat with her while she fondled unset and antique gems in a jeweller's, or inspected the china, miniatures, and embroideries in private collections. If the mere look of the books in the British Museum gave me a headache, it is curious that the Chamber of Horrors at Madame Tussaud's Wax Works did not. And yet I don't know; life itself had initiated me into this freemasonry. I surveyed the guillotine without a shudder, and eyed Mr. Hare and Charles Peace with far less discomposure than General Tom Thumb, or even Robert Burns in the respectable gallery above. My one misfortune was that I could look at no murderer without instantly recomposing the imaginary scene of his crime within my mind. And as after a while Mrs. Monnerie decided to rest on a chair set for her by the polite attendant under the scaffold, and we had the Chamber nearly to ourselves, I wandered on alone, and perhaps supped rather too full of horrors for one evening.

Mrs. Monnerie would often question me. 'Well, what do you think of that, Mammetinka?' or, 'Now, then, my inexhaustible little Miss Aristotle, discourse on that.'

And like a bullfinch I piped up in response to the best of my ability. My answers, I fear, were usually evasive. For I had begun to see that she was making experiments on my mind and senses, as well as on my manners and body. She was a 'fancier'. And one day I ogled up at her with the pert remark that she now possessed a pocket barometer which would do its very utmost to remain at 31 deg., if that was possible without being 'Very Dry'.

She received this little joke with extraordinary good humour. 'When I come down in the world, my dear,' she said, 'and these horrid anarchists are doing their best to send us all sky-high first, we'll visit the Courts of Europe together, like Count Boruwlaski. Do you think you could bring yourself to support your old friend in her declining years in a declining age?'

I smiled and touched her glove. 'Where thou goest, I will go,' I replied; and then could have bitten off my tongue in remorse. 'Pah,' gasped a secret voice, 'so that's going the same way too, is it?'

Yet heaven knows I was not a Puritan – and never shall be. I just adored things bright and beautiful. Music, too, in moderation, was my delight; and Susan Monnerie with her small, sweet voice would sometimes sing to me in one room while – in an almost unbearable homesickness – I listened in another. Concerts in general, however, left every muscle of my body as stiff with rheumatism as it was after my visit to Mr. Moss's farmhouse. The unexpected blare of a brass band simply froze my spine; and a really fine performance on the piano was sheer torture. Once, indeed, when Mrs. Monnerie's carriage was one of a mellay clustered together while the Queen drove by, in the appalling clamour of the Lancers' trombones and kettledrums, I fell prostrate in a kind of fit. So it was my silly nerves that cheated me of my one and only chance to huzza a Crowned Head not, if I may say so without disrespect, so very many sizes larger than my own.

Alas, Mrs. Monnerie was an enthusiast for all the pleasures

of the senses. I verily believe that it was only my vanity which prevented me from becoming as inordinately fat as Sir William Forbes-Smith's white meat threatened to make me.

Brightest novelty of all was my first visit to a theatre – the London night, the glare and clamour of the streets, the packed white rows of faces, the sea-like noise of talk, the glitter, shimmer, dazzle – it filled my veins with quicksilver; my heart seemed to be throbbing in my breast as fast as Mrs. Monnerie's watch. Fortunately she had remembered to take our seats on the farther side from the brass and drums of the orchestra. I restrained my shivers; the lights went out; and in the congregated gloom softly stole up the curtain on the ballet.

Perched up there in the velvet obscurity of our box, I surveyed a woodland scene, ruins, distant mountains, a rocky stream on which an enormous moon shone, and actually moved in the theatrical heavens. And when an exquisite figure floated, pale, gauzy, and a-tiptoe, into those artificial solitudes, drenched with filmy light, with a far cry of 'Fanny!' my heart suddenly stood still; and all the old stubborn infatuation flooded heavily back upon me once more.

Susan sat ghostlike, serenely smiling. Percy's narrow jaws were working on their hinges like those of a rabbit I had seen through my grandfather's spyglass nibbling a root of dandelion. Mrs. Monnerie reclined in her chair, hands on lap, with pursed-up mouth and weary eyes. There was nobody to confide in, then. But when from either side of the brightening stage flocked in winged creatures with lackadaisical arms and waxlike smilings, whose paint and powder caught back my mind rather than my feelings, my first light-of-foot was hovering beneath us close to the flaring footlights; and she was now no more Fanny than the circle of illuminated parchment over her head was the enchanting moon. What a complicated

world it was with all these *layers*! The experience filled me with a
hundred disquieting desires, and yet again, chiefest of them was
that which made sensitive the stumps where, if I turned into a
bird, my wings would grow, and which bade me 'escape'.

'She's getting devilish old and creaky on her pins,' yawned Percy,
when the curtain had descended, and I had sighingly shrunk back
into my own tasselled nook from the noise and emptiness of
actuality.

'No,' said Mrs. Monnerie, 'it is you, Percy, who are getting old.
You were born blasé. You'll be positively yawning your head off at
the Last Trump.'

'Dear Aunt Alice,' said Percy, squinting through his opera
glasses, 'nothing of the kind. I shall be helping you to find the mislaid knucklebones. Besides, it's better to be born – '

But the rest of his sentence – and I listened to him only
because I hated him – passed unheeded, for all my attention had
been drawn to Susan. The hand beside me had suddenly clutched
at her silk skirt, and a flush, gay as the Queen's Union Jacks in Bond
Street, had mounted into her clear, pale cheek, as with averted chin
she sat looking down upon someone in the stalls. At sight of her
blushing, a richer fondness for her lightened my mind. I followed
her eye to its goal, and gazed enthralled, now up, now down,
stringing all kinds of little beads of thoughts together; until, perhaps conscious that she was being watched, she turned and caught
me. Flamed up her cheeks yet hotter; and now mine too; for my
spirits had suddenly sunk into my shoes at the remembrance of
Wanderslore and my 'ghostly, gloating, little dwarfish creature'.
Then once more darkness stole over the vast, quieting house, and
the curtain reascended upon Romance.

Chapter Thirty-Five

Instead of its being a month as had been arranged, it was over six weeks before I was deposited again with my elegant dressing-case – a mere flying visitor – on Mrs. Bowater's doorstep. A waft of cooked air floated out into the June sunshine through the letter-box. Then, in the open door, just as of old, flushed and hot in her black clothes, there stood my old friend, indescribably the same, indescribably different. She knelt down on her own doormat, and we exchanged loving greetings. Once more I trod beneath the wreathing, guardian horns, circumnavigated the age-stained eight-day clock, and so into my parlour.

Nothing was changed. There stood the shepherdess ogling the shepherd; there hung Mr. Bowater; there dangled the chandelier; there angled the same half-dozen flies. Not a leg, caster, or anti-macassar was out of place. Yet how steadfastly I had to keep my back turned on my landlady lest she should witness my discomfiture. Faded, dingy, crowded, shrunken – it seemed unbelievable, as I glanced around me, that here I could have lived and breathed so many months, and been so ridiculously miserable, so tragically happy. All that bygone happiness and wretchedness seemed, for the moment, mere waste and folly. And not only that – 'common'.

I climbed Mr. Bates's clumsy staircase, put down my dressing-case, and slowly removing my gloves, faced dimly the curtained window. Beyond it lay the distant hills, misty in the morning sunbeams, the familiar meadows all but chin-high with buttercups.

'Oh, Mrs. Bowater,' I turned at last, 'here I am. You and the quiet sky – I wish I had never gone away. What is the use of being one's self, if one is always changing?'

'There comes a time, miss, when we don't change; only the outer walls crumble away morsel by morsel, so to speak. But that's not for you yet. Still, that's the reason. Me and the old sticks are just what we were, at least to the eye; and you – well, there! – the house has been like a cage with the bird gone.'

She stood looking at me with one long finger stretching bonily out on the black and crimson tablecloth, a shining sea of loving kindness in her eyes. 'I can see they have taken good care of you and all, preened the pretty feathers. Why, you are a bit plumper in figure, miss; only the voice a little different, perhaps.' The last words were uttered almost beneath her breath.

'My voice, Mrs. Bowater; oh, they cannot have altered *that*.'

'Indeed they have, miss; neater-twisted, as you might say; but not scarcely to be noticed by any but a very old friend. Maybe you are a little tired with your long drive and those two solemnities on the box. I remember the same thing – the change of voice – when Fanny came back from her first term at Miss Stebbings's.'

'How is she?' I inquired, in even tones. 'She has never written to me. Not a word.'

But, strange to say, as Mrs. Bowater explained, and not without a symptom of triumph, that's just what Fanny *had* done. Her letter was awaiting me on the mantelpiece, tucked in behind a plush-framed photograph.

'Now, let me see,' she went on, 'there's hot water in your basin, miss – I heard the carriage on the hill; a pair of slippers to ease your feet, in case in the hurry of packing they'd been forgot; and your strawberries and cream are out there icing themselves on the tray. So we shan't be no time, though disturbing news has come from Mr. Bowater, his leg not mending as it might have been foreseen – but that can wait.'

An unfamiliar Miss M. brushed her hair in front of me in the familiar looking-glass. It was not that her Monnerie raiment was particularly flattering, or she, indeed, pleasanter to look at – rather the contrary; and I gazed long and earnestly into the glass. But art has furtive and bewitching fingers. While in my home-made clothes I had looked just myself, in these I looked like one or other of my guardian angels, or perhaps, as an unprejudiced Fleming would have expressed it – the perfect lady. How gradual must have been the change in me to have passed thus unnoticed. But I didn't want to think. I felt dulled and dispirited. Even Mrs. Bowater had not been so entranced to see me as I had anticipated. It was tiresome to be disappointed. I rummaged in a bottom drawer, got out an old gown, made a grimace at myself in my mind, and sat down to Fanny's letter. But then again, what are externals? Who was this cool-tempered Miss M. who was now scanning the once heartrending handwriting?

> DEAR MIDGETINA – When this will reach you, I don't know. But somehow I cannot, or rather I can, imagine you the cynosure of the complete peerage, and prefer that my poor little letter should not uprear its modest head in the midst of all that Granjer. You may not agree – but if a few weeks of a High Life that may possibly continue into

infinity has made *no* difference to you, then Fanny is not among the prophets.

We have not met since – we parted. But did you ever know a yesterday entomb itself with such ingratiating rapidity? Have you in your sublime passion for Nature ever watched a Sexton Beetle? But, mind you, I have helped. The further all that slips away, the less I can see I was to blame for it. What's in your blood needs little help from outside. Cynical it may sound; but imagine the situation if I *had* married him! What could existence have been but a Nightmare-Life-in-Death? (*Vide* S. T. Coleridge.) Now the Dream continues – for us both.

Oh, yes, I can see your little face needling up at this. But you must remember, dear Midgetina, that you will never, never be able to see things in a truly human perspective. Few people, of course, try to. You do. But though your view may be delicate as gossamer and clear as a glass marble, it can't be full-size. Boil a thing down, it isn't the *same*. What remains has the virtues of an essence, but not the volume of its origin. This sounds horribly *school-booky*; but I am quite convinced you are too concentrated. And I, being what I am, only the full volume can be my salvation. Enough. The text is as good as the sermon – far better, in fact.

Now I am going to be still more callous. My own little private worries have come right – been made to. I'm tit for tat, that is, and wiser for it beyond words. Some day, when Society has taught you all its lessons, I will explain further. Anyhow, first I send you back £3 of what I owe you. And thank you. Next I want you to find out from Mrs. Mummery (as Mother calls her – or did), if among her distinguished acquaintance she knows anyone with one or two, or at most three, small and adorable children who need an excellent governess. Things have made it undesirable for me to stay on here much longer. It shall be I who give notice, or, shall we say, terminate the engagement.

Be an angel, then. First, wake up. Candidly, to think me better than I am is more grossly unfair than if I thought you taller than you are. Next, sweet cynosure, find me a sinecure. Don't trouble about salary. (You wouldn't, you positive acorn of quixoticism, not if I owed you half a million.) But remember! *Wanted by the end of August at latest, a Lady, wealthy, amiable, with two Cherubic Doves in family, boys preferred.* The simple, naked fact being that after this last bout of life's fitful fever, I pine for a nap.

Of course Mother can see this letter if she wishes to, and you don't mind. But personally I should prefer to have the bird actually fluttering in my hand before she contemplates it in the bush.

I said *pine* just now. Do you ever find a word suddenly so crammed with meaning that at any moment it threatens to explode? Well, Midgetina, them's my sentiments. Penitent I shall never be, until I take the veil. But I have once or twice lately awoke in a kind of glassy darkness – beyond all moonshine – alone. Then, if I hadn't been born just thick-ribbed, unmeltable ice – well … Vulgar, vulgar Fanny!

Fare thee well, Midgetina. 'One cried "God bless us", and "Amen" the other.' Prostituted though he may have been for scholastic purposes, w. s. knew something of Life.

Yours – F.

What was the alluring and horrifying charm for me of Fanny's letters? This one set my mind, as always, wandering off into a maze. There was a sour taste in it, and yet – it was all really and truly Fanny. I could see her unhappy eyes glittering through the mask. She saw *herself* – perhaps more plainly than one should. 'Vulgar Fanny'. As for its effect on me, it was as if I had fallen into a bed of nettles, and she herself, picking me up, had scoffed: 'Poor little Midgekin', and supplied the dock. Her cynicism was its own antidote, I suppose. The selfishness, the vanity, and impenetrable hardness – even love had never been so blind as to ignore all that, and now what love remained for her had the sharpest of sharp eyes.

And yet, though my little Bowater parlour looked cheap and dingy after the splendours of No. 2, Fanny somehow survived every odious comparison. She was very *intelligent*, I whispered to myself. Mrs. Monnerie would certainly approve of that. And I prickled at the thought. And I – I was too 'concentrated'. In spite of my plumping 'figure', I could never, never be full-size. If only Fanny had meant that as a compliment, or even as a kind of explanation to go on with. No, she had meant it for the truth. And it must be far easier for a leopard to change his spots than his inside. The accusation set all the machinery of my mind emptily whirring.

My glance fell on my Paris frock, left in a shimmering slovenly ring on the floor. It wandered off to Fanny's postal order, spread over my lap like an expensive antimacassar. She had worked for that money; while I had never been anything more useful than 'an angel'. In fancy I saw her blooming in a house as sumptuous as Mrs. Monnerie's. Bloom indeed! I hated the thought, yet realized, too, that it was safer – even if for the time being not so profitable – to be life-size. And, as if out of the listening air, a cold dart pierced me through. Suppose my Messrs. Harris and Harris and Harris might not be such honest trustees as Miss Fenne had vouched for. Suppose they decamped with my £110 per annum! – I caught a horrifying glimpse of the wolf that was always sniffing at Fanny's door.

Mrs. Bowater brought in my luncheon, and – as I insisted – her own, too. The ice from Mr. Tidy, the fishmonger's, had given a slightly marine flavour to the cream, and I had to keep my face averted as much as possible from the scorched red chop sprawling and oozing on her plate. How could she bring herself to eat it? We are such stuff as dreams are made on, said Hamlet. So then was Mrs. Bowater. What a mystery then was this mutton fat! But chop or no chop, it was a happy meal.

Having waved my extremely 'Fannyish' letter at her, I rapidly dammed that current of her thoughts by explaining that I had changed my clothes not (as a gleam from her eye had seemed to suspect) because I was afraid of spoiling my London finery, but in order to be really at home. For the first time I surprised her muttering a grace over the bone on her plate. Then she removed the tray, accepted a strawberry, folded her hands in her lap, and we began to talk. She asked a hundred and one questions concerning my health and happiness, but never once mentioned Mrs. Monnerie; and at last, after a small pause, filled by us both with the same thought, she remarked that 'that young Mr. Anon was nothing if not persistent'.

Since I had gone, not a week had passed, she told me, but he had come rapping at the door after dusk to inquire after me. 'Though why he should scowl like a pitchpot to hear that you are enjoying the lap of luxury –' The angular shoulders achieved a shrug at least as Parisian as my discarded gown.

'Why doesn't he write to me, then? Twice, in ten weeks!'

'Well, it's *six*, miss, I've counted, though *seemingly* sixty. But that being the question, he is there to answer it, at any time this evening, or at six to-morrow morning, if London ways haven't cured you of early rising.'

So we went off together, Mrs. Bowater and I, in the cool of the evening about half an hour after sunset – she, alas, a little ruffled because I had refused to change back again into my Monnerie finery. 'But Mrs. Bowater, imagine such a thing in a real wild garden!' I protested, but without mollifying her, and without further explaining – how could I do that? – that the gown which Miss Sentimentality (or Miss Coquette) was actually wearing was that in which she had first met Mr. Anon.

Chapter Thirty-Six

I trod close in Mrs. Bowater's track as she convoyed me through
a sea of greenery breaking here and there to my waist and even
above my hat. Summer had been busy in Wanderslore. Honey-
suckle and acid-sweet brier were in bloom; sleeping bindweed and
pimpernel. The air was liquidly sweet with uncountable odours.
And the fading skies dyed bright the frowning front of the house,
about which the new-come swifts shrieked in their play over my
wilderness. Mr. Anon looked peculiar, standing alone there.

Having bidden him a gracious good-evening, Mrs. Bowater
after a long, ruminating glance at us, decided that she would 'take
a stroll through the grounds'. We watched her black figure trail
slowly away up the overgrown terraces towards the house. Then
he turned. His clear, dwelling eyes, with that darker line encircling
the grey-black iris, fixed themselves on me, his mouth tight-shut.

'Well,' he said at last, almost wearily. 'It has been a long waiting.'

I was unprepared for this sighing. 'It has indeed,' I replied. 'But
it is exceedingly pleasant to see Beechwood Hill again. I wrote;
but you did not answer my letter, at least not the last.'

My voice dropped away; every one of the fine little speeches I
had thought to make forgotten.

'And now you are here.'

'Yes,' I said quickly, a little timid of any silence between us, 'and that's pleasant too. You can have no notion what a stiff, glaring garden it is up there – geraniums and gravel, you know, and windows, windows, windows. They are wonderfully kind to me – but I don't much love it.'

'Then why stay?' he smiled. 'Still, you are, at least, safely out of *her* clutches.'

'Clutches!' I hated the way we were talking. 'Thank you very much. You forget you are speaking of one of my friends. Besides, I can take care of myself.' He made no answer.

'You are so gloomy,' I continued. 'So – oh, I don't know – about everything. It's because you are always cooped up in one place, I suppose. One must take the world – a little – as it is, you know. Why don't you go away; travel; *see* things? Oh, if I were a man.'

His eyes watched my lips. Everything seemed to have turned sour. To have waited and dreamed; to have actually changed my clothes and come scuttling out in a silly longing excitement – for this. Why, I felt more lonely and helpless under Wanderslore's evening sky than ever I had been in my cedar-wood privacy in No. 2.

'I mean it, I mean it,' I broke out suddenly. 'You domineer over me. You pamper me up with silly stories – "trailing clouds of glory", I suppose. They are not true. It's every one for himself in this world, I can tell you; and in future, please understand, I intend to be my own mistress. Simply because in a little private difficulty I asked you to help me –'

He turned irresolutely. 'They have dipped you pretty deep in the dye-pot.'

'And what, may I ask, do you mean by that?'

'I mean', and he faced me, 'that I am precisely what your friend, Miss Bowater, called me. What more is there to say?'

'And pray, am I responsible for everything my friends say? And to have dragged up *that* wretched fiasco after we had talked it out to the very dregs! Oh, how I have been longing and longing to come home. And this is what you make of it.'

He turned his face towards the west, and its vast light irradiated his sharp-boned features, the sloping forehead beneath the straight, black hair. Fume as I might, resentment fainted away in me.

'You don't seem to understand,' I went on; 'it's the waste – the waste of it all. Why do you make it so that I can't talk naturally to you, as friends talk? If I am alone in the world, so are you. Surely we can tell the truth to one another. I am utterly wretched.'

'There is only one truth that matters; you do not love me. Why should you? But that's the barrier. And the charm of it is that not only the Gods, but the miserable Humans, if only they knew it, would enjoy the sport.'

'Love! I detest the very sound of the word. What has it ever meant to me, I should like to know, in this – this cage?'

'Scarcely a streak of gilding on the bars,' he sneered miserably. 'Still we are sharing the same language now.'

The same language. Self-pitying tears pricked into my eyes; I turned my head away. And in the silence, stealthily, out of a dark woody hollow nearer the house, as if at an incantation, broke a low, sinister, protracted rattle, like the croaking of a toad. I knew that sound; it came straight out of Lyndsey – called me back.

'S-sh!' I whispered, caught up with delight. 'A nightjar! Listen. Let's go and look.'

I held out my hand. His sent a shiver down my spine. It was

clammy cold, as if he had just come out of the sea. Thrusting our way between the denser clumps of weeds, we pushed on cautiously until we actually stood under the creature's enormous oak. So elusive and deceitful was the throbbing croon of sound that it was impossible to detect on which naked branch in the black leafiness the bird sat churring. The wafted fragrances, the placid dusky air, and, far, far above, the delicate, shallowing deepening of the faint-starred blue – how I longed to sip but one drop of drowsy mandragora and forget this fretting, inconstant self.

We stood, listening; and an old story I had read somewhere floated back into memory. 'Once, did you ever hear it?' I whispered close to him, 'there was a ghost came to a house near Cirencester. I read of it in a book. And when it was asked: "Are you a good spirit or a bad?", it made no answer, but vanished, the book said – I remember the very words – "with a curious perfume and most melodious twang". With a curious perfume', I repeated, 'and most melodious twang. There now, would you like *me* to go like that? Oh, if I were a moth, I would flit in there and ask that old Death-thing to catch me. Even if I cannot love you, you are part of all this. You feed my very self. Mayn't that be enough?'

His grip tightened round my fingers; the entrancing, toneless dulcimer thrummed on.

I leaned nearer, as if to raise the shadowed lids above the brooding eyes, 'What can I give you – only to be your peace? I do assure you it is yours. But I haven't the secret of knowing what half the world means. Look at me. Is it not *all* a mystery? Oh, I know it, even though they jeer and laugh at me. I beseech you be merciful, and keep me what I am.'

So I pleaded and argued, scarcely heeding the words I said. Yet I realize now that it was only my mind that wrestled with him there. It was what came after that took the heart out of me. There came a clap of wings, and the bird swooped out of its secrecy into the air above us, a moment showed his white-splashed, cinder-coloured feathers in the dusk, seemed to tumble as if broken-winged upon the air, squawked, and was gone. The interruption only hastened me on.

'Still, still listen,' I implored: 'if Time would but cease awhile and let me breathe.'

'There, there,' he muttered. 'I was unkind. A filthy jealousy.'

'But think. There may never come another hour like this. Know, know now, that you have made me happy. I can never be so alone again. I share my secretest thoughts – my imagination, with you; isn't that a kind of love? I assure you that it is. Once I heard my mother talking, and sometimes I have wondered myself, if I am quite like – oh, you know what they say: a freak of Nature. Tell me; if by some enchantment I were really and indeed come from those snow mountains of yours, and that sea, would you recognize me? Would you? No, no; it's only a story – why, even all this green and loveliness is only skin deep. If the Old World were just to shrug its shoulders, Mr. Anon, we should all, big and little, be clean gone.'

My words seemed merely to be like drops of water dripping upon a sponge. 'Wake!' I tugged at his hand. 'Look!' Kneeling down sidelong, I stooped my cheek up at him from a cool, green mat of grass, amid which a glow-worm burned: 'Is this a – a *Stranger's* face?'

He came no nearer; surveyed me with a long, quiet smile of infinitely sorrowful indulgence. 'A Stranger's? How else could it be, if I love you?'

Intoxicated in that earthy fragrance, washed about with the colours of the motionless flowers, it seemed I was merely talking to someone who could assure me that I was still in life, still myself. A strand of my hair had fallen loose, and smiling its gold pin between my lips, I looped it back. 'Oh, but you see – haven't I told you? – I can't love you. Perhaps; I don't know ...What shall I do? What shall I say? Now suppose', I went on, 'I like myself *that* much,' and I held my thumb and finger just ajar, 'then I like *you,* think of you, hope for you, why, that!' – and I swept my hand clean across the empty zenith. '*Now* do you understand?'

'Oh, my dear, my dear,' he said, and smiled into my eyes.

I laughed out in triumph at the success of my device. And he laughed too, as if in a conspiracy with me – and with Misery, I could see, sitting like an old hag at the door from which the sound came. And out of the distance the nightjar set again to its churring.

'Then I have made you a little – a little less unhappy?' I asked him, and hid my face in my hands, in a desolate peace and solitude.

He knelt beside me, held out his hand as if to touch me, withdrew it again. All presence of him distanced and vanished away in that small darkness. I prayed not to think any more, not to be exiled again into – how can I explain my meaning except by saying – Myself? Would some further world have withdrawn its veils and have let me in then and for ever if that lightless quiet could have continued a little longer? Is it the experience of every human being seemingly to trespass at times so close upon the confines of existence as that?

It was his own harsh voice that broke the spell.

'Wake, wake!' it called in my ear. 'The woman is looking for you. We must go.'

My hands slipped from my face. A slow, sobbing breath drew itself into my body. And there beneath evening's vacancy of twilight showed the transfigured scene of the garden, and, near me, the anxious, suffering face of this stranger, faintly greened by the light of the worm.

'Wake!' he bade me, rapping softly with his bony finger on my hand. I stared at him out of a dream.

Chapter Thirty-Seven

Time and circumstance have strangely divided me from the Miss M. of those days. I look back on her, not with shame, but with a shrug of my shoulders, a sort of incredulous tolerance – almost as if she too were a stranger. Perhaps a few years hence I shall be looking back with an equal detachment on the Miss M. seated here at this moment with her books and her pen in the solitude of her thoughts, vainly endeavouring to fret out and spin together mere memories that nobody will ever have the patience to read. Shall I then be able to tell myself what I want now, give words to the vague desires that still haunt me? Shall I still be waiting on for some unconceived eventuality?

There is, too, another small riddle of a different kind, which I cannot answer. In memory and imagination, as I steadily gaze out of this familiar room recalling the past, I am that very self in that distant garden of Wanderslore. But even as I look, I am not only *within* myself there, but also outside of myself. I seem, I mean, actually to be contemplating, as if with my own eyes, those two queer, silent figures returning through the drowsying, moth-haunted flowers and grasses to the black, vigilant woman awaiting them beside the garden house. 'Alas, you poor, blind thing,' I seem, like a ghost, to warn the one small creature, 'have a care; seize your happiness; it is vanishing!'

All that I write, then, is an attempt only to tell, not to explain. I realize that sometimes I was pretending things, yet did not know that I was pretending; that often I acted with no more conscience or consciousness, maybe, than has a carrion crow that picks out the eyes of a lamb, or a flower that draws in its petals at noon. Yet I know – know absolutely, that I was, and am, responsible not only for myself, but for everything. For my whole world. And I cannot explain this either. At times, as if to free myself, I had to stare at what appalled me. I am sure, for instance, that Mrs. Monnerie never dreamed that her mention of Mr. Crimble sent me off in fancy at the first opportunity to that woeful outhouse in his mother's garden to look in on him there – again. But I did so look at him, and was a little more at peace with him after that. Why, then, cannot I be at peace with one who loved me?

Maybe if I could have foreseen how I was to come to Wanderslore again, I should have been a less selfish, showy, and capricious companion to him that June evening. But I was soon lapped back into my life in London; and thought only of Mr. Anon, as I am apt to think of God: namely, when I needed his presence and his help. As a matter of fact, I had small time to think. Even the doubts and misgivings that occasionally woke me in the night melted like dreams in the morning. Every morrow blotted out its yesterday – as faded flowers are flung away out of a vase.

In that vortex of visits and visitors, that endless vista of amusements and eating and drinking – some hidden spring of life in me began to fail. What a little self-conscious affected donkey I became, shrilly hee-hawing away; the centre of a simpering throng plying me with flattery. What airs I put on.

If this Life of mine had been a Biography, the author of it would have had the satisfaction of copying out from a pygmy blue morocco diary the names of all the celebrated and distinguished people I met at No. 2. A few of them underlined in red! The amusing thing is that, like my father, I was still a Radical at heart and preferred low life – flea-bane and chick-weed – to the fine flowers of culture; which only means, of course, that in this I am a snob inside out. Nevertheless, the attention I had shunned I now began to covet, and, like a famous artist or dancer, would go sulky to bed if I had been left to blush at being unseen. I forced myself to be more and more fastidious, and tried to admire as little as possible. I would even imitate and affect languid pretentiousnesses and effronteries; and learned to be downright rude to people in a cultivated way. As for small talk, I soon accumulated a repertory of that, and could use the fashionable slang and current 'conversations' like a native. All this intensely amused Mrs. Monnerie. For, of course, the more like the general run of these high livers I was, the more conspicuous I became.

The truth is, the Lioness's head was in peril of being turned, and, like a blind kitten in a bucket of water, I came very near to being drowned in the social cream-bowl. For what little I gained in public by all this silly vanity I paid a heavy price when alone. I began to be fretful and utterly useless to myself – just lived on from excitement to excitement. And Fleming soon had better reasons for detesting me than merely because I was horribly undersized.

Perhaps I am exaggerating; but the truth is I find it extremely difficult to keep patience with Mrs. Monnerie's pampered *protégée*. She was weak and stupid. Yet learning had not lost its charm. My mind persisted in being hungry, however much satiated were my senses and fine feelings. I even infected Susan with my enthusiasm for indigestible knowledge. For since Mrs. Monnerie had begun to find my passion for shells, fossils, flints, butterflies, and stuffed animals a little wearisome, it was her niece who now accompanied me to my many Meccas in her stead. By a happy chance we often met on these pilgrimages the dark, straight-nosed young man whom I had looked down upon at my first ballet, and who also apparently was a fanatic.

However deeply engrossed in mementoes of the Dark or Stone Ages he might be, he never failed to see us the moment we entered his echoing gallery. He would lift his eyebrows; his monocle would drop out; and he would come sauntering over to meet us, looking as fresh as apples cold with dew. I liked Captain Valentine. So much so that I sent an almost rapturous description of him to Mr. Anon.

He did not seem in the least to mind being seen in my company. We had our little private jokes together. We both enjoyed the company of Susan. He was so crisp and easy and quick-witted, and yet – to my unpractised eye – looked delightfully domesticatable. Even the crustiest old caretaker, at a word and a smile from Captain Valentine, would allow me to seat myself on the glass cases. So I could gloat on their contents at leisure. And certainly of the three of us I was by far the most diligent student.

Long hours, too, of the none too many which will make up my life would melt away like snow in Mrs. Monnerie's library. A button specially fixed for me in the wainscot would summon a manservant. Having ranged round the lofty walls, I would point up at what books I wanted. They would be strewn around me on the floor – gilded and leathery volumes, some of them almost of my own height, and many times my weight. I would open the lid, turn the great pages, and carefully sprawling on my elbows between them, would pore for hours together on their coloured pictures of birds and flowers, gems and glass, ruins, palaces, mountains – hunting, cock-fighting, fashions, fine ladies, and foreign marvels. And I dipped into novels so like the unpleasanter parts of my own life that they might just as well have been autobiographies.

The secret charm of all this was that I was alone; and while I was reading I ceased to worry. I just drugged my mind with books. I would go rooting and rummaging in Mrs. Monnerie's library, like a little pig after truffles. There was hardly a subject I left untasted – old plays, and street ballads; Johnson's enormous dictionary, that extraordinary book on Melancholy with its borage and hellebore and the hatted young man in love; *Bel and the Dragon*, the *Newgate Calendar*. I even nibbled at Debrett – and clean through all its 'M's'. The more I read, the more ignorant I seemed to become; and quite apart from this smattering jumble of knowledge, I pushed my way through memoirs and romances at the very sight of which my poor godmother would have fainted dead off.

They may have been harmful; but I certainly can't say that I regret having read them – which may be part of the harm. You could tell the really bad ones almost at a sniff. They had bad smells, like a beetle cupboard or a scented old man. I read on of witchcraft and devils, yet hated the cloud they cast over me – like some horrible treacle in the mind. But as for the authors who just reasoned about Time and God and Miracles, and so on, I poked about in them willingly enough; but my imagination went off the other way – with my heart in its pocket. Possibly without knowing it. But I do know this: that never to my dying day shall I learn what a common-sized person with a pen or a pencil can *not* make shocking, or be shocked at. It seemed to me that to some of these authors the whole universe was nothing better than a Squid, and a very much scandalized young woman would attempt to replace their works on the shelves.

When in good faith I occasionally ventured to share (or possibly to show off) some curious scrap of information with Mrs. Monnerie, I thought her eyes would goggle out of her head. It was perhaps my old *mole* habit that prevented me from dividing things up into the mentionable and unmentionable. Possibly I carried this habit to excess; and yet, of course, remained the slave of my own small pruderies. Still, I don't think it was either Mrs. Monnerie's or Percy's pruderies that I had to be careful about. To make *him* laugh was one of the most hateful of my experiences at No. 2.

I have read somewhere that the human instincts are 'un-like Apollyon, since they always degrade themselves by their disguises. They dress themselves up as Apes and Mandrils; he as a ringed, supple, self-flattering, seductive Serpent'. Possibly that has something to do with it. Or is it that my instincts are also on a petty scale? I don't know. I hate and fear pain even more than most people, and have fought pretty hard in the cause of self-preservation. On the other hand, I haven't the faintest wish in the world to 'perpetuate my species'. Not that I might not have been happy in a husband and in my children. I suppose that kind of thing comes on one just as naturally as breathing. Nevertheless, I suspect I was born to be an Old Maid. Calling up Spirits from the vasty deep has always seemed to me to be a far more dreadful mystery than Death. It is not, indeed, the ghosts of the dead and the past which I think should oppress the people I see around me, but those of the children to come. I thank God from the bottom of my heart for the happiness and misery of having been alive, but my small mind reels when I brood on what the gift of it implies.

Well, well, well; of one burden at least I can absolve Mrs. Monnerie – that of making me so sententious. Somehow or other, but ever more sluggishly, those few crowded summer months of my twentieth year wore away. It is more of a mercy than a curse, I suppose, that Time never stands still.

Meanwhile two events occurred which, for the time being, sobered and alarmed me. A few days before I had actually planned to pay a second visit to Mrs. Bowater's, the almost incredible news reached me that she was sailing for South America. It would hardly have surprised me more to hear that she was sailing for Sirius. She came to bid me good-bye. It was *Mr.* Bowater, she told me. She had been too confident of the 'good nursing'. Far from mending in this world, his leg threatened 'to carry him off into the next'. At these tidings Shame thrust out a very ugly head at me from her retreat. I had utterly forgotten the anxiety my poor old friend was in.

She put on her spectacles with trembling fingers, and pushed her husband's letter across to me. The handwriting was bold and thick, yet I fancied it looked a little weak in the loops:

> DEAR EMILY – The leg's giving me the devil in this hole of a place. It looks as if I shouldn't get through with it. I should be greatly obliged if you would come out to me. They'll give you all the necessary information at the shipping office. Ask for Pullen. My love to Fanny. What's she looking like now? I should like to see her before I go; but better say nothing about it. You've got about a month or three weeks, I should think; if that.
>
> I remain, your affec. husband,
JOSEPH BOWATER

'Easy enough in *appearance*,' was Mrs. Bowater's comment, as she folded up this stained and flimsy letter again, and stuffed it into her purse, 'but it's past even Mr. Bowater to control what can be read between the lines.'

She looked at me dumbly; the skin seemed to hang more loosely on her face. In vain I tried to think of a comforting speech. The tune of *Eternal Father*, one of the hymns we used to sing on windy winter Sunday evenings together, had begun droning in my head. The thought, too, was worrying me, though I did not put it into words, that Mr. Bowater, far rather than in Buenos Ayres, would have preferred to find his last resting-place in Nero Deep or the Virgin's Trough – those enormous pits of blue in the oceans which I myself had so often gloated on in his Atlas. We were old friends now, he and I. He was Fanny's father. The very ferocity of his look had become a secret understanding between us. And now – at this very moment perhaps – he was dying. The jaunty '*devil*' in his letter, I am afraid, affected me far more than Mrs. Bowater's troubled face or even her courage.

Without a moment's hesitation she had made up her mind to face the Atlantic's thousands of miles of wind and water to join the husband she had told me had long been 'worse than' dead. The very tone in which she uttered the word 'steamer' was even more lugubrious than the enormous, mocking hoot of a vessel that had once alarmed me out of the sea one still evening at Lyme Regis. It was a horrifying prospect, yet she just quietly said 'steamer', and looked at me over her spectacles.

While she was away, the little house on Beechwood Hill, 'bought, thank God, with my own money', was to be shut up, but it was mine if I cared to return to it, and would ask a neighbour of hers, Mrs. Chantry, for the key. It would be Fanny's if anything 'happened' to herself. So dismal was all this that Mrs. Bowater seemed already lost to me, and I twice an orphan. We talked on together in low, cautious voices. After a single sharp, cold glance at my visitor, Fleming had left us to ourselves over an enormous silver teapot. I grew so nervous at last, watching Mrs. Bowater's slow glances of disapproval at her surroundings; her hot, tired face; and listening to her long-drawn sighs, that again and again I lost the thread of what she was saying, and could answer 'Yes' or 'No', only by instinct.

What with an antiquated time-table, a mislaid railway ticket, and an impudent bus-conductor, her journey had been a trying experience. I discovered, too, that Mrs. Bowater disliked the West End. She had first knocked at No. 4 by mistake. Its butler had known nothing whatever at all about any Miss M., and Mrs. Bowater had been too considerate to specify my dimensions. She had then shared a few hot moments in the porch of No. 2 with a more fashionable visitor – to neither's satisfaction. A manservant had admitted her to Mrs. Monnerie's marble halls and 'barefaced' statuary, and had apparently thought the large parcel she carried in her arms should have been delivered in the area.

She bore no resentment, though I myself felt a little uneasy. Life was like that, she seemed to imply, and she had been no party to it. There was no doubt a better world where things would be different – it was extraordinary what a number of conflicting sentiments she could convey in a pause or a shut of her mouth. Black and erect, she sat glooming over that alien teapot, sipping Mrs. Monnerie's colourless China tea, firmly declining to grimace at its insipidity, until she had told me all there was to tell.

At last, having gathered herself together, she exhorted me to write to that young Mr. Anon. 'I see a fidelity one might almost say dog-like, miss, on that face, apart, as I have reasons for supposing, from a sufficiency in his pocket. Though, the Lord knows, you are young yet and seemingly in no need of a home.'

Parcel, reticule, umbrella – she bent over me with closed eyes, and muttered shamefacedly that she had remembered me in her Will, 'and may God bless you, miss, I'm sure'.

I clutched the gloved hand in a sudden helpless paroxysm of grief and foreboding. 'Oh, Mrs. Bowater, you forgive –' I choked, and still no words would come.

She was gone, past recall; and all the love and gratitude and remorse I had longed to express flooded up in me. Yet, stuck up there in my chair, my chief apprehension had been that Fleming might come in again, and cast yet another veiled sneering glance at my visitor.

Peering between the gilded balusters, I watched my old friend droop away stiffly down the mild, lustrous staircase, bow to the man who opened the door for her, and emerge into the sunny emptiness.

Maybe the thought had drifted across her mind that I had indeed been dipped in the dye-pot. But now – these many years afterwards – there is no more risk of misunderstanding. It is eight o'clock; the light is fading. Chizzel Hill glows green. I hear her feebling step on the stairs. She will peer at me over spectacles that now always straddle her nose. I must put my pen and papers away; and I, too, have made my Will.

Chapter Thirty-Eight

Mrs. Bowater's departure from England – and it seemed as if its very map in my mind had become dismally empty – was not my only anxiety. My solicitors had hitherto been prompt; their remittances almost monotonously identical in amount. But my quarterly allowance on Midsummer Day had been followed by a letter a week or two after her good-bye. It seemed to be in excellent English, and yet it was all but unintelligible to me. Every re-reading of it – the paper had apparently been dipped in water and dried – increased its obscurity and my alarm. I knew nothing about money matters, and the encyclopædia I consulted only made me more dejected and confused. I remembered with remorse my poor father's last troubles. To answer the Harrises was impossible, and further study of their letter soon became unnecessary, for I had learned it by heart.

The one thing certain was that Fanny's wolf had begun scratching at my door! that my income was in imminent danger. I had long since squandered the greater part of what remained out of my savings (after Fanny had helped herself) on presents and fal-lals; merely, I am afraid, to show Mrs. Monnerie that I, too, could be extravagant. How much I owed her I could not even conjecture, and had not dared to inquire. To ask her counsel was equally impossible. She was almost as remote from me in this respect as Mrs. Bowater, now in the centre of the Atlantic. As for Fanny, I had returned her postal orders and had heard no more.

For days and days gloom hung over me like a thundercloud. Wherever I went I was followed by the spectres of the Harrises. Then, for a time, as do all things, foreboding and anxiety gradually faded off. I plunged back into the cream-bowl with the deliberate intention of drowning trouble.

Meanwhile, I had not forgotten Fanny's 'sinecure'. One mackerel-skied afternoon, Mrs. Monnerie and I and Susan were returning across the Park from an 'At Home' – 'to meet Miss M.' A small child of the house had richly entertained the company by howling with terror at sight of me, until he had been removed by his nurse. I bear him no grudge; he made a peg on which to hang Fanny's proposal.

'And what can Miss Bowater do? What are her qualifications?' Mrs. Monnerie inquired pleasantly.

'She is – dark and – pale,' I replied, staring a little giddily out of the carriage at the sheep munching their way over the London grass.

'Dark and pale?' mused Mrs. Monnerie. 'Well, that goes nearer the bone, perhaps, than medals and certificates and that sort of thing. Still, a rather Jane Eyreish kind of governess, eh, Susan?'

Unfortunately I was acquainted with only one of the Miss Brontës, and that not Charlotte.

'Miss Bowater is immensely *clever*, Mrs. Monnerie,' I hurried on, 'and extremely popular with – with the other mistresses, and that sort of thing. She's not a bit what you might guess from what you might suppose.'

'Which means, I gather,' commented Mrs. Monnerie affably,

'that Miss Bowater is the typical landlady's daughter. A perfect angel in – or out of – the house, eh, Miss Innocent?'

'No,' said I, 'I don't think Miss Bowater is an angel. She is so interesting, so *herselfish*, you know. She simply couldn't be happy at Miss Stebbings's – the school where she's teaching now. It's not salary, Mrs. Monnerie, she is thinking of – just two nice children and their mother, that's all.'

This vindication of Fanny left me uncomfortably hot; I continued to gaze fixedly into the green distances of the park.

Yet all was well. Mrs. Monnerie appeared to be satisfied with my testimonial. 'You shall give me her address, little Binbin; and we'll have a look at the young lady,' she decided.

Yet I was none too happy at my success. Those familiar old friends of mine – motives – began worrying me. Would the change be really good for Fanny? Would it – and I had better confess that this troubled me the most – would it be really good for me? I wanted to help her; I wanted also to show her off. And what a joy it would be if she should change into the Fanny of my dreams. On the other hand, supposing she didn't. On the whole, I rather dreaded the thought of her appearance at No. 2.

Susan followed me into my room. 'Who *is* this Miss Bowater?' she inquired, 'besides, I mean, being your landlady's daughter, and that kind of thing?'

But my further little confidences failed to satisfy her.

'But why is she so *not* an angel, then? Clever and lovely – it's a rather unusual combination, you know. And yet' – she reflectively smiled at me, all candour and gentleness – 'well, not unique.'

I ran away as fast as ever I could with so endearing a compliment – and tossed it back again over my shoulder: 'You don't mean, Susan, that *you* are not clever?'

'I do, my dear; indeed I do. I am so stupid that unless things are as plain and open as the nose on my face, I feel like suffocating. I'm dreadfully out of the fashion – a horrible discredit to my sex. As for Miss Bowater, I was merely being odious, that was all. To be quite honest and hateful – I didn't like the sound of her. And Aunt Alice is so easily carried away by any new scent. If a thing's a novelty, or just good to look at, or what they call a work of art – why, the hunt's up. There wouldn't have been any use for the Serpent in *her* Eden. Mere things, of course, don't matter much: except that they rather lumber up one's rooms; and I prefer not to live in a museum. It's when it comes to persons. Still, it isn't as if Miss Bowater was coming here.'

I remained silent, thinking this speech over. Had it, I speculated, 'come to' being a 'person' in my own case?

'Did you meet any other interesting people there?' Miss Monnerie went on, as if casually, turning off and on the while the little cluster of coloured electric globes that was on my table. 'I mean besides Miss Bowater and that poor, dreadful – you know?'

'No,' I said bluntly, 'not many.'

'You don't mind my asking all these questions? And just in exchange, you solemn thing, I'll tell *you* a secret. It will be like shutting it up in the delightfullest, delicatest little rosebud of a box.' In that instant's pause, it was as if a dream had passed swiftly, entrancingly, across the grave, smiling face.

'Look!' she said, stooping low, and laying her slim left hand, palm downwards, across my table. I did look; and the first thing I noticed was how like herself that hand was, and how much less vigorous and formidable than Fanny's. And then I caught her meaning.

'Oh, Susan,' I cried in a woeful voice, gazing at the smouldering stones ringing that long slim third finger, 'wherever I turn, I hear that.'

'Hear what?'

'Why, of love, I mean.'

'But why, why?' the narrow brows lifted in faint distress, 'I am going to be ever so happy.'

'Ah, yes, I know, I know. But why can't you be happy alone?'

She looked at me, and a faint red dusked the delicate cheek. 'Not *so* happy. Not *me*, I mean.'

'You do love him, then?' the words jerked out.

'Why, you strange thing, how curiously you speak to me. Of course I love him. I am going to marry him.'

'But how do you know?' I persisted. 'Does it mean more to you – well – than the secret of everything? I mean, what comes when one is almost nothing? Does it make you more yourself, or just break you in two, or melt you away? – oh, like mist that is gone, and to every petal and blade of grass its drop of burning water?'

A shade of dismay, almost of fear – the look a timid animal gives when startled – stole into her eyes. 'You ask such odd questions! How can I answer them? I know this – I would rather die than *not*. Is that what you mean?'

'Oh,' my voice fainted away – disappointment, darkness, ennui; 'only that!'

'But what do you mean? What are you saying? Have you been told all this? It disturbs me; your face is like –'

'Yes! what is it like?' I cried in distress, myself sinking back into myself, as if hiding in a lair.

'I can't say,' she faltered. 'I didn't know –'

We talked on. But though I tried to blur over and withdraw what I had said, she remained dissatisfied. A thin edge of formality had for the moment pushed in between us.

That night I addressed a belated letter to Wanderslore, reproaching Mr. Anon for not writing to me, telling him of Mrs. Bowater's voyage, and begging him to assure the garden-house and the fading summer flowers that they had not been deserted in my dreams.

At a quarter to twelve one morning, soon after this, I was sitting with Mrs. Monnerie on a stool beneath Chakka's cage, and Susan was just about to leave us – was actually smoothing on the thumb of her glove; when Marvell announced that a Miss Bowater had called. I turned cold all over and held my breath.

'Ah,' whispered Mrs. Monnerie, 'your future Mrs. Rochester, my pet.'

Every thought scuttled out of my head; my needle jerked and pricked my thumb. I gazed at the door. Never had I seen anything so untransparent. Then it opened; and – there was Fanny. She was in dark grey – a gown I had never seen before. A tight little hat was set demurely on her hair. In that first moment she had not noticed me, and I could steal a long, steady look at the still, light, vigilant eyes, drinking in at one steady draught their new surroundings. Her features wore the thinnest, unfamiliar mask, like a flower seen in an artificial light. What wonder I had loved her. My hands went numb, and a sudden fatigue came over me.

Then her quiet, travelling glance descended and hovered in secret colloquy with mine. She dropped me a little smiling, formal nod, moistened her lips, and composed herself for Mrs. Monnerie.

And it was then I became conscious that Susan had quietly slipped out of the room.

It was a peculiar experience to listen to the catechism that followed. From the absorption of her attitude, the large, side-long head, the motionless hands, it was clear that Mrs. Monnerie found a good deal to interest her in the dark, attentive figure that stood before her. If Fanny had been Joan of Arc, she could not have had a more single-minded reception. Yet I was enjoying a duel: a duel not of wits, but of intuitions, between the sagacious, sardonic, watchful old lady, soaked in knowledge of humanity but, as far as I could discover, with extraordinarily small respect for it, and – Fanny. And it seemed to me that Fanny easily held her own; just by being herself, without revealing herself. Face, figure, voice; that was all. I could not take my eyes away. If only, I thought, my own ghost would keep as quiet and hidden as that in the presence of others.

Perhaps I exaggerate. Love, living or dying, even if it is not blind, cannot, I suppose, focus objects very precisely. It sees only itself or disillusionment. Whether or not, the duel was interrupted. In the full light of the window, Fanny turned softly at the opening of the door. Marvell was announcing another caller. At his name my heart leapt up like William Wordsworth's at the rainbow. It was Sir Walter Pollacke.

'This is *your* visitor, Poppet,' Mrs. Monnerie waggishly assured me; 'you shall have half an hour's *tête-à-tête*.'

Chapter Thirty-Nine

So it was with a deep sigh – half of regret at being called away, and all of joy at the thought of seeing my old friend again – that I followed Marvell's coat-tails over the threshold. With a silly, animal-like affection I brushed purposely against Fanny's skirts as I passed her by; and even smirked in a kind of secret triumph at Percy Maudlen, who happened to be idling on the staircase as I hastened from room to room.

The door of the library closed gently behind me, as if with a breath of peace. I paused – looked across. Sir Walter was standing at the further end of its high, daylit, solemn spaciousness. He was deep in contemplation of a white marble bust that graced the lofty chimney-piece – so rapt, indeed, that until I had walked up into the full stream of sunshine from a nearer window and had announced my approach with a cough, he did not notice my entrance. Then he flicked round with an exclamation of welcome.

'My dear, dear young lady,' he cried, beaming down on me from between his peaked collar-tips, over his little black bow, the gold rim of his large eyeglasses pressed to his lip, 'a far – far more refreshing sight! Would you believe it, it was the pleasing little hobby of that oiled and curled monstrosity up there – Heliogabalus – to smother his guests in roses – literally, smother them? Now,' and he looked at me quizzically as if through a microscope, 'the one question is how have *you* survived what I imagine must have been a similar ordeal? Not quite at the last gasp, I hope? *Comparatively* happy? It's all we can hope for, my dear, in this world.'

I nodded, hungrily viewing him, meeting as best I could the bright blue eyes, and realizing all in a moment the dark inward of my mind.

Those other eyes began thinking as well as looking. 'Well, well, that's right. And now we must have a little quiet talk before his Eminence reappears. So our old friend Mrs. Bowater has gone husband-hunting? Gallant soul! she came to see me.'

Squatted up on a crimson leather stool, I must have looked the picture of astonishment.

'Yes,' he assured me, 'there are divinities that shape our ends; and Mrs. Bowater is one of them. If anything can hasten her husband's recovery – but never mind that. She has left *me* in charge. And here I am. The question is, can we have too many trustees, guardians? Perhaps not. Look at the Koh-i-Noor, now.'

I much preferred to continue to look at Sir Walter, even though, from the moment I had entered the room, at least five or six voices had begun arguing in my mind. And here, as if positively in answer to them, was his very word – *trustee*. I pounced on it like a wasp on a plum. It was a piece of temerity that saved me from – well, as I sit thinking things over in quiet and leisure in my old Stonecote, the house of my childhood, I don't know what it hasn't saved me from.

'Too many trustees, Sir Walter?' I breathed. 'I suppose, not – if they are *honest.*'

'But bless me, my dear young lady,' his face seemed to be

shining like the sun's in mist; 'whose heresies are these? Have they given you a French maid?'

'Fleming; oh, no,' I replied, laughing out, 'she's a Woman of Kent, all *but*. What I was really thinking is, that I would, if I may – and please forgive me – very much like to show you a letter. I simply can't make head or tail of it. But it's dreadfully – suggestive.'

'My dear, I came in certain hope of being shown nothing less vital than your heart,' he retorted gallantly.

So off I went – with my visitor all encouraging smiles as he opened the door for me – to fetch my lawyer's bombshell.

Glasses on tip of his small, hawklike nose, Sir Walter's glittering eyes seemed to master this obscure document at one swoop.

'H'm,' he said cautiously, and once more communed with the bust of Heliogabalus. 'Now what did you think of it all? Was it worth six and eightpence, do you think?'

'I couldn't think. It frightened me. 'The Shares', you know. Whose Shares? Of What? I'm terribly, terribly ignorant.'

'Ah,' he echoed, 'the Shares – as the blackbird said to the Cherry Tree. And there was nobody, you thought, to discuss the letter with? You didn't answer it?'

'Nobody,' said I, with a shake of my head, and smoothing my silk skirts over my knees.

'Why, of course not,' he sparkled. 'You see how admirably things work out. Miss Fenne, Mr. Pellew, Mrs. Bowater, my wife, Tom o' Bedlam, Hypnos, Mrs. Monnerie, Mr. Bowater, Mrs. Bowater, the Harrises, *Me*. 'Pon my word, you'd think it was a plot. Now, supposing I keep this letter – could you trust it with me for a while? – and supposing I see these gentlemen, and make a few inquiries; and that in the meantime – we – we bottle the Cherries? But first, I must have a little more information. Your father, my dear. Let's just unbosom ourselves of all this horrible old money-grubbing, and see exactly how we stand.'

I needed no second invitation, and poured out helter-skelter all (how very little, in my girlish folly) that I knew about my father's affairs, and of how I had been 'left'.

'And Miss Fenne, now?' he peered out, as if at my godmother herself. 'Why didn't she send word to France? Where is this providential step-grandfather, Monsieur Pierre de Ronvel, all this time? Not dead too?'

Shamefully I had to confess that I did not know; had not even inquired. 'It is my miserable ingratitude. I just blow hot and cold; that is my nature.'

'Well, well, it may be so.' He smiled at me, as if out of the distance, with the serenest kindliness. 'But you and I are going to share the temperate zone – a cool, steady Trade Wind.'

'If only,' I smiled, taking him up on this familiar ground, 'if only I could keep clear of the Tropics – and that Sargasso Sea!'

At this little sally he gleamed at me as goldenly as the spade guinea that dangled on his waistcoat. Then he rose and surveyed one by one a row of silent, sumptuous tomes in their glazed retreat: 'The Sargasso Sea; h'm, h'm, h'm; and one might suppose,' he cast a comprehensive glance at the taciturn shelves around and above us, 'one might suppose the tuppenny box would afford some of these a more sociable haven.'

But this was Greek to me. 'Mrs. Monnerie is generous?' he went on, 'indulgent? Groundsel, seed, sugar, *and* a Fleming. Yet perhaps the door might be pushed just an inch or two farther open, eh? What I'm meaning, my dear, is, will you perhaps wait in patience a little? And if anything should go amiss, will you make me a promise to send just a wisp of a word and a penny stamp to an old friend who will be doing his best? The first lawyer, you know, was a waif that was adopted by a tortoise and a fox. Now *I'm* going to be a mole – with its fur on the bias, as Miss Rossetti happened to notice – and burrow. So you see, all will come well!'

I must have been sitting very straight and awkward on my stool, and not heeding what my face was telling.

'Is there anything else distressing you, my dear?' he asked anxiously, almost timidly.

'Only myself,' I muttered. 'There doesn't seem to be any end to it all. I grope on and on, and – the kindness only makes it worse. *Can* there be a riddle, Sir Walter, that hasn't any answer? I remember reading in a book that was given me that Man "comes into the world like morning mushrooms". Don't you think that's true; even, I mean, of – everybody?'

But his views on this subject were not to be shared with me for many a long day. Our half-hour was over; and there stood Mrs. Monnerie, mushroom-shaped, it is true, but suggesting nothing of the evanescent, as she looked in on us from the mahogany doorway.

'How d'ye do, Sir Walter,' she greeted him. 'If it hadn't been for an exceedingly interesting young creature disguised, I understand, as a Miss Bowater, I should have had the happiness of seeing you earlier. And how is our Peri looking, do you think?'

'How is our Peri looking?' he repeated musingly, poising himself, and eyeing me, on his flat, gleaming boots; 'why, Mrs. Monnerie, as I suppose a Peri *should* be looking – into Paradise.'

'Then, my Peri,' said Mrs. Monnerie blandly, 'ask Sir Walter to be a complete angel, and stay to luncheon.'

Mrs. Monnerie, I remember, was in an unusually vivacious humour

at that meal; and devoured immense quantities of salmon mayon-
naise. One might have supposed that Fanny's influence had added
a slim crescent of silvery light to her habitual earthshine. None the
less, when our guest was gone, she seemed to subside into a shallow dejection; and I into a much deeper. We sat on together in
an uneasy silence, she pushing out her lips, restlessly prodding
Cherry with her foot, and occasionally uttering some inarticulate
sound that was certainly not intended as conversation.

I think Mrs. Monnerie was in secret a more remarkable woman
than she affected to be. However thronged a room might be, you
could never be unaware that she was in it. And in the gentle syl-
labub of polite conversation her silence was like that of an ancient
rock with the whispering of the wavelets on the sands at its base. I
remember once seeing a comic picture of an old lady with a large
feather in her bonnet placidly sitting on a camp-stool beneath a
pollard willow on one side of a stream, while a furious, frothing bull
stood snorting and rampaging on the other. I think the old lady in
the picture was meant to be Britannia; but, whoever or whatever
the bull might represent, Mrs. Monnerie reminded me of her. She
sat more heavily, more passively, in her chair than anyone I have
ever seen.

Of course – quite apart from intelligence – there must be many,
many *layers* in society, and I cannot say at all how far Mrs. Monnerie
was from the topmost. But I am sure she was able to look down on
a good many of them; while I was born always to be 'looking up'. I
was looking up at Mrs. Monnerie now from my stool. Widespread
in her chair, she had closed her eyes, and to judge from her face, she
was dreaming. It looked more faded than usual. The puckers gave it
a prunish look. Queer, contorting expressions were floating across
her features. Her soul seemed gently to rock in them, like an

empty boat at night on a dark river. In the pride of my youth – and a little uneasy over my confidences with Sir Walter – I examined my patroness with a slight stirring of dismay.

'Oh, no, no! never to grow old, not me,' a voice was saying in me. Yet, after all, I reminded myself, I was looking only at Mrs. Monnerie's outer case. But then, after all, was it only that? 'The Resurrection of the body.' One may see day at a little hole, says an old proverb – I hope a Kentish proverb. And from Mrs. Monnerie, my thoughts drifted away to Fanny. She would grow old too. Should we know one another then? Should we understand, and remember what it was to be young? We had had our secrets.

I came out of these reflections to find Mrs. Monnerie's sleepy eyes fixed full upon me; and herself marvellously cheered up by her nap. She had thought very well of Miss Bowater, she told me. So well that she not only very soon found her a charming engagement as a morning-governess to the two little girls of a rich fashionable widow – just Fanny's 'sinecure' – but invited her to stay at No.2 as a 'companion' to herself, until a more permanent post offered itself.

'You and I want more company,' she assured me; 'otherwise the flint will use up all the tinder, or vice versa, my dear. A pretty creature and no fool. She sings a little, too, she tells me. So we shall have music wherever she goes.'

That afternoon both flint and tinder – whichever of us was which – were kept very busy. Mrs. Monnerie fell into one of her long monologues, broken only by Chakka's griding on his bars, and Cherry's whimpering in his dreams. It was another kind of 'white meat' for me; and though, no doubt, I was incapable of digesting *all* Mrs. Monnerie's views on life, society, and the world at large, I realized that if in the course of time it might be my fate to wither and wizen away, I should still have my own company and plenty of internal entertainment. I actually saw myself a little bent-up, old, midget woman, creeping down some stone steps out of a porch, with a fanlight, under a street lamp. It curdled my blood, that picture. And yet, I thought, what must be, must be. I will *endure* to be a little, bent-up, old, midget woman, creeping down stone steps out of a porch with a fanlight. And I even nodded up at the street lamp.

In response to a high-spirited scrawl from Fanny, I sent her all that was left of my savings to purchase 'those horrible little etceteras that just feather down the scales, Midgetina. It would be saintlike of you, and you won't miss it *there*'. It was a desperate wrench to me to see the last of my money disappear. I knew no more than the Man in the Moon where the next was to come from.

I counted the days to Fanny's coming; and dressed myself for the occasion in the most expensive gold and blue afternoon gown I possessed. It must have been with a queer, mixed motive in my head. I sat waiting for her, while beyond the gloom-hung window raged a London thunderstorm, with dense torrents of rain. My little silver clock struck three, and she entered my room like a black swan, tossing from her small, velveted head, as she did so, a few beads of rain. From top to toe in deadest black. She must have noticed my glance of wonderment.

'When you want to make a favourable impression on your social superiors, Midgetina, the meeker you look the better,' she said.

But this was not the only reason for her black. Only a day or two before, she told me, a letter had come from her mother ... 'My father is dead.' The words dropped out as if they were quite accustomed to one another's company. But those which followed – 'blood-poisoning', 'mortification', hung up in my mind – in that interminable gallery – a hideous picture. I could only sit and stare at the motionless figure outlined against the sepulchral window.

'It is awful, awful, Fanny!' I managed to whisper at last. 'It never stops. One after another they all go. Think how he must have longed to be home. And now to be buried – out there – nothing but strangers.'

A vacancy came over my mind in which I seemed to see the dead Mr. Bowater of my photograph rising like Lazarus in his grave-cloths out of his foreign tomb, and looking incredulously around him.

'And your mother, Fanny! Out there, too – those miles and miles of sea away!'

Fanny made no movement, though I fancied that her eyes wandered uneasily towards the door. 'I quite agree, Midgetina; it's awful!' she said. 'But really and truly, it's worse for me. I think I am like my father in some ways. Mother never really understood him. You can't *talk* a man different; and for that matter holding your tongue at him is not much good either. You must just lie in wait for him with – well, with your charms, I suppose.'

The word sounded like a sneer. 'Still, I don't mean to say that it was all pure filial bliss for me when he *was* at home, until, at least, I grew up. Then he and I quarrelled too; but that's pleasure itself by comparison with listening to other people at it. He did his best to spoil me, I suppose. He wanted to make a lady of me.' She turned and smiled out of the window, her under-lip quivering and casting a faint shadow on the smooth skin beneath. 'So here I am; though I fear you can't make ladies of *quite* the correct consistency out of dressmaker's clothes and a smatter of Latin. The salt will out. But there,' she flung a little gesture with her glove, 'as I say, here I am.'

And as if for welcome, a gleam of lightning danced at the

window, illumining us there, and a crackling peal of thunder rolled hollowly off over the roof-tops of the square. We listened until the sound had emptied itself into quiet; and only the rain in the gutters gurgled and babbled.

'Do you know,' she went on, with a faraway challenging thrill in her low, mournful voice, 'I don't think I have a solitary relation left in the world now – except Mother. "They are all gone into a world of light" – though I've now and then suspected that a few of the disreputable ones have been buried alive. There's nothing very dreadful in that. Life consists, of course, in shedding various kinds of skin – and tanning the remainder.'

Fanny, then, *was* unaware that Mrs. Bowater was not her real mother. And I think she never guessed it.

'Nor have I,' I said, 'not one.' As I looked at it there, it seemed a fact more curious than tragic. Besides, in the brooding darkness of that room it was Fanny and I who were strange, external beings, not the memoried phantoms of my mother and father. We had still to go on, to live things out. 'So you see, Fanny,' I continued, after a pause, 'I do know what it means – a little; and we must try more than ever to be really one another's friend, mustn't we? I mean, if you think I can be.'

'Why, I owe you pounds and pounds,' cried Fanny gaily, pushing back her handkerchief into her bodice. 'Here we are – not quite in the same box, perhaps; still strangers and pilgrims. Of course we must help one another …Just think of this house! The servants! The folly of it, and all for Madame Monnerie – though I wouldn't mind being in her shoes, even for one season. Socialism, my dear, is all a question of shoes. And this is Poppetkin's little boudoir? A pygmy palace, my dear, and if only the lightning would last a little longer I might get a real glimpse of that elfin little exquisite over there in her beautiful blue brocade. But then; it will be roses all the way with you, Miss M. You are independent, and valued for yourself alone.'

'How different people are, Fanny. You always think first of the use of a thing, and I, stupidly, just of it – itself.'

'Do we?' she said indifferently, and rose from her chair.

'Anyhow I'm here to be of use. And who,' she remarked, with a little yawn, as she came to a pause again beside the streaming window. 'Who was that prim, colourless girl with the pale blue eyes? Engaged to be married.'

'But Fanny, she had her gloves on that morning, I remember it as clearly as – as I always remember everything where you are! how could you possibly tell that Susan Monnerie was engaged?'

It was quite a simple problem, Fanny tranquilly assured me! 'The ring bulged under the suède.'

Her scornfulness piqued me a little. 'Anyhow,' I retorted, 'Susan's eyes are not *pale* blue. They are almost cornflower – chicory colour; like the root of a candle-flame.'

'Please, Midgetina,' Fanny begged me, 'don't let me canker your new adoration. Perhaps you preened your pretty feathers in them when they were fixed on the demigod. "Susan!" I thought all the Susans perished in the 'sixties, or had fled down the area. And who is *he*?' But she did not follow up her question. All things come to him who waits, she had rambled on inconsequently, if he waits long enough; and no doubt God would temper the wind to the shorn orphan even if she did look a perfect frump in mourning.

'You know you could never look a frump,' I replied indignantly, 'even if you hadn't a rag on.'

Fanny shrugged her dainty shoulders. 'Alas!' she said.

But her 'orphan' had brought me back with a guilty shock to

MEMOIRS OF A MIDGET

what, no doubt, was an extremely fantastic panorama of Buenos Ayres; and that swiftly back again to Mr. Crimble. For an instant or two I looked away. Perhaps it was my caution that betrayed me.

'It's no use, Midgetina,' she sang across at me from her window. 'Whether it's because the chemical reactions of your pat little brain are more intense than ordinary people's, or because you and I are *en rapport*, I can't say. But there's one thing we must agree upon at once: never, never again to mention his name – at least in *this* house. The Crimble chapter is closed.'

Closed indeed. But so sharp were her tones I hadn't the courage to warn her that even Susan had read most of it. Fanny came near, and, stooping as Susan had stooped, began fidgeting with the button of my electric chandelier. The little lamps shone wanly in our faces in the cloud-darkened room.

'You see, my dear,' she said playfully, 'you think me all mockery and heartlessness. And no doubt you are right. But I want ease and security; just like that – as if I were writing an essay – "ease and security". I don't care a dash about affection – at least without the aforesaid E. and S. I intend to please Mrs. Monnerie, and she is going to be grateful to me. Don't think I am being "candid". I should have no objection to saying just the same thing to Mrs. Monnerie herself: she'd enjoy it. Wait, you precious inchy image – wait until you need a sup of fatted calf's-foot jelly, not because you are sick of husks, but because you are deadly poor. Then you will understand. These sumptuosities! Wait till they haven't a ha'penny in their pockets, real or moral, for their next meal. They only look at things – if that; they can't know what they are. Even to be decently charitable one must have been a beggar – and cursed the philanthropists. Oh, I know; and Fanny's race is for Success.'

'But surely, Fanny, a thing *is* its looks, if only you look long enough. And I should just like to hear you talking if you were in my place. Besides, what is the use of success – in the end, I mean? You should see some of the actresses and singers and authors and that kind of thing Mrs. Monnerie knows! You wouldn't have realized the actresses were even beautiful unless you had been told so. Why, you couldn't even say the *World* is a success, except in the country. What is truly the use of it, then?' I had grown so eager in my argument that I had got up from my chair.

'The use, you poor thing?' laughed Fanny; 'why, only as a kind of face-cream to one's natural pride.'

The day was lightening now; but at that the whole darkness of my own situation drew close about me. Success, indeed. What was I? Nothing but a halfpennyless, tame pet in No. 2. What salve could restore to me *my* natural pride?

Chapter Forty

In happier circumstances, the next morning's post might have reassured me. Two letters straddled my breakfast tray, for I always had this meal in my own room. One of them was from Wanderslore – a long, crooked, roundabout letter, that seemed to taunt, upbraid, and entreat me, turn and turn about. It ended with a proposal of marriage.

In most of the novels I have read, the heroine simply basks in such a proposal, even though scarcely her finger-tips are warmed by its rays. For my part, this letter, far from making me happy or even complacent, produced nothing but a feeling of fretfulness and shame. Thrusting it back into its envelope, I listened awhile as if an eavesdropper might have overheard my silent reading of it – as if I must hide. Then, with eyes fixed on my small coffee-pot, I sank into a low, empty reverie.

The world had not been so tender to my feelings as to refrain from introducing me to General Tom Thumb and Miss Mercy Lavinia Bump Warren.

'A pair of them! how quaint! how romantic! how *touching*!' I saw myself – gossamer veil, dwarfed orange blossom, and gypsophila bouquet, all complete. Perhaps Mr. Pellew – perhaps even

Miss Fenne's bishop, would officiate. Possibly Percy would be persuaded to 'give me away'. And what a gay little sniggling note in the *Morning Post*.

I came out of these sardonic thoughts with cold hands and a sneer on my lips, and the thought that I had seen quite as conspicuously paired human mates even though their size was beyond reproach. Thank goodness, when I read my letter again, slightly better feelings prevailed. After all, the merest cinder of love would have made my darkness light. I shouldn't have cared for a thousand 'touchings' then. I was still myself, a light-headed, light-hearted young woman, for all my troubles and follies. If I had loved him, the rest of the world – much truer and sweeter within than it looks from without – would have vanished like a puff of smoke. But not even love's ashes were in my heart, except, perhaps, those in which Fanny had scrawled her name.

I beat about, bruising wings and breast, hating life, hating the friend who had suddenly slammed-to another door in my gilded cage. 'You can never, never go back to Wanderslore now,' muttered my romantic heart. Friends we could have remained – only the closer for adversity. Now all that was over; and two human beings who might have been a refuge and reconciliation to one another, amused – as well as amusing – observers of the world at large, had been by this one piece of foolish excess divided for ever. I simply couldn't bear to look ridiculous in my own eyes.

My other letter was from Sir W. P. He had seen the Harrises. Those foxy tortoises had advanced a ridiculous £1 19s. 7d. of my September allowance – the price of a pair of Monnerie bedroom slippers! It was enclosed – and Sir Walter begged me not to worry. Might he be my bank? Would I be so kind as to break it as soon as ever I wished? Meanwhile he would be making further inquiries into my affairs.

Perhaps because Sir W. P. was a business man, he was less persuasive with his pen than with his tongue. I thought he was merely humouring me, fell into a violent rage, and tore up not only his letter, but – noodle that I was – the Harris Order too – into the tiniest pieces, and heaped them up, like a soufflé, on my tray. Mr. Anon's I locked up in my old money-box, with the nightgown and the Miss Austen. Both letters wore like acid into my mind. From that day on – except for a few half-stifled or excited hours – they were never out of remembrance.

Even the most valuable and expensive pet may become a vexation if it is continually showing ill-temper and fractiousness. Mrs. Monnerie merely puckered her lips or shrugged her shoulders at my outbursts of vanity and insolence. But drops of water will wear away a stone. From being Court Favourite I gradually sank to being Court Fool. In sheer ennui and desperation I waggled my bells and brandished my bladder. A cat may look at a Queen, but it should, I am sure, make faces only at her Ladies-in-waiting.

Fanny inherited yet another sinecure; and it was not envy on my side that helped her to shine in it, though I had my fits of jealousy. She was determined to please; and when Fanny made up her mind, circumstances seemed just to fawn at her feet. Life became a continuous game of chess, the moves of which at times kept me awake and brooding in a far from wholesome fashion in my bed. Pawn of pawns, and one at the point of being sacrificed, I could only squint at the board. Indeed, I deliberately shut my eyes to my own insignificance, strutted about, sulked, sharpened my tongue like a serpent, and became a perfect pest to myself when alone. Yet

I knew in my heart that those whom I hoped to wound merely laughed at me behind my back, that I was once more proving to the world that the smaller one is, the greater is one's vanity.

In the midst of this nightmare, by a curious coincidence rose like a Jack-in-the-box from out of my past the queerest of phantoms – and proved himself real.

I was sullenly stewing in my thoughts in the library one morning over a book which to this day I never weary of reading: Gilbert White's *Natural History of Selborne*. It was the nearest I could get to the country. The whim took me to try and become a little better acquainted with 'William Markwick, Esq., F.L.S.' who had himself seen the *sphinx stellatarum* inserting its proboscis into the nectary of a flower while 'keeping constantly on the wing'. There seemed to be something in common, just then, between myself and the *Sphinx*.

I pressed my wainscot bell. After an unusual delay in a drastically regulated household, the door behind me gently opened. I began simpering directions over my shoulder in the Percy way with servants – and presently realized that all was not quite as it should be. I turned to look, and saw thrust in at the doorway an apparently bodiless, protuberant head, with black, buttony eyes on either side a long, long nose. Then the remainder of this figure squeezed reluctantly in. It was Adam Waggett.

Guy Fawkes himself, caught lantern in hand among his powder barrels, must have looked like Adam Waggett at this moment. For a while I could only return his stare from the midst of a vortex of memories. When at last I found my tongue and inquired peremptorily how he came there, and what he was doing in the house, he broke into a long, gurgling, strangulated guffaw of laughter. I was already in a sour temper – in spite of the sweetness of Selborne.

As a boy he had been my acute aversion; and here he was a grown man and as doltish and ludicrous as when he had roared at me in the moonlight from outside the kitchen window at Stonecote. His stupidity and disrespect made me almost inarticulate with rage.

Maybe the foolish creature, feeling as strange as a cat in a new house, was only expressing his joy and affection at sight of a familiar face. But I had no time to consider motives. In a fever of apprehension that his noise might be overheard, my one thought now was to bring him to his senses. I shook my fists at him and stamped my foot on the Turkey carpet – as if in snow. He watched me in a stupefaction of admiration, but at length his face solemnified, and he realized that my angry gestures were not intended for his amusement.

His mouth stood open, he shook his head, and, unless my eyes deceived me, set back his immense ears.

'Beg pardon, miss, I'm sure,' he stuttered, 'it was the sh-hock, and you inside the book there, and the old times like; and even though they was telling me that there was such a – such a young lady in the house ... But I won't utter a word, miss, not me. Only,' he stared round at the closed door and lowered his voice to an even huskier whisper, 'except to tell you that Pollie's doing very nicely, and whenever I sees her – well, miss, that thunderstorm and the old cow!'

At this his features gathered together for another outburst, which I succeeded in stifling only by warning him that so long as he remained at Mrs. Monnerie's he must completely forget the old cow and the thunderstorm, and never address me in company, or even glance in my direction if we happened to be together in the same room.

'Mrs. Monnerie would be extremely angry, Adam, to hear you laughing in the library; and I am anxious that you should be a credit to Lyndsey in your new situation.'

'But you rang, miss – at least the library did,' he replied, now thoroughly contrite, 'and Mr. Marvell said: "You go along, there, Waggett, second door right, first staircase," so I come.'

'Yes,' I said, 'but it was a mistake. A mistake, you understand. Now go away; and remember!'

A few minutes afterwards, Marvell himself discreetly entered the room, merely, as it would appear, to adjust the angles of a copy of the *Spectator* that lay on the table.

'It's very close this morning,' I remarked, with as much dignity as I could muster.

'It is indeed, miss,' said Marvell, stooping sedately to examine my bell-push. He rose and brushed his fingers.

'They say, miss, the electricity gets into the wires, when thunder's in the air. A wonderful invention, but not, as I am told, entirely independent of changes in the weather. I hope, miss, you haven't been disturbed.'

When Susan, even paler and quieter than usual, presently looked into the library, she found its occupant still on the floor and brooding over the browns and greys, the roses and ochres, of a complete congregation of *Sphingidæ*. She stooped over me, sprawling in so ungainly a fashion across my book.

'Moths, this morning? What a very learned person you will become.' Her voice was a little flat, yet tender; but I was still in the sulks, and made no answer.

'I suppose,' she began again, as if listlessly, and straying over to the window, 'I suppose it is very pleasant for you, seeing so much of your friend, Miss Bowater?'

Caution whispered a warning, and I tried to wriggle out of an answer by remarking that Fanny's mother was the kindest woman in the whole world.

'Where is she now?'

'In Buenos Ayres.'

'Really? How curious family traits are. The very moment I saw Miss Bowater I was quite certain that she was intended for an adventurous life; and didn't you say that her father was an officer in the merchant service? What is he like?'

'Mr. Bowater? He died – out there, only a week or two ago.'

'How very, very sad,' breathed Susan. 'And for Miss Bowater. I never even guessed from her manner that she was in trouble of that kind. And that, I suppose, shows a sort of courage. You were perfectly right; she is lovely and clever. The face a little hard, don't you think, but *very* clever. She seems to be prepared for what Aunt Alice is going to say long before she says it. And I, you know, sometimes don't notice even the sting till – till the buzzing is over.' She paused. 'And you were able to make a real friend of her?'

Susan had not the patience to wait until I could sort out an answer to this question. 'I don't want to be intrusive,' she went on hurriedly, 'to – to ask horrid questions; but is it true, you dear thing, that you may some day be leaving us?'

'Leaving you?' I echoed, my thoughts crouching together like chicks under a hen.

The reply came softly and reluctantly in that great cistern of air.

'Why, I understood – to be married.'

I leant heavily on my hands, seeing not the plumes and colours of the Sphinxes that swam up at me from the page, but, as if in a mist between them and me, the softly smiling face of Fanny. At last I managed to overcome the slight physical sickness that had swept over me. 'Susan,' I said, 'if a friend betrayed the very soul out of your body, what would you do? where would you go?'

'Betray! I, my dear?' and she broke into a confused explanation.

It was a remark of Percy's she had been referring to, a silly, trivial remark, not, she was sure, intended maliciously. Why, every one teased every one. Didn't she know it? And especially about the things that were most personal, 'and, Well, sacred'. It was nothing. Just that; and she should not have repeated it.

'Tell me exactly, please,' said I.

'Well, Aunt Alice was talking of marriage; and Miss Bowater smiled. And Aunt Alice – you know her mocking way – asked how, at her age – Miss Bowater's – she had learned to look at the same time both charming and cynical. "Don't forget, my dear," they were her very words, "that the cynicism wears the longer." But Miss Bowater laughed, and changed the subject by asking if she could do anything for your headache. It was the afternoon, you remember, when you were lying down. That was all.'

'And Mr. Maudlen?'

The fair cheek reddened. 'Oh, Percy made a joke – about you. Just one of his usual horrid jokes. My dear' – she came and knelt down beside me and laid her gentle hand on my shoulder – 'don't look so – so awful. It's only how things go.'

I drew the hand down. It smelled as fresh and sweet as jessamine.

'Don't bother about me; Susan,' I said coldly. 'Just leave me to my moths. I could show you scorpions and hornets ten times more dangerous than a mere Death's Head. You don't suppose I care? Why, as you say, even God has His little joke with some of us. I'm quite used to it.'

'Don't, don't,' she implored me. 'You are over-tired, you poor little thing. You go on reading and reading. Why, your teeth are chattering.'

A faint brazen reverberation from out of the distance increased in intensity and died away. It was Adam performing on the gong. Susan had tried to be kind to me, to treat me as if I were a normal fellow-being. I pressed the cool fingers to my lips.

'There, Susan,' I said, with cheerful mockery, 'except for my father and mother, I do believe you are the first life-size or any size person I have ever kissed. A midget's gratitude!'

Ever so slightly the fingers constricted beneath my touch. No doubt there was a sensation of the spidery in my embrace.

Chapter Forty-One

But a devil of defiance had entered into me. With a face as snakily sweet as I could make it, I made my daintiest bow to Mrs. Monnerie's guests – to Lord Chiltern, a tall, stiffish man, who blinked at our introduction almost as solemnly and distastefully as had Mrs. Bowater's Henry, and to Lady Diana Templeton. A glance at this lady reminded me spitefully of an old suspicion of mine that Mrs. Monnerie usually invited her duller friends to luncheon and the clever to dinner. Not that she failed to enjoy the dull ones, but it was in a different way.

A long, gilded Queen Anne mirror hung opposite my high chair, so that whenever I glanced across I caught sight not only of myself with cheeks like carnations above my puffed blue gown, but also of Adam Waggett. Ever and again his red hand was thrust over my shoulder – the hand that had held the wren. And I was so sick at heart – on yet another wren's behalf – that I could hardly repress a shudder. Poor Adam; whenever I think of him it is of a good, yet weak and silly man. He has found his Eden, so I have heard, in New Zealand now, and I hope he has forgiven my little share in his life.

Throughout that dull luncheon my tongue went mincing on

and on – in sheer desperation lest anyone should detect the state of mind I was in. With pale eyes Percy sniggered over his soup. Susan was silent and self-conscious. Captain Valentine frowned and nibbled his small moustache. Lady Diana Templeton smiled like a mauve-pink snapdragon, and Mrs. Monnerie led me on. It was my last little success. Luncheon over, I was helped down from my chair, and allowed 'to run away'.

What was it Lord Chiltern was saying? I paused on the threshold: 'An exquisite little performance. But isn't it a little selfish to hide her light under your admirable bushel, Mrs. Monnerie? The stage, now?'

'The stage!' exclaimed Mrs. Monnerie in consternation. 'The child's as proud as Lucifer. She would faint at the very suggestion. You have heard her deliciously sharp little tongue; but her tantrums! Still, she's a friendly and docile little creature, and I am very well satisfied with her.'

'And not merely that,' paced on the rather official voice. 'I was noticing that something in the eyes. Almost disconcertingly absent yet penetrating. She thinks. She comes and goes in them. I noticed the same peculiarity in poor Willie Arbuthnot's. And this little creature is scarcely more than a child.'

'I think it is *perfectly* sad, Lord Chiltern,' broke in a reedy, vibrating voice. 'In some circumstances it would be *tragic*. It's a mercy she does not realize ... *habit*, you know ...'

Listeners seldom hear such good things of themselves. Why, then, was it so furious an eavesdropper that hastened away with a face and gesture worthy of a Sarah Siddons!

No: my box remained locked. Yet, thought I, as I examined its contents, any dexterous finger could have opened that tiny lock – with a hairpin. And how else could my secret have been discovered? Fleming or Fanny – or both of them: it maddened me to think of them in collusion. I would take no more risks. I tore Mr. Anon's letter into fragments, and these again into bits yet smaller, until they were almost like chaff. These I collected together and put into an envelope, which I addressed in sprawling capitals to Miss Fanny Bowater, at No. 2.

Then for a sombre half hour I communed intensely at the window with my Tank. It was hot and taciturn company – not a breath of air stirred my silk window-blind – yet it managed to convey a few home truths, and even to increase the light a little in which I could look at the 'bushel'. There *were* 'mercies', I suppose. Out of the distance rolled the vague reverberation of the enormous city. I watched the sparrows, and they me. When the time came for my afternoon walk, I put on my hat, with eyes fixed on my letter, and, finally – left it behind me.

Was it for discretion's sake, or in shame? I cannot say, but I remember that during my slow descent to the empty hall I kept my eyes fixed with peculiar malignity on the milk-white figure of a Venus (not life-size, thank Heaven), who had been surprised apparently in the very act of entering the water for a bathe. Why I singled her out for contempt I cannot say; for she certainly looked a good deal more natural and modest than many of the fine ladies who heedlessly passed her by. It was merely my old problem of the Social Layers over again. And my mind was in such a state of humiliation and discomfort that I hadn't the energy even to smile at a marble goddess.

Fanny was awaiting me on my return. A strand of hair was looped demurely and old-fashionedly round each small ear; her clear, unpowdered skin had the faint sheen of a rose. She stood, still and

MEMOIRS OF A MIDGET

shimmering, in the height of pleasant spirits, yet, I thought, watchful and furtive through it all. She had come, she said, to congratulate me on my 'latest conquest'.

Mrs. Monnerie, she told me, had been pleased with my entertainment of the late First Commissioner of – was it Good Works? But I must beware. 'Once a coquette, Midgetina, soon *quite* heartless,' she twitted me.

To which I called sourly, as I stood drying my hands, that pretty compliments must be judged by where they come from.

'Come from, indeed,' laughed Fanny. 'He's a positive Peer of the Realm, and bathes, my dear, every morning in the Fount of Honours. You wouldn't be so flippant if ... hallo! what's this? A letter – addressed to Me! Where on earth did this come from?'

Heels to head, a sudden heat swept over me. 'Oh,' said I hollowly, 'that's nothing, Fanny. Only a little joke. And now you are here – but surely,' I hurried on, 'you don't really like that starched-up creature?'

But Fanny was holding up my envelope between both her thumbs and forefingers, and steadily smiling at me, over its margin. 'A joke, Midgetina; and one of your very own. How exciting. And how bulgy. May I open it? I wouldn't miss it for the world.'

'Please, Fanny, I have changed my mind. Let me have it. I don't feel like jokes now.'

'But honestly, *I* do. Some jokes have such a deliciously serious side. Besides, as you have just come in, why didn't this go out with you?' To which I replied stubbornly that it was not her letter; that I had thought better of it; and that she had no right to question me if I didn't want to answer.

'I see.' Her voice had glided steadily up the scale of suavity. 'It's a bit more of the dead past, is it? And you don't like the – the fragrance. But surely, if we are really talking about rights – and, according to my experience, there are none too many of them knocking about in this world – surely I have the right to ask what pulpy mysteries are enclosed in an envelope addressed to me in what appears to be a feigned ca – calligraphy? Look. I am putting the thing on the floor so that we shall be on – well – fairly equal terms. Even your sensitive Sukie could not be more considerate than that, could she? All I want to know is, what's inside that envelope? If you refuse to say, well and good. I shall retire to my maidenly couch and feed on the blackest suppositions.'

It was a cul-de-sac; and the only thing to do was to turn back boldly and get out of it.

'Well, Fanny; I have told you that I thought better of sending it. But I am not ashamed. Even if I am wrong, I suppose you are at liberty to have your little jokes too, and so is Percy Maudlen. It's a letter, torn up; that's all.'

'A letter – so I guessed. Who from?'

I gazed at her silently.

'Yes?'

'It's hateful of you, Fanny ... From the hunchback.'

Her astonishment, surely, could not have been pretence. 'And what the devil, you dear, stammering little midgelet, has your miserable little hunchback to do with me? Why send his scrawls to *me* – and in bits?'

'Because,' said I, 'I thought you had been making fun of him and me to – the others.'

The light hands lifted themselves; the dark head tilted a little back and askew. '*What* a roundabout route,' she sighed. But her face was false to the smooth, scornful accents. 'So you suspected me of spying on you? *I* see. And gentle Susan Monnerie was kind enough to smear a little poison on the fangs. Well, Midgetina love, I tell you this. It's safer sometimes to lose your reputation than your temper. But there's a limit –'

'Hush,' I whispered, for I had sharper ears than Fanny even when rage had not deafened her own. I pounced on the envelope – but only just in time.

'It's Mr. Percy, miss,' announced Fleming, 'and may he come in?'

'Hallo!' said that young man, lounging greyly into view, 'a bad penny, Miss M. I happened to be passing Buszard's just now, and there was the very thing! Miss Bowater says you have a sweet tooth, and they really are rather neat.' He had brought me the daintiest little box of French doll bonbons. I glared at it; I glared at him – hardly in the mood for any more of his little jokes – not even one tied up with pale-blue ribbon.

'There's another thing,' he went on. 'Susan told us that your birthday was coming along – August 25th, isn't it? And I have proposed a Grand Birthday Party, sort of general rag. Miss M. in the Chair. Don't you think it's a ripping idea of mine, Miss Bowater?'

'*Most* ripping,' said Fanny, meeting his long, slow, sneaking glance with a slight and seeming involuntary lift of her narrow shoulder. A long look I could not share passed between them; I might have been a toy on the floor.

'But you don't look positively in the pink,' he turned to me. 'Now, does she? Late hours, eh? You look crumpled, doesn't she? Cherry, too: we must have in another vet.' The laugh died on his long lips. His eyes roved stealthily from point to point of the basking afternoon room, then once more sluggishly refastened on Fanny. I sat motionless, watching his every turn and twist, and repeating rapidly to myself: 'Go away, my friend; go away, go away.' Some nerve in him must have taken the message at last, or he found Fanny's silence uneasy. He squinnied a glinting, curious look at me, and as jauntily as self-consciousness permitted, took his departure.

The door shut. His presence fainted out into a phantasm, and that into nothing at all. And for sole evidence of him basked on my table, beneath a thread of sunlight, his blue-ribboned box.

'*Is*n't he a ninny?' sighed Fanny. 'And yet, my dear: *there* – but for the grace of God – goes Mr. Fanny Bowater.'

Her anger had evaporated. There stood my familiar Fanny again, slim as a mast, her light eyes coldly shining, her bearing, even the set of her foot showing already a faint gilding of Mrs. Monnerie. She laughed – looking straight across at me, as if with a challenge.

'Yes, my dear, it's quite true. I'm not a bit cross now. Milk and Honey. So you see even a fool may be a lightning conductor. I forgive,' she pouted a kiss from the tips of her fingers, 'I forget.'

And then she was gone too, and I alone. What an easy, consoling thing – not to care. But though Fanny might forgive, she must have found it unamusing to forget. The next evening's post brought me an exquisitely written little fable, signed 'F. B.' and entitled *Asteroida and the Yellow Dwarf*. I couldn't enjoy it very much; though no doubt it must have been exceedingly entertaining when read aloud.

Still Fanny did not care. While I myself was like those railway lines under the green bank I had seen on my journey to Lyme Regis. A day's neglect, a night's dews, and I was stained thick with rust. A dull and heedless wretchedness took possession of me. The one thought that kept recurring in every instant of solitude, and most sharply in those instants which pounced on me in the midst of strangers, was, how to escape.

I put away the envelope and its contents into my box again. And late that night, when I was secure from interruption, I wrote to Wanderslore. Nibbling a pen is no novelty to me, but never in all my life have I spent so blank and hideous an hour merely in the effort to say no to one simple question so that it should sound almost as pleasant as yes, and far more unselfish. 'Throw the stone', indeed; when my only desire was to heal the wound it might make.

Thank goodness my letter was kinder than I felt. My candelabra burned stilly on. Cold, in the blues, I stood in my dressing-gown and spectacling my eyes with my hands, looked out of the chill glass into the London night. Only one high garret window shone out in the dark face of the houses ... Who and where was Willie Arbuthnot with the peculiar eyes? Had Lord Chiltern a tank on his roof – his back yard? What a fool I had been to abandon myself and come here. If they only knew how I despised them. And the whole house asleep.

So much I despised them that not until I was dressing the following morning did I stoop into my Indian mirror to see if I could discover what Lord Chiltern had meant.

During the next few weeks Mrs. Monnerie – with ample provocation – almost yawned at sight of me. In a bitter instant of rebellion our eyes met. She detected the 'ill-wish' in mine, and was so much taken aback by it that I should hardly have recognized the set face that glared at me as hers at all. Well, the fancier had wearied of her fancy – that was all. If I had been just an ordinary visitor, she would soon have washed her hands of me. But I was notorious, and not so easily exchanged as bronchitic Cherry had been for her new Pekinese, Plum.

Possibly, too, the kind of aversion she now felt against me was a closer bond than even virtuosity or affection. She would sit with a sullen stare under her heavy eyelids watching me grow more and more heated and clumsy over my scrap of embroidery or my game of Patience. Meanwhile Chakka would crack his nut, and with stagnant eye sidle thievishly up and down the bars of his cage; while Plum gobbled up dainties or snored on his crimson cushion. We three.

Usually I was left pretty much alone; and what plans Mrs. Monnerie was turning over to dispose of me were known only to herself. What to do; where to hide; how to 'make myself small' during those torpid August days, I hardly knew. My one desire was to keep out of sight. One afternoon, I remember, after brooding for some hours under a dusty lilac bush in the Square garden, I strayed off – my eyes idly glancing from straw to hairpin to dead match in the dust – down a narrow deserted side street that led to a Mews. A string of washing hung in the sunlight from the windows. Skirting a small public house, from which the smell of beer and spirits vapoured into the sunshine, I presently found myself in a black-green churchyard among tombstones.

A clear shadow slanted across the porch, the door of the church stood open, and after pausing for a moment on its flagstones, I went in. It was empty. Stone faces gazed sightlessly from its walls. Two red sanctuary lamps hung like faint rubies in the distant chancel. I dragged out a cushion and sat down under the font. The thin, cloudy fragrance that hung in the gloom of the coloured windows stole in through my nostrils, drugged my senses. Propping my chin on my hands, I looked up through the air into the dark roof. A pendulum ticked slowly from on high. Quiet began to steal over me – long centuries of solitude had filled this vacancy as with a dream.

It was as if some self within me were listening to the unknown – but to whom? I could not answer; I might as well have been born a pagan. Was this church merely the house of a God? There were gods and temples all over the world. Was it a house of *the* God? Or only of 'their' God? In a sense I knew it was also *my* God's, but how much more happily confident of His secret pres- ence I had been in wild-grown Wanderslore. Did this mean that I was actually so much alone in my world as to be different from all other human beings?

A fluttering panic swept through my mind at the muffled thumping of the invisible pendulum. I had forgotten that time never ceased to be wasting. And the past stretched its panorama before my eyes: No. 2; the public house with the solitary think- ing man I had seen, pot in hand, staring into the sawdust; and this empty, cavernous silence. Then back and back – Lyme Regis, Mrs. Bowater's – and Fanny, Lyndsey, my mother and father, the garden. No sylphs of the air, no trancing music out of the waters now! It was as if the past were surrounded with a great wall; and the future clear and hard as glass. You might explore the past in memory: you couldn't scale its invisible walls.

And there was Mr. Crimble – an immeasurable distance away; yet he had still the strange power to arrest me, to look out on me in my path. Must the future be all of its piece? I stopped thinking again, and my eyes wandered over my silk skirt and shoes.

My ghost! there was no doubt I was an exceedingly small human being. It may sound absurd, but I had never *vividly* real- ized it before. And how solemnly sitting there – like a spider in wait for flies. 'For goodness sake, Miss M.,' I said to myself, 'cheer

up. You are being deadly dull company – always half afraid. They
daren't really do anything to you, you know. Face it out.' And even
while I was muttering, I was reading the words cut into a worn
tombstone at my feet: 'Jenetta Parker' – only two-and-twenty, a
year older than I. Yet she had lain here for two whole centuries
and more. And beneath her name I spelled out her epitaph:

> Ah, Stranger, breathe a sigh:
>   For, where I lie,
> Is but a handful of bright Beauty cast:
>   It was; and now is past.

I repeated the words mechanically again and again; and, as if in
obedience to her whisper, a much more niggardly handful of none
too bright a beauty did breathe a sigh and a prayer – part pity, part
melancholy, and all happiness and relief. I kissed my hand to Jenetta; crossed myself and bowed to the altar – dulled gems of light
the glass – and emerged into the graveyard. A lamp had been lit.
An old man was shuffling along behind me; he had come to lock
up the church. For an instant I debated whether or not to scuttle
off down the green-bladed cobbles of the Mews and – trust my
luck. No: the sight of a Punch and Judy man gobbling some food
out of a newspaper at the further corner, scared me out of *that*
little enterprise. Dusk was settling; and I edged back as fast as I
could to No. 2.

But it did me good, that visit. It was as if I had been looking up
at my own small skull on a high shelf in some tranquil and dingy old
laboratory – a few bottles, a spider's web, and an occasional glint of
moonlight. How very brief the animation for so protracted a peace.

Chapter Forty-Two

Susan's visits to her aunt were now less frequent. Percy's multiplied. Duty seemed to have become a pleasure to him. Mrs. Monnerie's gaze would rest on him with a drowsy vigilance which it was almost impossible to distinguish from mere vacancy of mind. He was fortunate in being her only nephew; unfortunate in being himself, and the son of a sister to whom Mrs. Monnerie seemed very little attached. Still, he appeared to be doing his best to cultivate his aunt's graces, would meander 'in attendance' round and round the Square's square garden, while Fanny's arm had now almost supplanted Mrs. Monnerie's ebony cane. When Mrs. Monnerie was too much fatigued for this mild exercise, or otherwise engaged, there was still *my* health to consider. At least Fanny seemed to think so. But since Percy's conversation had small attractions for me, it was far rather he who enjoyed the experience; while I sat and stared at nothing under a tree.

At less than nothing – for I was staring, as usual, chiefly at myself. I seemed to have lost the secret of day-dreaming. And if the quantity of aversion that looked out of my eyes had matched its quality, those piebald plane-trees and poisonous laburnums would have been scorched as if with fire. I shall never forget those interminable August days, besieged by the roar and glare and soot and splendour and stare of London. All but friendless, absolutely penniless, I had nothing but bits of clothes for bribes to keep Fleming from mutiny. I shrank from making her an open enemy; though I knew, as time went on, that she disrelished me more and more. She would even keep her nose averted from my clothes.

As for Fanny, to judge from her animation when Susan and Captain Valentine broke in upon us, I doubt if anybody less complacent than Percy would not have realized that she was often bored. She would look at him with head on one side, as if she had been painted like that for ever and ever in a picture. She could idly hide behind her beauty, and Percy might as well have gone hunting Echo or a rainbow. She could make corrosive remarks in so seducing a voice that the poor creature hardly knew where the smart came from. He would exclaim: 'Oh, I say, Miss Bowater!' and gape like a goldfish. Solely, perhaps, to have someone to discuss herself with, Fanny so far forgave and forgot my shortcomings as to pay me an occasional visit, and had yawned how hideously expensive she found it to live with the rich. But the only promise of help I could make was beyond any possibility of performance. I promised, none the less, for my one dread was that she should guess what straits I was in for money.

It is all very well to accuse Percy Maudlen of goldfishiness. What kind of fish was I? During the few months of my life at Mrs. Monnerie's – until, that is, Fanny's arrival – she had transported her 'Queen Bee', as she sometimes called me, to every conceivable social function and ceremony, except a deathbed and a funeral. Why had I not played my cards a little more skilfully? Had not Messrs. de la Rue designed a pack as if expressly for me, and for my own particular little game of Patience? If perhaps I had shown more sense and less sensibility; and had not been, as I suppose, in spite of all my airs and flauntings, such an inward young woman, what altitudes I might have scaled. Mrs. Monnerie, indeed, had once made me a promise to present me at Court in the coming May. It is true that this was a distinction that had been enjoyed by many of my predecessors in my own particular 'line' – but I don't think my patroness would have dished me up in a Pie.

That being so, my proud bosom might at this very moment be heaving beneath a locket adorned with the royal monogram in seed pearls, and inscribed: 'To the Least of her Subjects from the Greatest of Queens.' Why, I might have been the most talked-of and photographed débutante of the season. But I must beware of sour grapes. 'There was once a Diogenes whom the gods shut up in a tub' – poor Mr. Wagginhorne, he had been, after all, comparatively frugal with his azaleas.

In all seriousness I profited far too little by Mrs. Monnerie's generosities, by my 'chances', while I was with her. I just grew hostile, and so half-blind. Many of her friends, of course, were merely wealthy or fashionable, but others were just natural human beings. As Fanny had discovered, she not only delighted in people that were pleasant to look at. She enjoyed also what I suppose is almost as rare – intelligence.

The society 'Beauties', now? To be quite candid, and I hope without the least tinge of jealousy, I think they liked the look of me – well, no better than I liked the look of excessively handsome men. These exotics of either sex reminded me of petunias – the headachy kind, that are neither red nor blue, but a mixture. I always felt when I looked at them that they knew they were making me dizzy. Yet, as a matter of fact, I could hardly see their beauty for their clothes. It must, of course, be extremely difficult to endure *pure* admiration. True, I never remember even the most tactful person examining me for the first time without showing some little symptom of discomposure. But that's a very different thing.

There was, however, another kind of beauty which I loved with all my heart. It is difficult to express what I mean, but to see a woman whose face seemed to be the picture of a dream of herself, or a man whose face was absolutely the showing of his own mind – I never wearied of that. Or, at any rate, I do not now; in looking back.

So much for outsides. Humanity, our old cook Mrs. Ballard used to say, is very like a veal and ham pie: its least digestible part is usually the crust. I am only an amateur veal and ham Pieist; and the fact remains that I experienced just as much difficulty with what are called 'clever' people. They were like Adam Waggett in his Sunday clothes – a little too much of something to be quite all there. I firmly believe that what one means is the best thing to say, and the very last thing, however unaffected, most of these clever people said was seemingly what they meant. Their conversation rarely had more than an intellectual interest. You asked for a penny, and they gave you what only looked like a threepenny-bit.

Perhaps this is nothing but prejudice, but I have certainly always got on very much better with stupid people. Chiefly, perhaps, because I could share experiences with them; and the latest thoughts did not matter so much. Clever men's – and women's – experiences all seem to be in their heads; and when I have seen a rich man clamber through the eye of a needle, as poor Mr. Crimble used to say, I shall keep my eyes open for a clever one attempting the same feat. It had been one of my absurd little amusements at Mrs. Bowater's to imagine myself in strange places – keeping company with a dishevelled Comet in the cold wilds of space, or walking about in the furnaces of the Sun, like Shadrach and

Abednego. Not so now. Yet if I had had the patience, and the far better sense, to fix my attention on anyone I disliked at Mrs. Monnerie's so as to enter *in*, no doubt I should so much have enlarged my inward self as to make it a match at last even for poor Mr. Daniel Lambert.

On the other hand, I sometimes met people at No. 2, or when I was taken out by Mrs. Monnerie, whose faces looked as if they had been on an almost unbelievably long journey – and one not merely through this world, though that helps. I did try to explore *those* eyes, and mouths, and wrinkles; and solitudes, stranger than any comet's, I would find myself in at times. Alas, they paid me extremely little attention; though I wonder they did not see in my eyes how hungry I was for it. They were as mysterious as what is called genius. And what would I not give to have set eyes on Sir Isaac Newton, or Nelson, or John Keats – all three of them comparatively little men.

However absurdly pranked up with conceit I might be, I knew in my heart that outwardly, at any rate, I was nothing much better than a curio. To care for me was therefore a really difficult feat. And apart from there being very little time for anything at Mrs. Monnerie's, I never caught anyone making the attempt. When the novelty of me had worn off, I used to amuse myself by listening to Mrs. Monnerie's friends talking to one another – discussing plays and pictures and music and so on – anything that was new, and, of course, each other. Often on these occasions I hardly knew whether I was on my head or my heels.

Books had always been to me just a part of my life; and music very nearly my death. However much I forgot of it, I wove what I could remember of my small reading round myself, so to speak; and I am sure it made the cocoon more comfortable. As often as not these talkers argued about books as if their authors had made them – certainly not 'out of their power and love' – but merely for their readers to pick to pieces; and about 'beauty', too, as if it were something you could eat with a spoon. As for poetry, one might have guessed from what they said that it meant no more than – well, its 'meaning'. As if a butterfly were a chrysalis. I have sometimes all but laughed out. It was so contrary to my own little old-fashioned notions. Certainly it was not my mother's way.

But there, what presumption this all is. I had never been to school, never been out of Kent, had never 'done' anything, nor 'been' anything, except – and that half-heartedly – myself. No wonder I was censorious.

If I could have foreseen how interminably difficult a task it would prove to tack these memoirs together, I am sure I should have profited a little more by the roarings of my fellow lions. As a matter of fact I used merely to watch them sipping their tea, and devouring their cake amid a languishing circle of admirers, and to wonder if they found the cage as tedious as I did. If they noticed me at all, they were usually polite enough; but – like the Beauties – inclined to be absent and restless in my company. So the odds were against me. I had one advantage over them, however, for when I was no longer a novelty, I could occasionally slip in, unperceived, behind an immense marquetry bureau. There in the dust I could sit at peace, comparing its back with its front, and could enjoy at leisure the conversation beyond.

Nevertheless, there was one old gentleman, with whom I really made friends. He was a bachelor, and was not only the author of numbers of books, but when he was a little boy had been presented by Charles Dickens himself with a copy of *David Copperfield*, and had actually sat on the young novelist's knee. No matter who it was he might be talking to, he used to snap his fingers at me in the most exciting fashion whenever we saw each other in the distance, and we often shared a quiet little talk together (I standing on a highish chair, perhaps, and he squatting beside me, his hands on his knees) in some corner of Mrs. Monnerie's enormous drawing-room, well out of the mob.

I once ventured to ask him how to write.

His face grew very solemn. 'Lord have mercy upon me,' he said, '*to write*, my dear young lady. Well, there is only one recipe I have ever heard of: take a quart or more of life-blood; mix it with a bottle of ink, and a teaspoonful of tears; and ask God to forgive the blots.' Then he laughed at me, and polished his eyeglasses with his silk pocket handkerchief.

I surveyed this grisly mixture without flinching, and laughed too, and said, tapping his arm with my fan: 'But, dear Mr. – , would you have me die of anæmia?'

And he said I was a dear, valuable creature, and, when next 'Black Pudding Day' tempted us, we would collaborate.

Having heard *his* views, I was tempted to push on, and inquired as flatteringly as possible of a young portrait painter how he mixed his paints: 'So as to get exactly the colours you want, you know?'

He gently rubbed one long-fingered hand over the other until there fell a lull in the conversation around us. 'What I mix my paints with, Miss M.? Why – merely with brains,' he replied. My old novelist had forgotten the brains. But I discovered in some book or other long afterwards that a still more celebrated artist had said that too; so I suppose the *mot* is traditional.

And last, how to 'act'; for some mysterious reason I never asked any theatrical celebrity, male or female, how to do that.

More or less intelligent questions, I am afraid, are not the only short-cut to good, or even to polite, conversation. And I was such a dunce that I never really learned what topics are respectable, and what not. In consequence, I often amused Mrs. Monnerie's friends without knowing why. They would exchange a kind of little ogling glance, or with a silvery peal of laughter like bells, cry: 'How naïve!'

How I detested the word. Naïve – it was simply my ill-bred earnestness. Still, I made one valuable discovery: that you could safely laugh or even titter at things which it was extremely bad manners to be serious about. What you *could* be serious about, without letting skeletons out of the cupboard – that was the riddle. I had been brought up too privately ever to be able to answer it.

How engrossing it all would have been if only the Harrises could have trebled my income, and if Fanny had not known me so well. There was even a joy in the ladies who shook their lorgnettes at me as if I were deaf, or looked at me with their noses, as one might say, as if I were a bad or unsavoury joke. On my part, I could never succeed in forgetting that, in spite of appearances, they must be of flesh and blood, and therefore the prey of them, and of the World, and the Devil. So I used to amuse myself by imagining how they would look in their bones, or in rags, or in heaven, or as when they were children. Or again, by an effort of fancy I would reduce thïem, clothes and all, to *my* proportions; or even a little less. And though these little inward exercises made me absent-minded, it made them ever so much more interesting and entertaining.

How I managed not to expire in what, for a country mouse, was extremely like living in a bottle of champagne, I don't know. And if my silly little preferences suggest cynicism – well, I may be smug enough, but I don't, and won't, believe I am a cynic. Remember I was young. Besides I love human beings, especially when they are very human, and I have even tried to forgive Miss M. her Miss M-ishness. How can I be a cynic if I have tried to do that? It is a far more difficult task than to make allowances for the poor, wretched, immortal waxwork creatures in Madame Tussaud's Chamber of Horrors, or even for the gentleman naturalist who shot and stuffed Kent's last golden oriole.

Nor have I ever, for more than a moment, shared with Lemuel Gulliver his none too nice disgust at the people of Brobdingnag, even at kind-hearted Glumdalclitch. Am I not myself – not one of the quarrelsome 'Fair Folks of the Woods' – but a Yahoo? Gulliver, of course, was purposely made unaccustomed to the gigantic; while I was born and bred, though not to such an extreme, in its midst. And habit is second nature, or, as an old Lyndsey proverb goes: 'There's nowt like eels for eeliness.'

I am, none the less, ever so thankful that neither my ears, nose, nor eyes, positively magnify, so to speak. I may be a little more sensitive to noises and smells than some people are, but that again is probably only because I was brought up so fresh and quiet and privately. I am far more backward than can be excused, and in some things abominably slow-witted. Whether or not my feelings are pretty much of the usual size, I cannot say. What is more to the point is that in some of my happiest moments my inward self seems to be as remote from my body as the Moon is from Greenland; and, at others – even though that body weighs me down to the earth like a stone – it is as if memory and consciousness stretched away into the ages, far, far beyond my green and dwindling Barrow on Chizzel Hill, and had shaken to the solitary night-cry of Creation: 'Let there be Light.'

But enough and to spare of all this egotism. I must get back to my story.

Chapter Forty-Three

The fact is, Miss M.'s connection with good society was rapidly drawing to a close. My smoky little candle had long since begun to gutter and sputter and enwreathe itself in a winding sheet. It went out at last in a blaze of light. For once in his life Percy had conceived a notion of which his aunt cordially approved – my Birthday Banquet. Heart and soul, all my follies and misdemeanours forgotten, she entered into this new device to give her *Snippety,* her *Moppet*, her *Pusskinetta*, her little *Binbin*, her *Fairy*, her *Petite Sereine*, an exquisite setting.

Invitations were sent out to the elect on inch-square cards embossed with my family crest and motto – a giant, head and shoulders, brandishing a club, and *Non Omnis Moriar*.[1] She not only postponed her annual departure from town, but, as did the great man in the parable, *compelled* her friends to come in. She exhausted her ingenuity on the menu. The great, on this occasion, were to feast on the tiny. A copy of it lies beside me now, though, unfortunately, I did not examine it when I sat down to dinner.

---

1 To be truthful, this is not my family motto (*nor* crest); but the real motto seemed a little too satirical to share with Mrs. Monnerie; and however overweening its substitute may appear, I have now hopes, and now misgivings, that it is true.

Last, but not least, Percy's pastrycooks, Messrs. Buszard, designed a seven-tiered birthday cake, surrounded on its lowermost plateau by one-and-twenty sugar-figures, about a quarter life-size, and each of them bearing on high a silver torch.

Their names were inscribed on their sugar pediments: Lady Morgan (the Windsor Fairy); Queen Elizabeth's Mrs. Tomysen; the Empress Julia's Andromeda; the great little, little great Miss Billing of Tilbury; Anne Rouse and poor Ann Colling; the Sicilian Mlle. Caroline Crachami (who went to the anatomists); Nannette Stocker (33 inches, 33 lbs. avoirdupois at 33); the blessed and tender Anastasia Boruwlaski; Gaganini; the gentle Miss Selby of Bath; Alethea (the Guernsey Nymph); Madame Teresa (the Corsican Fairy); Mrs. Jekyll Skinner; the appalling Nono; Mrs. Anne Gibson (*née* Shepherd); and the rest.

It was a joke, none the worse, maybe, for being old; and Peter the Great must have turned in his grave in envy of Mrs. Monnerie's ingenuity.

It may scarcely be believed, but I had become so hardened to such little waggeries that under the genial eye of Mrs. Monnerie I made the circuit of this cake with a smile; and even scolded her for omitting the redoubtable Mrs. Bellamy with her life-size family of nine. I criticised the images too, as not to be compared even as sugar, with the alabaster William of Windsor and Blanche, in the Tower.

The truth is, when real revulsions of body and soul come, they come, in a gush, all at once. Fleming, on the Night, was actually putting the last touches to my coiffure when suddenly, with a wicked curse, I turned from the great glass and announced my decision. Tiny tortoiseshell comb uplifted, she stood in the clear lustrousness looking in at my reflection, queer thoughts darting about in her eyes. At first she supposed it was but another fit of petulance. Then her hatred and disgust of me all but overcame her.

She quietly argued. I insisted. But she was mortally afraid of Mrs. Monnerie, and rather than deliver my message to her, sought out Susan. Poor Susan. She, too, was afraid: and it was her face rather than her love that won me over at last. Then she had to rush away to make what excuse she could for my unpunctuality. It thus came about that Mrs. Monnerie's guests had already sat down to table, and were one and all being extremely amused by some story she was entertaining them with, when Marvell threw open the great mahogany doors for me, and I made my solitary entry.

In primrose silk, *à la Pompadour*, a wreath of tight-shut pimpernels in my hair – it is just possible that Mrs. Monnerie suspected I had chosen to come in late like this merely for effect. But that would have been an even feebler exhibition of vanity than *I* was capable of. All her guests were known to me, even though only one of them was of my choosing; for Mrs. Bowater was in the Argentine, Sir Walter in France, Miss Fenne on her deathbed, Mr. Pellew in retreat, and Mr. Crimble in his grave. Fanny was my all.

She was sitting four or five chairs away from me on my left, between Percy (who had on his right hand a beautiful long-faced girl in turquoise green) and Captain Valentine. Further down, and on the other side of the table, sat Lady Maudlen – a seal-like lady, who, according to Fanny, disapproved of me on religious grounds – while I was on Mrs. Monnerie's left, and next to Lord Chiltern. Alas, even my old friend the 'Black Pudding' was too far distant to do more than twinkle 'Courage!' at me, when our eyes met.

Recollections of that disastrous evening are clouded. So evil with dreams my nights had been that I hardly knew whether I was awake or asleep. But I recall the long perspective of the table, the beards, the busts, the pearls, the camellias and gardenias, the cornucopias, and that glistening Folly Castle, my Birthday Cake. Marvell is behind me, and Adam Waggett is ducketing in the luminous distance. The clatter of many tongues beats on my ear. Mrs. Monnerie murmurs and gently rocks. The great silver dishes dip and withdraw. Corks pop, and the fumes of meat and wine cloud into the air. In memory it is as if I myself were far away, as if I had read of the scene in a book.

But two moments stand vividly out of its unreality – and each of them to my shame. A small, wreathed, silver-gilt dish was placed before me. Automatically I thrust my spoon into its jelly, and pecked at the flavourless morsels. Sheer nervousness had deprived me of my sense of taste. But there was something in Mrs. Monnerie's sly silence, and Lord Chiltern's solemn monocle, and Percy's snigger, that set me speculating.

'Angelic Tomtitiska!' sighed Mrs. Monnerie, 'I wager when she returns to Paradise, she will sit in a corner and forget to tune her harp.'

There was no shade of vexation in her voice, only amiable amusement; but those sitting near had overheard her little pleasantry, and smilingly watched me as, casting my eye down the menu – *Consommé aux Nids d' Hirondelles, Filets de Blanchailles à la Diable, Ailes de Caille aux petits pois Minnie Stratton, Sauterelles aux Caroubes Saint Jean*, it was caught at last by a pretty gilt flourishing around the words, *Suprême de Langues de Rossignols*. This, then, was the dainty jest, the *clou du repas*. The faint gold words shimmered back at me. In an instant I was a child again at Lyndsey, lulling to sleep on my pillow amid the echoing songs of the nightingales that used to nest in its pleasant lanes. I sat flaming, my tongue clotted with disgust. I simply couldn't swallow; and didn't. But never mind.

This was my first mishap. Though her own appetite was capricious, ranging from an almost incredible voracity to a scrap of dry toast, nothing vexed Mrs. Monnerie so much as to see my poor, squeamish stomach revolting at the sight of meat. She drew up a naked shoulder against me, and the feast proceeded with its chief guest in the shade. Once I could soon have regained my composure. Now I languished, careless even of the expression on my face. Not even the little mincing smile Fanny always reserved for me in company could restore me, and it was at her whisper that Percy stole down and filled my acorn glass with a translucent green liquid which he had himself secured from the sideboard. I watched the slow, green flow of it from the lip of the decanter without a thought in my head. Lord Chiltern endeavoured to restore my drooping spirits. I had outrageously misjudged him. He was *not* one of Mrs. Monnerie's stupid friends, and he really did his utmost to be kind to me. If he should ever read these words, may he be sure that Miss M. is grateful. But his kindness fell on stony ground. And when, at length, he rose to propose my health, I crouched beneath him, shameful, haggard, and woebegone.

It was as minute a speech as was she whom it flattered, and far more graceful. Nothing, of course, would satisfy its audience when the toast had been honoured, but that Miss M. should reply. One single, desperate glance I cast at Mrs. Monnerie. She sat immovable as the Sphinx. There was no help for it. Knees knocking together, utterly tongue-tied, I stood up in my chair, and surveyed the two converging rows of smiling, curious faces. Despair gave me counsel. I stooped, raised my glass, and half in dread, half in bravado, tossed down its burning contents at a gulp.

The green syrup coursed along vein and artery like molten lead. A horrifying transparency began to spread over my mind. It seemed it had become in that instant empty and radiant as a dome of glass. All sounds hushed away. Things near faded into an infinite distance. Every face, glossed with light as if varnished, became lifeless, brutal and inhuman, the grotesque caricature of a shadowy countenance that hung somewhere remote in memory, yet was invisible and irrevocable. In this dead moment – the whole blazing scene like a nowhere of the imagination – my wandering eyes met Fanny's. She was softly languishing up at Captain Valentine, her fingers toying with a rose. And it seemed as though her once loved spirit cried homelessly out at me from space, as if for refuge and recognition; and a long-hidden flood broke bounds in my heart. All else forgotten, and obeying mechanically the force of long habit, I stepped up from my chair on to the table, and staggered towards her, upsetting, as I went, a shallow glass of bubbling wine. It reeked up in the air around me.

'Fanny, Fanny,' I called to her out of my swoon, 'Ah, Fanny. Holy Dying, Holy Dying! *Sauve qui peut!*' With empty, shocking face, she started back, appalled, like a wounded snake.

'Oh!' she cried in horror into the sleep that was now mounting my body like a cloud, 'oh!' Her hand swept out blindly in my direction as if to fend me off. At best my balance was insecure; and though the velvet petals of her rose scarcely grazed my cheek, the insane glaze of my mind was already darkening, I toppled and fell in a heap beside her plate.

Monk's House

* * *

Chapter Forty-Four

Thus, then, I came of age, though not on St. Rosa's day. However dramatic and memorable, I grant it was not a courteous method of acknowledging Lord Chiltern's courtesy. In the good old days the drunken dwarf would have been jovially tossed from hand to hand. From mind to mind was my much milder penalty. And yet this poor little *contretemps* was of a sort that required 'hushing up'; so it kept tongues wagging for many a day. It was little comfort that Percy shared my disgrace, and even Susan, for 'giving way'.

She it was who had lifted my body from the table and carried it up into darkness and quiet. In the half light of my bedroom I remember I opened my eyes for a moment – eyes which refused to stay still in their sockets, but were yet capable of noticing that the left hand which clasped mine had lost its ring. I tried to point it out to her. She was crying.

Philippina sober was awakened the next morning by the fingers of Mrs. Monnerie herself. She must have withdrawn the kindly sheet from my face, and, with nightmare still babbling on my lips, I looked up into the familiar features, a little grey and anxious, but creased up into every appearance of goodwill.

'Not so excessively unwisely, then,' she rallied me, 'and only the least little thought too well. We have been quite anxious about Bébé, haven't we, Fleming?'

'Quite, madam. A little indigestion, that's all.'

'Yes, yes; a little indigestion, that's all,' Mrs. Monnerie agreed: 'and I am sure Poppet doesn't want those tiresome doctors with their horrid physic.'

I sat up, blinking from one to the other. 'I think it was the green stuff,' I muttered, tongue and throat as dry as paper. I could scarcely see out of my eyes for the racking stabs of pain beneath my skull.

'Yes, yes,' was the soothing response. 'But you mustn't agitate yourself, silly child. Don't open your eyes like that. The heat of the room, the excitement, some little obstinate dainty. Now, one of those darling little pills, and a cooling draught, perhaps. Thank you, Fleming.'

The door closed, we were left alone. Mrs. Monnerie's scrutiny drifted away. Their shutters all but closed down on the black-brown pupils. My head pined for its pillows, my shoulders for some vestige of defence but pined in vain. For the first time I felt afraid of Mrs. Monnerie. She was thinking so densely and heavily.

Yet, as if out of a cloud of pure absent-mindedness, dropped softly her next remark. 'Does pretty Pusskin remember what she *said* to Miss Bowater? ... No? ... Well, then, if she can't, it's quite certain nobody else can – or wishes to. I inquired merely because the poor thing, who has been really nobly devoting herself to her duties, seems so hurt. Well, it shall be a little lesson – to us all. Though one swallow does not make a summer, my child, one hornet can make things extremely unpleasant. Not that I –' A vast shrug of the shoulders completed the sentence. 'A little talk and tact will soon set *that* right; and I am perfectly satisfied, perfectly satisfied with things as they are. So that's settled. Some day you must tell me a little more about your family history. Meanwhile, rest and quiet. No more excitement, no more company, and no more' – she bent low over me with wagging head – 'no more *green stuff*. And then' – her eyes rested on me with a peculiar zest rather than with any actual animosity – 'then we must see what can be done for you.'

There came a tap – and Percy showed in the doorway.

'I thought, Aunt Alice, I thought –' he began, but at sight of the morose, heavy countenance lifted up to him, he shut his mouth.

'Thank you,' said Mrs. Monnerie, 'thank you, Sir Galahad; you did nothing of the kind.'

Whereupon her nephew wheeled himself out of the room so swiftly that I could not detect what kind of exotics he was carrying in a little posy in his hand.

So the invalid, now a burden on the mind of her caretaker many times her own weight, was exiled for ever from No. 2. Poor Fleming, sniffier and more disgusted than ever, was deputed to carry me off to the smaller of Mrs. Monnerie's country retreats, a long, low-roofed, shallow-staired house lying in the green under the downs at Croomham. There I was to vegetate for a time and repent of my sins.

Percy's fiery syrup took longer to withdraw its sweet influences than might have been foreseen. Indeed, whenever I think of him, its effects are faintly renewed, though not, I trust, to the detriment of my style! None too strong physically the Miss M. that sat up at her latticed window at Monk's House during those few last interminable August days, was very busy with her thoughts. As she looked down for hours together on the gnarled, thick-leafed old mulberry-tree in the corner of the lawn that swept up to the very stones of the house, and on the walled, sun-drugged garden beyond, she was for ever debating that old, old problem: what could be done *by* herself *with* herself?

The doves crooned; the cawing rooks flapped back into the blue above the neighbouring woods; the earth drowsed on. It was a scene of peace and decay. But I seemed to have lost the charm that could have made it mine. I was an Ishmael. And worse – I was still a prisoner. No criminal at death's door can have brooded more laboriously on his chances of escape. No wonder the voices of childhood had whispered 'Away!'

There came a long night of rain. I lay listening to the whisper and clucking of its waters. Far away the lapwings called: 'Ee-ooeet! Ee-ooeet!' What follies I had been guilty of. How wilily circumstance had connived at them. Yet I was no true penitent. My heart was empty, so parched up that neither love nor remorse had any place in it. Revenge seemed far sweeter. Driven into this corner, I sent a desperate word to Sir W. It remained unanswered, and this friend followed the rest into the wilderness of my ingratitude.

But that brought me no relief. For of all the sins I have ever committed, envy and hatred seem to me the most unpleasant to practise. I was to learn also that 'he who sows hatred shall gather rue', and 'bed with thistles'. With eyes at last as anxious as Jezebel's, I resumed my watch at the window. But even if Percy had ridden from London solely to order Fleming to throw me down, she would not have 'demeaned' herself to set hands on me. She might be bold, but she, too, was fastidious.

Then Fleming herself one afternoon softly and suddenly vanished away – on her summer's holiday. Poor thing; so acute was the chronic indigestion caused by *her* obstinate little dainty that she did not even bid me good-bye.

She left me in charge of the housekeeper, Mrs. French, a stout, flushed, horse-faced woman, who now and then came in and bawled good-humouredly at me as if I were deaf, but otherwise ignored me altogether. I now spent most of my time in the garden, listlessly wandering out of sight of the windows (and gardeners), along its lank-flowered, rose-petalled walks, hating its beauty. Or I would sit where I could hear the waterdrops in a well. The very thought of company was detestable. I sat there half-dead, without book or needle, with scarcely a thought in my head. In my library days at No. 2 I had become a perfect slave to pleasures of the intellect. But now dyspepsia had set in there too.

My nights were pestered with dreams and my days with their vanishing spectres; and I had no Pollie to tell me what they forecast. I suppose one must be more miserable and hunted in mind even than I was, *never* to be a little sentimental when alone. I would lean over the cold mouth of the well, just able to discern in the cold mirror of water, far beneath, the face I was almost astonished to find reflected there. 'Shall I come too?' I would morbidly whisper, and dart away.

Still, just as with a weed in winter, life was beginning to renew the sap within me; and Monk's House was not only drowsy with age but gentle with whispers. Once at least in every twenty-four hours I would make a pilgrimage to its wrought-iron gates beside the square white lodge, to gloat out between the metal floriations at the dusty country lane beyond – with its swallows and wagtails and dragon-flies beneath the heat-parched tranquil elms. A slim, stilted greyhound on one such visit stalked out from the lodge. Quite unaware of his company, I turned about suddenly and stared clean down his arched throat – white teeth and lolling tongue. It was as if I had glanced into the jaws of destiny.

He turned his head, whiningly yawned, and stalked back into the shade.

A day or two afterwards I made the acquaintance of the lodge-keeper's daughter, a child named Rose, about five years of age, with a mop of copper-coloured curls bound up with a pale blue bow. At first glimpse of me she had hopped back as if on springs into the house. A moment after, her white-aproned mother appeared in the porch, and with a pleasant nod at me bade the child smile at the pretty little lady. Finger in mouth, Rose wriggled and stared. In a few days she grew accustomed to my small figure. And though I would sometimes discover her saucer-blue eyes fixed on me with a peculiar intensity, we almost came to be friends. She was not a very bright little girl; yet I found myself wooing her with all the arts I knew – in a scarcely conscious attempt, I suppose, to creep back by this small lane into the world's and my own esteem.

I made her wristlets of little flowers, hacked her out cockle boats from the acorns, told her half-forgotten stories, and once had to trespass into the kitchen at the back of the lodge to tell her mother that she was fallen asleep. Was it mere fancy that read in the scared face she twisted round on the pretty little lady from over her sauce-pan: 'Avaunt, Evil Eye!' I had become abominably self-conscious.

Chapter Forty-Five

One such afternoon Rose and I were sitting quietly together in the sunshine on the green grass bank when a smart, short step sounded in the lane, and who should come springily pacing out of the country through the gates but Adam Waggett – red hands, black boots, and Londonish billycock hat all complete. Adam must have been born in a fit of astonishment; and when he dies, so he will enter Paradise. He halted abruptly, a ring of shifting sunshine through the leaves playing on his purple face, and, after one long glance of theatrical astonishment, he burst into his familiar guffaw.

This time the roar of him in the open air was nothing but a pleasure, and the mere sound and sight of him set Rose off laughing, too. Her pink mouth was as clustered about with milk-teeth as a fragment of honeycomb is with cells.

'Well, there I never, miss,' he said at last, with a slow, friendly wink at the child. 'Where shall us three meet again, I wonder?' He flicked the dust off his black button boots with his pocket-handkerchief, mopped his high, bald forehead, and then positively exploded into fragments of information – like my father's fireworks on Guy Fawkes Day.

He talked of young Mr. Percy's 'goings-on', of the august Mr.

Marvell, of life at No. 2. 'That Miss Bowater, now, she's a bit of all right, she's toffee, she is.' But, his hat! there *had* been a row. And the Captain, too. Not that there was anything in that – 'just a bit of silly jealousy; *like* the women!' He could make a better guess than that. He didn't know what 'the old lady' would do without that Miss Bowater – the old lady whose carriage would in a few days be rolling in between these very gates. And then – He began this thing a Highland Reel.

The country air had evidently got into his head. Hand over hand he was swarming up the ladder of success. His '*joie de vivre*' gleamed at every pore. And I? – I just sat there, passively drinking in this kitchen-talk, without attempting to stop him. After all, he was out of my past; we were children of Israel in a strange land; and that hot face, with its violent pantomime, and hair-plastered temples, was as good as a play.

He was once more settling his hat on his head and opening his mouth in preparation for a last bray of farewell, when suddenly in the sunny afternoon hush a peculiar, melancholy, whining cry rose over the treetops, and slowly stilled away. As if shot from a bow, Rose's greyhound leapt out of the lodge and was gone. With head twisted over his shoulder, Adam stood listening. Somewhere – where? when? – that sound had stirred the shadows of my imagination. The day seemed to gather itself about me, as if in a plot.

In the silence that followed I heard the dust-muffled grinding of heavy wheels approaching, and the low, refreshing talk of homely, Kentish, country voices. Adam stepped to the gate. I clutched Rose's soft, cool fingers. And spongily, ponderously there, beyond the bars, debouched into view a huge-shouldered, mole-coloured elephant, its trunk sagging towards the dust, its small, lash-fringed eye gleaming in the sun, its bald, stumpy, tufted tail stiff and still behind it.

On and on, one after another, in the elm-shaded beams of the first of evening, the outlandish animals, the wheeled dens, the gaudy, piled-up vans of pasteboard scenery, the horses and ponies and riff-raff of a travelling circus wound into, and out of, view before my eyes. It was as if the lane itself were moving, and all the rest of the world, with Rose and myself clutched hand in hand on our green bank, had remained stark still. Probably the staring child supposed that this was one of my fairy-tales come true. My own mind was humming with a thought far more fantastic. Ever and again a swarthy face had glanced in on our quiet garden. The lion had glared into Africa beyond my head. But I was partly screened from view by Rose, and it was a woman, and she all but the last of the dusty, bedraggled company, that alone caught a full, clear sight of me.

One flash of eye to eye – we knew each other. She was the bird-eyed, ear-ringed gipsy of my railway journey with Pollie from Lyndsey to Beechwood. Even more hawklike, bonier, striding along now like a man in the dust and heat in her dingy coloured petticoats and great boots, with one steel-grey dart of remembrance, she swallowed me up, like flame a moth. Her mouth relaxed into a foxy smile while her gaze tightened on me. She turned herself about and shrilled out a strange word or two to someone who had gone before. A sudden alarm leapt up in me. In an instant I had whisked into hiding, and found myself, half-suffocated with excitement, peeping out of a bush in watch for what was to happen next.

So swift had been my disappearance she seemed doubtful of her own senses. A cage of leopards, with a fair-skinned, gold-haired girl in white stockings lolling asleep on the chained-up tailboard, trundled by; and then my gipsy was joined by a thick-set, scowling man. His face was bold and square, and far more lowering than that of the famous pugilist, Mr. Sayers – to whose coloured portrait I had become almost romantically attached in the library at No. 2. This dangerous looking individual filled me with a tremulous excitement and admiration. If, as in a dream, my past seemed to have been waiting for that solitary elephant; then my future was all of a simmer with *him*.

He drew his thick hand out of his stomach-pocket and scratched his cheek. The afternoon hung so quiet that I heard the rasp of his finger nail against his sprouting beard. He turned to mutter a sullen word or two at the woman beside him. Then, more civilly, and with a jerk of his squat thumb in my direction, he addressed himself to Adam. Adam listened, his red ears erect on either side of his hat. But his only answer was so violent a wag of his head that it seemed in danger of toppling off his body. Softly I laughed to myself. The woman yelped at him. The man bade her ferociously 'shut her gob'. Adam clanged-to the gates. They moved on. Beast, cage, and men were vanished like a daydream. A fitful breeze rustled the dry elm-leaves. The swifts coursed on in the shade.

When the last faint murmur had died away, I came out from behind my bush. 'A country circus,' I remarked unconcernedly. 'What did the man want, Adam?'

'That hairy cat frowned at Rosie,' whispered the child, turning from me to catch at Adam's coat-tails. 'Not *eat* Rosie?'

Adam bent himself double, and with an almost motherly tenderness stroked her bright red hair. He straightened himself up, spat modestly in the dust, and, with face still mottled by our recent experience, expressed the opinion that the man was 'one of them low blackguards – excusing plain English, miss – who'd steal your chickens out of the very saucepan'. As for the woman – words failed him.

I waited until his small, round eye had rolled back in my direction. 'Yes, Adam,' I said, 'but what did he *say*? You mean she told him about *me*?'

'Well, miss, to speak equal-like, that was about the size of it. The old liar said she had seen you before, that you were – well, there you are – a gold mine, a – a blessed gold mine. Her very words nearabout.' At that, in an insuppressible gush of happiness I laughed out with him, like a flageolet in a concourse of bassoons.

'But he didn't see me, Adam. I took good care of that.'

'That's just', said Adam, with a tug at his black cravat, 'what's going to give the pair of them a mighty unpleasant afternoon.'

I dismissed him, smiled at the whimpering greyhound, smiled at Rose, whose shyness at me had unaccountably whelmed over her again, and followed in Adam's wake towards the house. But not to enter it. 'A blessed' – oh, most blessed '*Gold Mine*!' The word so sang in me that the whole garden – espaliered wall, and bird, and flower – leapt into life and beauty before my eyes. Then my prayer (*what* prayer?) had been answered. I squared my shoulders, shuddered – a Lazarus come to life. Away I went, and seating myself in a sunny corner, a few paces from a hive of bees, plucked a nectarine, and surrendered myself to the intoxication of an idea. Not 'Your Master is dead', but 'Your mistress is come to life again!' I whispered to the bees. And if I had been wearing a scarlet garter I would have tied it round their skep.

Money! Money! – a few even of my handfuls of that, and I was free. I would teach 'them' a lesson. I would redeem myself. Ah, if only I had had a fraction of Fanny's courage, should I so long have remained wilting and festering at No. 2? The sweet, sharp juices of the clumsy fruit quenched my thirst. To and fro swept the bees along their airy highway. A spiked tree of late-blooming bugloss streamed its blue and purple into my eyes. A year ago, the very thought of exhibiting myself for filthy (or any kind of) lucre would have filled me with unspeakable shame. But what else had I been doing those long, dragging months? What had Miss M. hired herself out to be but a pot of caviare to the gourmets? Puffed up with conceit and complacency, I had been merely feeding on the world's contempt sauced up as flattery. Nonsensical child.

'Ah, I can make honey, too,' I nodded at the bees; whereupon a wasp pounced out of nowhere upon my oozy fruit, and I thrust it away into the weeds. But how refreshing a draught is the thought of action, how comforting the first returning trickle of self-esteem. My body sank into motionlessness. The shadows lengthened. The August sun slid down the sky.

Dusk was abroad in the colder garden, and the last bee home, when, with plans resolved on, I stretched my stiffened limbs and made my way into the house. Excellent augury – so easy had been my daily habits that no one had noticed my absence. Supper was awaiting me. I was ravenous. Up and down I stumped, gnawing my biscuit and sipping my sweet country milk. I had suddenly realized what the world meant to Fanny – an oyster for her sword. Somewhere I have read that every man of genius hides a woman in his breast. Well, perhaps in mine a *man* was now stirring – the man that had occupied my Aunt Kitilda's skirts. It was high time.

A moon just past its quarter was sinking in the heavens and silvering the jessamine at my window. My bosom swelled with longing at the breath of the slow night airs. Monk's House – I, too, had my ghosts and would face them down, would vanquish fate with the very weapons it had forged for my discomfiture.

In that sheltered half-light I stood myself before a down-tilted looking-glass. If I had been malshapen, limbless, contorted, I would have drowned myself in mud rather than feed man's hunger for the monstrous and obscene. No, I was a beautiful thing, even if God had been idly at play, when He had shaped me, and had then flung away the mould; even if to Mrs. Monnerie I was nothing much better than a disreputable marionette. So I boasted myself. Percy's Chartreuse had been mere whey compared with the fleeting glimpse of a tame circus elephant.

I tossed out on to the floor the old Lyndsey finery which some homesick impulse had persuaded me to bring away in my trunk. Seated there with busy needle under the window, sewing in every gewgaw and scrap of tinsel and finery I could lay hands on, I prepared for the morrow. How happy I was. Bats in the dewy dusklight cast faint, flitting shadows on the casements. A large dark moth hawked to and fro above my head. It seemed I could spend eternity in this gentle ardent busyness. To think that God had given me what might have been so dreadful a thing as solitude, but which in reality, while my thoughts and fingers were thus placidly occupied, could be so sweet. When at length I leaned out on the cold sill, my work done, wrists and shoulders aching with fatigue, Croomham clock struck two. The moon was set. But there, as if in my own happy mind – away to the east shone Orion. Why, Sirius, then, must be in hiding under that quiet shoulder of the downs. A dwindling meteor silvered across space; I breathed a wish, shivered, and drew in.

And there came that night a curious dream. I dreamt that I was a great soldier, and had won an enormous unparalleled battle. Glaring light streamed obliquely across a flat plain, humped and hummocked with the bodies of the dead lying in disorder. I was standing in arrogant reverie alone, a few paces distant – though leagues away in being – from a group of other officers, who were looking at me. And I suffered the streaming light to fall upon me, as I gazed into my joy and triumph with a kind of severe nonchalance. But though my face under my three-cornered hat can have expressed only calmness and resolution, I knew in my heart that my thoughts were merely a thin wisp of smoke above the crater of a suppressed volcano. Lest I should be detected in this weakness, I turned out of the glare, and without premeditation, began to step lightly and abstractedly from huddling mound to mound. And, as these heaps of the dead increased in size in the gloom after the white western light was gone, so I diminished, until I was but a kind of infinitesimal will-o'-the wisp gliding from peak to peak of an infernal mausoleum of which every eye, though dead, was watching me. But there was *one* Eye ...

And that is all of the dream that I could remember. For then I awoke, looking into the dark. A pencil ray of moonlight was creeping across my bed. Peace unutterable. Over my drowsy eyes once more the clouds descended, and once more I fell asleep.

Chapter Forty-Six

Next day, after a long lying-in-wait, I intercepted Adam Waggett and beckoned him into the shrubbery. First I questioned him. A bill of the circus, he told me, had already been left at the lodge. Its tents and booths and Aunt Sallies were even now being pitched in a meadow three or four miles distant and this side the neighbouring town. So far, so good. I told him my plan. He could do nothing but look at me like a fish, with his little black eyes, as I sat on a tree stump and marshalled my instructions.

But my first crucial battle had been fought with Adam Waggett in the garden at Lyndsey. He had neither the courage nor even the cowardice to gainsay me. After a tedious siege of his sluggish wits, greed for the reward I promised him, the assurance that if we were discovered the guilt should rest on me, and maybe some soupçon of old sake's sake won him over. The branches of the trees swayed and creaked above us in the sunshine; and at last, looking down on me with a wry face, Adam promised to do my bidding.

Six had but just struck that evening when there came the rap of his knuckles on my bedroom door. He found me impatiently striding up and down in a scintillating bodice and skirts of scarlet, lemon, and silver – as gay and gaudy an object as the waxen Russian

Princess I had seen in one of Mrs. Monnerie's cabinets. My flaxen hair was plaited German-wise, and tied in two thumping pigtails with a green ribbon; I stood and looked at him. He fumblingly folded his hands in front of him as he stood and looked back at me. I was quivering like a flame in a lamp. And never have I been so much flattered as by the silly, stupefied stare on his face.

How I was to be carried to the circus had been one of our most difficult problems. This cunning creature had routed out from some lumber room in the old house a capacious old cage – now rusty, but stout and solidly made – that must once have housed the aged Chakka.

'There, miss,' he whispered triumphantly; 'that's the ticket, and right to a hinch.'

I confessed I winced at his 'ticket'. But Adam had cushioned and padded it for me, and had hooded it over with a stout piece of sacking, leaving the ring free. Apart from our furtive preparations, evening quiet pervaded the house. The maids were out sweethearting, he explained. Mrs. French had retired as usual to her own sitting-room; Fortune seemed to be smiling upon me.

'Then, Adam,' I whispered, 'the time has come. Jerk me as little as possible; and if questions are asked, you are taking the cage to be mended, you understand? And when we get there, see no one but the man or the woman who spoke to you at the gates.'

'Well, miss, it's a rum go,' said Adam, eyeing me with a grotesque grimace of anxiety.

I looked up at him from the floor of the cage. 'The rummer the go is, Adam, the quicker we ought to be about it.'

He lowered the wiry dome over my head; I bunched in my skirts; and with the twist of a few hooks I was secure. The faint squeak of his boots told me that he had stolen to the door to listen.

'All serene,' he whispered hoarsely through the sacking. I felt myself lifted up and up. We were on our way. Then, like flies, a cloud of misgivings settled upon my mind. As best I could I drove them away, and to give myself confidence began to count. A shrill false whistling broke the silence. Adam was approaching the lodge; a mocking screech of its gates, and we were through. After that, apart from the occasional beat of hoofs or shoes, a country 'good-night', or a husky cough of encouragement from Adam, I heard nothing more. The gloom deepened. The heat was oppressive; I became a little seasick, and pressing my mouth to a small slit between the bars, sucked in what fresh air I could.

Midway on our journey Adam climbed over a stile to rest awhile, and, pushing back a corner of the sacking, he asked me how I did.

'Fine, Adam,' said I, panting. 'We are getting along famously.'

The fields were sweet and dusky. It was a clear evening, and refreshingly cool.

'You may smoke a pipe, Adam, if you wish,' I called softly. And while he puffed, and I listened to the chirping of a cricket, he told me of a young housemaid that was always chaffing and ridiculing him at No. 2. 'It may be that she has taken a passing fancy to you,' said I, looking up into the silent oak tree under which we were sitting. 'On the other hand, you may deserve it. What is she like, Adam?'

'Black eyebrows,' said Adam. 'Shows her teeth when she laughs. But that's no reason why she should make a fool of a fellow.'

'The real question is, is she a nice modest girl?' said I, and my bangles jangled as I raised my hand to my hair. 'Come, Adam, there's no time to waste; are you ready?'

He grunted, his mind still far away. 'She's a fair sneak,' he said, rapping his pipe-bowl on a stone. And so, up and on.

Time seemed to have ceased to be, in this jolting monotony, unbroken except by an occasional giddying swing of my universe as Adam transferred the cage from hand to hand. Swelteringly hot without, but a little cold within, I was startled by a faraway blare of music. I clutched tight the slender bars; the music ceased, and out of the quiet that followed rose the moaning roar of a wild beast.

My tongue pressed itself against my teeth; the sacking trembled, and a faint luminousness began to creep through its hempen strands. Shouting and screaming, catcalls and laughter swelled near. And now by the medley of smells and voices, and the glint of naked lights floating in on me, I realized that we had reached our goal.

Adam came to a standstill. 'Where's the boss?' The tones were thick and muffled. A feeble smile swept over my face: I discovered I was holding my breath.

A few paces now; the din distanced a little and the glare diminished. Then sounded another voice hoarse and violent, high above my head.

The cage bumped to the ground. And I heard Adam cringingly explain: 'I've got a bird here for you, mister.'

'A bird,' rang the jeer, 'who wants your bloody bird? Be off.'

'Ay, but it won't be a bloody bird', gasped Adam cajolingly, 'when you've seen her pretty feathers.'

At this, apparently, recollection of Adam's face or voice returned to the showman. He remained silent while with palsied fingers Adam unlatched my bolts and bars. Bent almost double and half-stifled, I sat there in sight, my clothes spread brightly out about me. The cool air swirled in, and for a while my eyes dazzled at the bubbling blaze of a naphtha-lamp suspended from the pole of the tent above the criss-cross green-bladed grass at my feet. I lifted my head.

There stood Adam, in his black tail-coat, rubbing his arm; and there the showman. Still to the tips of my fingers, I sat motionless, gazing up into the hard, high-boned, narrow-browed face with its small restless eyes voraciously taking me in. Fortunately the choked beating of my heart was too small a sound for his ear; and he was the first to withdraw from the encounter.

'My God,' he muttered, and spat into a corner of the canvas booth – with its one dripping lamp, its rough table and chair, and a few oddments of his trade.

'And what, my handsome young lady,' he went on in a low, car-neying tone, and fidgeting with his hands, 'what might be your little imbroglio?'

In a gush, presence of mind returned to me, and fear passed away. I quietly listened to myself explaining without any concealment precisely what was my little imbroglio. He burst out laughing.

'Stage-struck, eh? There's a young lady now! Well, who's to blame 'ee?'

He asked me my age, my name, where I came from, if I could dance, sing, ride; and stared so roundly at me that I seemed to see my garish colours reflected in the metallic grey of his eyes.

All this was on his side of the bargain. Now came mine. I folded tight my hands in my lap, glanced up at the flaming lamp. How much would he pay me?

It was as if a shutter had descended over his face. 'Drat me,' said he, 'when a young lady comes selling anything, she *asks* her price.'

So I asked mine – fifteen guineas for four nights' hire ... To look at that human animal you might have supposed the actual guineas had lodged in his throat. It may be that Shylock's was a more modest bargain. I cannot say.

At first thought it had seemed to me a monstrous sum, but at that time I was ignorant of what a really fine midget fetched. It was but half my old quarterly allowance, with £2 over for Adam. I should need every penny of it. And I had not come selling my soul without having first decided on its value. The showman fumed and blustered. But I sat close on Chakka's abandoned stage, perfectly still, making no answer; finding, moreover, in Adam an unexpected stronghold, for the wider gawked his frightened eyes at the showman's noise and gesticulations, the more resolved I became. With a last dreadful oath, the showman all but kicked a hole in my cage.

'Take me away, Adam,' I cried quaveringly; 'we are wasting this gentleman's time.'

I smiled to myself, in spite of the cold tremors that were shaking me all over; with every nerve and sinew of his corpulent body he was coveting me; and with a curse he at last accepted my terms. I shrugged my shoulders, but still refused to stir a finger until our contract had been written down in black and white. Maybe some tiny lovebird of courage roosts beneath *every* human skull, maybe my mother's fine French blood had rilled to the surface. However that may be, there could be no turning back.

He drew out a stump of pencil and a dirty envelope. 'That, my fine cock,' he said to Adam, as he wrote, 'that's a woman, and you make no mistake about it. To hell with your fine ladies.'

It remains, if not the most delicate, certainly one of the most substantial compliments I ever earned in my life.

'That's that,' he pretended to groan, presenting me with his scrawl. 'Ask a shark for a stamp, and if ruined I must be – ruined I am.'

I leapt to my feet, shook out my tumbled finery, smiled into his stooping face, and tucked the contract into my bodice. 'Thank you, sir,' I said, 'and I promise you shan't be ruined if *I* can help it.' Whereupon Adam became exceedingly merry, the danger now over.

Such are the facts concerning this little transaction, so far as I can recall them; yet I confess to being a little incredulous. Have I, perhaps, gilded my side of the bargaining? If so, I am sure my showman would be the last person to quarrel with me. I am inclined to think he had taken a fancy to me. Anyhow, I had won – what is, perhaps, even better – his respect. And though the pay came late, when it was no longer needed, and though it was the blackest money that ever touched my fingers, it came. And if anybody was the defaulter, it was I.

There was no time to lose. My gipsy woman was sent for from the shooting gallery. I shook hands with her; she shook hands with Adam, who was then told to go about his business and to return to the tent when the circus was over. The three of us, showman, woman, and I, conferred together, and with extreme cordiality agreed what should be my little part in the performance. The booth in which we had made our bargain was hastily prepared for my 'reception'. Its table was to be my daïs. A loose flap of canvas was hung to one side of it to screen me off from prying eyes when

I was not on show. My only dangerous rival, it appeared, was the Spotted Boy.

There followed a deafening pealing of panpipes, drumming of drum, and yelling of voices. In that monstrous din I was past thinking, just *being*; and I bridled to myself like a schoolgirl caught in a delicious naughtiness, to hear the fine things – the charms and marvels – which my showman was bawling about me. Then one by one, at first a little owlishly, the Great Public, at the charge of 6d. per adult and half price for children (or 'full-growns under 3 foot') were admitted to the presence of the '*Signorina Donna Angélique, the Fairy Princess of Andalusia in Spain*'. So at any rate declares the printed handbill.

In the attitude of Madame Recamier in the picture, I reclined on a lustrous spread of crimson satin and rabbit skin draped over a small lump of wood for bolster to give support to my elbow. And out of my paint and powder, from amid this oasis – and with repeated warnings 'not to touch' screamed by my gipsy – I met as pleasantly and steadily as I could the eyes of the grinning, smirking, awestruck faces – townsfolk and village folk, all agape and all sound Kentish stock.

'That isn't real, she's a doll,' lisped a crêpe-bonneted little girl who with skimpy legs dangling out of her petticoat had been hoisted up under her armpits for a clearer view. I let a little pause come, then turned my head on my hand and smiled, leaned over and eased my tinselled slippers. An audible sigh, sweet as incense, went up under the hollow of the booth. I looked on softly from face to face – another dream. Some captive beast mewed and brushed against the sides of a cage drawn up a yard or two from where I lay. The lamp poured flame and smoke. The canvas quietly flapped, and was still. Wild ramped the merry-go-round with its bells and hootings;

and the panpipes sobbed their liquid decoy. The Signorina's first reception was over.

News of her spread like wildfire. I could hear the showman bellowing at the press of people. His guineas were fructifying. And a peculiar rapturous gravity spread over me. When one's very self is wrapt in the ordeal of the passing moment, is lost like that, out of time and space, it seems, well – another presence had stolen into my mind, had taken possession. I cannot explain. But in this, it may be, all men *are* equal, whatever their lot. So, I suppose, a flower breaks out of the bud, and butterflies put off the mask of the chrysalis, and rainbows mount the skies. But I must try not to rhapsodize. All I know is that even in that low self-surrender, some tiny spark of life in me could not be content to let my body remain a mere mute stock for the ignorant wonder of those curious eyes.

The actual impulse, however, came from a young woman who, when next the people had streamed in, chanced to be standing close beside me. She was a weak-looking thing, yet reminded me in a sorrowful fashion of Fanny. Caught back by her melancholy, empty eyes, I seemed to lose myself in their darkness; to realize that she, too, was in trouble. I craned up from my wooden bolster and whispered in her hair: 'Patience, patience. There shall be a happy issue, my dear, out of all your afflictions.'

Only she herself and a weedy, sallow young man in her company could have heard these words. A glint of fright and desperation sprang into her large-pupilled eyes. But I smiled, and we exchanged kindness. She moistened her lips, turned from me, and clutching at the young man's arm, edged her way out of the throng and vanished.

'And what sort be this un?' roared an ox-faced, red-haired man from the back. 'This un' hung on his shoulder, tiptoe, fair, young and blowsy.

'She'll *coin* you money,' I cried pleasantly, 'and spend it. The hand that rocks the cradle rules the world.'

'And him, and him? the toad!' cried the girl half-angrily at the shout of merriment that had shaken the tent.

'Why, pretty maid,' piped I, 'the nearer the wine the sweeter the cork; the plumper the pig the fatter the pork.' The yell that followed was a better advertisement than drum or panpipes. The showman had discovered an oracle! For the next half-hour my booth was a mass of 'Sixpennies' – the squirming Threepennies were told to wait. It filled and emptied again and again like a black bottle in the Dog Days. And when the spirit moved me, I singled out a tell-tale face and told its fortune – not less shrewdly on the whole, I think, than Mrs. Ballard's *Book of Fate*.

But it was a strangely exhausting experience. I was inexpressibly relieved when it was over; when the tent-flap descended for the last time, and I could rest from my labours, puffed up, no doubt, with far too rich a conceit of myself, but immeasurably grateful and happy. Comparative quiet descended on the meadows. From a neighbouring tent broke shattering bursts of music, clapping and thumping, the fretful growling of the beasts, the elephant's trumpeting, the firing of guns, whoops, caterwauling, and the jangling of harness. The Grand Circus was in progress, and fantasy made a picture for me of every sound.

Presently my showman reappeared, leading in a pacing, smooth-skinned, cinnamon-and-milk-dappled pony, bridled and saddled with silver and scarlet, his silky mane daintily plaited, his tail a sweeping plume. He stood, I should guess, about half a hand higher than my childhood's Mopsa – the prettiest pygmy creature, though obviously morose and unsettled in temper. I took a good long look at his pink Albino eye. But a knack once acquired is quickly recovered. I mounted him. The stirrup was adjusted, one of my German plaits was dandled over my shoulder, and after a leisurely turn or two in the open, I nodded that the highborn Angelique was ready.

The showman, leering avariciously at me out of his shifty eyes, led us on towards the huge ballooning tent, its pennon fluttering darkly against the stars. I believe if in that spirituous moment he had muttered 'Fly with me, fairest!' all cares forgotten, I'd have been gone. He held his peace.

The brass band within wrenched and blared into the tune of *The Girl I Left behind Me*. Chafing, pawing, snorting, my steed, with its rider, paused in the entry. Then with a last smirk of encouragement from the gipsy woman, the rein was loosed, I bowed my head, and the next moment, as if in a floating vat of light, I found myself cantering wellnigh soundlessly round the ring, its circumference thronged tier above tier in the smoke-laden air with ghost-white rings of faces.

I smiled fixedly, tossing my fingers. A piebald clown came wambling in to meet me, struck his hand on his foolish heart, and fell flat in the tan. Love at first sight. Over his prostrate body we ambled, the ill-tempered little beast naggling at its bit, and doing his utmost to unseat me. The music ceased. The cloud of witnesses loured. Come Night, come Nero, I didn't care! Edging the furious little creature into the centre of the ring, I mastered him, wheeled him, in a series of obeisances – North, South, East, West. A hurricane – such as even Mr. Bowater can never have outridden – a hurricane of applause burst bounds and all but swept me out of the saddle. 'Good-bye, Sweetheart, Good-bye!' sang cornet and trombone. With a toss, I swept my plaits starwards, brandished my whip at the faces, and galloped out into the night.

My *début* was over. I confess it – the very memory of it carries me away even now. And even now I would maintain that it was at least a little more successful than that other less professional *début* which poor Mr. Crimble and Lady Pollacke had left unacclaimed in Beechwood High Street.

Chapter Forty-Seven

My showman, his hard face sleek with sweat, insisted on counting out three huge plate-like crown pieces into my lap – for a douceur. I brushed them off on to the ground. 'Only to clinch the bargain,' he said. His teeth grinned at me as if he would gladly have swallowed me whole.

'Pick up the money,' said I coldly, determined once and for all to keep him in his place. 'It's early days yet.' But when my back was turned, covetous Adam took charge of it.

While we trudged along homeward – for in the deserted night the cage was unnecessary, until I was too tired to go further – I listened to the coins clanking softly together in Adam's pocket. It was an intoxicating lullaby. But such are the revulsions of success, for hours and hours that night I lay sleepless. Once I got up and put my hand in where the crowns were, to assure myself I was awake. But the dream which visited me – between the watches of remorse – I shall keep to myself.

With next day's sun, the Signorina had become the talk of the countryside, and Adam's vacant face must have stood him in good stead. She had been such 'a draw', he told me, that the showman had decided to stay two more nights on the same pitch: which

was fortunate for us both. Especially as on the third afternoon
heavy rain fell, converting the green field into a morass. With
evening the clouds lifted, and a fulling moon glazed the puddles,
and dimmed the glow-worm lamps. Impulse is a capricious master.
I did my best, for even when intuition fails my sex, there's obstinacy to fall back upon; but all that I had formerly achieved with
ease had to be forced out of me that night with endless effort. The
Oracle was unwilling. When a genteel yet foxy-looking man, with
whiskers and a high stiff collar under his chin, sneakishly invited
me to tell his fortune, and I replied that 'Prudent chickens roost
high', the thrust was a little too deft. My audience was amused, but
nobody laughed.

He seemed to be well known, and the green look he cast me
proved that the truth is not always palatable or discreet. Unse-
duced by the lumps of sugar which I had pilfered for him my
peevish mount jibbed and bucked and all but flung the Princess of
Andalusia into the sodden ring. He succeeded in giving a painful
wrench to her wrist, which doubled the applause.

A strange thing happened to me, too, that night. When for
the second or third time the crowd was flocking in to view me,
my eyes chanced to fall on a figure standing in the clouded light
a little apart. He was dressed in a high-peaked hat and a long and
seemingly brown cassock-like garment, with buttoned tunic and
silver-buckled leather belt. Spurs were on his boots, a light whip
in his hand. Aloof, his head a little bowed down, his face in profile, he stood there, framed in the opening, dusky, level-featured,
deep-eyed – a Stranger.

What in me rushed as if on wings into his silent company? A
passionate longing beyond words burned in me. I seemed to be
carried away into a boundless wilderness – stunted trees, salt in

the air, a low, enormous stretch of night sky, space; and this man, master of soul and solitude.

He never heeded me; raised not an eyelid to glance into my tent. If he had, what then? I was a nothing. When next, after the press of people, I looked, he was gone; I saw him no more. Yet the girlish remembrance remains, consoling this superannuated heart like a goblet of flowers in that secret chamber of the mind we call the imagination.

The fall from that giddy moment into this practical world was abrupt. Sulky, tired with the rain and the cumbersome cage and the showman's insults, on our arrival at Monk's House Adam was completely unnerved when he found our usual entry locked and bolted.

He gibbered at me like a mountebank in the windy moon-light, his conical head blotting out half the cloud-wracked sky. These gallivantings were as much as his place was worth. He would wring the showman's neck. He had a nail in his shoe. He had been respectable all his life; and what was I going to do about it? A nice kettle of fish. Oh, yes, he had had 'a lick or two of the old lady's tongue' already, and he didn't want another. What's more, there was the mealy-mouthed Marvell to reckon with.

Once free of the cage, I faced him and desired to know whether he would be happier if I wrote at once to Mrs. Monnerie and absolved him there and then. 'Look at yourself in your own mind,' I bade him. 'What a sight is a coward!' And I fixed him with none too friendly an eye under the moon.

His clumsiness in opening a window disturbed Mrs. French. She came to the head of the staircase and leaned over, while we crouched in a recess beneath. But while the beams of the candle she carried were too feeble to pierce the well of darkness between us, by twisting round my head I could see every movement and changing expression of the shape above me – the frilled, red-flannel dressing-gown, the shawl over her head, and her inflamed peering face surmounted with a 'front' of hair in pins. She was talking to herself in peculiar guttural mutterings. But soon, either because she was too sleepy or too indolent to search further, she withdrew again; and Adam and I were free to creep up the glooming shallow staircase into safety.

Last but not least, when I came to undress, I found that my grandfather's little watch was gone. In a fever I tumbled my clothes over again and again. Then I sat down and in memory went over the events of the evening, and came at last to the thief. There was no doubt of him – a small-headed, puny man, who almost with tears in his eyes had besought me to give him one of my buttons to take home to his crippled little daughter. He had pressed close: my thoughts had been far away. I confess this loss unnerved me – a haggard face looked out of my glass. I scrambled into bed, and sought refuge as quickly as possible from these heart-burnings.

After such depressing experiences Adam's resolution was at an even lower ebb next morning. We met together under the sunny whispering pine-trees. I wheedled, argued, adjured him in vain. Almost at my wits' end at last, I solemnly warned him that if we failed the showman the following evening, he would assuredly have the law against us. 'A pretty pair we shall look, Adam, standing up there in the dock – with the black cap and the wigs and the policemen and everything. And not a penny for our pains.'

He squinted at me in unfeigned alarm at this; the lump in his throat went up and down; and though possibly I had painted the picture in rather sombre colours, this settled the matter. I hope it taught Adam to fight shy ever afterwards of adventuresses. It certainly taught *this* adventuress that the mind may be 'subdued to what it works in, like the dyer's hand'. I cast a look of hatred after the weak, silly man as he disappeared between the trees.

The circus, so the showman had warned me, was moving on that day to another market town, Whippington – six miles or so from its present pitch, though not more than four miles further away from Croomham. This would mean a long and wearisome trudge for us the next evening, as I found on consulting an immense map of Kent. Yet my heart sighed with delight at the discovery that, as the dove flies, we should be a full five miles nearer to Beechwood. If this little church on the map was St. Peter's, and this faint shading the woody contour of the Hill, why, then, that square dot was Wanderslore. I sprawled over the outspread county with sublime content. My very 'last appearance' was at hand; liberty but a few hollow hours away.

It is true I had promised my showman to think over his invitation to me to 'sign on' as a permanent member of his troupe of clowns, acrobats, wild beasts, and monstrosities. He had engaged in return to pay me in full, 'with a bit over', at the close of the last performance. But I had merely laughed and nodded. Not that I was in any true sense ashamed of what I had done. Not *ashamed*.

But you cannot swallow your pride and your niceness without any discomfort. I was conscious of a hardening of the skin, of a grimness stealing over my mouth, and of a tendency to stare at the world rather more boldly than modesty should. At least, so it seemed. In reality it may have been that Life was merely scraping off the 'cream'. Quite a wholesome experience.

On the practical side, all was well. Two pounds to Adam, which I had promised to make three if he earned it, would leave me with thirteen or twelve pounds odd, apart from my clumsy 'douceur'.

I thirsted for my wages. With that sum – two five-pound notes and say four half-sovereigns – sewn up, if possible, in my petticoat, I should once more be my own mistress; and I asked no more for the moment. The future must take care of itself. On one thing I was utterly resolved – never, never to return to Monk's House, or to No. 2 – to that old squalid luxury, dissembling and humiliation.

No; my Monnerie days were over; even though it had taken a full pound of their servile honey to secrete this ounce of rebellious wax.

How oddly chance events knit themselves together. That very morning I had received a belated and re-addressed letter which smote like sunbeams on my hopes and plans. It was from Mrs. Bowater:

> DEAR MISS M. – I send this line to say that I am still in the land of the living. I have buried my poor husband but have hopes some day of bringing him home. England is England when all's said and done, and I can't say I much approve of foreign parts. It's a fine town and not what you might call foreign to look at the buildings, but moist and flat and the streets like a draughtboard. And the thought of the cattle upsets me. Everything topsy-turvy too with Spring coming along and breaking out and we here on the brink of September. It has been an afflicting time though considering all things he made a peaceful end, with a smile on his face as you would hardly consider possible.
>
> The next fortnight will see me on board the steamer again, which I can scarcely support the thought of, though, please God, I shall see it through. I have spent many days alone here and the strangeness of it all and the foreign faces bring up memories which are happier forgotten. But I'm often thinking what fine things you must be doing in that fine place. Not as I think riches will buy everything in this world – and a mercy too – or that I'm not anxious at times you don't come

to harm with that delicate frame and all. Wrap up warm, miss, be watchful of your victuals and keep early hours. Such being so, I'm still hoping when I come home, if I'm spared, you may be of a mind to come to Beechwood Hill again and maybe settle down.

I may say that I had my suspicions for some time that that young Mr. Anon was consumptive in the lungs. But from what I gathered he isn't, only suffering from a stomach cough – bad cooking and exposing himself in all weathers. I will say nothing nearer. I shall be easier off as money goes, but you and me needn't think of that. Fanny doesn't write much and which I didn't much expect. She is of an age now which must reap as it has sown, though even allowing for the accident of birth, as they say, a mother's a mother till the end of the chapter. I must now close. May the Lord bless you, miss, wherever you may be.

Yours truly,

E. BOWATER (Mrs.)

Surely this letter was a good omen. It cheered me, and yet it was disquieting, too. That afternoon I spent in the garden, wandering irresolutely up and down under the blue sky, and fretting at the impenetrable wall of time that separated me from the longed-for hour of freedom. On a sunny stone near a foresty bed of asparagus I sat down at last, tired, and a little dispirited. I was angry with myself for the last night's failure, and for a kind of weakness that had come over me. Yet how different a creature was here today from that of only a week ago. From the darkened soil the stalks sprang up, stiffened and green with rain. A snail reared up her horns beneath my stone. An azure butterfly alighted on my knee, slowly fanning its turquoise wings, patterned with a delicate narrow black band on the one side, and spots of black and orange like a Paisley shawl beneath. Between silver-knobbed antennæ its furry perplexed face and shining eyes looked out at me, sharing my warmth. I watched it idly. How long we had been strangers. And surely the closer one looked at anything that was not of man's making ...My thoughts drifted away. I began day-dreaming again.

And it seemed that life was a thing that had neither any plan nor any purpose; that I was sunk, as if in a bog, in ignorance of why or where or who I truly was. The days melted on, to be lost or remembered, the Spring into Summer, and then Winter and death. What was the meaning of it all – this enormous ocean of time and space in which I was lost? Never else than a stranger. That couldn't be true of the men and women who really keep the world's 'pot boiling'. All *I* could pray for was to sit like this for a while, undisturbed and at peace with my own heart. Peace – did I so much as know the meaning of the word? How dingy a patchwork I had made of everything. And how customary were becoming these little passing fits of repining and remorse. The one sole thing that comforted me – apart from my blue butterfly – was an echo in my head of those clapping hands, whoops and catcalls – and the white staring faces in the glare. And a few months ago this would have seemed an incredible degradation.

There stole into memory that last evening at Wanderslore. What would he think of me now? I had done worse than forget him, had learned in one single instant that for ever and ever, however dearly I liked and valued him and delighted in his company, I could not be 'in love' with him. I hid my face in my hands. Yet a curious quiet wish for his company sprang up in me. How stiff-necked and affected I had been. Love was nothing but cheating. Let me but confess, explain, ask forgiveness, unburden myself. Those hollow temples, that jutting jaw, the way he stooped on his hands and coughed. My great-aunt, Kitilda, had died in her youth of consumption. A sudden dread, like a skeleton out of the sky, stood up in my mind. There was no time to delay. To-morrow night, Adam or no Adam, I would set off to find him: all would be well.

As if in response to my thought, a shadow stole over the stones beside me. I looked up and – aghast – saw Fanny.

Chapter Forty-Eight

Her head was turned away from me, a striped parasol leaned over her shoulder. With a faintly defiant tilt of her beautiful head, as if exclaiming 'See, Strangeness, I come!' she stepped firmly on over the turf. A breath of some delicate indoor perfume was wafted across to my nostrils. I clung to my stone, watching her.

Simply because it seemed a meanness to play the spy on her in her solitude, I called her name. But her start of surprise was mere feigning. The silk of her parasol encircled her shoulders like an immense nimbus. Her eyes dwelt on me, as if gathering up the strands of an unpleasing memory.

'Ah, Midgetina,' she called softly, 'it is you, is it, on your little stone? Are you better?' The very voice seemed conscious of its own cadences. 'What a delicious old garden. The contrast!'

The contrast. With a cold gathering apprehension at my heart I glanced around me. Why was it that of all people only Fanny could so shrink me up like this into my body? And there floated back to remembrance the vast, dazzling room, the flower-clotted table, and, in that hideous vertigo, a face frenzied with disgust and rage, a hand flung out to cast me off. But I entered her trap none the less.

'Contrast, Fanny?'

'No, *no,* now, my dear! Not quite so disingenuous as all that, *please.* You can't have quite forgotten the last time we met.'

'There was nothing in that, Fanny. Only that the midge was drunk. You should see the wasps over there in the nectarines.'

'Only?' she echoed lightly, raising her eyebrows. 'I am not sure that everyone would put it quite like that. You couldn't see yourself, you see. They call you little Miss Cassandra now. Woe! Woe! you know. Mrs. Monnerie asked me if I thought you were – you know – "all there", as they say.'

'I don't care what they say.'

'If I weren't an old friend,' she returned with crooked lip, 'you might be made to care. I have brought the money you were kind enough to lend me; I'll give it you when I have unpacked – to-morrow night.'

My body sank into a stillness that might well have betrayed its mind's confusion to a close observer. *Had* she lingered satirically, meaningly, on those two last words? 'I don't want the money, Fanny: aren't you generous enough to accept a gift?'

'Well,' said she, 'it needs a good deal of generosity sometimes. Surely, a gift depends upon the spirit in which it is given. That last little message, now – was that, shall we say, an acceptable gift?' Her tones lost their silkiness. 'See here, Midgetina,' she went on harshly, 'you and I are going to talk all this out. But I'm thirsty. I hate this spawning sun. Where are the nectarines?'

Much against my will I turned my back on her, and led her off to the beehives.

'One for you,' she said, stooping forward, balancing the sheeny toe of her shoe on the brown mould, 'and the rest for me. Catch!' She dropped a wasp-bitten, pulpy fruit into my hands. 'Now then.

It's shadier here. No eavesdroppers. Just you and me and God. *Please* sit down?'

There was no choice. Down I sat; and she on a low wooden seat opposite me in the shade, her folded parasol beside her, the leaf-hung wall behind. She bit daintily into the juicy nectarine poised between finger and thumb, and watched me with a peculiar fixed smile, as if of admiration, on her pale face.

'Tell me, pretty Binbin,' she began again, 'what is the name of that spiked red and blue and violet thing behind your back? It colours the edges of your delicate china cheeks. Most becoming!'

It was viper's bugloss – a stray, I told her, shifting my head uneasily beneath her scrutiny.

'Ah, yes, *viper's* bugloss. Personally I prefer the common variety. Though no doubt that may stray, too. But fie, fie! You naughty thing,' she sprang up and plucked another nectarine, 'you have been blacking your eyebrows. I shouldn't have dreamt it of you. What would mother say?'

'Listen, Fanny,' I said, pronouncing the words as best I could with a tongue that seemed to be sticking to the roof of my mouth; 'I am tired of the garden. What do you really want to say to me? I don't much care for your – your fun.'

'And I just beginning to enjoy it! There's contrariness! – To *say*? Well, now, a good deal, my dear. I thought of writing. But it's better – safer to talk. The first thing is this. While you have been malingering down here I have had to face the whole Monnerie orchestra. It hasn't been playing quite in tune; and you know why. That lovesick Susan, now, and her nice young man. But since you seem to be quite yourself again – more of yourself than ever, in fact – listen.' I gazed, almost hypnotized, through the sunshine into her shady face.

'What I am going to suggest', she went on smoothly, 'concerns only you and me. If you and I are to go on living in the same house – which heaven forbid – I give you fair warning that we shall have nothing more to do with one another than is absolutely inevitable. I am not so forgiving as I ought to be, Midgetina, and insults rankle. Treachery, still more.' The low voice trembled.

'Oh, yes, you may roll your innocent little eyes and look as harmless as a Chinese god, but answer me this: Am *I* a hypocrite? Am I? And while you are thinking it over, hadn't you better tumble that absurd little pumpkin off your knee? It's staining your charming frock.'

'I never said you were a hypocrite,' I choked.

'No?' The light gleamed on the whites of her eyes as they roved to and fro. 'Then I say, *you* are. Fair to face, false to back. Who first trapped me out star-gazing in the small hours, then played informer? Who wheedled her way on with her mincing humbug – poof! *naïveté*! – and set my own mother against me? Who told some-one – *you* know who – that I was not to be trusted, and far better cast-off? Who stuffed that lackadaisical idiot of a Sukie Monnerie with all *those* old horrors? Who warned that miserable little piece of deformity that I might come – borrowing? Who hoped to betray me by sending an envelope through the post packed with mousey bits of paper? Who made me a guy, a laughing-stock and poisoned – Oh, it's a long score, Miss M. When I think of it all, what I've endured – well, honestly when a wasp crawls out of my jam, I remind myself that it's stinged.'

The light smouldering eyes held me fast. 'You mean, I suppose, Fanny, that you'd just kill it,' I mumbled, looking up into her dis-torted face. 'I don't think I should much mind even that. But it's no use. It would take hours to answer your questions. You have only put them your own way. They may sound true. But in your heart you know they are false. Why should you bother to hurt me? You know – you know how idiotically I loved you.'

'*Loved me, false, kill*,' echoed Fanny scornfully, with a leer which transformed her beauty into a mere vulgar grimace. 'Is there any end to the deceits of the little gaby? Do you really suppose that to be loved is a new experience for me; that I'm not smeared with it wherever I go; that I care a snap of my fingers whether I'm loved or not; that I couldn't win through without that? Is that what you suppose? Well, then, here's one more secret. Open your ears. I am going to marry Percy Maudlen. Yes, *that* weed of a creature. You may remember my little prophecy when he brought his Aunt Alice's manikin some lollipops. Well, the grace of God is too leisurely, and since you and I are both, I suppose, of the same sex, I tell you I care no more for him than that –' She flung the nectarine stone at the beehive. 'And I defy you, defy you to utter a word. I am glad I was born what I am. All your pretty little triumphs, first to last, what are they? – accidents and insults. Isn't half the world kicking down the faces of those beneath them on the ladder? *I* have had to fight for a place. And I tell you this: I am going to teach these supercilious money-smelling ladies a lesson. I am going to climb till I can sneer down on *them*. And Mrs. Monnerie is going to help me. She doesn't care a jot for God or man. But she enjoys intelligence, and loves a fighter. Is that candour? Is it now?'

'I detest Percy Maudlen,' I replied faintly. 'And as for sneering, that only makes another wall. Oh, Fanny, do listen to yourself, to what you are. I swear I'm not the sneak you think me. I'd help you, if I could, to my last breath. Indeed, I would. Yes, and soon I *can*.'

'Thank you; and I'd rather suffocate than accept your help – now. Listen to myself, indeed! That's just the pious hypocrite all over. Well, declarations of love you know quite enough about for your – for your age. Now you shall hear one of a different kind. I tell you, Midgetina, I hate you: I can't endure the sight or sound or creep or thought of you any longer. Why? Because of your unspeakable masquerade. You play the pygmy; pygmy you are: carried about, cosseted, smirked at, fattened on nightingale's tongues – the last, though, you'll ever eat. But where have you come from? What are you in your past – in your mind? I ask you that: a thing more everywhere, more thief-like, more detestable than a conscience. Look at me, as we sit here now. *I* am the monstrosity. You see it, you think it, you hate even to touch me. From first moment to last you have secretly despised me – me! I'm not accusing you. You weren't your own maker. As often as not you don't know what you are saying. You are just an automaton. But these last nights I have lain awake and thought of it all. It came on me as if my life had been nothing but a filthy, aimless nightmare; and chiefly because of you. I've worked, I've thought, I've contrived and forced my way. Oh, that house, the wranglings, the sermons. Did I make myself what I am, *ask* to be born? No, it's all a devilish plot. And I say this, that while things are as they are, and this life is life, and this world *my* world, I refuse to be watched and taunted and goaded and defamed.'

Her face stooped closer, fascinating, chilling me like a cold cloud with its bright, hunted, malevolent stare. She stretched out a hand and wrung my shoulder. 'Listen, I say. Come out of that trance! I loathe you, you holy imp. You haunt me!'

My eyes shut. I sat shivering, empty of self, listening, as if lost in a fog in a place desperately strange to me; and only a distant sea breaking and chafing on its stones far below. Then once more I became conscious of the steady and resolute droning of the bees: felt the breathing of actuality on my hair, on my cheek. My eyes opened on a garden sucked dry of colour and reality, and sought her out. She had left me, was standing a few paces distant now, looking back, as if dazed, her lips pale, her eyes dark-ringed.

'Perhaps you didn't quite hear all that, Midgetina. You led me on. You force things out of me till I am sick. But some day, when you are as desperate as I have been, it will come back to you. Then you'll know what it is to be human. But there can't be any misunderstanding left now, can there?'

I shook my head. 'No, Fanny. I shall know you hate me.'

'And I am free?'

What could she mean? I nodded.

She turned, pushed up her parasol. 'What a talk! But better done with.'

'Yes, Fanny,' said I obediently. 'Much better done with.'

She gave me an odd glance out of the corner of her eye. 'The queer thing is,' she went on, 'what I wanted to say was something quite, quite different. To give you a friendly word of warning, entirely on your own account ... You have a rival, Midgetina.'

The words glided away into silence. The doves crooned on the housetop. The sky was empty above the distant hills. I did not stir, and am thankful I had the cowardice to ask no questions.

'Her name is Angélique. She lives in a Castle in Spain', sighed the calm, silky voice, with the odd break or rasp in it I knew so well. 'Oh, I agree a circus-rider is nothing better than a mongrel, a pariah, worse probably. Yet this one has her little advantages. As Midgets go, she beats you by at least four inches, and rides, sings, dances, tells fortunes. Quite a little Woman of the World. The only really troublesome thing about it is that she makes you jiltable, my dear. They are so very seductive, these flounced-up, painted things. *No* principle! And, oh, my dear, all this just as dear Mrs. Monnerie has set her heart on finding her Queen Bee a nice little adequate drone for a husband!'

It was her last taunt. It was over. I had heard the worst. The arrow I had been waiting for had sprung true to its mark. Its barb was sticking there in my side. And yet, as I mutely looked up at her, I knew there was a word between us which neither could utter. The empty air had swallowed up the sound of our voices. Its enormous looking-glass remained placid and indifferent. It was as if all that we had said, or, for that matter, suffered, was of no account, simply because we were not alone. For the first instant in the intimacy of my love and hatred, Fanny seemed to be just any young woman standing there, spiteful, meaningless. The virtue had gone out of her. She made up her mouth, glanced uneasily over her shoulder and turned away.

We were never again to be alone together, except in remembrance.

I sat on in the garden till the last thin ray of sunlight was gone. Then, in dread that my enemy might be looking down from the windows of the house, I slipped and shuffled from bush to bush in the dusk, and so at last made my way into the house, and climbed the dark polished staircase. As, stealthily, I passed a bedroom door ajar, my look pierced through the crevice. It was a long, stretching, shallow room, and at the end of it, in the crystal quiet, stood Fanny, her arms laid on the chimney-piece, her shoulder blades sticking out of her muslin gown, her face hidden in her hands.

Why did I not venture in to speak to her? I had never seen a figure so desolate and forsaken. Could things ever be so far gone as to say no to that? I hesitated; turned away: she would think I had come only to beg for mercy.

For hours I sat dully brooding. What a trap I was in. In my rummagings in the Monnerie library I had once chanced on a few yellow cardboard-covered novels tucked away in a cupboard, and had paddled in one or two of them. Now I realized that my life also was nothing but 'a Shocker'. So people actually suffered and endured the horrible things written about in cheap, common books.

One by one I faced Fanny's charges in my mind. None was true, yet none was wholly false. And none was of any consequence beside the fact that she execrated the very self in me of which I could not be conscious. And what would she do? What did all those covert threats and insinuations mean? A 'husband' – why had that such a dreadful power to wound me? I heard my teeth begin to chatter again. There was no defence, no refuge anywhere. If I could get no quiet, I should go mad. I looked up from my stool. It was dark. It was a scene made for me. I could watch the miserable little occupant of its stage roving to and fro like one of my showman's cowed, mangy beasts.

The thought of the day still ahead of me, through which I must somehow press on, keep alive, half stupefied me with dread. We can shut our eyes and our mouths and our hearts; why cannot we stop thinking? The awful passive order of life: its mechanicalness. All that I could see was the blank white face of its clock – but no more of the wheels than of the Winder. No haste, no intervention, no stretching-out beyond one's finger tips. So the world wore away; life decayed; the dunghill smoked. Mrs. Monnerie there; stepping into her brougham, ebony cane in hand, Marvell at her elbow; Mrs. Bowater languishing on board ship, limp head in stiff frilling; Sir Walter dumb; the showman cursing his wretched men; the bills being posted, the implacable future mutely yawning, the past unutterable. Everything in its orbit. Was there no help, no refuge?

The door opened and the skimpy little country girl who waited on me in Fleming's absence, brought in my supper. She bobbed me a scared curtsey, and withdrew. Then she, too, had been poisoned against me. I flung myself down on the floor, crushing my hands against my ears. Yet, through all this dazed helplessness, in one resolve I never faltered. I would keep my word to the showman, and this night that was now in my room should be the last I would spend alive in Monk's House. Fanny must do her worst. Thoughts of her, of my unhappy love and of her cruelty, could bring no good. Yet I thought of her no less. Her very presence in the house lurked in the air, in the silence, like an apparition's.

Still stretched on the floor, I woke to find the September constellations faintly silvering the pale blue crystal of the Northern Lights; and the earth sighing as if for refuge from the rising moon. My fears and troubles had fallen to rest beneath my dreams, and I prepared myself for the morrow's flight.

Chapter Forty-Eight

When next Fanny and I met, it was in the cool grey-green summery drawing-room at Monk's House, and Mrs. Monnerie and Susan shared tea with us. One covert glance at Mrs. Monnerie's face had reassured me. That strange mask was as vigilant and secretive, but as serene, as when it had first smiled on me in the mauves and gildings of Brunswick House. She had set her world right again and was at peace with mankind. As complacently as ever she stretched me out her finger. She had not even taken the trouble to forgive me for my little 'scene'; had let it perish of its own insignificance. Oh, I thought, if I could be as life-size as that! I did not learn till many days afterwards, however, that she had had news of me from France. *Good* news, which Sir W., trusting in my patience and commonsense, had kept back from me until he could deliver it in person and we could enjoy it together.

Only one topic of conversation was ours that afternoon – that 'amazing Prodigy of Nature', the Spanish Princess; Mrs. Monnerie's one regret that she herself had not discovered a star of such ineffably minute magnitude. Yet her teasing and sarcasm were so nimble and good-humoured; she insinuated so pleasantly her little drolleries and innuendoes, that even if Miss M. had had true cause for envy and malice, she could have taken no offence. Far from it.

I looked out of the long open windows at the dipping, flittering wagtails on the lawn; shrugged my shoulders; made little mouths at her with every appearance of wounded vanity. Did she really think, I inquired earnestly, that that shameless creature was as lovely as the showman's bills made her out to be? Mightn't it all be a cheat, a trick? Didn't they always exaggerate – just to make money? The more jovially she enjoyed my discomfiture, nodding her head, swaying in her chair, the more I enjoyed my duplicity. The real danger was that I should be a little too clever, over-act my part, and arouse her suspicions.

'Ah, you little know, you little know,' I muttered to myself, sharply conscious the while of the still, threatening presence of Fanny. But she meant to let me go – that was enough. It was to be good riddance to bad rubbish. There was nothing to fear from her – yet. Her eyes lightly dwelling on me over her Chelsea teacup, she sat drinking us in. Well, she should never taunt me with not having played up to her conception of me.

'Well, well,' Mrs. Monnerie concluded, 'all it means, my dear, is that you are not quite such a rarity as we supposed. Who is. There's nothing unique in this old world; though character, even bad character, never fails to make its mark. Ask Mr. Pellew.'

'But, surely, Mrs. Monnerie,' said I, 'it isn't character to sell yourself at twopence a look.'

'Mere scruples, Poppet,' she retorted. 'Think of it. If only you could have pocketed that pretty little fastidiousness of yours, the newspapers would now be ringing with *your* fame. And the fortune! You are too pernickety. Aren't we all of us on show? And aren't nine out of ten of us striving to be more on show than we are entitled to be? If man's first disobedience and the rest of it doesn't mean that, then what, I ask you, Mademoiselle *Bas Bleu*, was the sour old Puritan so concerned about? Assist me, Susan, if I stumble.'

'I wish I could, Aunt Alice,' said Susan sweetly, cutting the cake. 'You must ask Miss Bowater.'

'*Please*, Miss Monnerie,' drawled Fanny.

'Whether or not,' said Mrs. Monnerie crisply, 'I beseech you, children, don't quarrel about it. There is our beloved Sovereign on her throne; and there the last innocent little victim in its cradle; and there's the old sun waggishly illuminating the whole creaking stage. Blind beggar and dog, Toby, artists, authors, parsons, statesmen – heart and everything else, or everything else *but* heart, on sleeve – and all on show – every one of them – at *something* a look. No, my dear, there's only one private life, the next; and, according to some accounts, that will be more public than ever. And so twirls the Merry-go-Round.'

Her voice relapsed, as it were, into herself again, and she drew in her lips. She looked about her as if in faint surprise; and in returning to its usual expression, it seemed to me that her countenance had paused an instant in an exceedingly melancholy condition. Perhaps she had caught the glint of sympathy in my eye.

'But isn't that all choice, Mrs. Monnerie?' I leaned forward to ask. 'And aren't some people what one might call conspicuous, simply because they are really and truly, as it were, superior to other people? I don't mean better – just superior.'

'I *think*, Mrs. Monnerie,' murmured Fanny deprecatingly, 'she's referring to that "*ad infinitum*" jingle – about the fleas, you know. Or was it Dr. Watts, Midgetina?'

'Never mind about Dr. Watts,' said Mrs. Monnerie flatly.

'The point from which we have strayed, my dear, is that even if you were not born great, you were born exquisite; and now here's this Angélique rigmarole –' Her face creased up into its old good-humoured facetiousness: 'Was it three inches, Miss Bowater?'

'Four, Mrs. Monnerie,' lipped Fanny suavely.

'Four! pooh! Still, that's what they say; half a head or more, my dear, more exquisite! Perfect nonsense, of course. It's physically impossible. These Radical newspapers! And the absinthe, too.' Her small black-brown eyes roamed round a little emptily. Absinthe! was that a Fanny story? 'But there, my child,' she added easily, 'you shall see for yourself. We dine with the Padgwick-Steggals; and then go on together. So that's settled. It will be my first travelling circus since I was a child. Most amusing: if the lion doesn't get out, and there's none of those horrible accidents on the trapeze one goes in hope to see. By the way, Miss Bowater, your letter was posted?'

'Oh, yes, Mrs. Monnerie – this afternoon; but, as you know, I was a little doubtful about the address.' She hastened to pass me a plate of button-sized ratafias; and Mrs. Monnerie slowly turned a smiling but not quite ingenuous face aside.

'What a curious experience the circus will be for you, Midgetina,' Fanny was murmuring softly, glancing back over her shoulder towards the tea-table. 'Personally, I believe the Signorina Angélique and the rest of it is only one of those horrible twisted up prodigies with all the bones out of place. Mightn't it, Mrs. Monnerie, be a sort of shock, you know, for Miss M.? She's still a little pale and peaky.'

'She shall come, I say, and see for herself,' replied Mrs. Monnerie petulantly.

There was a pause. Mrs. Monnerie gazed vacantly at the tiers of hothouse flowers that decorated the window-recess. Susan sat with a little forked frown between her brows. She never seemed to derive the least enjoyment from this amiable, harmless midget-baiting. Not at any rate one hundredth part as much as I did. Fanny set Plum begging for yet another ratafia. And then, after a long, deep breath, my skin all 'goose-flesh', I looked straight across at my old friend.

'I don't think, Mrs. Monnerie,' I said, 'if you don't mind – I don't think I really *wish* to go.'

As if Joshua had spoken, the world stood still.

Mrs. Monnerie slowly turned her head. 'Another headache?'

'No, I'm perfectly well, thank you. But, whatever I may have said, I don't approve of that poor creature showing herself for – for money. She is selling herself. It *must* be because there's no other way out.'

Finger and thumb outstretched above the cringing little dog, Fanny was steadily watching me. With a jerk of my whole body I turned on her. 'You agreed with me, Fanny, didn't you, in the garden yesterday afternoon?'

Placidly, Fanny drooped her lids: 'Trust, Plum, trust!'

'What!' croaked Mrs. Monnerie, 'you, Miss Bowater! Guilty of that silly punctilio! She was merely humouring you, child. It will be a most valuable experience. You shall be perfectly protected. Pride, eh? Or is it jealousy? Now what would you say if I promise to try and ransom the poor creature? – buy her out? pension her off? Would *that* be a nice charitable little thing to do? She might make you quite a pleasant companion.'

'Ah, Mrs. Monnerie, please let *me* buy her out. Let me be the intermediary!' I found myself, hands clasped in lap, yearningly stooping towards her, just like a passionate young lady in a novel.

She replied ominously, knitting her thick, dark eyebrows. 'And how's that to be done, pray, if you sulk here at home?'

'I think, Aunt Alice, it's an excellent plan,' cried Susan, 'much, much more considerate. She could write. Think of all those horrible people! The poor thing may have been kidnapped, forced to do her silly tricks like one of those wretched, little barbered-up French poodles. Anyhow, I don't suppose she's there – or anywhere else, for that matter – for *fun*!'

Even Susan's sympathy had its sting.

'Thank you, Susan,' was Mrs. Monnerie's acid retort. '*Your* delicate soul can always be counted on. But advice, my child, is much the more valuable when asked for.'

'Of course I mustn't interfere, Mrs. Monnerie,' interposed Fanny sweetly; 'but wouldn't it perhaps be as well for you to see the poor thing first? She mayn't be quite – quite a proper kind of person, may she? At least that's what the newspapers seem to suggest. Not, of course, that Miss M. wouldn't soon teach her better manners.'

Mrs. Monnerie's head wagged gently in time to her shoe. 'H'm. There's something in that, Miss Worldly-Wise. Reports don't seem to flatter her. But still, I like my own way best. Poppet must *come and see*. After all, she should be the better judge.'

Never before had Mrs. Monnerie so closely resembled a puffed-out tawny owl.

I looked at her fixedly: shook my head. 'No, no, judge,' I spluttered. 'I'm sorry, Mrs. Monnerie, but I *won't* go.'

There was no misdoubting her anger now. The brows forked. The loose-skinned hands twitched. She lifted herself in her chair. '*Won't*,' she said. 'You vex me, child. And pray don't wriggle at me in that hysterical fashion. You are beside yourself; trembling like a mouse. You have been mooning alone too much, I can see. Run away and nurse that silly head, and at the same time thank heaven that you have more time and less need of the luxury than someone else we know of. It may be a low life, but it needs courage. I'll say *that* for her.'

She swept her hands to her knees over her silken lap, and turned upon Susan.

Wanderslore

* * *

Chapter Fifty

I had been dismissed. But Mrs. Monnerie's anger had a curious potency. For a moment I could scarcely see out of my eyes, and the floor swayed under me as I scrambled down from my chair. It took me at least a minute, even with the help of a stool, to open the door.

Like a naughty child I had been put in the corner and then sent to bed. Good. There could be no going back now. I could count on Fanny – the one thing she asked was to be free of me. As for Mrs. Monnerie, her flushed and sullen countenance convinced me that my respite would be undisturbed. There was only impulsive Susan to think of. And as if in answer, there came a faint tap, and the door softly opened to admit her gentle head and shoulders.

'Ah, my dear,' she whispered across at me. 'I'm *so* sorry; and so helpless. Don't take it too hardly. I have been having my turn, too.'

I twisted round, wet face and hands, as I stood stooping over my washbowl on its stool, scrutinized her speechlessly, and shook a dizzy head. The door shut. Dearest Susan: as I think of her I seem to see one of those tiny, tiny 'building rotifers' collecting out of reality its exquisite house. Grace, courage, loving kindness. If I had been the merest Miss Hop-o'-my-Thumb, I should still have been the coarsest little monster by comparison.

Scarce three safe hours remained to me; I must be off at once. To go looking for Adam was out of the question. Even if I could find him, I dared not risk him. Would it be possible for me to cover my six miles or more across undiscovered country in a hundred and eighty minutes? In my Bowater days, perhaps; but there had been months of idle, fatted, indoor No. 2 in between. A last forlorn dishonest project, banished already more than once from my mind, again thrust itself up – to creep off to the nearest Post Office and with one of my crown pieces for a telegram, cast myself on the generosity of Mr. Anon. No, no: I couldn't cheat myself like that.

I was ready. I pinned to the carpet a message for Adam, in case he should dare to be faithful to me – just four scribbled uncompromising words: 'The Bird is flown.' With eyes fixed on a starry knot of wood at the threshold, I stood for a while, with head bent, listening at my door. I might have been pausing between two worlds. The house was quiet. No voice cried 'Stay'. I bowed solemnly to the gentle, silent room behind me, and, with a prayer between my teeth, bundle in hand, stepped out into the future.

Unchallenged, unobserved, I slipped along the blue-carpeted corridor, down the wide stairs and out of the porch. After dodging from tree to tree, from shrub to shrub, along the meandering drive, I turned off, and, skirting the lodge through a seeding forest of weeds and grasses, squeezed through the railings and was in the lane. From my map of Kent I had traced out a rough little sketch of the route I must follow. With the sun on my left hand I set off almost due north. How still the world was. In that silk-blue sky with its placid, mountainous clouds there was no heed of human doings.

The shoes I had chosen were good sound Bowaters, and as I trudged on my spirits rose high. I breathed in deep draughts of the sweet September air. Thomasina of Bedlam had been 'summoned to tourney'. 'The wide world's end ...No journey!' In sober fact, it was a sorry little wretch of a young female, scarcely more than a girl, that went panting along in the dust and stones, scrambling into cover of ditch and hedge at every sound or sight of life. I look at her now, and smile. Poor thing; it needed at any rate a pinch of 'courage'.

Cottages came into sight. At an open door I heard the clatter of crockery, and a woman scolding a child. Two gates beyond, motionless as a block of wood, an old, old man stood leaning out of his garden of dahlias and tarnishing golden-rod. In an instant in the dumb dust I was under his nose. His clay pipe shattered on the stone. Like a wagtail I flitted and scampered all in a breath. That little danger was safely over; but it was not ruminating old gentlemen who caused me apprehension. Youthful Adam Waggetts were my dread.

At the foot of the slope there came a stile, and a footpath winding off north-west but still curving in my direction. I hesitated. Any risk seemed better than the hedged-in publicity of this dusty lane. Ducking under the stile, I climbed the hill and presently found myself clambering across an immense hummocky field, part stubble, part fresh plow. Then a meadow and cows. Then once more downhill, a drowsy farmyard, with its stacks and calves and chickens, to the left, and at bottom of the slope a filthy quagmire where an immense sow wallowed, giving suck to her squalling piglets. Her glinting, amorous eyes took me in. Stone on to stone, I skipped across a brook, dowsing one leg to the thigh in its bubbling water. It was balm in Gilead, for I was in a perfect fume of heat, and my lungs were panting like bellows.

I sat down for a breathing space on the sunset side of a haystack. In the shade of the hazels, on the verge of the green descending field, rabbits were feeding and playing. And I began to think. Supposing I did reach the new pitch in time: the wreck I should be. Then Mrs. Monnerie – and Fanny; my thoughts skimmed hastily on. What then? As soon as my showman had paid me I must creep away by myself out of sight *at once*; that was certain. I must tell him that Adam was waiting for me. And then? Well, after a few hours' rest in some shed or under a haystack, somehow or other I should have to find out the way, and press on to Wanderslore. There'd be a full moon. That would be a comfort. I knew the night. Once safely there, with money in my pocket, I could with a perfectly free conscience ask Mr. Anon to find me a lodging, perhaps not very far from his own. A laughable situation. But we would be the best of friends; now that all that – that nonsense was over. A deep sigh, drawn, as it were, from the depths of my bowels, rose up and subsided. What a strange thing that one must fall in love, couldn't jump into it. And then? Well, Mrs. Bowater would soon be home, and perhaps Sir Walter had circumvented the Harrises. Suppose not. Well, even at the very worst, at say ten, say even fifteen shillings a week, my thirteen pounds would last me for months and months ...Say *four*.

And as I said 'four', a gate clacked-to not many yards distant and a slow footfall sounded. Fortunately for me, the path I had been following skirted the other side of my haystack. Gathering myself close under the hay, I peeped out. A tall, spare man, in a low, peaked cap and leather leggings, came cautiously swinging along. His face was long, lean, severe. His eyes were fixed in a steady gaze, as if he were a human automaton stalking on. And the black barrel of a gun sloped down from under his arm. I drew in closer. His footsteps passed, died away; the evening breeze blew chill. A few moments afterwards a shattering report came echoing on from wood to wood, seeming to knock on my very breastbone. This was no place for me. With one scared glance at the huddling wood, I took to my heels, nor paused until the path through the spinney became so rutted that I was compelled to pick my way.

A cold gloom had closed in on my mind. I cursed clod-hopping shoes and bundle; envied the dead rabbit that had danced its airy dance and was done. As likely as not, I had already lost my way. And I plodded on along the stony paths, pausing only to quench my thirst with the rough juice of the blackberries that straggled at the wayside. I wonder if the 'Knight of Furious Fancies' was as volatile!

But yet another shock was awaiting me. The footpath dipped, there came a hedge and another stile, and I scuffled down the bank into the very lane which I had left more than an hour ago. I knew that white house on the hill; had seen it with Adam under the moon. It stood not much more than a mile from the lodge gates. My short cut had been a detour; and now the sun was down.

I drew back and examined my scribble of map. There was no help for it. Henceforward I must keep to the road. My thick shoes beat up the dust, one of my heels had blistered, my bundle grew heavier with every step. But fear had left me. Some other master cracked his whip at me as I shambled on, as doggedly and devil-may-care as a tramp.

I was stooping in the wayside ditch in one more attempt to ease my foot, when once again I heard hoofs approaching. With head pushed between the dusty tussocks, I stared along the flat, white road. A small and seemingly empty cart was bowling along in the dust. As it drew near, my ears began to sing, my heart stood still. I knew that battered cart, that rough-haired, thick-legged pony. Suddenly I craned up in horror, for it seemed that the face peering low over the splashboard in my direction was that of a death's-head, grinning at me out of its gloom. Then with a cry of joy I was up and out into the road. 'Hi, hi!' I screamed up at him.

It was Mr. Anon. The pony was reined back on to its haunches; the cart stood still. And my stranger and I were incredulously gazing at one another as if across eternity, as if all the world beside were a dream that asked no awakening.

Half dragged and half lifted into the cart, by what signs I could, for speech was impossible, I bade him turn back. It unmanned me to see the quiet and love in his face. Without a word he wheeled the rearing pony round under the elmboughs, and for many minutes we swung on together at an ungainly gallop, swaying from this side to that, the astonishment of every wayfarer we met or overtook on our way. At length he turned into a grass-track under a rusting hedge festooned with woodbine and feathery travellers' joy; and we smiled at one another as if in all history there had never been anything quite so strange as this.

'You are ill,' he said. 'Oh, my dear, what have they done to you?'

I denied it emphatically, wiping my cheeks and forehead with the hem of my skirt – for my handkerchief was stuffed into my shoe. 'Look at me!' I smiled up at him, confident and happy. Was my face lying about me? Oh, I knew what a dreadful object I must be, but then: 'I've been tramping for hours and hours in the dust; and why! – haven't you come to meet me; to give me a *lift*?'

What foolish speeches makes a happy heart. Indeed, Mr. Anon *had* come to meet me, but not exactly there and then. He fetched out of his pocket the minute note that had summoned him. Here it is, still faintly scented:

> Mrs. Monnerie sends her compliments, and would Miss M.'s friend very kindly call at Monk's House, Croomham, at three o'clock on Friday afternoon. Mrs. Monnerie is anxious about Miss M.'s health.

Oh, Fanny, Fanny! Precisely how far she had taken Mrs. Monnerie's name in vain in this letter I have never inquired. And now, I suppose, Mrs. Percy Maudlen would not trouble to tell me. But I can vow that in spite of the grime on my face the happiest smile shone through as I stuffed it into my bodice. So this was all that her harrowing 'husband' had come to – a summoning of friend to friend. If every little malicious plot ended like this, what a paradise the world would be. All tiredness passed away, though perhaps it continued to effervesce in my head a little. It seemed that I had been climbing on and on; and now suddenly the mist had vanished, and mountain and snow lay spread out around me in eternal peace and solitude. If Susan Monnerie's was my first stranger's kiss, Mr. Anon's were my quietest tears.

His crazy cart seemed more magical than all the carpets of Arabia. I poured out my story – though not quite to its dregs. 'This very afternoon,' I told him, 'I was writing to you – in my mind. And you see, you have come.' The shaggy pony tugged at the coarse grass. I could hear the trickling sands in the great hour-glass, and chattered on in vain hope to hold them back.

'You are not listening, only watching,' I blamed him.

His lips moved; he glanced away. Yet I had already foreseen the conflict awaiting me. And all his arguments and entreaties that I should throw over the showman, and drive straight on with him into the gathering evening towards Wanderslore, were in vain.

'Look,' he said, as if for straw to break the camel's back, and drew out by its ribbon my Bowater latchkey.

'No,' said I, 'not even that. I sleep out to-night.' And surely, surely I kept repeating, he must understand. How could I possibly be at rest with a broken promise? What cared I now for what was past and gone? Think what a joy, what sheer fun it would be to face Mrs. Monnerie for the last time, and she unaware of it! Nothing, nothing could amuse her more when she hears of it. He should come and see; hear the crowd yell. He mustn't be so solemn about things. 'Do try and see the humour of it,' I besought him.

But the money – that little incentive – I kept to myself.

He stared heavily into the silvery copse that bordered the track. Motionless in their bright, withering leaves, its trees hung down their tasselled branches beneath the darkening sky. Then, much against his will, he turned his pony towards the high road. The wheel gridded on a stone, he raised his whip.

'Hst!' I whispered, clutching at the arm that held the rein. Crouching low, we watched the great Monnerie carriage, with its stiff-necked, blinkered, stepping greys and gleaming lamps sweep by.

'There,' I laughed up at him, lifting myself, one hand upon his knee, 'there but for the Grace of God goes Miss M.'

The queer creature frowned into my smiling face and flicked the pony with his whip. 'And here,' he muttered moodily, 'who knows but by the Grace of God go I?'

Anxiety gone now, and responsibility but a light thing, my tongue rattled on quite as noisily as the cart. Kent's rich cornfields were around us, their stubble a pale washed-out gold in the last light of evening. Here and there on the hills a row or two of ungarnered stooks stood solemnly carved out against the sky. Most of the hop-gardens, too, had been dismantled, though a few we passed, with their slow-twirling dusky vistas and labyrinths, were still wreathed with bines. Their scent drifted headily on the stillness. And as with eyes peeping over the edge of the cart I watched these beloved, homelike hills and fields and orchards glide by, I shrilled joyfully at my companion every thought and fancy that came into my head, many of them, no doubt, recent deposits from the library at No. 2.

I told him, I remember, how tired I was of the pernicketiness of my life; and amused him with a description of my Tank. 'You would hardly believe it, but I have never once heard the least faint whisper of water in it, and if I had been a nice, simple savage, I dare say I should have prayed to it. Instead of which, when one night I saw a star over the housetop I merely shrugged my shoulders. My mind was so rancid I hated it. I was so shut in; that's what it was.'

He stroked the little, thick-coated horse with the lash of his whip, and smiled round at me.

On I went. Shouldn't life be a High Road, didn't he think; surely not a hot, silly zigzag of short cuts leading back to the place you started from, and you too old or stupid, perhaps, to begin again? Didn't he hunger, too, to see the *great* things of the world, the ruins of Babylon, the Wall of China, the Himalayas, and the Pyramids – at night – black; and sand?

'My ghost!' said I, had he ever thought of the enormous solitudes of the Sahara, or those remote places where gigantic images stare blindly through the centuries at the stars – their builders just a pinch of dust? Some day, I promised him out of the abandonment of my heart, we would sail away, he and I, to his Pygmy Land. Surf and snow and singing sand-dunes, and fruits on the trees and birds in the air: we would live – 'Oh, happy as all this!' (and I swept my hands across hill and dale), 'ever, ever afterwards. As they do, Mr. Anon, in those absurd, incredible fairy-tales, you know.'

He smiled again, cast a look into the distance, touched my hand.

Perhaps he was wishing the while that that piercing, pining voice of mine would keep silence, so that my presence might not disturb his own brooding thoughts. I could only guess at pleasing him. Yet I felt, still feel, that he was glad of my company and never for a moment sorry we had met.

Chapter Fifty-One

But our brief hour was drawing to an end. We were now passing little groups of country people and children in the quiet evening. We ourselves talked no more. The old pony plodded up yet another hill; we went clattering down its deep descent; and there, in the green bowl of a meadow sloping down from its woody fringes above, lay scattered the bellying booths, the gaudy wagons and cages of the circus. All but hidden in the trees above them, a crooked, tarnished weathercock glinted in the sunset afterglow. Lights twinkled against the dying daylight. The bright-painted merry-go-round with its staring, motionless, galloping horses was bathed in the shine of its flares, a thin plume of steam softly ascending from its brass-rimmed funnel.

A knot of country boys, gabbling at one another like starlings, shrilled a cheer as we came rattling over a stone bridge beneath which a stream shallowly washed its bank of osiers. I laughed at them, waved my hand. At this they yelled, danced in the road, threw dust into the air. Not, perhaps, a very friendly return; but how happy I was, all anxiety and responsibility gone now.

The faint, rank smell of the wild beasts mingling with the evening air was instilling its intoxication in my brain. I longed for darkness, the din and glare; longed for my tent and the gaping faces, for the smoky wind to fan my cheek as I bobbed cantering round the ring. It must have been a ridiculously childish face that ever and again scrutinized my companion's. Nothing for me in *that* looking-glass! How slow a face his was; he was refusing to look at me. It dismayed and fretted me to find him so sombre and dour.

His glance shifted to and fro under a frown that expressed a restless anxiety. His silence seemed to reproach me. Oh, well, when the day was over, and Mademoiselle's finery packed up in its bundle again, and the paint washed off, and the last echo of applause from the crowded benches had died away, and my pay was safe in my pocket, then he would know that the stake I had played for had been my freedom, my very self. Then surely his heart would lighten, and he would praise me, and we could go in peace. Would he not realize, too, that even my small body had its value, and was admired in a dismal world that cared not a jot for the spirit that inhabited it?

The showman stood by the tent, a gaudy silk scarf knotted round his neck. My lean-breasted gipsy woman spangled there beside him, with her black hair looped round her narrow bony head, and her loose, dusty, puckered boots showing beneath her skirts. There was a clear lustre in the lamp-starred air; and the spectacle of man and woman, of resting wheel and cropping horse, meadow and hill, poured a livelong blessing into my heart. Even the cowed, enfeebled lion with the mange of age and captivity in his skin, seemed to drowse content, and the satin-skinned leopards – almost within pat of paw of the flaxen-haired girl in the white stockings who leaned idly against the wheel – paced their den as if in pride. It was the same old story: my heart could not contain it all. Yet to whom tell its secrets?

A roomier tent had been prepared for me. We were ushered into it by the showman with a mock obeisance that swelled the veins on his forehead almost to bursting. The gipsy's birdlike eyes pierced and darted from one to the other of us, her skinny hand concealing her mouth. I felt as light as a feather, and thankful that my mud-caked shoes and petticoats were hardly discernible as none too elegantly I scrambled down from the cart.

The showman watched me with that sly, covetous grin about his mouth that I knew so well, though the stare with which he had greeted Mr. Anon had been more insolent than friendly. I had cut the time rather close, he told me, but better late than never! As for that long-nosed rat with the cage, he hadn't been much smitten with the looks of him; and he was not the man to ask questions of a lady, not he. Here I was, and he hoped I had come for good. A rough life but a merry. Up with the lark until down under the daisies; and every man jack of them ready to kiss the ground I walked on. And the Fat Woman – just pining good money away she was, with longing to mother the little stranger!

I nodded my head at him with a smile as worldly-wise as I could make it. 'It's the last taste that counts, Mr. Showman,' I said politely. 'Everyone has been exceedingly kind to me; and my love, please, to the Fat Woman. This is my friend, Mr. Anon. He has come to take care of me. We shall go back – go on together.'

The showman broke into a laugh, but his face hardened again, as, grinding one jaw slowly on the other, he turned to Mr. Anon. Maybe 'the young gentleman' was anxious to enjoy a taste of the life on his own account, he asked me. Could he ride? A bit of steeple-chasing? There was plenty of horseflesh – a double turn: Beauty and the Beast, now? Or perhaps another Spotted Boy? Love or money; just name the figure. Treat him fair and square, and he wouldn't refuse a genuine offer; though, naturally, every inch made a difference, and a foot twelve times as much. And looks were looks.

There was little enough to enjoy in the sound of all this. Apparently the mere sight of Mr. Anon had soured the showman. Many of his words were Greek to me, and to judge from the woman's yelps of laughter their meaning was none of the daintiest. I shrugged my shoulders, smiled, spread out my hands, and with a word or two fenced him off, pretending to be flattered. He looked at the woman as if to say 'There's manners for you!' She made a sudden, ferocious grimace. We were a singular four in the tent.

But it would be false to profess that I hadn't a sneaking admiration for the man; and I kept glancing uneasily at the 'young gentleman' who was so blackly ignoring his advances. To say the least of it, it was a little unintelligent of Mr. Anon not to take things as they came, if only for my sake.

'But you must please try and help me a little,' I pleaded, when the showman and the gipsy had left us to ourselves for a moment. 'It's only his fun. He's really not a bad sort of man underneath. You can't say there's a Spirit of Evil in that great hulking creature, now can you? I am not the least bit afraid of him.'

He glanced at me without turning his head. Involuntarily I sighed. Things never were so easy as one supposed or hoped they would be.

Already my fingers were busy at the knots of my bundle, and for a while, simply because what Mr. Anon was saying was so monstrous and incredible, I continued to fumble at them without attempting to answer him. He was forbidding me to keep my word; forbidding me to show myself; just ordering me to come away. No, no; he must be crazy; I had never understood him. There must be some old worm in his mind. He was telling me in so many words that to lie a prey to the mob's curiosity had been a disgrace – soiling me for ever.

The cruel stupidity of it! With head bent low and burning cheek I heard his harsh voice knell on and on – not persuading or conciliating, or pleading with me – I could have forgiven him that easily enough; but flatly commanding me to listen and obey.

'For mercy's sake,' I broke in hurriedly at last, 'that's enough of that. If just sitting here and talking to one's fellow-creatures has smeared me over, as you say it has, why, I must wait till Jordan to be clean. You should have seen that great wallowing sow this evening. *She* wasn't ashamed of herself. Can't you understand that I simply had to get free? You'd see it was for your sake, too, perhaps, if you had had the patience to listen. But there; never mind. I understand. You can't endure my company any longer. That's what it means. Well, then, if that is so, there's no help for it. You must just go. And I must be alone again.'

But no: there was a difference, he stubbornly maintained. What was done, was done. He was not speaking of the past. I knew nothing about the world. It was my very innocence that had kept me safe; 'and – well, the courage'. My innocence! and the 'courage' thrown in! But couldn't I, wouldn't I *see*? he argued. The need was over now; he was with me; there was nothing to be afraid of; he would protect me. 'Surely – oh, you know in your heart you couldn't have enjoyed all that!'

'Oh,' said I poisonously, 'so you don't think that to cheat the blackguard, as you call him, at the last moment – and please don't suppose I have forgotten what you have called other friends of mine – you don't think that to break every promise I have made wouldn't be wallowing worse than – Oh, thank you for the *wallowing*, I shall remember that.'

'But, my dear, my dear,' he began, 'I never –'

'I say I am *not* your dear,' I broke in furiously. 'One moment you dictate to me as if I were a child, and the next – As if I hadn't been used to that pretence, that wheedling all my life long. As if I had ever been treated like an ordinary human being – coddled up, smuggled about, whispered at! Why, a scullery maid's is Paradise compared with the life *I*'ve led. And as for the vile mob and the rest of it, I tell you I've enjoyed every minute of them. I *make* them clap their great ugly hands; I *make* them ashamed of themselves; they can't help themselves; they just – And I've comforted some of them, too. What's more, I tell you I love them. They are my own people; and I'd die for them if they would only forget what's between us and – and share it all. You be careful; maybe I shall stay here for good. *They* don't wince at my company; *they* don't come creeping and crawling. Why! aren't we all on show? Who set the world spinning? I tell you I hate that – that hypocrisy. What does it amount to, pray, but that you'd like the pretty, simpering doll all to yourself?'

A hooting screech broke the quiet that followed. The merry-go-round had set to its evening's labours. Faster and faster jangled the pipes and chiming:

> I dreamt that I dwe-elt in mar-ar-ble halls,
> With vassals and serfs by my si-i-ide ...

And at the sound, anger and pride died down in me. I lifted my face from the ground.

'I'm sorry,' I muttered. 'But you don't know what I have gone through these last weeks. And even if I were a hundred times as ashamed of myself as you think I ought to be, I couldn't – I can't go back. I have promised. It's written down. Only once more – this one night, and I swear it shall be the last.' My mouth crooked itself into a smile. 'You shall pray for me on the hill,' I said, 'then lead me off to a Nunnery yourself.'

And still I could not whisper – Money. The word stuck in my throat.

He seemed not to have heard the miserable things I had been saying. Without a syllable of retaliation, he came a little nearer, and stood over me. We were all but in darkness now, though lights were beating on the canvas of our tent. It was quite, quite simple, he said. The showman was no fool. He couldn't compel me to exhibit myself against my will. A contract was a contract, of course, but what if both parties to it agreed to break it? And supposing the showman refused to agree – what then? There was a far better plan, if only I would listen. As soon as he had been made to realize that nothing on earth could persuade me to show myself again, he would accept any alternative: 'I'll take your place,' smiled Mr. Anon.

Take my place!

So this was the plan he had been brooding over on our journey. No wonder he had been absent-minded. Cold with dread I gazed at him in the obscurity of the tent. A glimpse of Adam's rabbit face as he had stood brazening out his fears of the showman on that first night of adventure had darted through my mind. And this man – dwarfed, shrunken, emaciated.

A terrifying compassion gushed up into my heart, breaking down barriers that I never knew were there. It was the instant in my life, I think, when I came nearest to being a mother.

'S-sh,' I implored him. 'You don't understand. You can have no notion of what you are saying. I am a woman. They daren't harm me. But you! They – and besides,' the craftier argument floated into my mind, 'besides, Mrs. Monnerie ...'

But the sentence remained unfinished. The flap of the tent had lifted. The figure of the showman loomed up in the entry against the lights and the darkening sky. He was in excellent humour. He rattled the money in his pocket and breathed the smell of whisky into the tent, peering into it as if he were uncertain whether it was occupied or not.

'That's right, then,' he began huskily, 'that's as it should be. Ten minutes, your ladyship! And maybe the young gentleman would give a hand with the drum outside, while you get through with the titivating.'

His shape was only vaguely discernible as he stood gently rocking there. It was Mr. Anon who answered him. For a little while the showman seemed to be too much astounded to reply. Then he lost control of himself. A torrent of imprecations spouted out of his mouth. He threatened to call in the police, the mob. He shook his brass-ringed whip in our faces. I had never seen a man of his kind really angry before. He looked like a beast, like the Apollyon straddling the path in my *Pilgrim's Progress*. His roaring all but stunned me, swept over me, as if I were nothing – a leaf in the wind. I think I could have listened to him all but in mere curiosity – as to an equinoctial gale when one is safe in bed – if he had not been so near, and the tent so small and gloomy, and if Mr. Anon had not been standing in silence within reach of his hands. But his fury spent itself at last. Slowly his head turned on his heavy shoulders. He seemed suddenly to have forgotten his rage and became coaxing and conciliatory. He had a sounding, calf-like voice, and it rose up and down. An eavesdropper outside the tent would have supposed he was on the verge of tears.

He was sure the young lady had no intention of cheating him, of 'doing the dirty'. Why, he'd as lief send off there and then to the great house for the flunkey and the cage. What had I to complain of? Wasn't it private enough? Should he make it a level bob-a-nob, and no thrupennies? There was nothing to be afraid of. 'God bless you, sir, she wouldn't cheat an honest man, not she.'

People were swarming into the Fair from miles around, and real gentry in their carriages amongst them, like as had never been seen before. Did we want to ruin him? What should we think, now, if we had paid down good money to come and see the neatest little piece of female shape as ever God Almighty smuggled out of heaven; and in we went, and stuck up there was a gent – 'a nice-spoken, respectable gent', he agreed, with a contemptuous heave of his massive shoulders, 'but a gent no less, and him gowked up on the table, there, why, half as big again, and mouthing, mouthing like a ...?' The hideous words poured on.

His great body gently rocked above me; his thumbs hooked-in under his armpits, his whip dangling. Till that moment I had scarcely realized that the scene in which I sat was real, I had been so harassed and stupefied by his noise. But now he had begun to think of what he was saying. In those last words an unnameable insult lurked. He was looking at us, *seeing* us, approaching us as if in a dream.

A horror of the spirit came over me, and, as if rapt away from myself, I stared sheer up at him.

'Beware, my friend,' I cried up at him. 'Have a care. I see a rope round your neck.'

It was the truth. In the gloom, actually with my own eyes, I saw a noose loosely dangling there over his round, heavy shoulders.

So to this day I see my showman. His circus, I believe, continues to roam the English countryside, and by the mercy of heaven he will die in his bed, or, better still, in the bracken. But I suppose, like most of us, he was a slave to his own superstitions, or perhaps it was my very littleness, combined with the memory of some old story he had heard as a boy, that intimidated him. His mouth opened; his whip shook; the grin of a wild beast swept over his face. But he said no more.

Yet his, none the less, was half the victory. Nothing on earth could now have dissuaded me from keeping my bargain. His words had bitterly frightened me. No one else should be 'gowked' up there. I turned my back on him. He could go; I was ready.

But if I could be obstinate, so too could Mr. Anon. And when at last our argument was over, in sheer weariness I had agreed to a compromise. It was that I should show myself, and he take my place in the circus. The showman's money was safe; that was all *he* cared about. If 'Humpty' liked to petticoat himself up like a doxy and take my 'turn' in the ring – why, it was a rank smelling robbery, but let him – let him. He bawled for the woman, flung a last curse at us, and withdrew.

We were alone – only the vacancy of the tent between us. Beyond the narrow slit I could see the merry jostling crowds, hoydens and hobbledehoys, with their penny squirts and pasteboard noses and tin trumpets. A strange luminousness bathed their faces and clothes, beautifying them with light and shadow, carpeting with its soft radiance the rough grey-green grass. The harvest moon was brightening. I went near to him and touched his sleeve. His lips contracted, his shoulder drew in from my touch.

'Listen,' I pleaded. 'One hour – that is all. That evening in Wanderslore – do you remember? All my troubles over. Yes, I know. I have brought you to this. But then we can talk. Then you shall forgive me.'

He stretched out his hand. A shuffling step, a light were approaching. I fled back, snatched up my bundle, and climbed up into the darkness behind my canvas curtain. The next moment gigantic shadows rushed furiously into hiding, the tent was swamped with the flaring of the naphtha-lamp which the gipsy woman had come to hang to the tent-pole to light my last séance.

A few hasty minutes, and, stealing out, I bade Mr. Anon look. All Angélique's fair hair had been tied into a bob and draped mantilla-fashion with a thick black veil. A black, coarse fringe torn from the head of a doll which I had found in the bottom of my trunk, dangled over her forehead. Her eyebrows were angled up like a Chinaman's. Her cheeks were chalk-white, except for a dab of red on the bone, and she was dressed in a flounced gown, jet black and yellow, which I had cobbled up overnight and had padded out, bust, hips, and shoulders to nearly double my natural size. A spreading topaz brooch was on her breast, chains of beads and coral dangled to her waist, and a silk fan lay on her arm.

I swept him a curtsey. 'I dreamt that I dwe-elt in mar-ar-ble halls,' I piped out in a quavering falsetto. The folly of taking things so solemnly. What was humanity but a dressed-up ape? Had not my fair saint, Isobel de Flores, painted her cheeks, and garlanded her hair? And all his answer was to clench his teeth. He turned away with a shudder.

The drum reverberated, the panpipes squealed. I signed to him to hide himself in the recess among my discarded clothes, out of sight of peeping eyes, and arranged my person on the satin and rabbit-skins.

The tent flap lifted and the mob pressed in. Stretching out in a queue like a serpent, I caught a glimpse in the pale saffron moon-light of the crowd beyond. The sixpences danced in the tray. Once more the flap descended; my audience stilled. I looked from one to the other, smiling, defiant.

'Why, Bob said she was a pale, pinched-up snippet of a thing with golden hair,' whispered a slip of a girl to a smooth little woman at her side.

'Ay, my Goff! And a waist like a wedding-ring,' responded a wide mouth in a large red face, peering over.

'Ah, lady,' warbled the Signorina, 'fair today and foul to-morrow. "Believe what you are told," clanked the bell in the churchyard. Stuffing, my pretty; ask the goose!'

So went the Signorina's last little orgy. It would be a lie to pro-fess that she, or rather some black hidden ghost in her, did not enjoy it. My monstrous disguise, that ferment of humanity, those owlish faces, the lurking shame, the danger, the poisonous excite-ment swept me clean out of myself. Anything to be free for a while from 'pernickety' Miss M. But that, I suppose, is the experience of every gambler and wastrel and jezebel in the world, every one of his kind. One must not open the door too wide.

But this was not all. On other nights I had been alone. Now I was fervidly conscious of unseen, hungering eyes, watching every turn, and glance, and gesture. My dingy daïs was no longer in actu-ality. I lived in that one watcher's mind – in his imagination. And deep beneath this insane excitement lay a gentle, longing happi-ness. Oh, when this vile tinsel show was over, and these swarming faces had melted into thin air, and the moonlit empty night was ours, what would I not pour out for his peace and comfort. What gratitude and tenderness for all that he had been to me, and done, and said. Why, we seemed never even to have spoken to each other – not self to self, and there was all the world to tell.

Hotter, ranker grew the fetid atmosphere. I could scarcely breathe in my monstrous mummery. But clearly, the showman was making a rich bargain of me, and rumour of a Midget that was golden as Aphrodite one night, and black as pitch the next, only thickened the swarm. At length – long expected – there came a pause. Yet another country urchin flat on his stomach in the grass, with head goggling up at me from the hem of the canvas, was dragged out, screeching and laughing, by his breeches. But I had caught the accents of a well-known voice, and, crouching, with head wrenched aside to listen, I heard the gipsy's whining reply.

My moment had come. A pulse began its tattoo in my head. To remain helplessly lying there was impossible. I thrust myself on to my feet and, drawing back a pace or two, stood hunched up on the crimson spread of satin beside my wooden bolster. The canvas lifted, and one by one, the little party of 'gentry' stooped and filed in.

Chapter Fifty-Two

Mrs. Monnerie had paid for elbow room. It was the last 'Private View' in this world we were to share together. The sight of her capacious figure with its great bonnet and the broad, dark face beneath, now suddenly become strange and hostile, filled me with a vague sense of desolation. Yet I know she has forgiven me. Had I not pocketed my 'pretty little fastidiousness'?

What Fanny had planned to do if Miss M., plain and simple, had occupied the Signorina's table, I cannot even guess. For the spectacle of the squat, black, gloating guy she actually found there, she was utterly unprepared. It seemed, as I looked at her, that myself had fainted – had withdrawn out of my body – like the spirit in sleep. Or, maybe, not to be too nice about it, I merely 'became' my disguise. With mind emptied of every thought, I sank into an almost lifeless stagnancy, and with a heavy settled stare out of my black and yellow, from under the coarse fringe that brushed my brows, I met her eyes. Out of time and place, in a lightless, vacant solitude, we wrestled for mastery. At length the sneering, incredulous smile slowly faded from the pale, lovely face, leaving it twisted up as if after a nauseous draught of physic. Her gaze faltered, and fell. Her bosom rose; she coughed and turned away.

'Hideous! monstrous!' murmured Mrs. Monnerie to the tall, expressionless figure that stood beside her. 'The abject evil of the creature!'

Her dark, appraising glance travelled over me – feet, hands, body, lace-draped head. It swept across my eyes as if they were less significant than bits of china stuck in a cocoanut.

'No, Miss Bowater,' she turned massively round on her, 'you were perfectly right, it seems. As usual – but a dangerous habit, my dear. My little ransoming scheme must wait a bit. Just as well, perhaps, that our patient's dainty nerves should have been spared this particular little initiation – Could one have imagined it?'

Mr. Padgwick-Steggall merely raised his eyebrows. 'I shouldn't have cared to try,' he drawled. And the lady beside him made a little mouth and laid her gloved hand on his arm. 'But, Madame is forgetting,' whined the Signorina in a broken nosy English over her outspread fan, 'Madame is forgetting. It's alive! Oh, truly!' and I clasped my arms even tighter across my padded chest, my body involuntarily rocking to and fro, though not with amusement.

'Madame is forgetting nothing of the kind,' retorted Mrs. Monnerie heartily. 'The princess is an angel – Angélique – adorable.' She turned to the gipsy woman and slipped a coin into the clawlike fingers. 'Well, good-night,' she nodded at me. 'We are perfectly satisfied.'

'La, la, Madame,' my stuttering voice called after her, the words leaping out from some old hiding-place in my mind. '*Je vous remercie, madame. Rien ne va plus ...Noir gagne!*'

Her ebony stick shook beneath her hand. 'Unspeakable,' she angrily ejaculated, stumping her way out. 'A positive outrage against humanity.'

I shut my eyes, but the silent laughter that had once overtaken me in my bedroom at Mrs. Bowater's scarcely sounded in my head. And Mrs. Monnerie could more easily survive the little exchange than I. My body was dull and aching as if after a severe fall. The booth was filling for the last time.

Little life was left in the inert figure that faced this new assortment of her fellow-creatures: how strangely dissimilar one from another; how horrifyingly alike. A faint premonition bade me be on my guard. Under the wavering flame of the lamp, my glance moved slowly on from face to face, eye on to eye; and behind every one a watcher whom now I dared not wait to challenge. Empty or cynical, disgusted, malevolent, or blankly curious, they met me: none pitiful; none saddened or afflicted. On former nights – Why had they grown so hostile? This, then, was to smother in the bog.

But one face there was known to me, and that known well. Hoping, perhaps, to take me unaware, or may it have been to snatch a secret word with me; Fanny had slipped back into the tent again, and was now steadily regarding me from behind the throng. A throng so densely packed together that the canvas walls bulged behind them, and the tent-pole bent beneath the strain. Yet so much alone were she and I in that last infinite moment that we might have been whispering together after death. And this time, suddenly overwhelmed with self-loathing, it was I who turned away.

When, stretching my cramped limbs, I drew back, exhausted and shivering, from the empty tent, I thought for an instant that the figure which sat crouching in the corner of the recess was asleep. But no: with head averted, sweat gleaming on his forehead, he rose to his feet. His consciousness had been my theatre in a degree past even my realization.

'Then, that is over,' was all he said. 'Now it is my turn.'

The voice was flat and indifferent, but he could not conceal his disgust of what had passed, nor his dread of what was to come. Why, I thought angrily once more as I looked at him, why did he exaggerate things like this? Even a drowning man can sink three times, and still cheat the water. What cared I? – the night was nearly over. We should have won release. Why consider it so deeply? But even while I pleaded with him to let me finish the wretched business – every savour of adventure and daring and romance gone from it now – I was conscious of the trussed-up monstrosity that confronted him. He could not endure even a glance at my painted face. I stepped back from him with a hidden grimace. Past even praying for, then. So be it.

I heard the nimble stepping of the pony's hoofs on the worn turf. A sullen malice smouldered in its reddish, luminous eyes. When I clutched at its bridle it jerked back its sensitive head as if teased with a gadfly. The gipsy daubed vermilion on my friend's sallow cheeks. She shook out the tarnished finery she had brought with her and hung it round the stooping shoulders. She plastered down his black hair above his eyes, and thrust a riding-whip into his hand.

'There, my fine pretty gentleman,' she smirked at him. 'King of the Carrots! I lay even your own mammie wouldn't know you now, not even if you tried it straddle-legs. Tug at the knot, lovey; it's fast, but it won't strangle you. As for you, you –!' she suddenly flamed at me, 'all very fly and cunning, but if I'd had the fixing of it, you wouldn't have diddled me: not you. I know *your* shop. Slick off double quick, I warn you, or you'll have the mob at your heels. Now then, master!'

She grasped at the bridle, slapped the tooth-bared sensitive muzzle with her hand. I drew back, cowed and speechless. The sour thought died in my mind – Better, perhaps, if we had missed each other on the road. The pony jerked and snatched back its head.

He was gone, and now I was quite alone. What was there to fear? Only his contempt, his loathing of this last humiliation? But that, too, would soon be nothing but a memory. As always, the present would glide into the past. Yet a dreadful foreboding daunted me. Coarse canvas, walls and roof, table, beaten grass, my very hands and clothes had become menacing and unreal. The lamp hissed and bubbled as if at any moment it would burst asunder. Alone, afraid, ashamed, in the foulness of the tent, I looked around me in the silence; and beyond, above – the Universe of night and space. All my life but the feeble rustlings of a mouse in straw.

As I stripped off my miserable gewgaws I discovered myself talking into my solitude, weeping, beseeching, though eyes were dry and tongue silent. I scoured away the chalk and paint: and cleansed as far as possible my travel-stained clothes. From my bit of looking-glass a scared and shining face looked out. 'Oh, my dear,' I whispered, but not to its reflection, 'it is as clean now and for ever as I can make it.' I tied up my bundle.

It was impossible to cheat away the moments any longer. I sat down and listened. A distant roar of welcome, like that of a wave breaking over a wreck, had been borne across as the band broke into its welcoming tune. I saw the ring, its tall, lank-cheeked 'master' in his white shirt and coat-tails, the lights, the sidling, squalling clown, and the slim, exquisite creature with its ungainly rider ambling on and on. Where sat Fanny amidst that rabble? What were her thoughts? Was Mrs. Monnerie already yawning over the low, beggarly scene? A few minutes now. I began to count. A scream, human or animal, rose faint and awful in the distance, and died away.

I climbed down the ladder and looked out of the tent. Far-spread the fields and wooded hills lay, as if in a swoon beneath the blazing moonlight. The scattered lamps on the slope shone dim as glow-worms. Only a few figures loitered in the gleam of the side-shows, and so engrossed and still sat the watching multitude beneath the enormous mushroom of the tent, so thinly floated out its strains of music, that the hollow clucking of the stream over its pebbles beneath the wanstoned bridge was audible. A few isolated stars glittered faintly in the heights of the sky. What was happening now? Why did he not hasten? I was ready: my life prepared. I could bear no more waiting. A whip cracked. The music ceased: silence. One moment now.

Again the whip cracked. And then, as if at a signal, a vast, protracted, unanimous bawl poured up into space, a spout of sound, like a gigantic, invisible flower. 'That wasn't applause. But, you know, that wasn't applause,' I heard myself muttering. There can be no mistaking the sound of human mockery. There can be no mistaking that brutal wrench at the heart, under one's very ribs. I leapt round where I stood, in a kind of giddiness.

The shout died away. An indiscriminate clamour broke out – clapping of hands, beating of feet, whistling, hootings, booings, catcalls, and these all but drowned by cymbal, drum, trombone: 'Good-bye, Sweetheart, Good-bye.' It was over. Unlike Mrs. Monnerie, the mob was imperfectly satisfied. But all was well. The elephant, massive, imperturbable – the sagacious elephant with the hurdy-gurdy, must now be swinging into the ring.

I ran out over the trampled grass to meet the approaching group – showman, gipsy, trembling, sweating pony. Its rider stooped forward on the saddle, clutching its pommel, as if afraid of falling. He pushed himself off, lurched unsteadily, lifted and let fall his arm in an attempt to stroke the milk-white snapping muzzle. The strings of his cloak were already broken. He edged from beneath it, and with his left hand clumsily brushed the dust and damp from his face.

'He hadn't quite the knack of it,' the showman was explaining. 'Stirrup a morsel too short, maybe. All the strength, lady, and the ginger, by God, but not the knack, you understand. And we offered him a quieter little animal too. But what I say is, a bargain's a bargain, that's what I say. A bit dazed-like, sir, eh? My, you did come a cropper.'

'Sst! are you hurt?' I whispered.

The head shook; his moon-washed face smiled at me.

'Come now, come *now*,' I implored him, tugging at his arm, 'before the crowd ...'

He recoiled as if my touch had scalded him.

'We go –' I turned to the showman.

Hands thrust under his leathern belt, he looked fixedly at me, and then at the woman. Her eyes glittered glassily back at him.

'That's it. The young lady knows best. He's twisted his shoulder, lady, wrenched it; more weight than size, as you might say. She'll know where to make her friend comfortable. Trust the ladies. Never you be afraid of that. Now, then, Mary, fetch up the gentleman's cart.'

The woman, with one wolfish glance into his face, obeyed.

'There, sir! Is that easier? Push the rags in there behind his back. It'll save the jolts. Lord love you, I wouldn't split on the pair of you, not me. I know the old, old story. There, that's it! Now then, your ladyship. No more weight in the hand than a mushroom! All serene, Mary. Home sweet home; that's the tune, sir, ain't it? Drive easy now: and off we go.'

•

Chapter Fifty-Three

Noiselessly turned the wheels in the grass. We were descending the hill. A jolt, and we were in the road. A hedgerow shut us out from the two shrouded watchers by the tent. The braying music fainted away; and apart from the trotting hoofs and the grinding of the wheels in the dust, the only sound I heard was an occasional lofty crackle in space, as a rocket – our last greeting from the circus – stooping on its fiery course, strewed its coloured stars into the moonlight. Then the rearing hillside shut us out.

Speechlessly, from the floor of the cart, I watched the stooping figure above me. Ever and again, at any sudden lurch against a stone, he shrank down, then slowly lifted himself, turned his head and smiled.

'That's the tune, sir; that's the tune, sir.' The words aimlessly repeated themselves in my brain, as if bringing me a message I could not grasp or understand. 'What was I thinking about?' a voice kept asking me. A strange, sluggish look dwelt in the dilated pupils under the drooping lids when the moonbeams struck in on us from between the branches. His right hand hung loosely down. I clasped it – stone cold.

'Listen, tell me,' I entreated, 'you fell? I heard them calling and

– and the clapping, what then?' I could speak no louder, but he seemed scarcely able to hear me.

'My shoulder,' he answered thickly, as if the words came sluggishly and were half-strange to him. 'I fell ...Nothing: nothing. Only that I love you.'

The breath sighed itself away. I leaned my cheek against the unanswering hand, and chafed it with mine. Where now? Where now?

'We must keep awake,' I called beguilingly into the slumbrous face, after a long silence, as if to a child. 'Awake!'

A sigh, as he smiled in answer, shook him from head to foot.

'You are thirsty? What's this on your coat? Look, there is a gate. I'll creep through and get help.' I scrambled up, endeavouring in vain to clutch at the reins.

But no; his head stirred its no; the left hand still held them fast. 'Only ...wait.'

Was it 'wait' – that last faint word? It fell into my mind like a leaf into a torrent, and before I could be sure of it, the sound was gone.

Instinct, neither his nor mine, guided us on through the winding lanes, up hill and down, along the margin of sleeping wood and light-dappled stream, over a level crossing whose dew-rusted rails gleamed in the moon, then up once more, the retreating hillside hollowly echoing to every clap of hoof against stone. There was no strength or will left in me, only thoughts which in the dark within, between waking and sleeping, seemed like hovering flies to veer and dart – fantasies, fragments of dream, rather than thoughts.

I realized how sorely he was hurt, yet not then in my stupidity and horror – or is it that I refused to confess it to myself? – that his hurt was mortal. Morning would come soon. I grasped tight the hand in mine. Then help. In this monotony and weariness of mind and body, the passing trees seemed to dance and gesticulate before my eyes. A torturing drowsiness crept over me which in vain, thrusting up my eyelids with my fingers, beating my senseless feet on the floor of the cart, I tried to dispel. Once, I remember, I rose and threw my cape over his shoulder. At last I must have slept.

For the next thing I became conscious of was that the cart was at a standstill, and that the pony stood cropping the thyme-sweet turf by the wayside. I touched the cold dark hand. 'Hush, my dear, we are here!'

But I expected no answer. The head was sunken between the heavy shoulders; the pallid features were set in an empty stare. There wasn't a sound in the whole world, far or near.

'Oh, but you haven't said a single word to me!' It was the only speech in my mind – a reproach. It died on my lips; I drew away. What was this? – a dreadful fear plucked at my sleeve, fear of the company I was in, of a solitude never so much as tasted before. I leapt out of the cart, stood up in the dust, and in the creeping light stared about me.

Every window of the creeper-hung cottage was shrouded, its gate latched. I struggled to climb the fence, to fling a stone through the casement. The moon shone glassily in the cold skies, but daybreak was in the east; I must wait till morning. With eyes fixed on the motionless head I sat down in the grass by the wayside. Ever and again, after solemnly turning to survey me, the pony dragged the cart on a foot or two under the willows, nibbling the dewy grass.

Roused suddenly from stupor by the howling of a dog, I leapt up. Who called? Where was I? What had I forgotten? In renewed and dreadful recognition I looked vacantly around me. A strangeness had come. His company was mine no longer.

Dawn brightened. The voice of a thrush pealed out of the orchard beyond the stone wall – wild and sweet as in Spring. I crouched on the ground, elbows and knees, and now kept steady watch upon those night-hung upper windows. At last a curtain was drawn aside. An invisible face within must have looked down upon us in the lane. The casement was unlatched and thrust open, and a grey, tousled head pushed out as if in alarm into the keen morning. At sight of it a violent hiccoughing seized me, so that when an old woman appeared at her door and hobbled out to the cart, I could not make myself understood. Her sleep-bleared, faded eyes surveyed me with horror and suspicion – as if in my smallness there I looked scarcely human. She shook her crooked fingers at me, to scare me off; then, stooping, put her head into the cart. I cried out, and ran.

Chapter Fifty-Four

The sun had burned for some hours in the heavens, when bleeding with thorns and on fire with nettles and stinking mayweed, I dragged myself out of the undergrowth into a low-lying corner of the desolate garden. Nearby lay a pool of water under an old ruinous wall, swept by the foliage of an ash. On a flat, shelving stone at its brink I knelt down, bathed my face, and drank.

All that day I spent in the neighbourhood of the water, overhung with the colourless trumpets of convolvulus. Occasionally I edged on, but only to keep pace with the sun-beams, for I was deathly cold, and as soon as shadow drew over me, fits of shivering returned. For some hours I slept, but so shallowly that I heard my own voice gabbling in dreams.

When I awoke, the western sky was an ocean of saffron and gold. Amidst its haze, stood up the distant clustered chimneys of Wanderslore: and I realized I must be in an outlying hollow of the park – farthest from Beechwood Hill. I sat up, bound back my hair, and, bathing my swollen feet in the dark, ice-cold water, I watched the splendour fade.

While there was still light in the sky I set out for the cottage again, but soon found myself in such distress amongst the tangled weeds and grasses, which at every movement flung their stifling dust and seeds and pollen over me, that I was compelled to give up the attempt. With senseless tears dropping down my cheeks, I returned to the pool, and made my bed in the withered bracken.

So passed the next day. When once more the cloudless heat of the sun had diminished, I made another attempt to press back by the way I had come, if only to look up at those windows again. But I was dazed and exhausted; lost my way; and, keeping watch until daybreak, I returned again to the pool. Sitting there I tried to control my misery, and be calm. 'Wait, wait; I am coming,' was my one inarticulate thought. Surely that other solitude must be the easier to bear. But it was in vain. He was dead; and I had killed him – pride, vanity, greed, obstinacy, lovelessness. Every flower and fading leaf bore witness against me.

Now and again I quenched my thirst and rambled off a little way in search of a few fallen hazel nuts and blackberries, and attempted to ease the pain and distress I was in. But I knew in my heart that a few such days must see the last of me, and I had no other desire. Evening came with its faint stars. My mind at last seemed to empty itself of thought; and until dark fell, a self sat at the windows of my eyes gazing heedlessly out over that peace and beauty without consciousness even of grief and despair. Nocturnal creatures began to stir in weed and thicket; a thin mist to rise. For a while I kept watch until sense left me, and I slept.

A waning misshapen moon hung over the garden when I awoke, my mind clear, still, empty. So empty that I might but just have re-entered the world after the lapse of ages. In this silvery hush of night, winged shapes were wheeling around and above me, piercing the air with mad, strident cries. With sight strangely sharpened and powerful, I gazed tranquilly up, and supposed for a while these birds were swallows. Idly I watched them, scarcely conscious whether they were real or creatures of the imagination.

Darting, swooping in the mild blaze of the moonlight, with gaping beaks and whirring wings, they swept, wavered, tumbled above their motionless pastures; ghostly-fluttering, feathery-plumed moths their prey. At last, a continuous churring, like the noise of a rattle, near at hand, betrayed them, I lay in my solitude in the midst of a whirling flock of nightjars, few in number, but beside themselves with joy, on the eve of their autumnal flight.

I can only grope my way now through vague and baffling memories. Maybe it was the frenzied excitement of these madly happy birds that shed itself into my defenceless mind, after rousing me into the night I knew too well. With full, vigilant eyes I am standing again a few paces from the brink of the pool, looking up into a moonlit bush of deadly nightshade, its noxious flowering over, and hung with its black, gleaming, cherry-like fruit. I cannot recall having ever given a thought to this poisonous plant in Wanderslore during my waking hours, though in my old happy reconnoitrings of the garden I had sometimes chanced on the coral-red clusters of the woody nightshade – the bitter-sweet, and had afterwards seen it in blossom.

It may be that only a part of my mind was fully awake, while the rest dreamed on. Yet, as I strive to return in imagination to that solitary hour, I am certain that a complete realization was mine of the power distilled into those alluring light-glossed berries; and, slave of my drowsy senses, I fixed gaze and appetite on them as though, from childhood up, they had been my one greed and desire. Even then, as if for proof that they were real, my eyes wandered: recognized, low in the west, glaring Altair amid the faint outspread wings of Aquila; pondered on the spark-like radiance struck out by the moonbeams from the fragments of tile that protruded here and there from the crumbling wall beyond the pool; and softly returned once more to the evil bush.

Then, for an instant, I fancied that out of the nearer shadows a half-seen form had stolen up close behind me, and was watching me. Fancy or not, it caused me no fear. I turned about where I stood, and from this gentle eminence scanned the immense autumnal garden with its coursing nightbirds and distant motionless woods. No; I was alone; by my self; conscious only of an unfathomable quiet; and I stooped and took up one of the ripe fuits that had fallen to the ground. 'Ah, ah!' called a far-away voice within me. 'Ah, ah! What are you at now?' – a voice like none I had ever heard in the world until that moment. Yet I raised the fruit to my lips.

Its bitter juices jetted out upon cheek, mouth, and tongue, for ever staining me with their dye. Their very rancour shocked my body wideawake. Struck suddenly through with frightful cold and terror, I flung the vile thing down, and scoured my mouth with the draggled hem of my skirt. 'Oh God; oh God!' I cried; then turned, ran a few steps, tripped, turned back and cast myself down, crushing my eyes with my hands; and in helpless confusion began to pray.

Minutes, hours, passed – I know not. But at last, with throat parched and swollen, and hands and cheeks and scalp throbbing with an unnatural heat, I raised my eyes. Two moons were in the sky, hideously revolving amid interwoven arcs of coloured light, and running backward and forward. I called out in the silence. A gigantic nightjar swirled on me, plucking at my hair. A maddening vertigo seized me. I went stumbling and staggering down to my stone and drenched head and breast in the flashing black and silver water.

It was a momentary refreshment, and in its influence memory began droning of the past. Confused abhorrent images mocked my helpless dreamings. There was a place – beyond – out of these shadows, unattainable. A piercing, vindictive voice was calling me. No hope now. I was damned. In senseless hallucination I began systematically, laboriously, a frenzied search. Leaf, pebble, crawling night-creature – with slow, animal-like care, I turned them over one by one, seeking and seeking.

Lyndsey

* * *

Chapter Fify-Five And Last

And yet again I pause – long after these last words were written – to look back across the intervening years at that young woman. What, indeed, was her insane mind seeking: what assurance; reconciliation? I know not, but there she herself was found, nails worn to the quick, feet shoeless, a hunted anatomy. Her fret and fever were to pass away; but what has all this experience done for me? – that wildest, happiest, cruellest, dearest, blackest twelvemonth of my life? One more unanswerable question. But, thank God, I live on; have even finished the task I set myself; and in spite of fits and moods of depression, distaste, and weariness, have been happy in it. Even when most contemptuous and ashamed of myself, I have still found comfort in the belief that truth is a wholesome medicine, though in essence it be humanly unattainable. And my work has taught me this too – not to fret so foolishly as once I did, at being small and insignificant in body; to fear a great deal more remaining pygmy-minded, and pygmy-spirited. I used to try to set myself against the World – but no need to enter further into that. We *cannot* see ourselves as others see us, but that is no excuse for not wearing spectacles; and even up here, in my peaceful lonely old Stonecote, I must beware of a mind swept and garnished. Moreover my hour must come again: and his.

That being so, of this I am certain; that it will be impossible to free myself, to escape from this world, unless in peace and amity I can take every shred of it, every friend and every enemy, all that these eyes have seen, these senses discovered with me. I *know* that. And perhaps for that very reason, in spite of the loving gratitude that overcomes me at the thought of what my existence might have been, I sometimes dread the ease and quiet and seclusion in which I live. And this tale itself? As Mrs. Monnerie had said, what is it but once more to have drifted into being on show again – in a book? That is so; and so I must leave it, hoping against hope that one friend at any rate will consent in his love and wisdom to take me seriously, and to remember me, not with scorn or even with pity, but as if, life for life, we had shared the world on equal terms.

M.